SNOOPY™

BOOGIE DOWN!

Other *Peanuts* Kids' Collections

Snoopy: Cowabunga!

Charlie Brown and Friends

Charlie Brown: Pow!

Woodstock: Master of Disguise

Snoopy: Contact!

Snoopy: Party Animal

Charlie Brown: Here We Go Again

Snoopy to the Rescue

Snoopy: What's Wrong with Dog Lips?

I'm Not Your Sweet Babboo!

SNOOPY™
BOOGIE DOWN!

A **PEANUTS**™ Collection

CHARLES M. SCHULZ

Andrews McMeel
PUBLISHING®

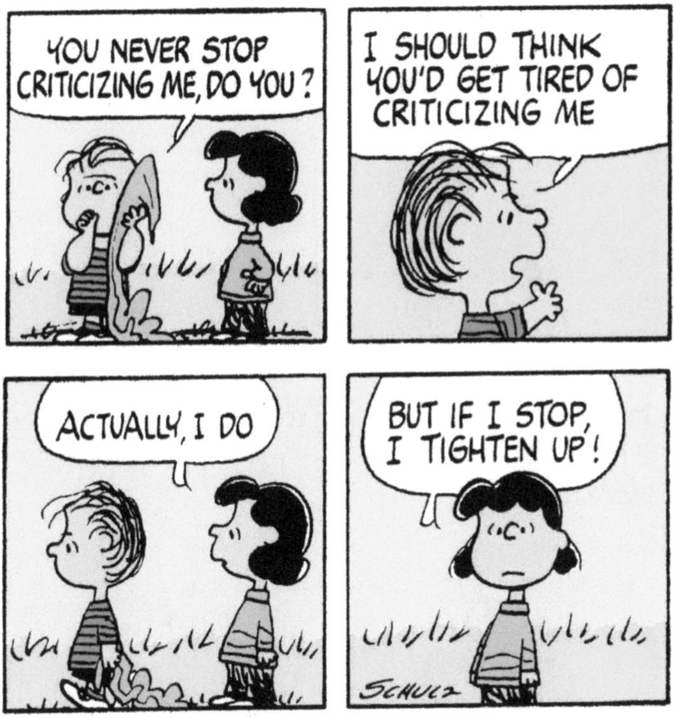
YOU NEVER STOP CRITICIZING ME, DO YOU?
I SHOULD THINK YOU'D GET TIRED OF CRITICIZING ME
ACTUALLY, I DO
BUT IF I STOP, I TIGHTEN UP!
SCHULZ

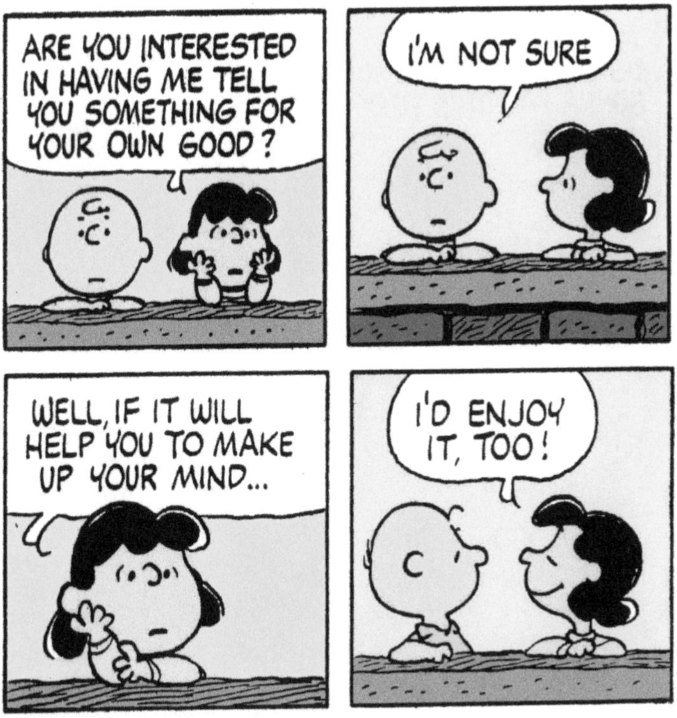
ARE YOU INTERESTED IN HAVING ME TELL YOU SOMETHING FOR YOUR OWN GOOD?
I'M NOT SURE
WELL, IF IT WILL HELP YOU TO MAKE UP YOUR MIND...
I'D ENJOY IT, TOO!

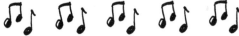

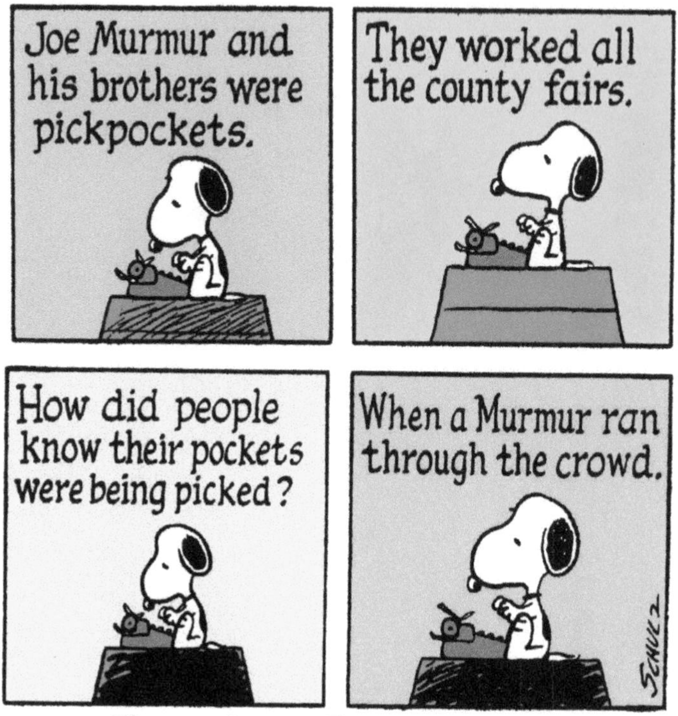
Joe Murmur and his brothers were pickpockets.
They worked all the county fairs.
How did people know their pockets were being picked?
When a Murmur ran through the crowd.
SCHULZ

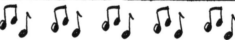

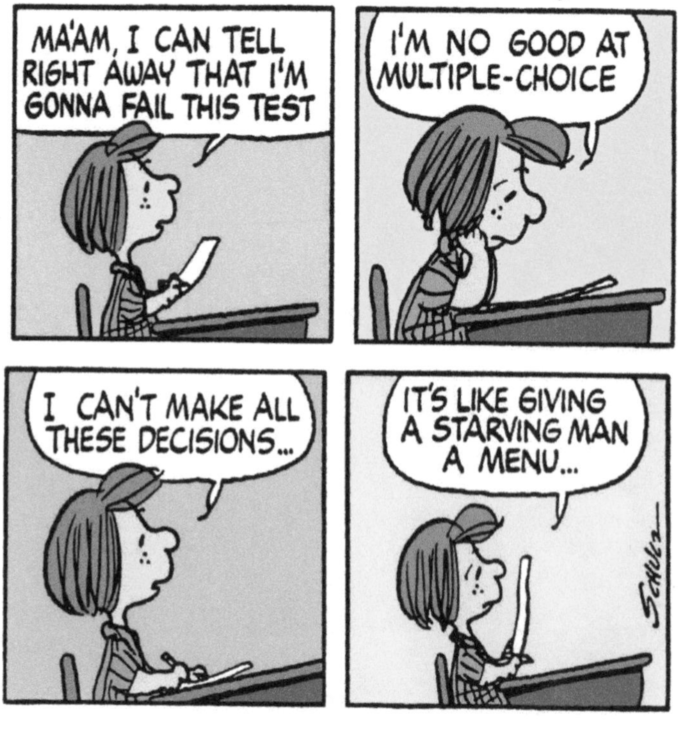
MA'AM, I CAN TELL RIGHT AWAY THAT I'M GONNA FAIL THIS TEST
I'M NO GOOD AT MULTIPLE-CHOICE
I CAN'T MAKE ALL THESE DECISIONS...
IT'S LIKE GIVING A STARVING MAN A MENU...
SCHULZ

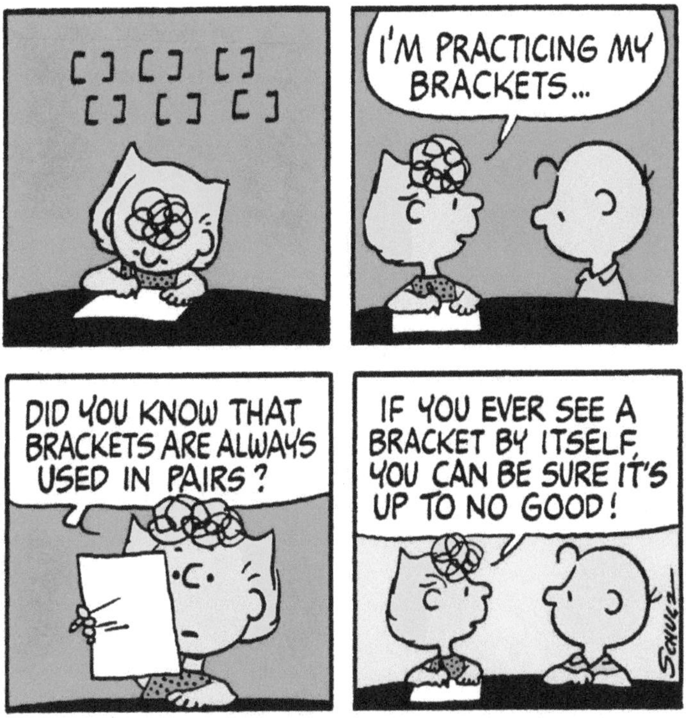
[ ] [ ] [ ]
[ ] [ ] [ ]
I'M PRACTICING MY BRACKETS...
DID YOU KNOW THAT BRACKETS ARE ALWAYS USED IN PAIRS ?
IF YOU EVER SEE A BRACKET BY ITSELF, YOU CAN BE SURE IT'S UP TO NO GOOD !
SCHULZ

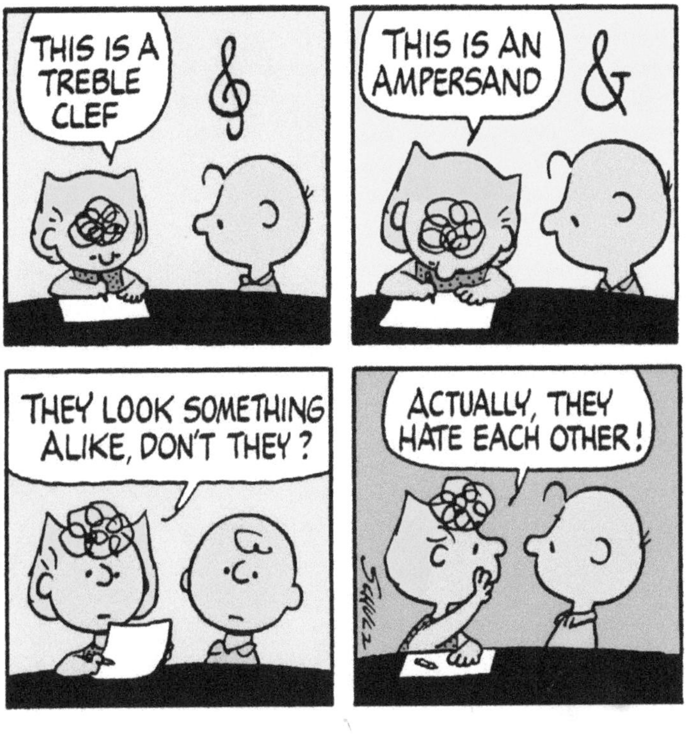
THIS IS A TREBLE CLEF
THIS IS AN AMPERSAND
&
THEY LOOK SOMETHING ALIKE, DON'T THEY ?
ACTUALLY, THEY HATE EACH OTHER !
SCHULZ

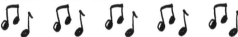

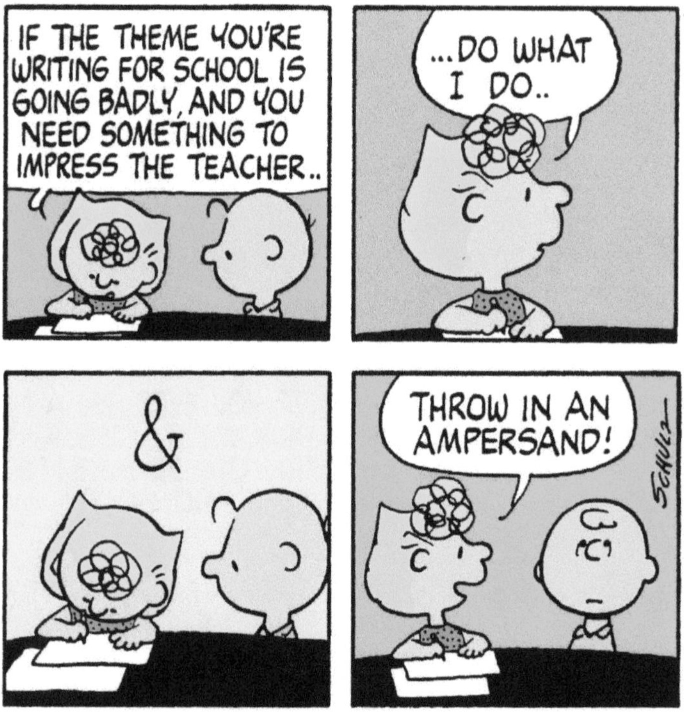
IF THE THEME YOU'RE WRITING FOR SCHOOL IS GOING BADLY, AND YOU NEED SOMETHING TO IMPRESS THE TEACHER..
...DO WHAT I DO..
&
THROW IN AN AMPERSAND!
SCHULZ

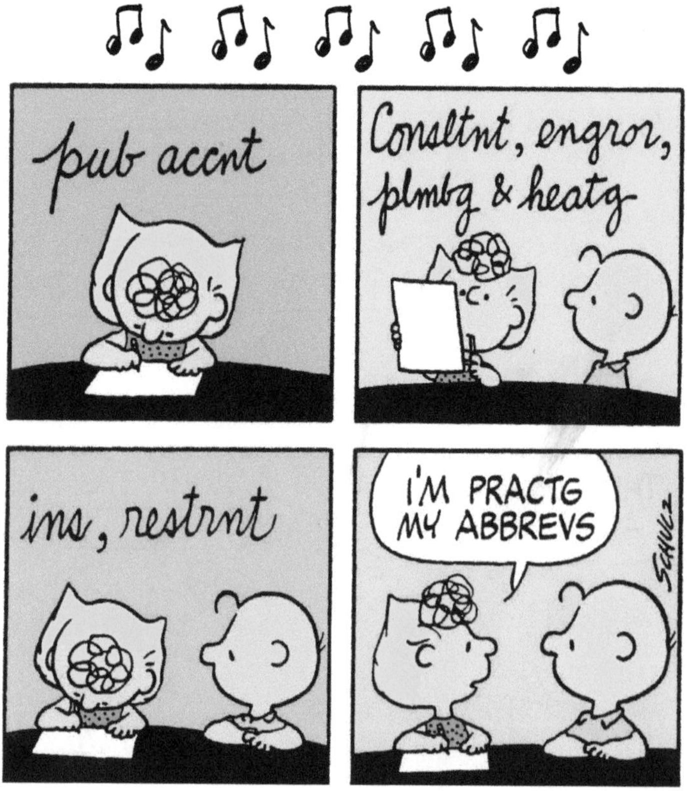
pub accnt
Consltnt, engnr, plmbg & heatg
ins, restrnt
I'M PRACTG MY ABBREVS
SCHULZ

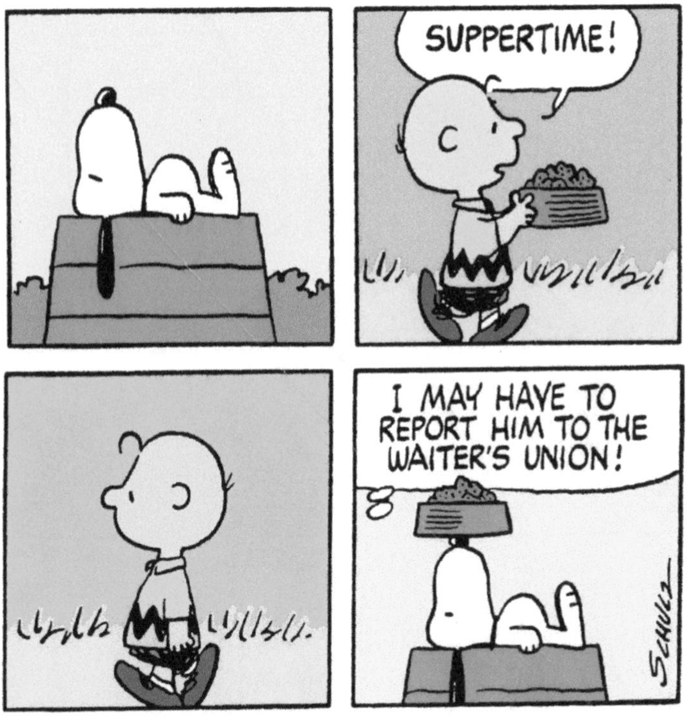
SUPPERTIME!
I MAY HAVE TO REPORT HIM TO THE WAITER'S UNION!
SCHULZ

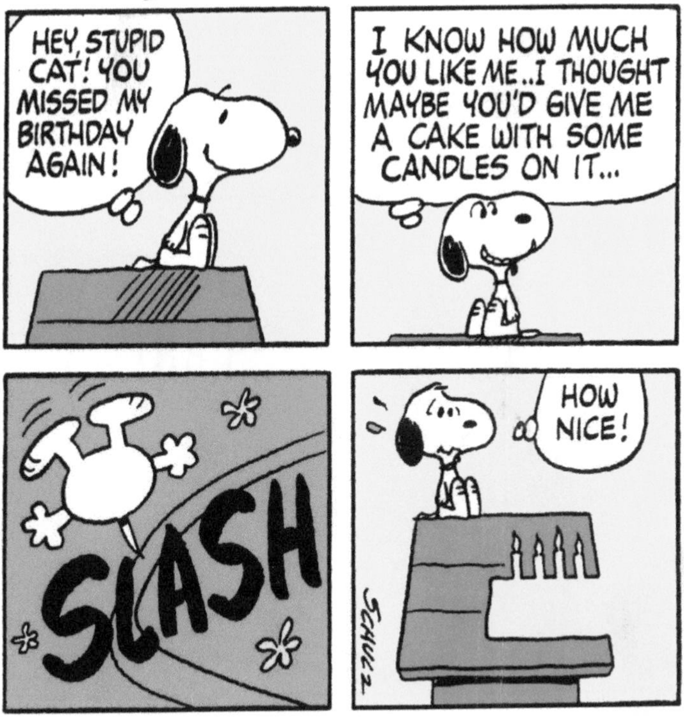
HEY, STUPID CAT! YOU MISSED MY BIRTHDAY AGAIN!
I KNOW HOW MUCH YOU LIKE ME..I THOUGHT MAYBE YOU'D GIVE ME A CAKE WITH SOME CANDLES ON IT...
SLASH
HOW NICE!
SCHULZ

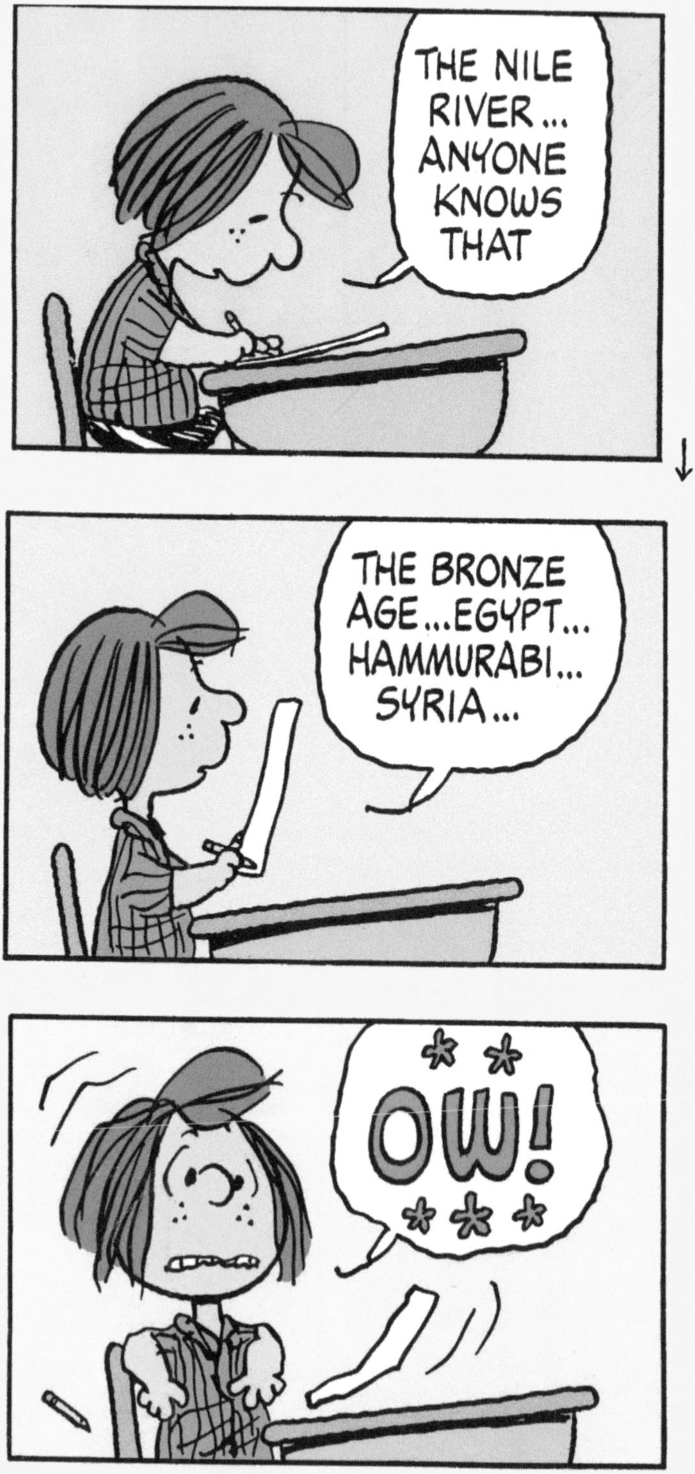
THE NILE RIVER... ANYONE KNOWS THAT
THE BRONZE AGE...EGYPT... HAMMURABI... SYRIA...
OW!

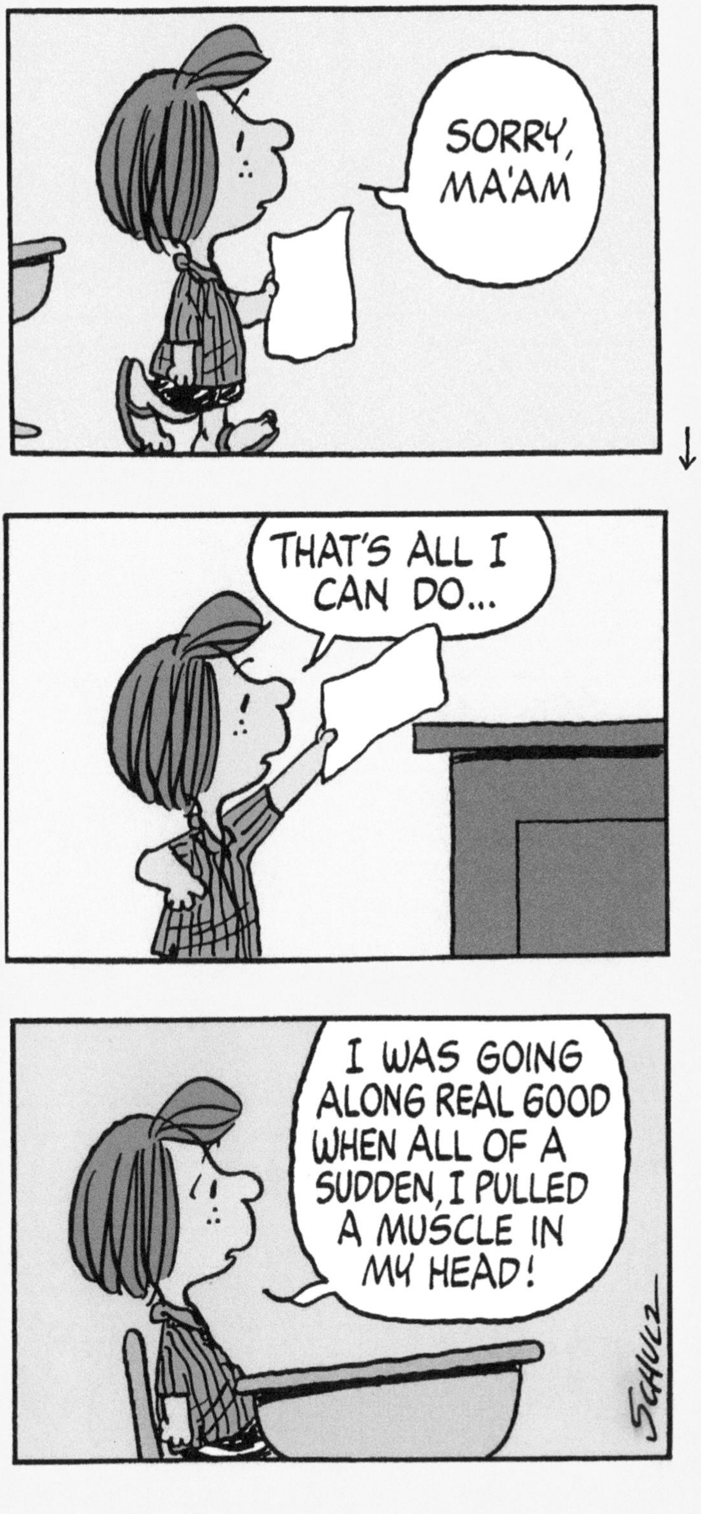
SORRY, MA'AM
THAT'S ALL I CAN DO...
I WAS GOING ALONG REAL GOOD WHEN ALL OF A SUDDEN, I PULLED A MUSCLE IN MY HEAD!
SCHULZ

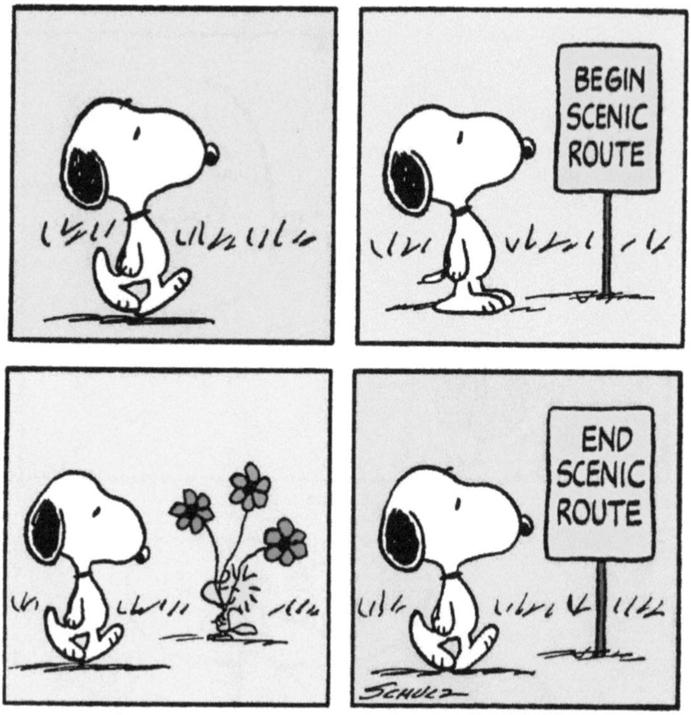
BEGIN SCENIC ROUTE
END SCENIC ROUTE
SCHULZ

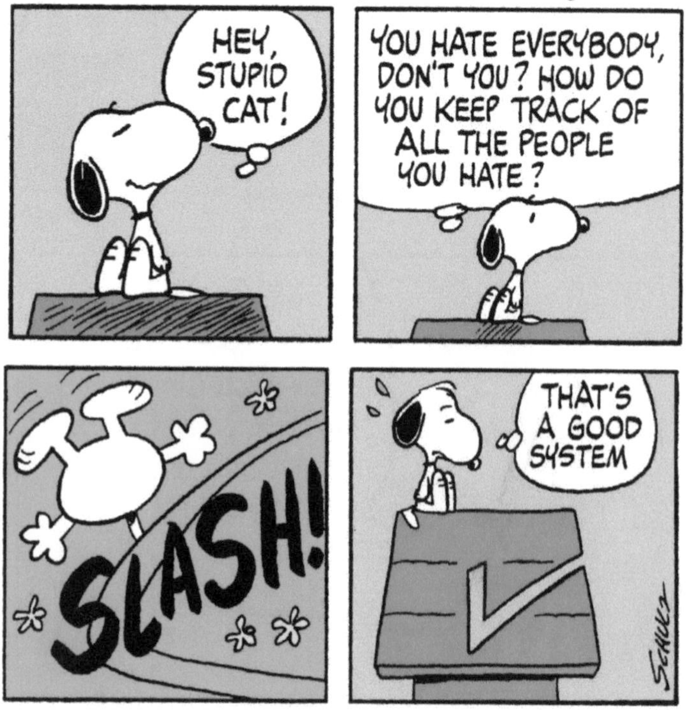
HEY, STUPID CAT!
YOU HATE EVERYBODY, DON'T YOU? HOW DO YOU KEEP TRACK OF ALL THE PEOPLE YOU HATE?
SLASH!
THAT'S A GOOD SYSTEM
SCHULZ

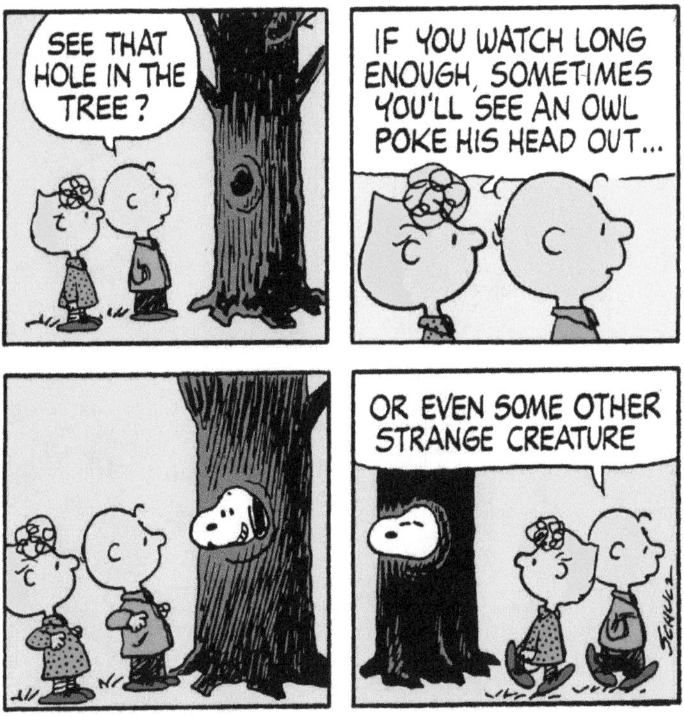
SEE THAT HOLE IN THE TREE?
IF YOU WATCH LONG ENOUGH, SOMETIMES YOU'LL SEE AN OWL POKE HIS HEAD OUT...
OR EVEN SOME OTHER STRANGE CREATURE
SCHULZ

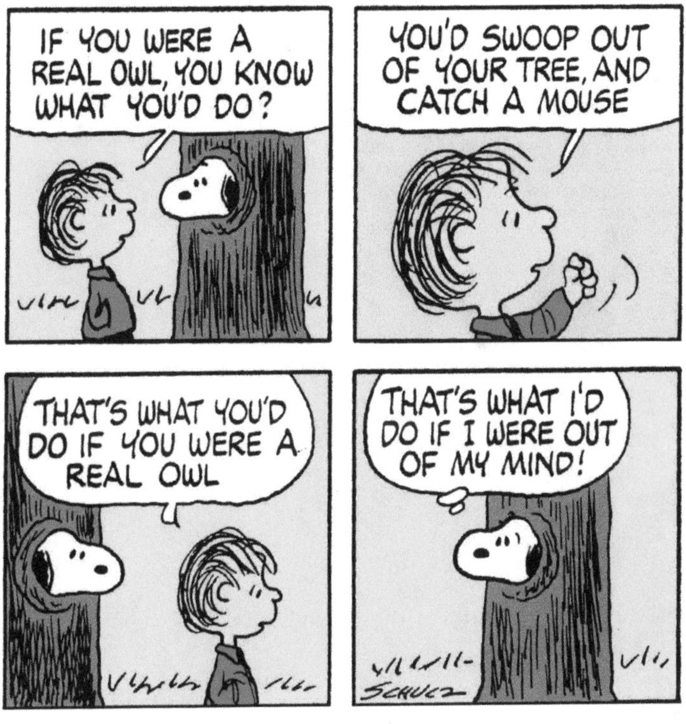
IF YOU WERE A REAL OWL, YOU KNOW WHAT YOU'D DO?
YOU'D SWOOP OUT OF YOUR TREE, AND CATCH A MOUSE
THAT'S WHAT YOU'D DO IF YOU WERE A REAL OWL
THAT'S WHAT I'D DO IF I WERE OUT OF MY MIND!
SCHULZ

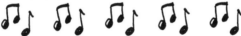

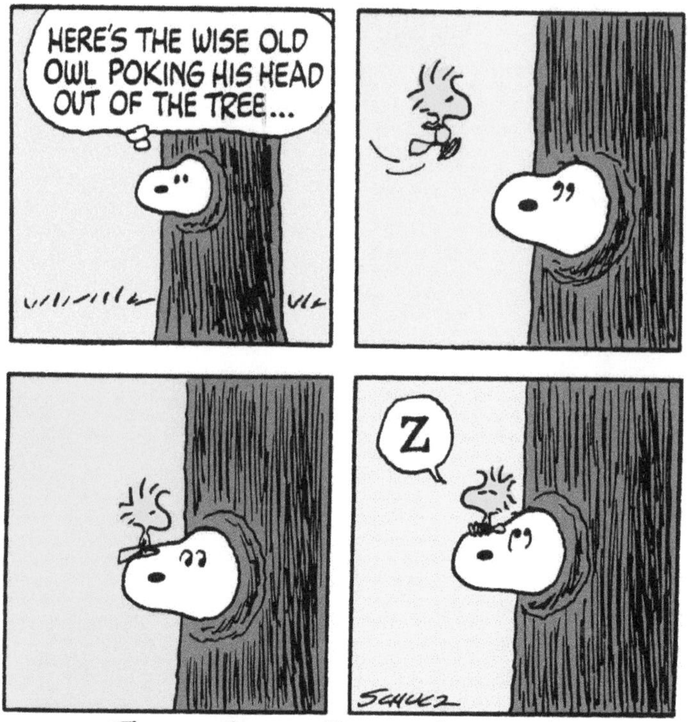
HERE'S THE WISE OLD OWL POKING HIS HEAD OUT OF THE TREE...
Z

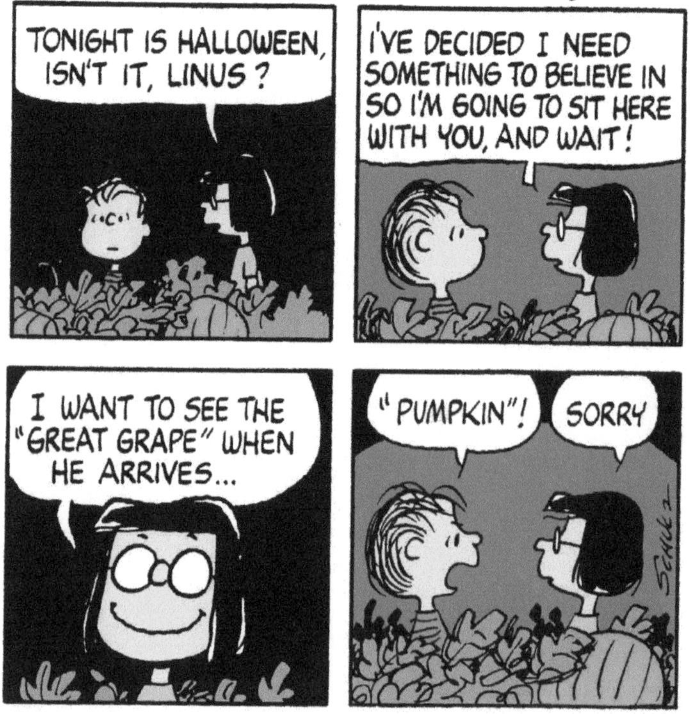
TONIGHT IS HALLOWEEN, ISN'T IT, LINUS?
I'VE DECIDED I NEED SOMETHING TO BELIEVE IN SO I'M GOING TO SIT HERE WITH YOU, AND WAIT!
I WANT TO SEE THE "GREAT GRAPE" WHEN HE ARRIVES...
"PUMPKIN"!
SORRY

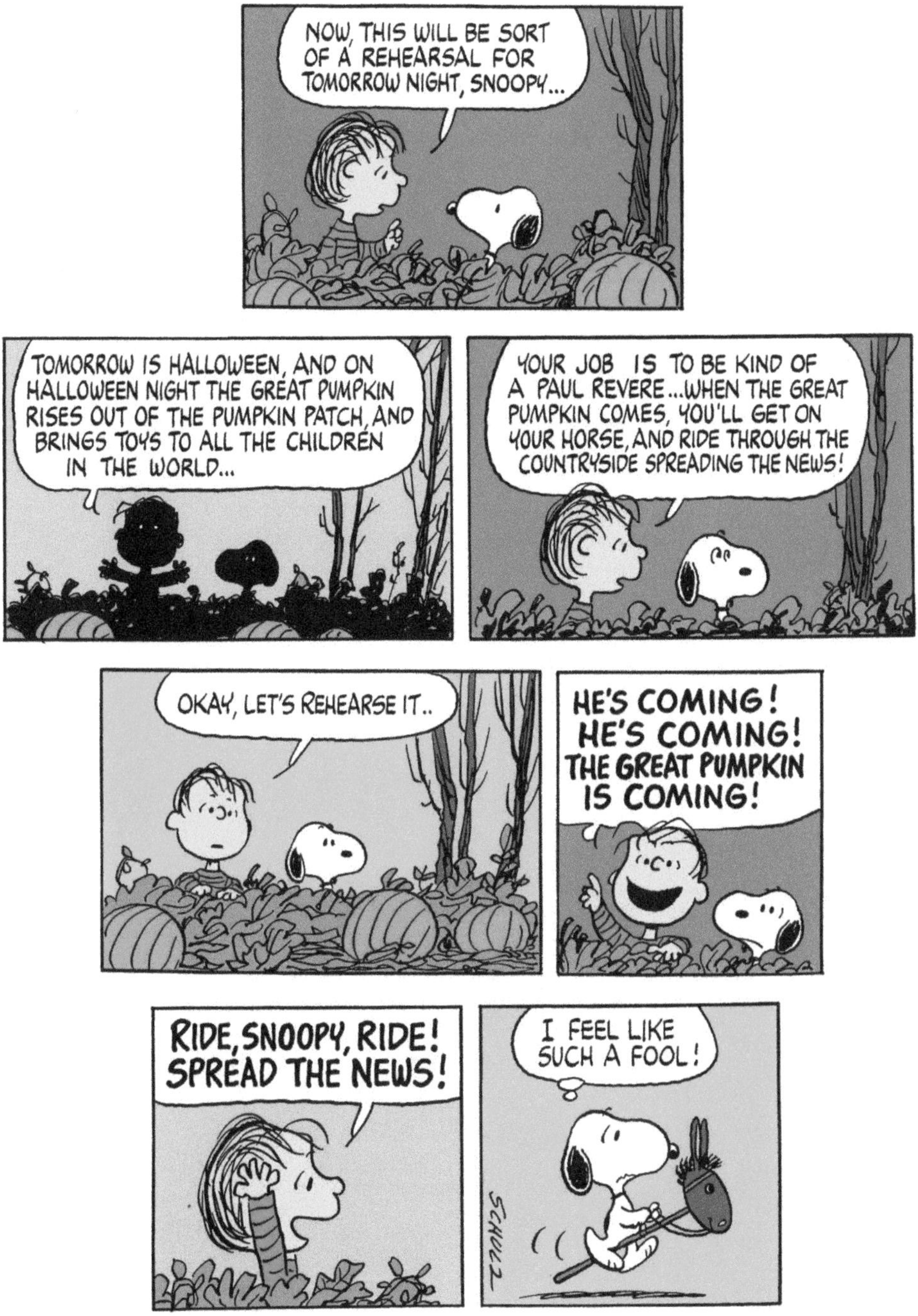
NOW, THIS WILL BE SORT OF A REHEARSAL FOR TOMORROW NIGHT, SNOOPY...
TOMORROW IS HALLOWEEN, AND ON HALLOWEEN NIGHT THE GREAT PUMPKIN RISES OUT OF THE PUMPKIN PATCH, AND BRINGS TOYS TO ALL THE CHILDREN IN THE WORLD...
YOUR JOB IS TO BE KIND OF A PAUL REVERE...WHEN THE GREAT PUMPKIN COMES, YOU'LL GET ON YOUR HORSE, AND RIDE THROUGH THE COUNTRYSIDE SPREADING THE NEWS!
OKAY, LET'S REHEARSE IT..
HE'S COMING! HE'S COMING! THE GREAT PUMPKIN IS COMING!
RIDE, SNOOPY, RIDE! SPREAD THE NEWS!
I FEEL LIKE SUCH A FOOL!

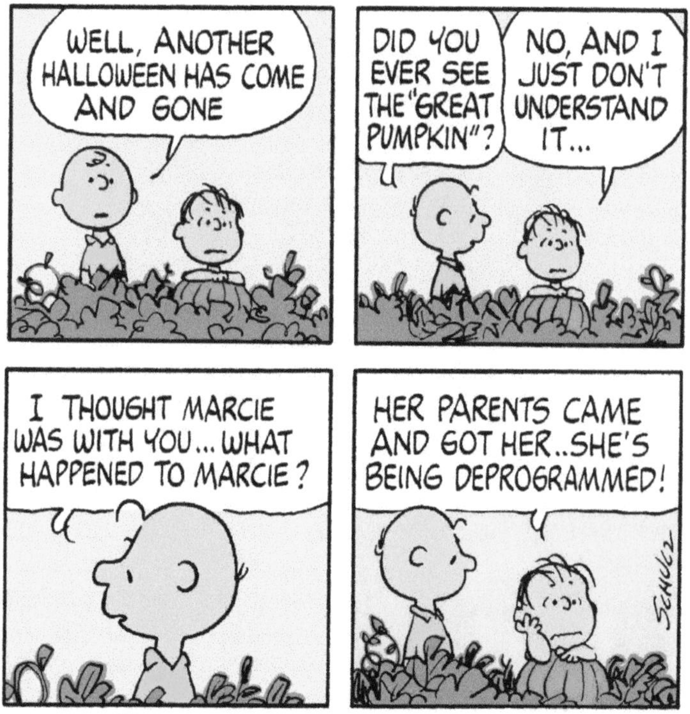
WELL, ANOTHER HALLOWEEN HAS COME AND GONE
DID YOU EVER SEE THE "GREAT PUMPKIN"?
NO, AND I JUST DON'T UNDERSTAND IT...
I THOUGHT MARCIE WAS WITH YOU... WHAT HAPPENED TO MARCIE?
HER PARENTS CAME AND GOT HER..SHE'S BEING DEPROGRAMMED!
SCHULZ

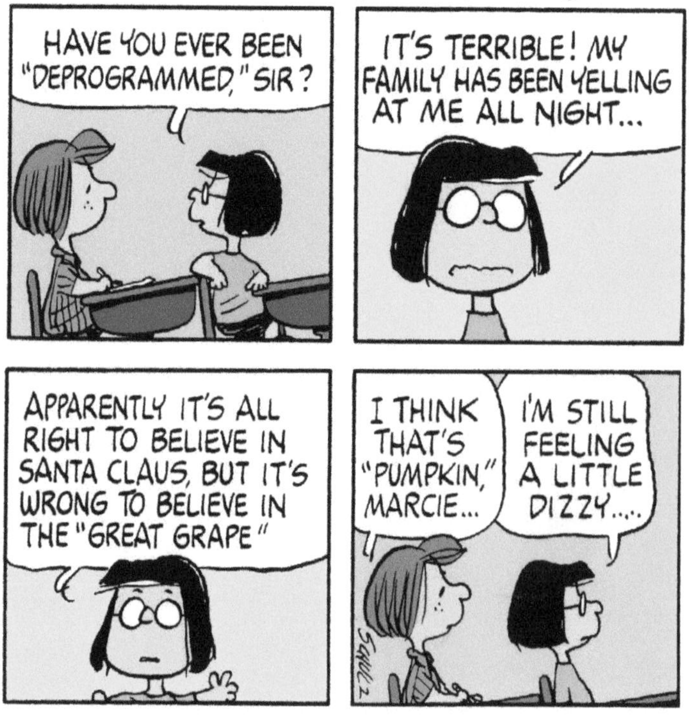
HAVE YOU EVER BEEN "DEPROGRAMMED," SIR?
IT'S TERRIBLE! MY FAMILY HAS BEEN YELLING AT ME ALL NIGHT...
APPARENTLY IT'S ALL RIGHT TO BELIEVE IN SANTA CLAUS, BUT IT'S WRONG TO BELIEVE IN THE "GREAT GRAPE"
I THINK THAT'S "PUMPKIN," MARCIE...
I'M STILL FEELING A LITTLE DIZZY.....
SCHULZ

I HEAR THEY'VE BEEN CALLING YOU A FALSE PROPHET
WHO CARES?
I HAVE AN IDEA
NO ONE IN MY CLASS HAS EVER SEEN A FALSE PROPHET...
HOW ABOUT JOINING ME FOR "SHOW AND TELL"?
SCHULZ

THIS IS MY REPORT ON CLEOPATRA...
ALL MY LIFE I HAVE ADMIRED CLEOPATRA
THEN I DISCOVERED A COUPLE OF THINGS ABOUT HER
MY ROLE MODEL LET ME DOWN!
SCHULZ

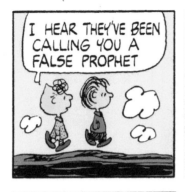

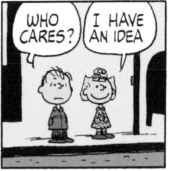

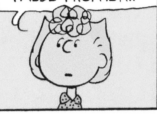

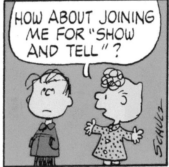

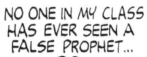

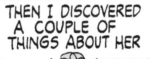

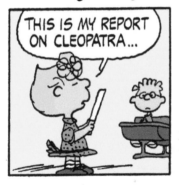

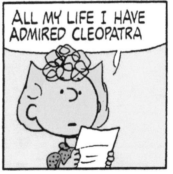

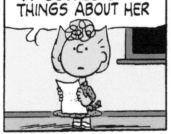

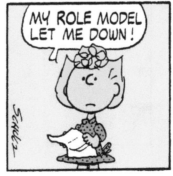

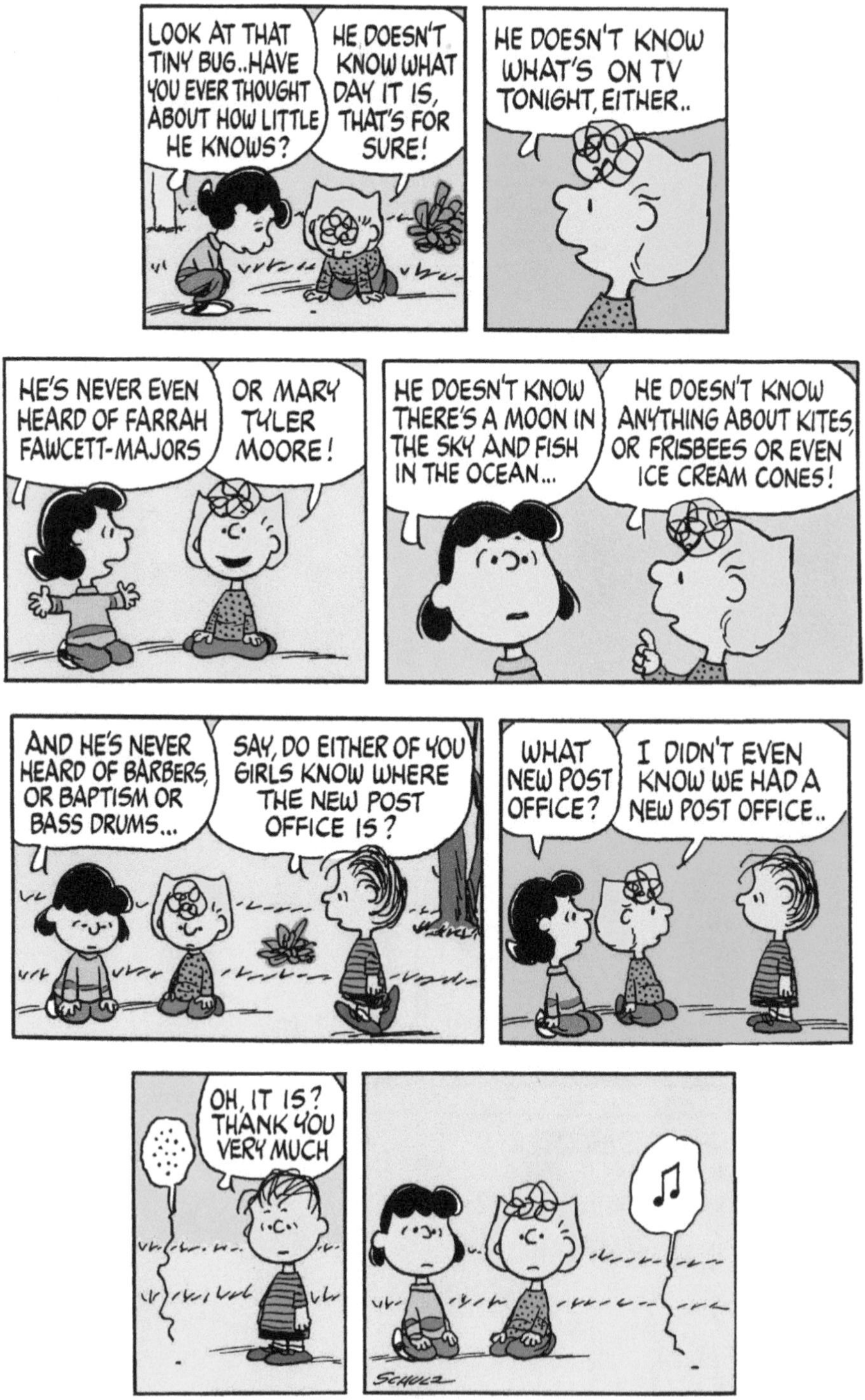
LOOK AT THAT TINY BUG..HAVE YOU EVER THOUGHT ABOUT HOW LITTLE HE KNOWS?
HE DOESN'T KNOW WHAT DAY IT IS, THAT'S FOR SURE!
HE DOESN'T KNOW WHAT'S ON TV TONIGHT, EITHER..
HE'S NEVER EVEN HEARD OF FARRAH FAWCETT-MAJORS
OR MARY TYLER MOORE!
HE DOESN'T KNOW THERE'S A MOON IN THE SKY AND FISH IN THE OCEAN...
HE DOESN'T KNOW ANYTHING ABOUT KITES, OR FRISBEES OR EVEN ICE CREAM CONES!
AND HE'S NEVER HEARD OF BARBERS, OR BAPTISM OR BASS DRUMS...
SAY, DO EITHER OF YOU GIRLS KNOW WHERE THE NEW POST OFFICE IS?
WHAT NEW POST OFFICE?
I DIDN'T EVEN KNOW WE HAD A NEW POST OFFICE..
OH, IT IS? THANK YOU VERY MUCH
SCHULZ

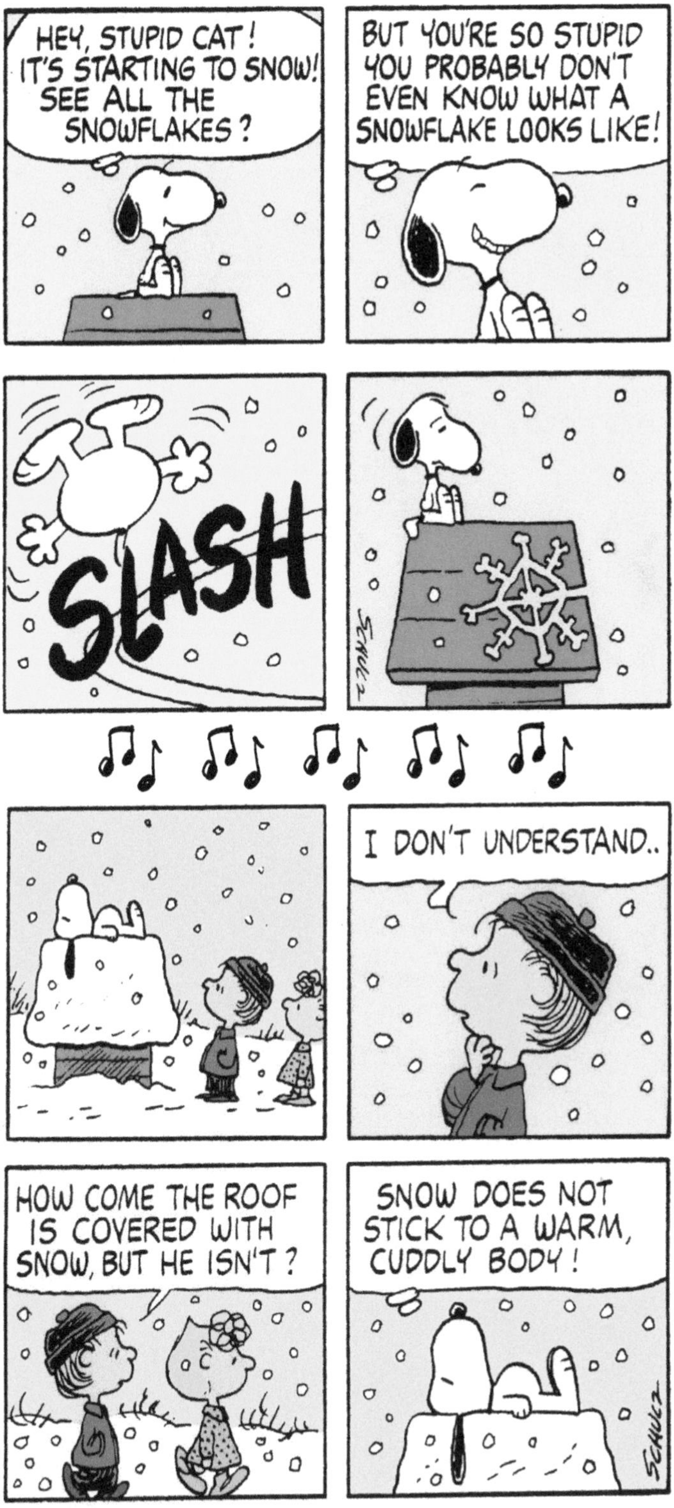
HEY, STUPID CAT! IT'S STARTING TO SNOW! SEE ALL THE SNOWFLAKES?
BUT YOU'RE SO STUPID YOU PROBABLY DON'T EVEN KNOW WHAT A SNOWFLAKE LOOKS LIKE!
SLASH
SCHULZ
I DON'T UNDERSTAND..
HOW COME THE ROOF IS COVERED WITH SNOW, BUT HE ISN'T?
SNOW DOES NOT STICK TO A WARM, CUDDLY BODY!
SCHULZ

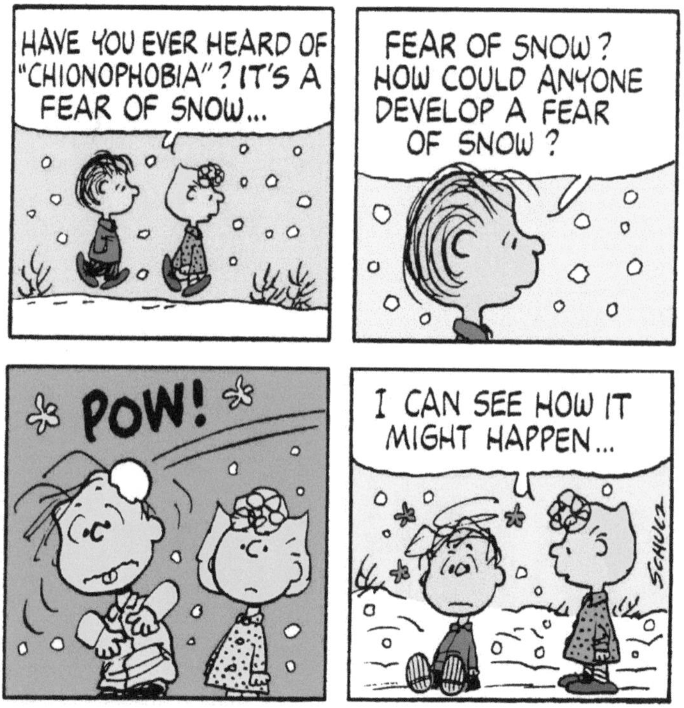
HAVE YOU EVER HEARD OF "CHIONOPHOBIA"? IT'S A FEAR OF SNOW...
FEAR OF SNOW? HOW COULD ANYONE DEVELOP A FEAR OF SNOW?
POW!
I CAN SEE HOW IT MIGHT HAPPEN...
SCHULZ

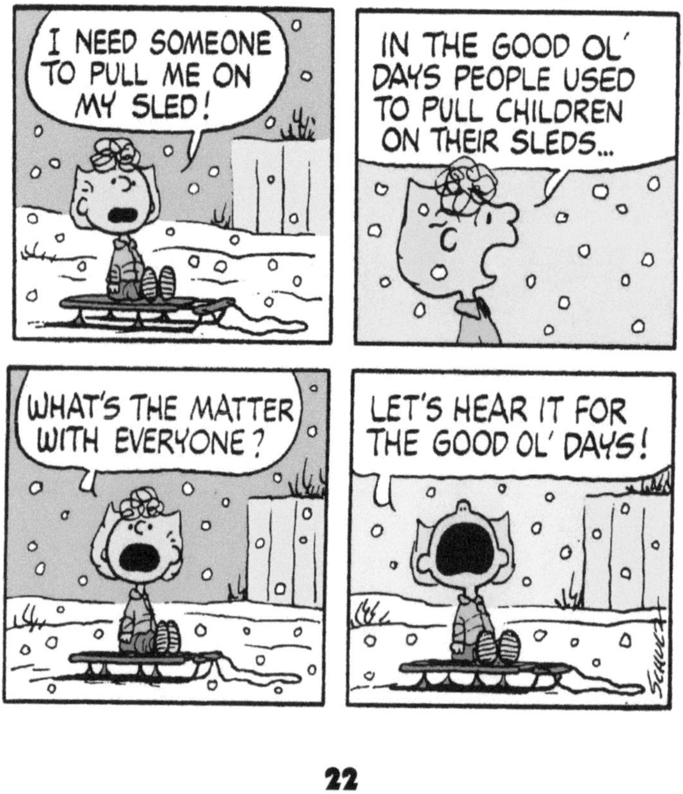
I NEED SOMEONE TO PULL ME ON MY SLED!
IN THE GOOD OL' DAYS PEOPLE USED TO PULL CHILDREN ON THEIR SLEDS...
WHAT'S THE MATTER WITH EVERYONE?
LET'S HEAR IT FOR THE GOOD OL' DAYS!
SCHULZ

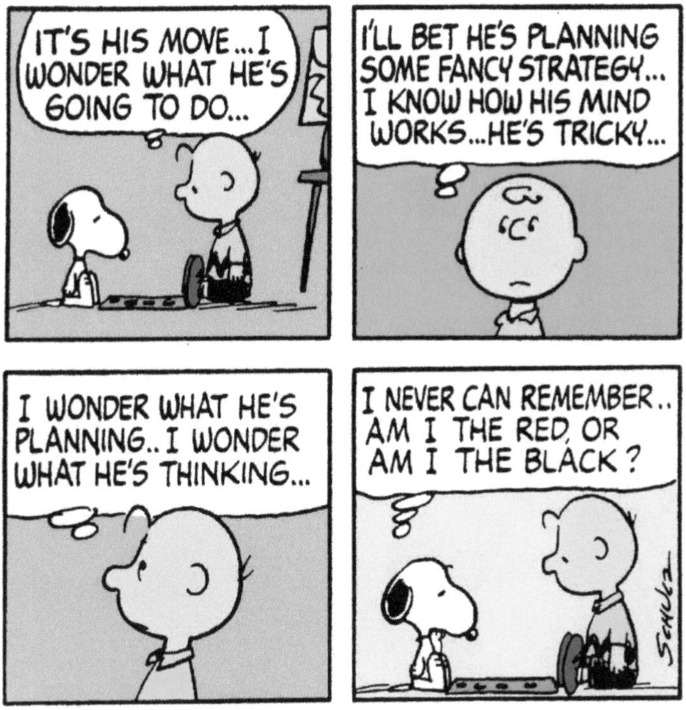
IT'S HIS MOVE...I WONDER WHAT HE'S GOING TO DO...
I'LL BET HE'S PLANNING SOME FANCY STRATEGY... I KNOW HOW HIS MIND WORKS...HE'S TRICKY...
I WONDER WHAT HE'S PLANNING..I WONDER WHAT HE'S THINKING...
I NEVER CAN REMEMBER.. AM I THE RED, OR AM I THE BLACK?
SCHULZ

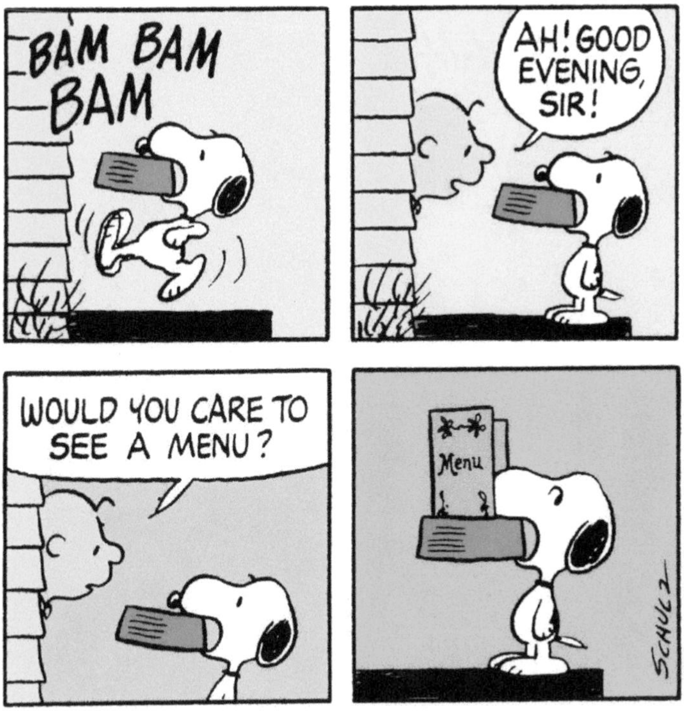
BAM BAM BAM
AH! GOOD EVENING, SIR!
WOULD YOU CARE TO SEE A MENU?
Menu
SCHULZ

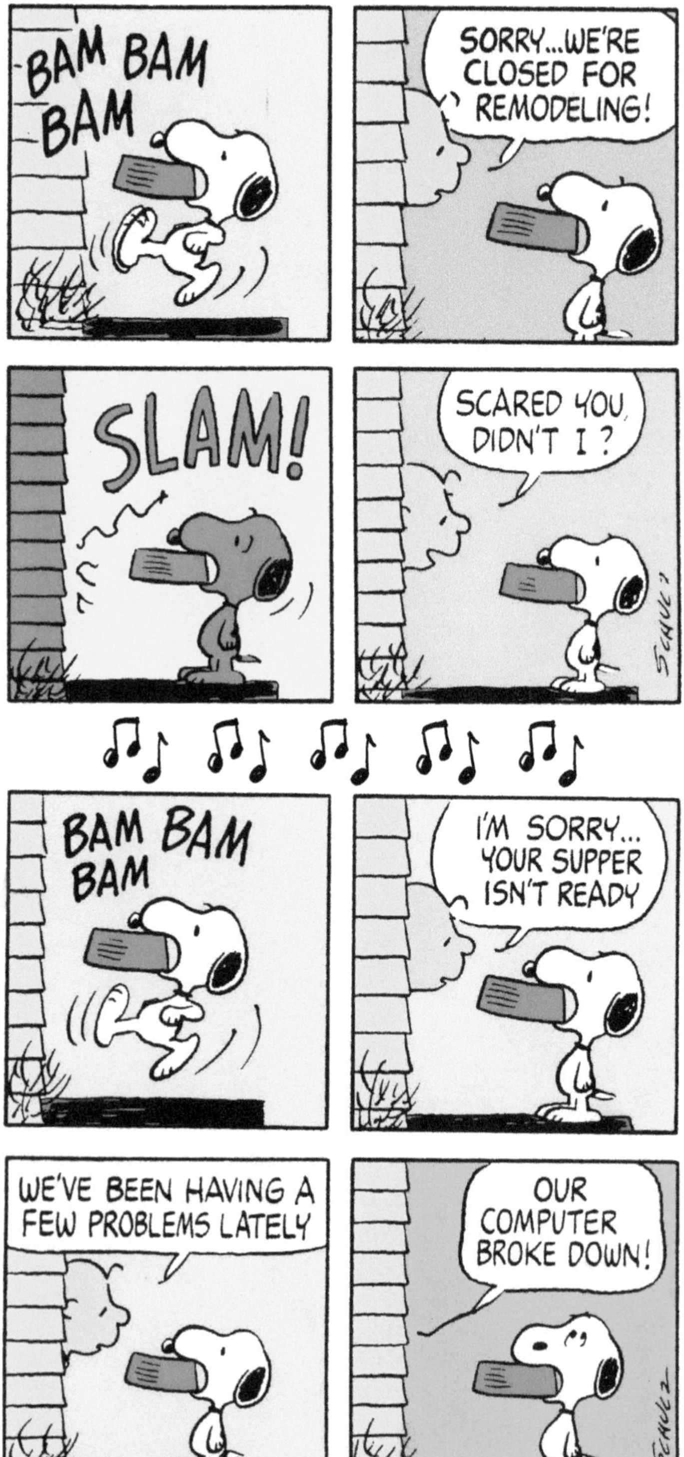
BAM BAM BAM
SORRY...WE'RE CLOSED FOR REMODELING!
SLAM!
SCARED YOU, DIDN'T I ?
BAM BAM BAM
I'M SORRY... YOUR SUPPER ISN'T READY
WE'VE BEEN HAVING A FEW PROBLEMS LATELY
OUR COMPUTER BROKE DOWN!

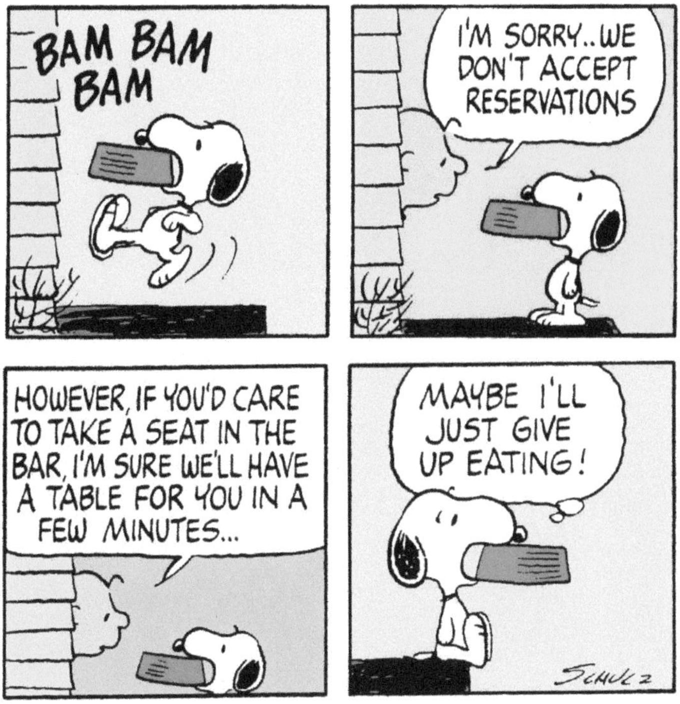
BAM BAM BAM
I'M SORRY..WE DON'T ACCEPT RESERVATIONS
HOWEVER, IF YOU'D CARE TO TAKE A SEAT IN THE BAR, I'M SURE WE'LL HAVE A TABLE FOR YOU IN A FEW MINUTES...
MAYBE I'LL JUST GIVE UP EATING!

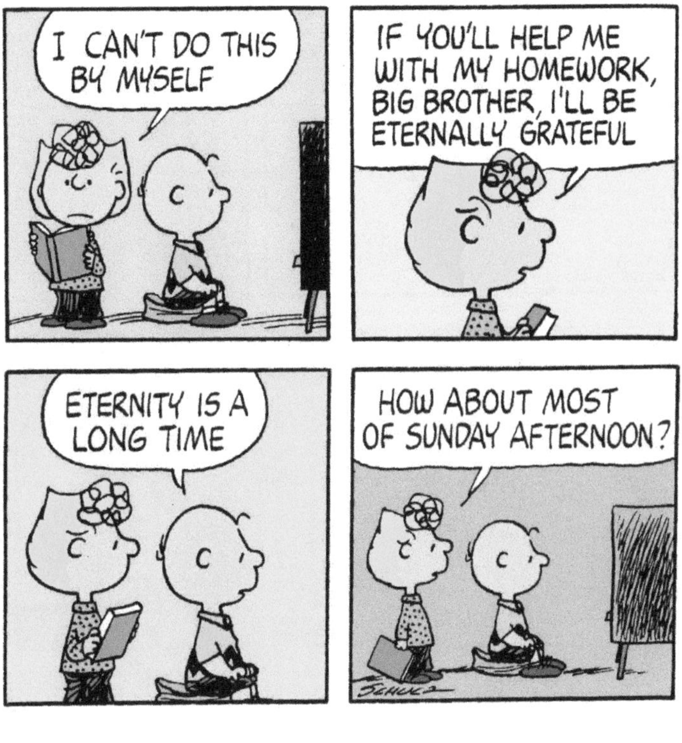
I CAN'T DO THIS BY MYSELF
IF YOU'LL HELP ME WITH MY HOMEWORK, BIG BROTHER, I'LL BE ETERNALLY GRATEFUL
ETERNITY IS A LONG TIME
HOW ABOUT MOST OF SUNDAY AFTERNOON?

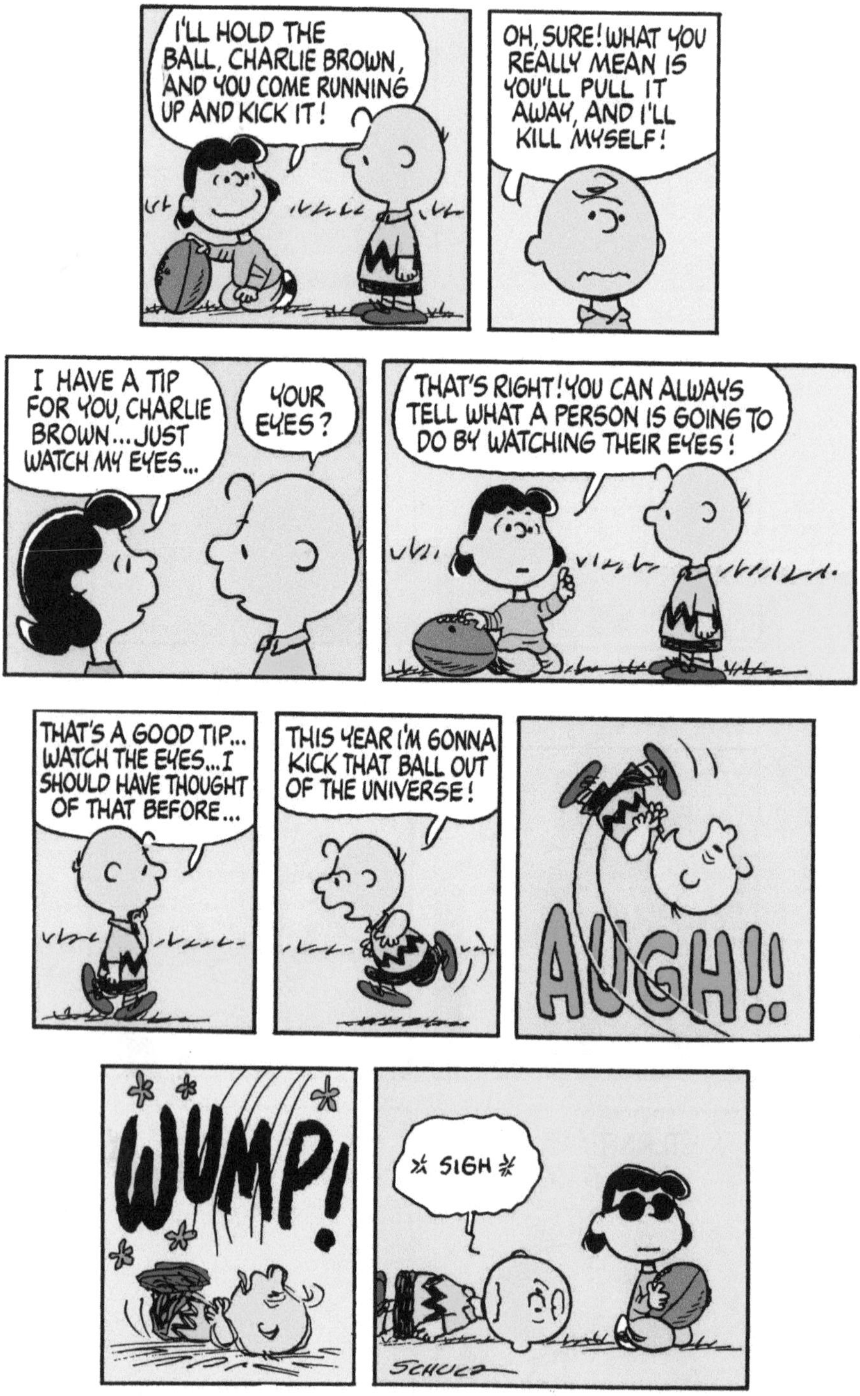
I'LL HOLD THE BALL, CHARLIE BROWN, AND YOU COME RUNNING UP AND KICK IT!
OH, SURE! WHAT YOU REALLY MEAN IS YOU'LL PULL IT AWAY, AND I'LL KILL MYSELF!
I HAVE A TIP FOR YOU, CHARLIE BROWN... JUST WATCH MY EYES...
YOUR EYES?
THAT'S RIGHT! YOU CAN ALWAYS TELL WHAT A PERSON IS GOING TO DO BY WATCHING THEIR EYES!
THAT'S A GOOD TIP... WATCH THE EYES... I SHOULD HAVE THOUGHT OF THAT BEFORE...
THIS YEAR I'M GONNA KICK THAT BALL OUT OF THE UNIVERSE!
AUGH!!
WUMP!
SIGH
SCHULZ

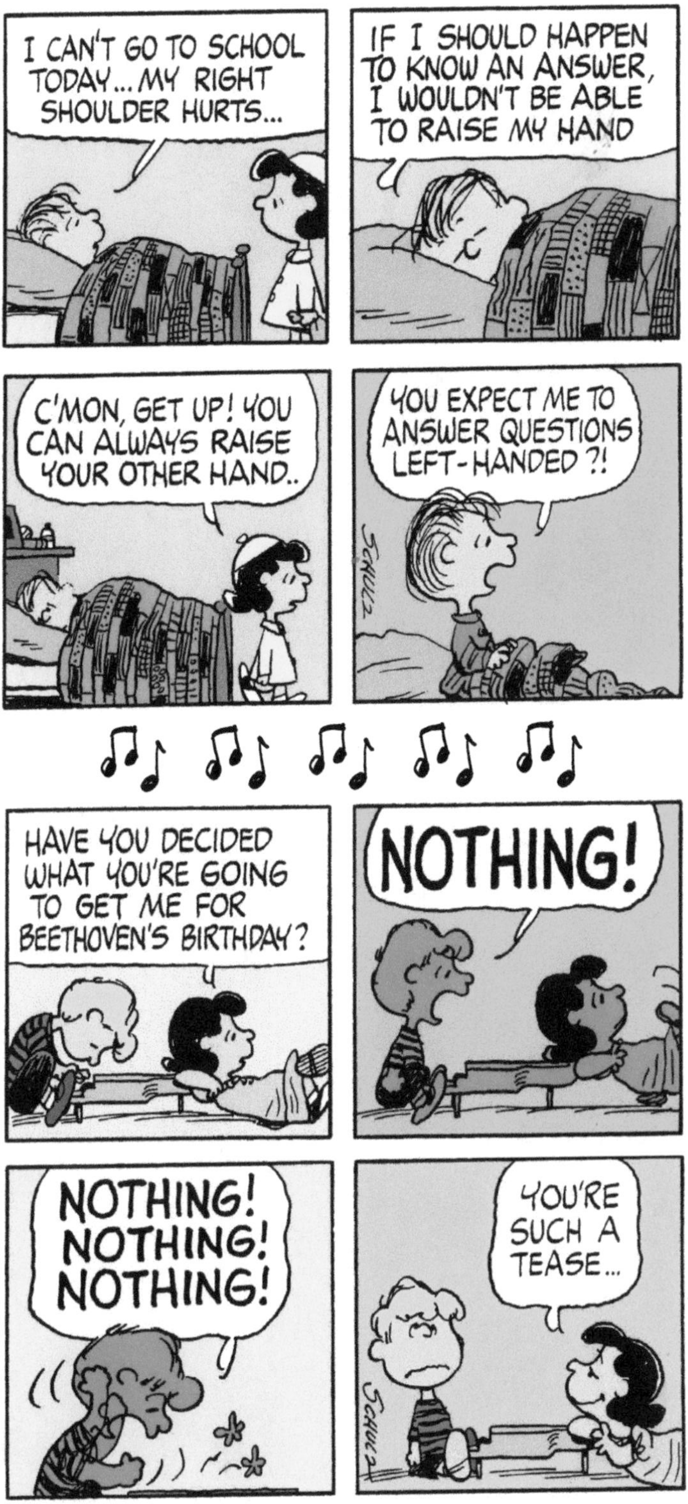
I CAN'T GO TO SCHOOL TODAY... MY RIGHT SHOULDER HURTS...
IF I SHOULD HAPPEN TO KNOW AN ANSWER, I WOULDN'T BE ABLE TO RAISE MY HAND
C'MON, GET UP! YOU CAN ALWAYS RAISE YOUR OTHER HAND..
YOU EXPECT ME TO ANSWER QUESTIONS LEFT-HANDED ?!
SCHULZ
HAVE YOU DECIDED WHAT YOU'RE GOING TO GET ME FOR BEETHOVEN'S BIRTHDAY ?
NOTHING!
NOTHING! NOTHING! NOTHING!
YOU'RE SUCH A TEASE...
SCHULZ

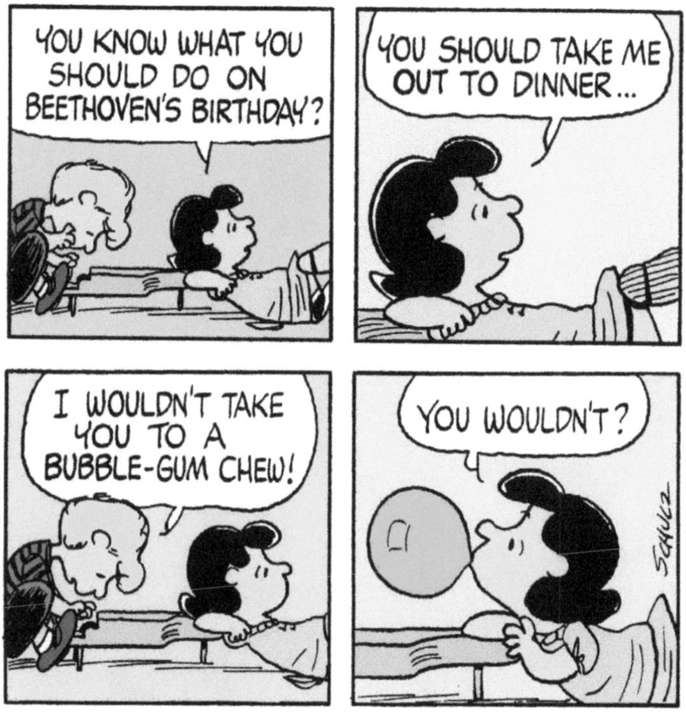
YOU KNOW WHAT YOU SHOULD DO ON BEETHOVEN'S BIRTHDAY?
YOU SHOULD TAKE ME OUT TO DINNER...
I WOULDN'T TAKE YOU TO A BUBBLE-GUM CHEW!
YOU WOULDN'T?
SCHULZ

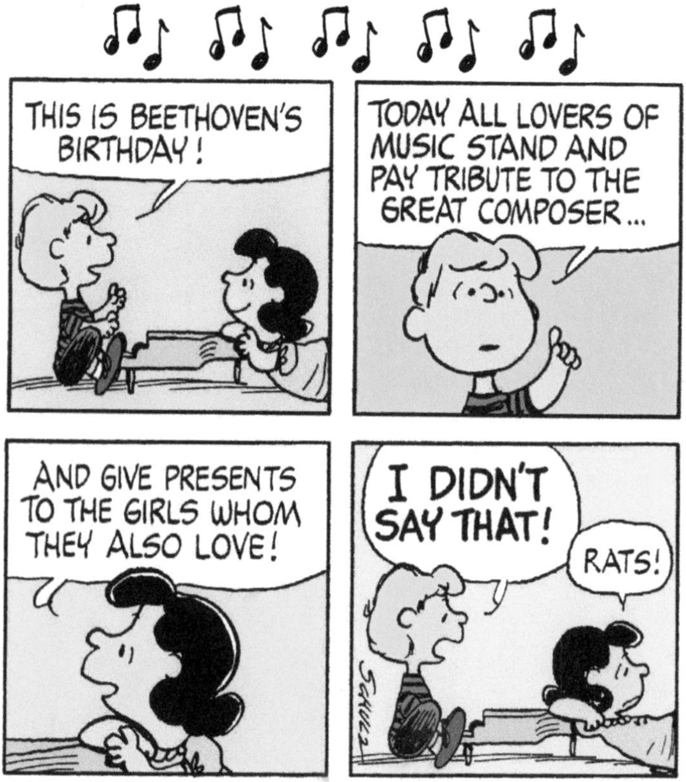
THIS IS BEETHOVEN'S BIRTHDAY!
TODAY ALL LOVERS OF MUSIC STAND AND PAY TRIBUTE TO THE GREAT COMPOSER...
AND GIVE PRESENTS TO THE GIRLS WHOM THEY ALSO LOVE!
I DIDN'T SAY THAT!
RATS!
SCHULZ

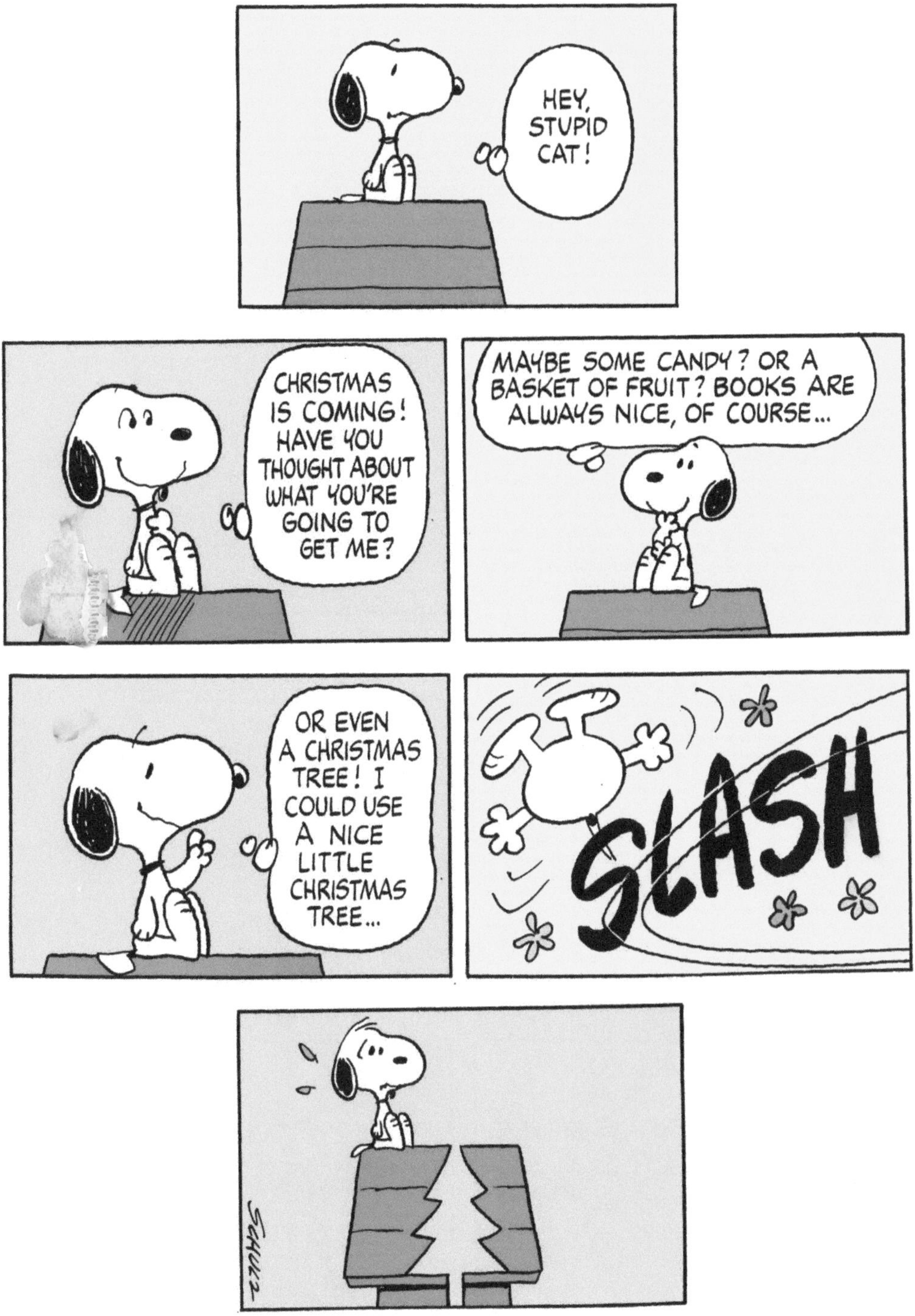
HEY, STUPID CAT!
CHRISTMAS IS COMING! HAVE YOU THOUGHT ABOUT WHAT YOU'RE GOING TO GET ME?
MAYBE SOME CANDY? OR A BASKET OF FRUIT? BOOKS ARE ALWAYS NICE, OF COURSE...
OR EVEN A CHRISTMAS TREE! I COULD USE A NICE LITTLE CHRISTMAS TREE...
SLASH
SCHULZ

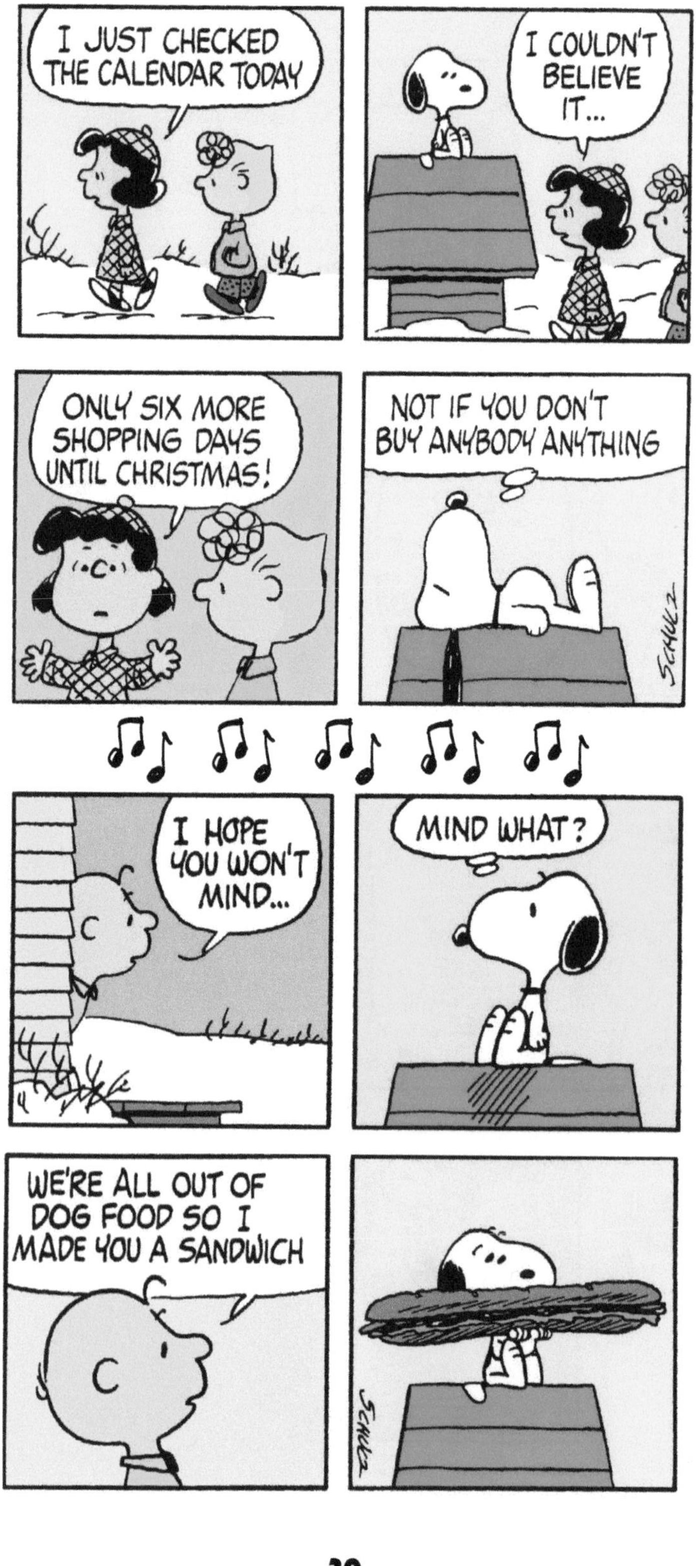
I JUST CHECKED THE CALENDAR TODAY
I COULDN'T BELIEVE IT...
ONLY SIX MORE SHOPPING DAYS UNTIL CHRISTMAS!
NOT IF YOU DON'T BUY ANYBODY ANYTHING
SCHULZ
I HOPE YOU WON'T MIND...
MIND WHAT?
WE'RE ALL OUT OF DOG FOOD SO I MADE YOU A SANDWICH
SCHULZ

SOMEHOW, I DON'T FEEL LIKE EATING
ACTUALLY, I'M MORE TIRED THAN HUNGRY...
WHAT I REALLY NEED IS A LITTLE NAP BEFORE DINNER...
SCHULZ

HEY, STUPID CAT!
I'M NOT AFRAID OF YOU ANY MORE..
IF YOU COME NEAR ME AGAIN, YOU KNOW WHAT I'LL DO?
I'LL HIT YOU WITH MY SANDWICH!
SCHULZ

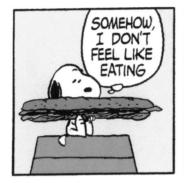

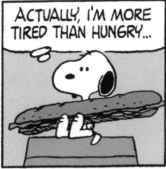

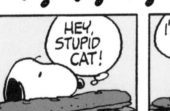

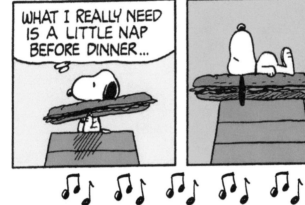

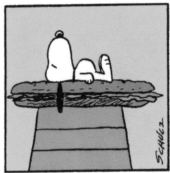

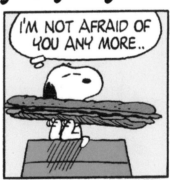

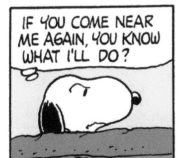

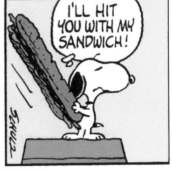

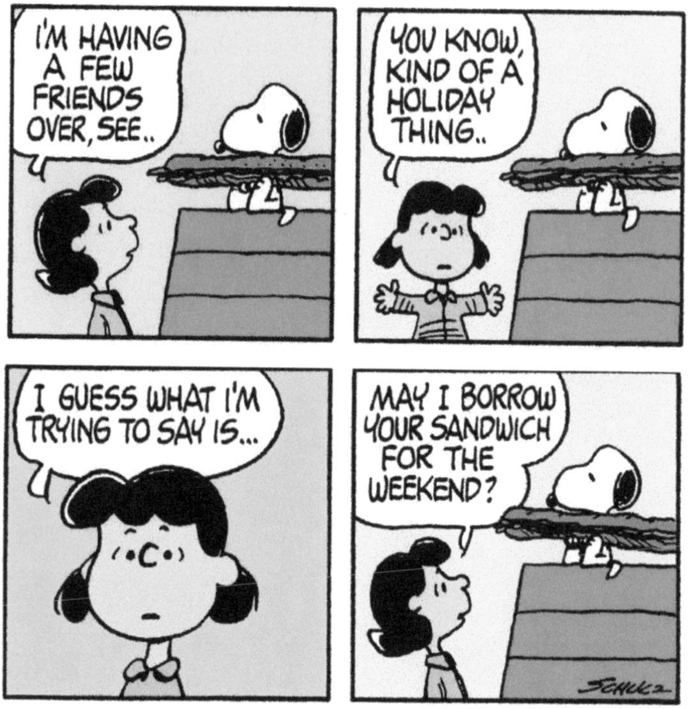
I'M HAVING A FEW FRIENDS OVER, SEE..
YOU KNOW, KIND OF A HOLIDAY THING..
I GUESS WHAT I'M TRYING TO SAY IS...
MAY I BORROW YOUR SANDWICH FOR THE WEEKEND?

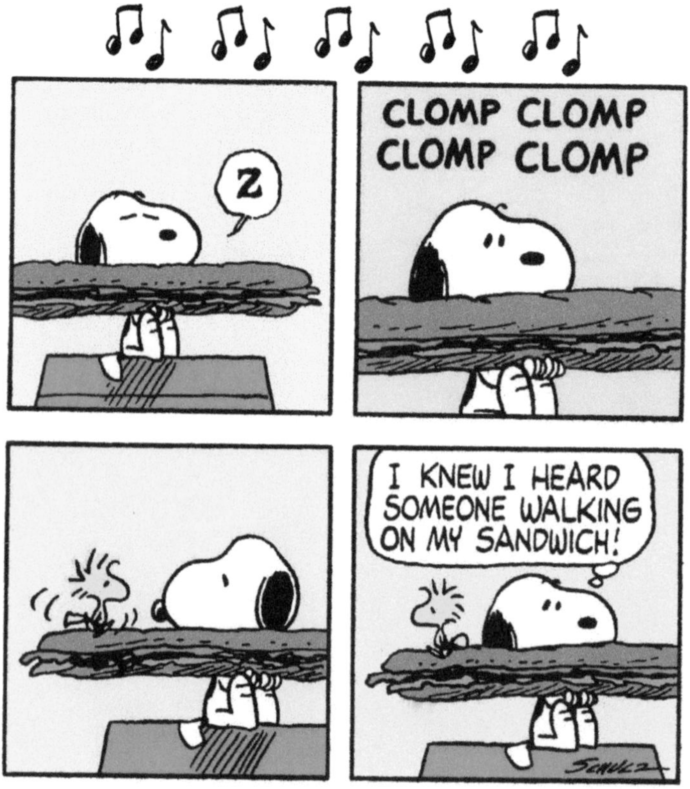
Z
CLOMP CLOMP CLOMP CLOMP
I KNEW I HEARD SOMEONE WALKING ON MY SANDWICH!

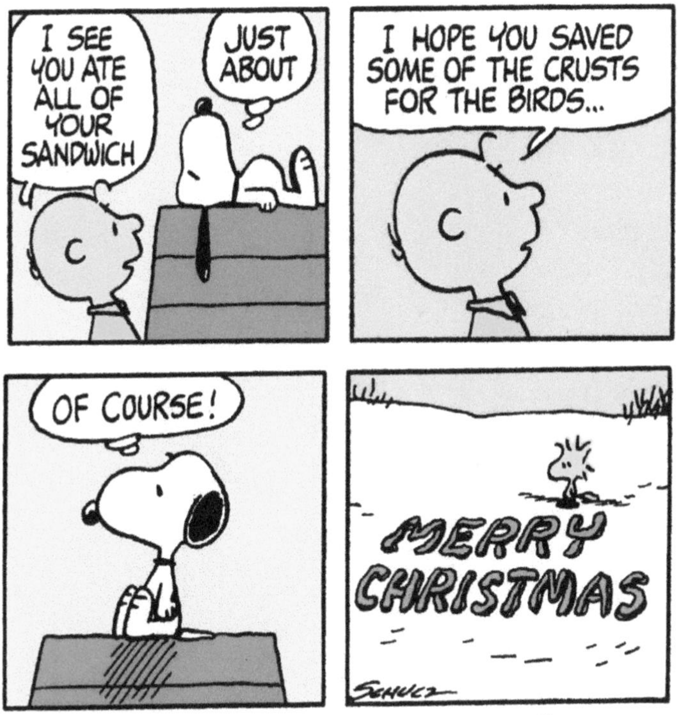
I SEE YOU ATE ALL OF YOUR SANDWICH
JUST ABOUT
I HOPE YOU SAVED SOME OF THE CRUSTS FOR THE BIRDS...
OF COURSE!
MERRY CHRISTMAS
SCHULZ

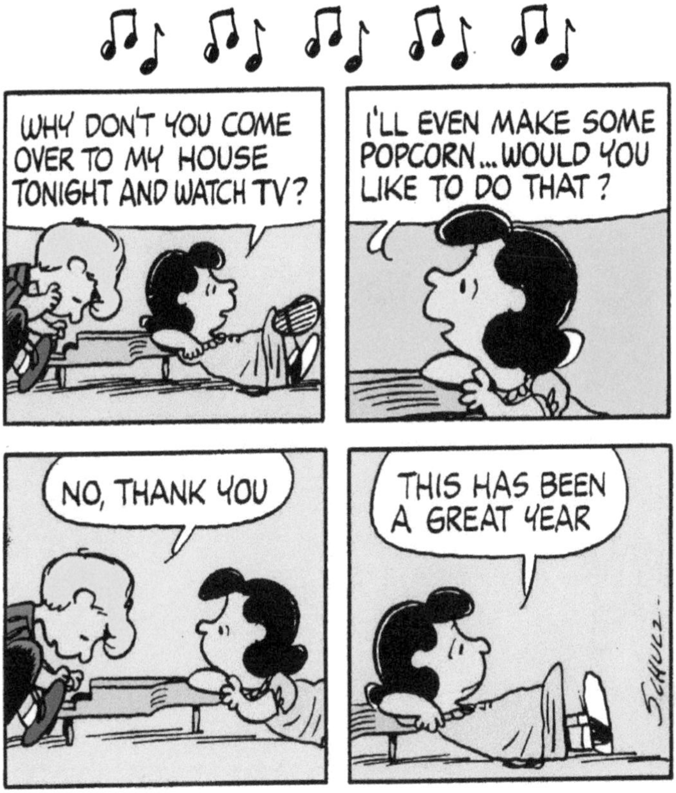
WHY DON'T YOU COME OVER TO MY HOUSE TONIGHT AND WATCH TV?
I'LL EVEN MAKE SOME POPCORN...WOULD YOU LIKE TO DO THAT?
NO, THANK YOU
THIS HAS BEEN A GREAT YEAR
SCHULZ

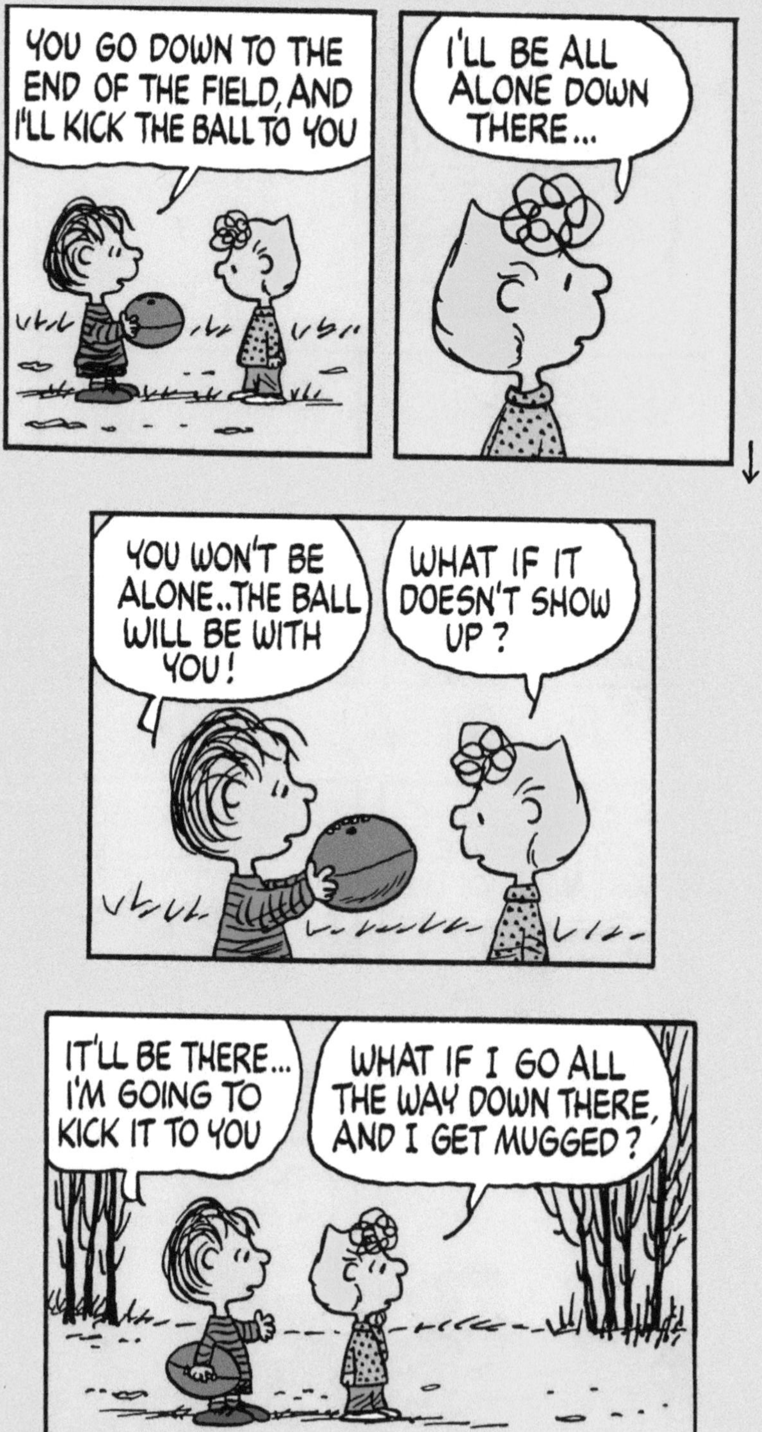
YOU GO DOWN TO THE END OF THE FIELD, AND I'LL KICK THE BALL TO YOU
I'LL BE ALL ALONE DOWN THERE...
YOU WON'T BE ALONE..THE BALL WILL BE WITH YOU!
WHAT IF IT DOESN'T SHOW UP?
IT'LL BE THERE... I'M GOING TO KICK IT TO YOU
WHAT IF I GO ALL THE WAY DOWN THERE, AND I GET MUGGED?

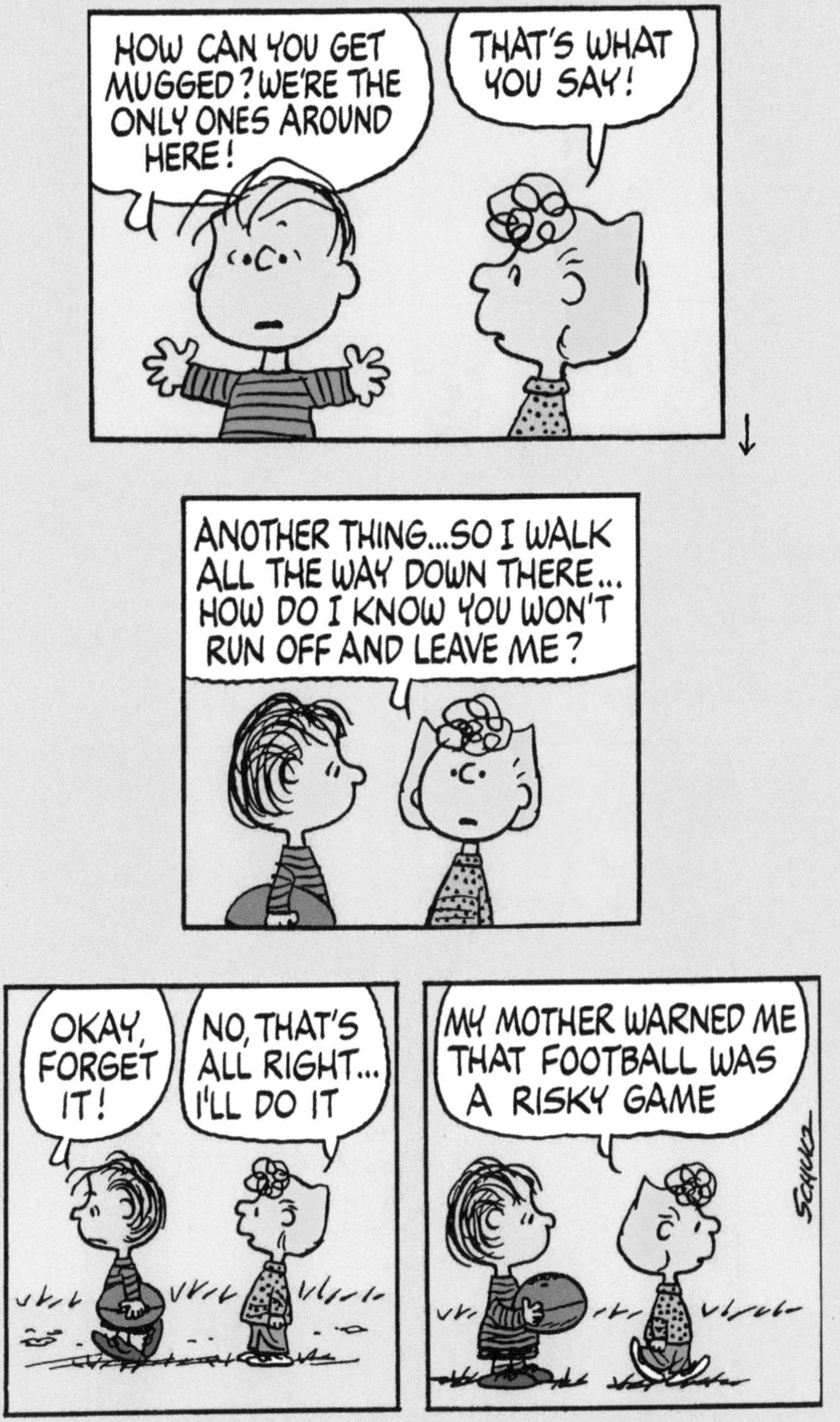
HOW CAN YOU GET MUGGED? WE'RE THE ONLY ONES AROUND HERE!
THAT'S WHAT YOU SAY!
ANOTHER THING...SO I WALK ALL THE WAY DOWN THERE... HOW DO I KNOW YOU WON'T RUN OFF AND LEAVE ME?
OKAY, FORGET IT!
NO, THAT'S ALL RIGHT... I'LL DO IT
MY MOTHER WARNED ME THAT FOOTBALL WAS A RISKY GAME
SCHULZ

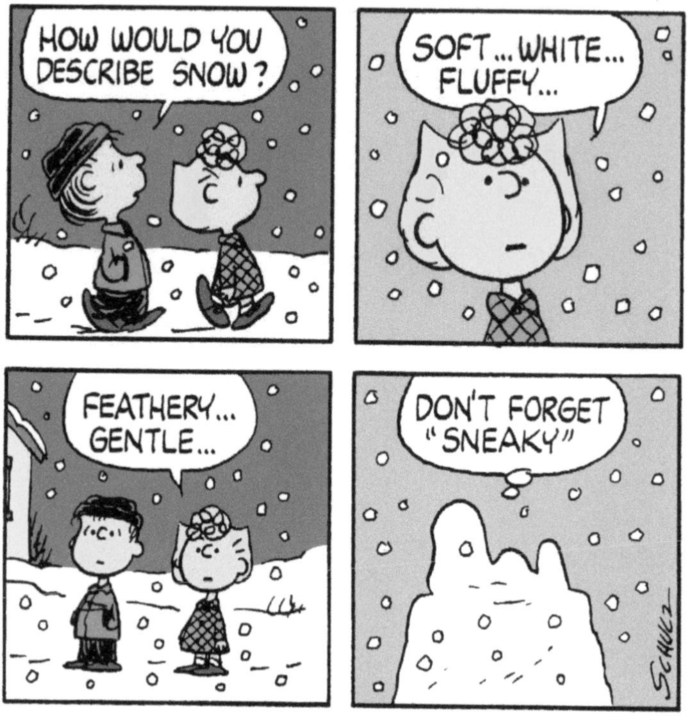
HOW WOULD YOU DESCRIBE SNOW?
SOFT... WHITE... FLUFFY...
FEATHERY... GENTLE...
DON'T FORGET "SNEAKY"
SCHULZ

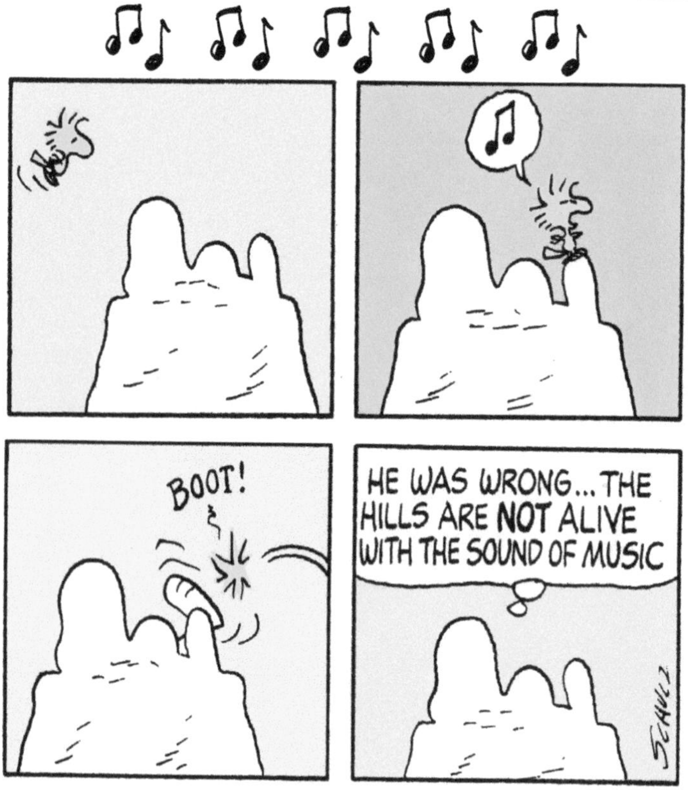
BOOT!
HE WAS WRONG... THE HILLS ARE NOT ALIVE WITH THE SOUND OF MUSIC
SCHULZ

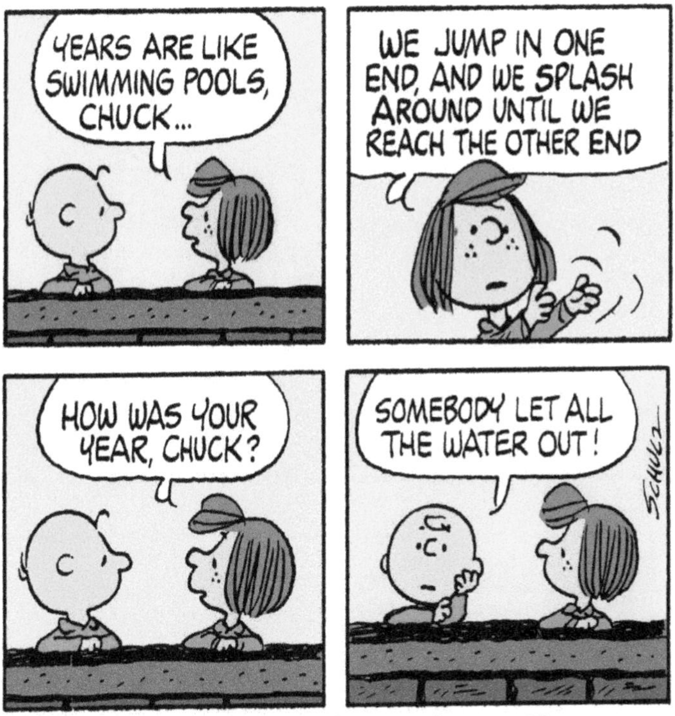
YEARS ARE LIKE SWIMMING POOLS, CHUCK...
WE JUMP IN ONE END, AND WE SPLASH AROUND UNTIL WE REACH THE OTHER END
HOW WAS YOUR YEAR, CHUCK?
SOMEBODY LET ALL THE WATER OUT!
SCHULZ

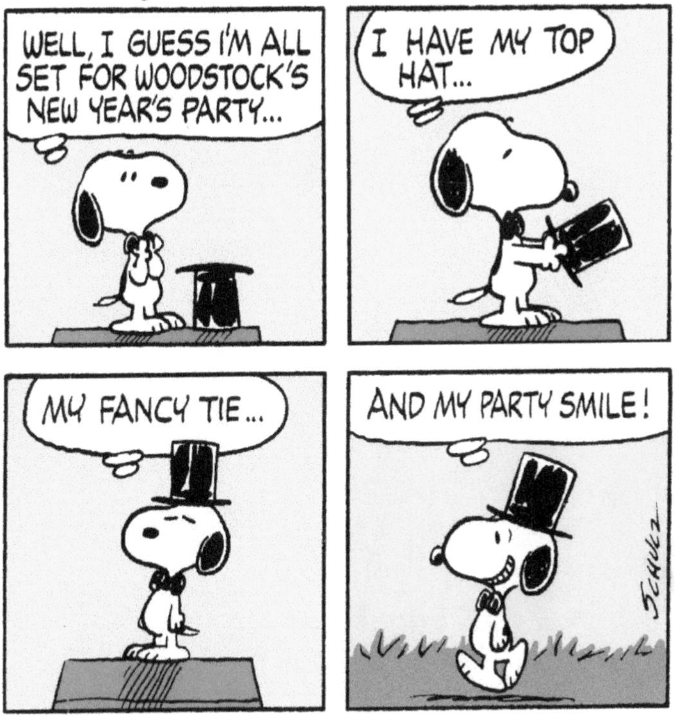
WELL, I GUESS I'M ALL SET FOR WOODSTOCK'S NEW YEAR'S PARTY...
I HAVE MY TOP HAT...
MY FANCY TIE...
AND MY PARTY SMILE!
SCHULZ

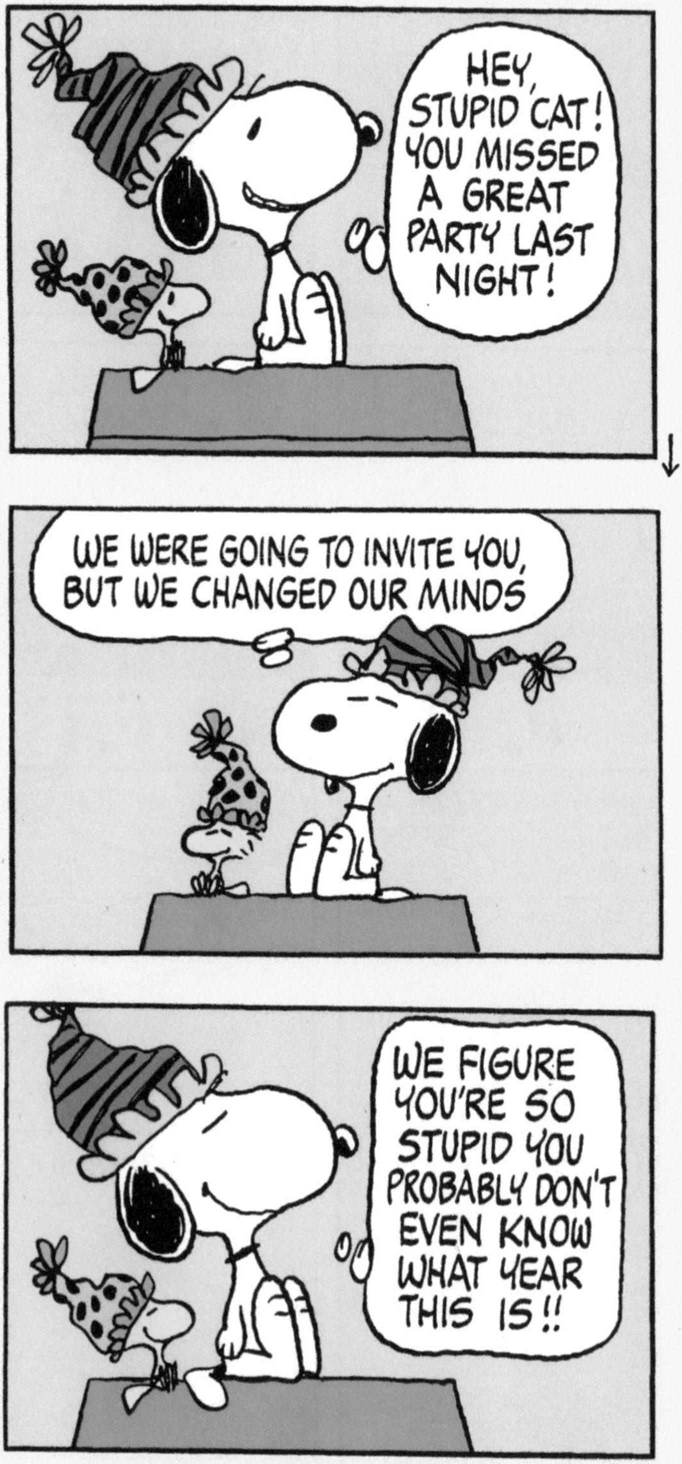
HEY, STUPID CAT! YOU MISSED A GREAT PARTY LAST NIGHT!
WE WERE GOING TO INVITE YOU, BUT WE CHANGED OUR MINDS
WE FIGURE YOU'RE SO STUPID YOU PROBABLY DON'T EVEN KNOW WHAT YEAR THIS IS!!

HEE HEE HEE HEE
HEE HEE HEE HEE
SLASH!
1978
SCHULZ

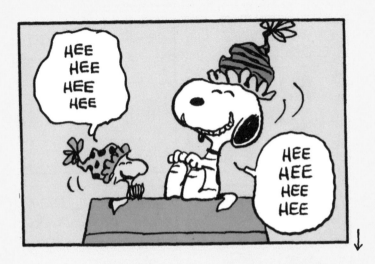

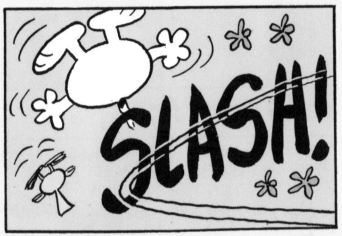

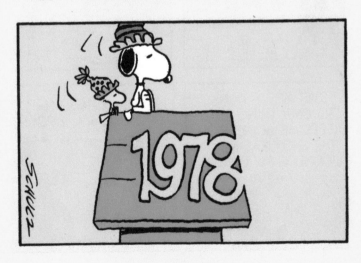

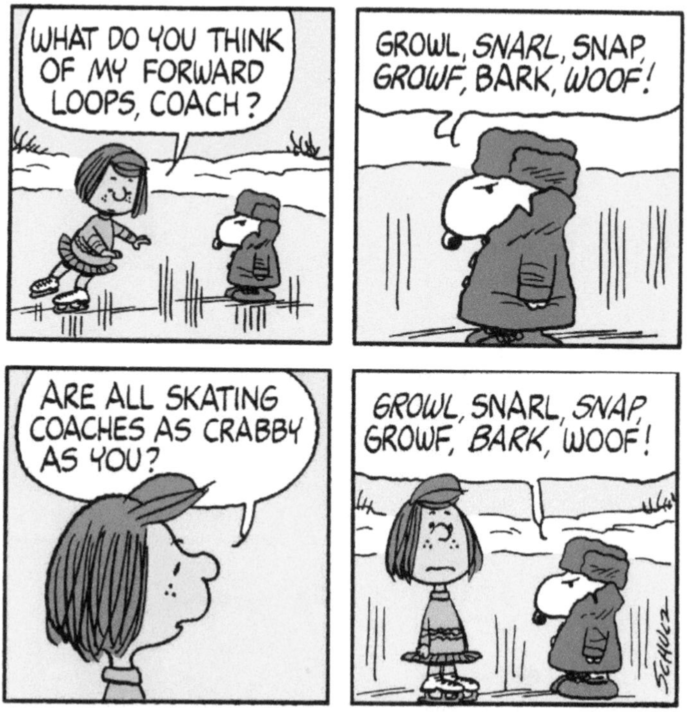
WHAT DO YOU THINK OF MY FORWARD LOOPS, COACH?
GROWL, SNARL, SNAP, GROWF, BARK, WOOF!
ARE ALL SKATING COACHES AS CRABBY AS YOU?
GROWL, SNARL, SNAP, GROWF, BARK, WOOF!
SCHULZ

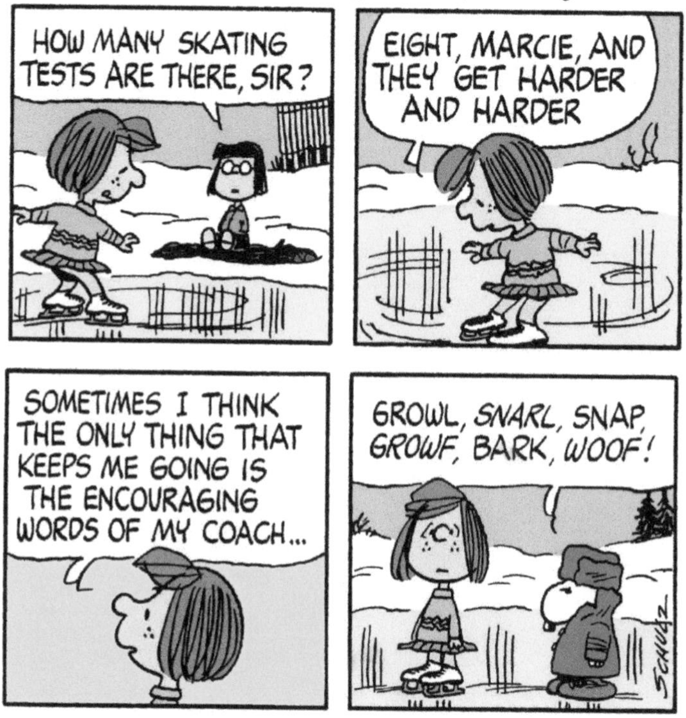
HOW MANY SKATING TESTS ARE THERE, SIR?
EIGHT, MARCIE, AND THEY GET HARDER AND HARDER
SOMETIMES I THINK THE ONLY THING THAT KEEPS ME GOING IS THE ENCOURAGING WORDS OF MY COACH...
GROWL, SNARL, SNAP, GROWF, BARK, WOOF!
SCHULZ

OKAY, BEAUTIFUL, GET OFF THE ICE!! WE'RE GONNA PLAY HOCKEY!

HOCKEY?! GET LOST, NECKHEAD! I WAS HERE FIRST!!

YOU WOULDN'T LIKE TO GET HIT WITH A HOCKEY STICK WOULD YOU, BEAUTIFUL?

HOW WOULD YOU LIKE TO BE FORCE-FED A PAIR OF GOALIE PADS?!

LISTEN, BEAUTIFUL, GET YOUR STUPID FIGURE SKATES OFF THE ICE! WE WANNA PLAY HOCKEY, SEE?

WE HAVE TEN HOCKEY STICKS HERE TELLING YOU TO "GET OFF THE ICE!"

OH, YEAH? COME ON AND TRY SOMETHING! ME AND MY COACH'LL TAKE YOU ALL ON!!

I THINK I'LL GO HOME.. I HAVE SOME CHAIN LETTERS TO WRITE...

41

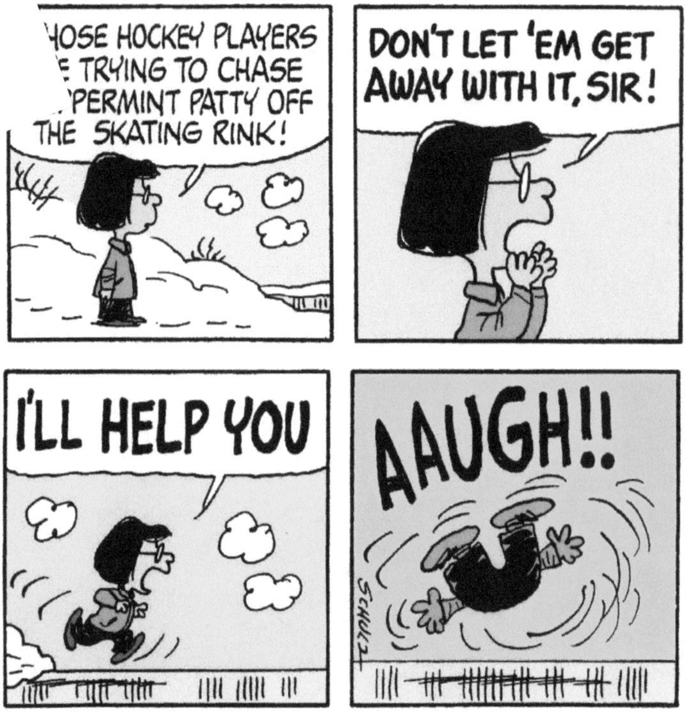
HOSE HOCKEY PLAYERS
E TRYING TO CHASE
PPERMINT PATTY OFF
THE SKATING RINK!
DON'T LET 'EM GET AWAY WITH IT, SIR!
I'LL HELP YOU
AAUGH!!
SCHULZ

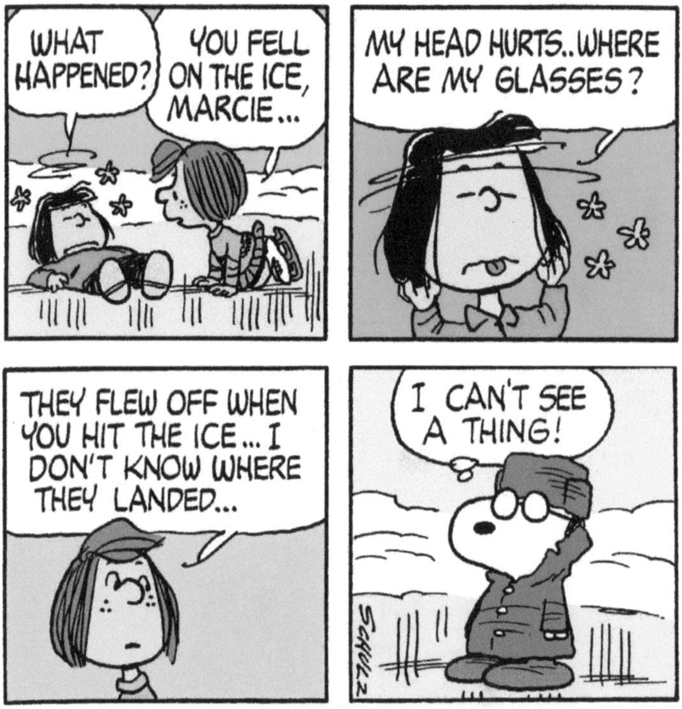
WHAT HAPPENED?
YOU FELL ON THE ICE, MARCIE...
MY HEAD HURTS..WHERE ARE MY GLASSES?
THEY FLEW OFF WHEN YOU HIT THE ICE... I DON'T KNOW WHERE THEY LANDED...
I CAN'T SEE A THING!
SCHULZ

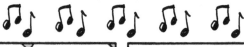

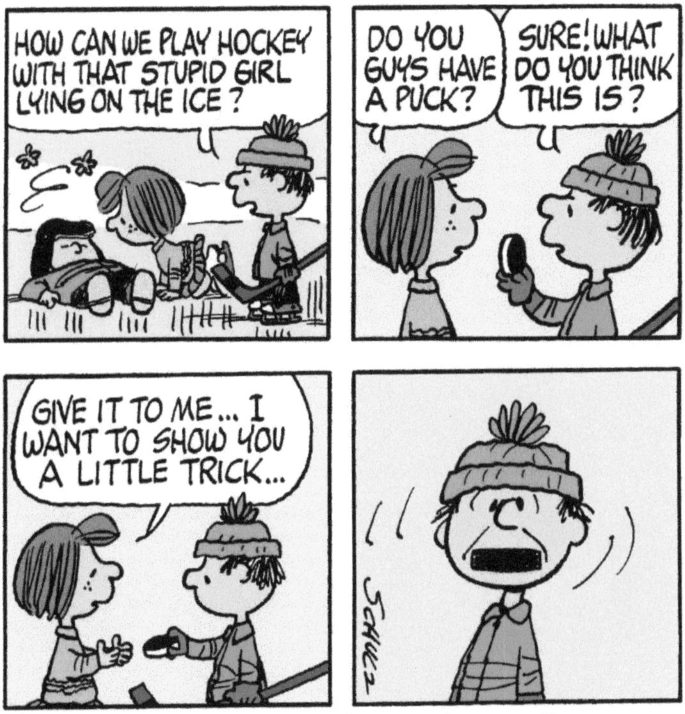
HOW CAN WE PLAY HOCKEY WITH THAT STUPID GIRL LYING ON THE ICE?
DO YOU GUYS HAVE A PUCK?
SURE! WHAT DO YOU THINK THIS IS?
GIVE IT TO ME... I WANT TO SHOW YOU A LITTLE TRICK...
SCHULZ

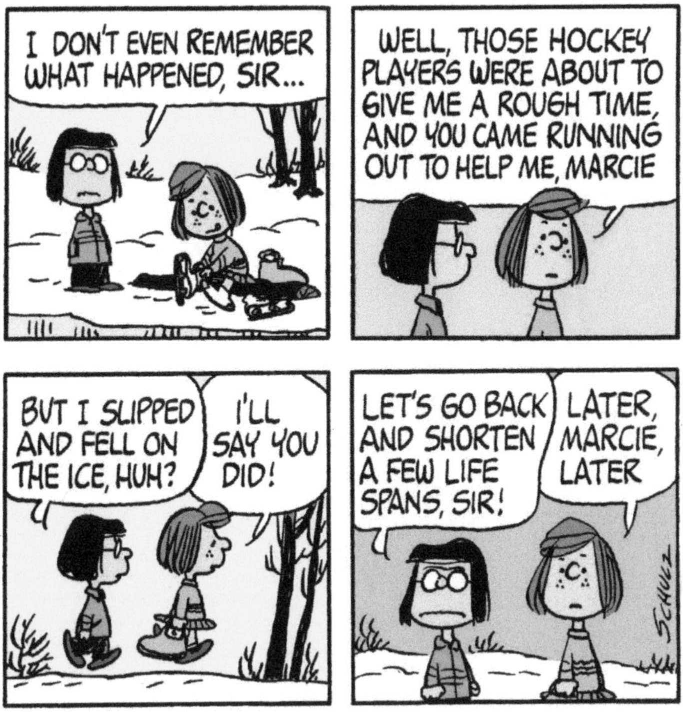
I DON'T EVEN REMEMBER WHAT HAPPENED, SIR...
WELL, THOSE HOCKEY PLAYERS WERE ABOUT TO GIVE ME A ROUGH TIME, AND YOU CAME RUNNING OUT TO HELP ME, MARCIE
BUT I SLIPPED AND FELL ON THE ICE, HUH?
I'LL SAY YOU DID!
LET'S GO BACK AND SHORTEN A FEW LIFE SPANS, SIR!
LATER, MARCIE, LATER
SCHULZ

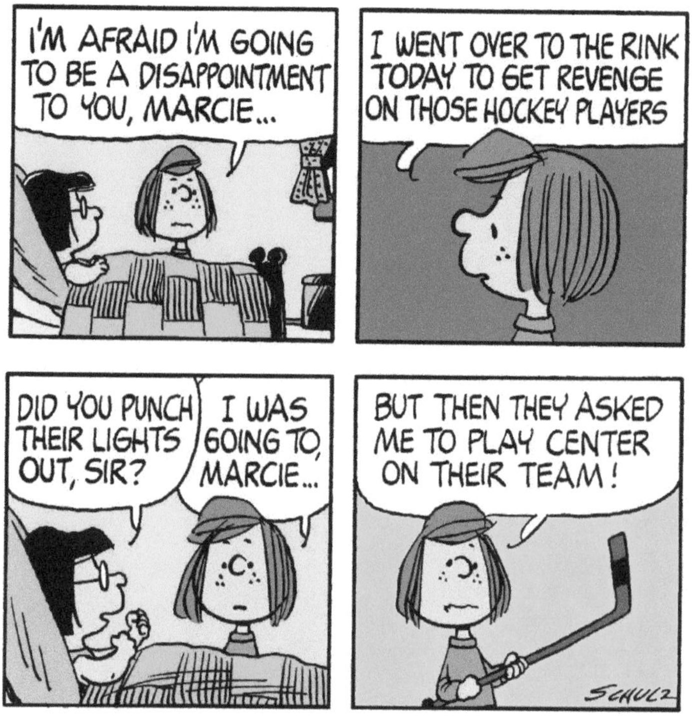
I'M AFRAID I'M GOING TO BE A DISAPPOINTMENT TO YOU, MARCIE...
I WENT OVER TO THE RINK TODAY TO GET REVENGE ON THOSE HOCKEY PLAYERS
DID YOU PUNCH THEIR LIGHTS OUT, SIR?
I WAS GOING TO, MARCIE...
BUT THEN THEY ASKED ME TO PLAY CENTER ON THEIR TEAM!
SCHULZ

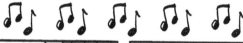

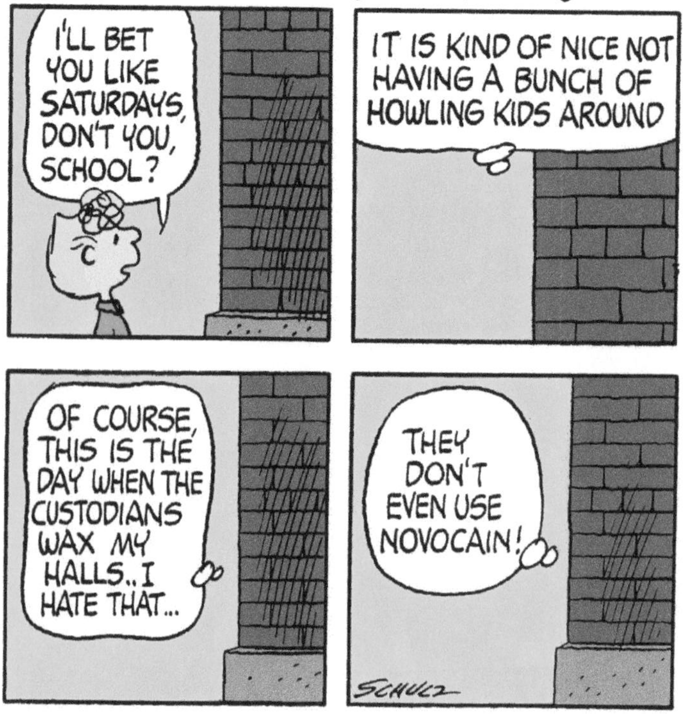
I'LL BET YOU LIKE SATURDAYS, DON'T YOU, SCHOOL?
IT IS KIND OF NICE NOT HAVING A BUNCH OF HOWLING KIDS AROUND
OF COURSE, THIS IS THE DAY WHEN THE CUSTODIANS WAX MY HALLS.. I HATE THAT...
THEY DON'T EVEN USE NOVOCAIN!
SCHULZ

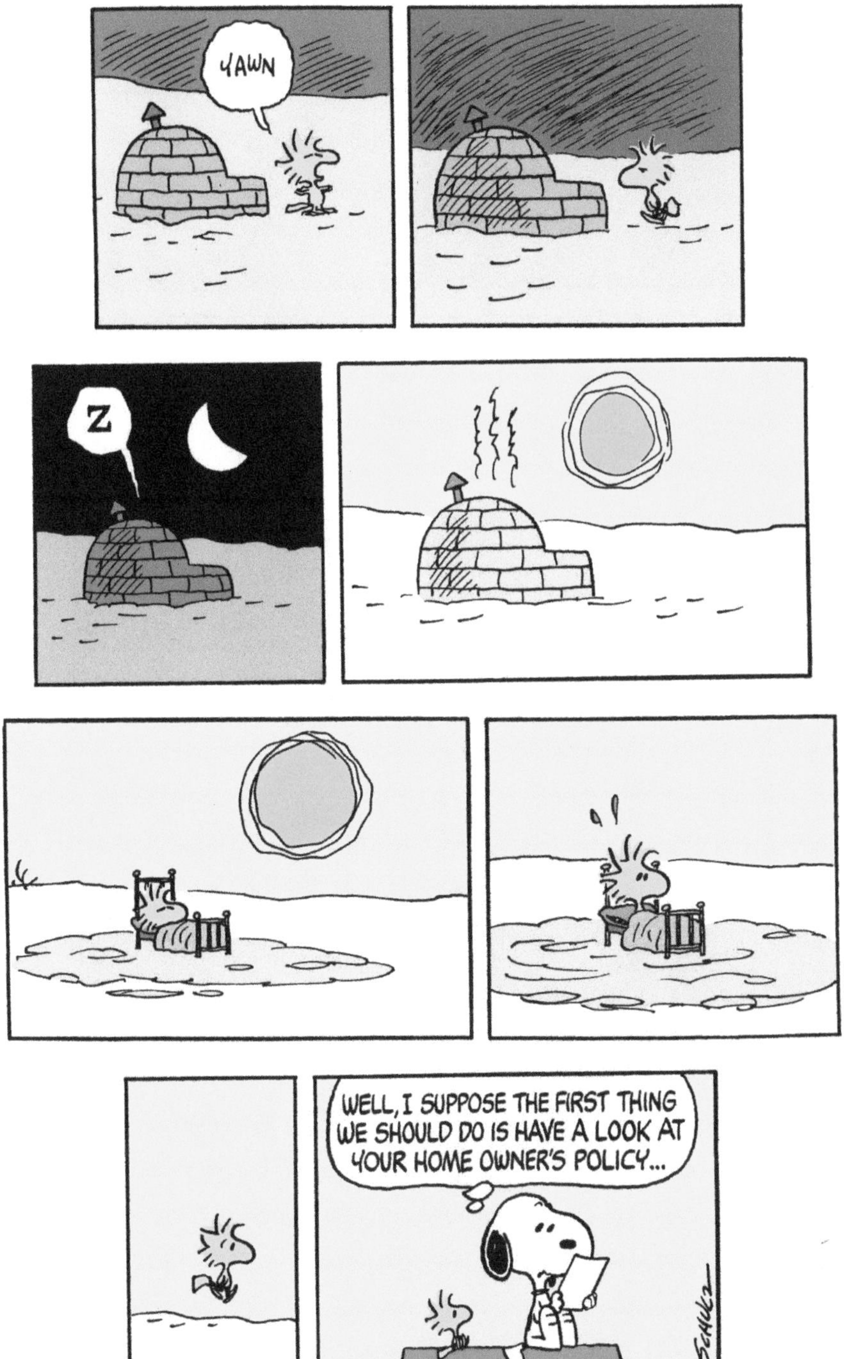
YAWN
Z
WELL, I SUPPOSE THE FIRST THING WE SHOULD DO IS HAVE A LOOK AT YOUR HOME OWNER'S POLICY...

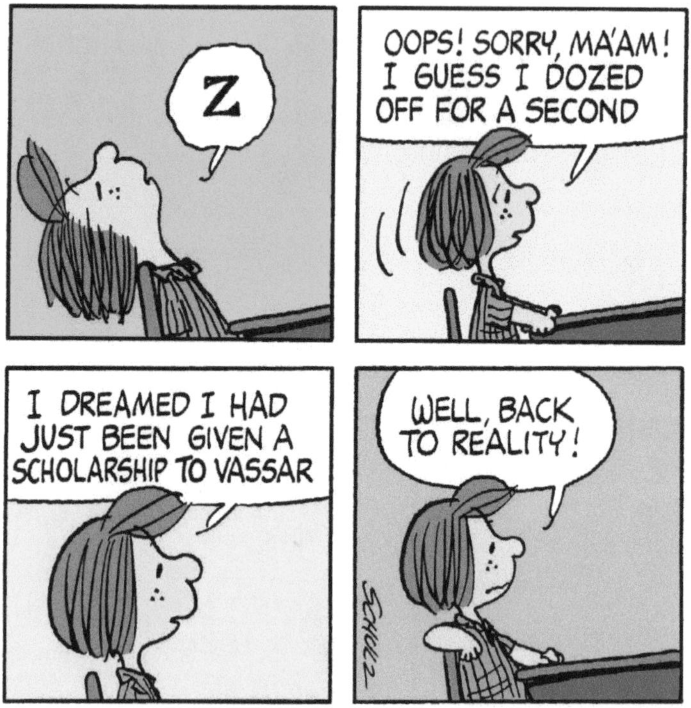
Z
OOPS! SORRY, MA'AM! I GUESS I DOZED OFF FOR A SECOND
I DREAMED I HAD JUST BEEN GIVEN A SCHOLARSHIP TO VASSAR
WELL, BACK TO REALITY!
SCHULZ

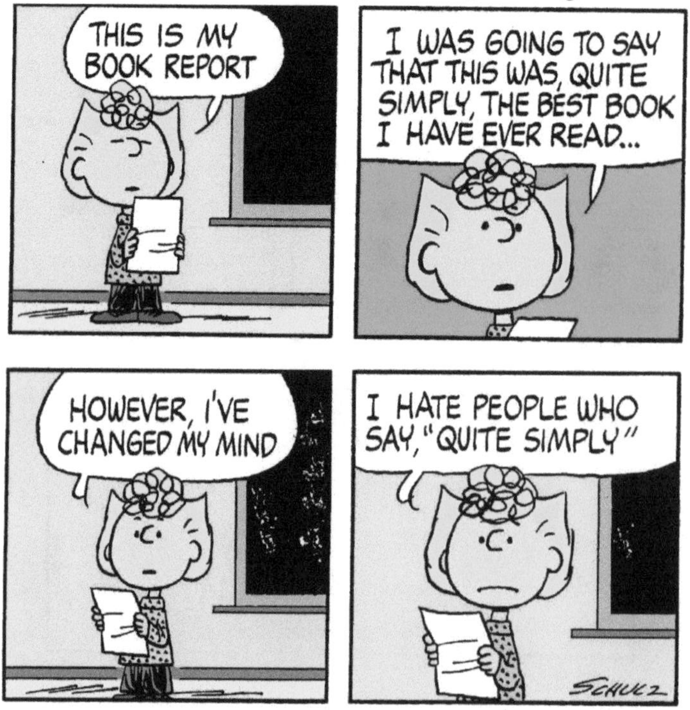
THIS IS MY BOOK REPORT
I WAS GOING TO SAY THAT THIS WAS, QUITE SIMPLY, THE BEST BOOK I HAVE EVER READ...
HOWEVER, I'VE CHANGED MY MIND
I HATE PEOPLE WHO SAY, "QUITE SIMPLY"
SCHULZ

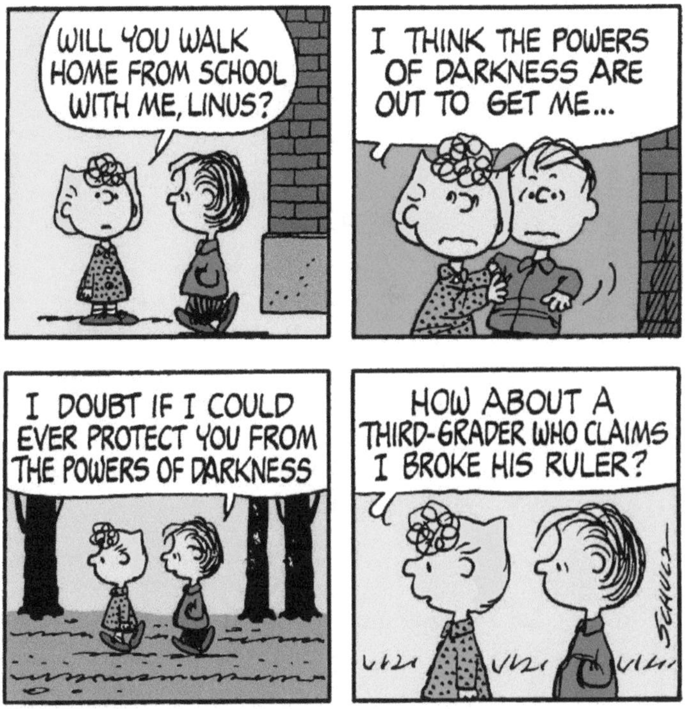
WILL YOU WALK HOME FROM SCHOOL WITH ME, LINUS?
I THINK THE POWERS OF DARKNESS ARE OUT TO GET ME...
I DOUBT IF I COULD EVER PROTECT YOU FROM THE POWERS OF DARKNESS
HOW ABOUT A THIRD-GRADER WHO CLAIMS I BROKE HIS RULER?
SCHULZ

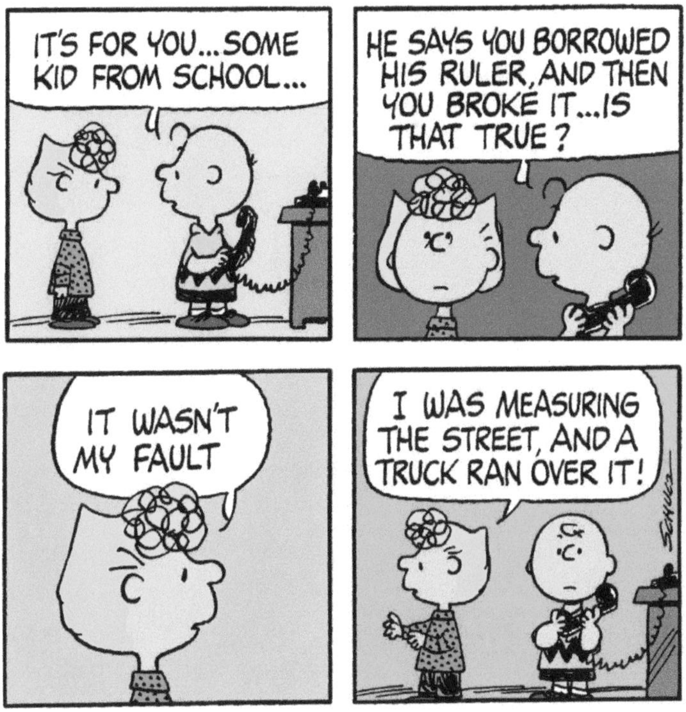
IT'S FOR YOU...SOME KID FROM SCHOOL...
HE SAYS YOU BORROWED HIS RULER, AND THEN YOU BROKE IT...IS THAT TRUE?
IT WASN'T MY FAULT
I WAS MEASURING THE STREET, AND A TRUCK RAN OVER IT!
SCHULZ

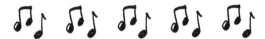

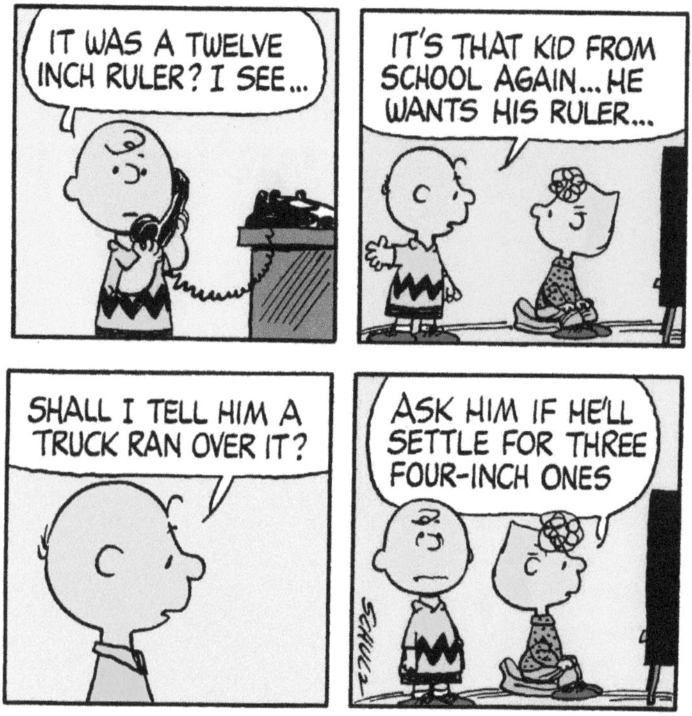
IT WAS A TWELVE INCH RULER? I SEE...
IT'S THAT KID FROM SCHOOL AGAIN... HE WANTS HIS RULER...
SHALL I TELL HIM A TRUCK RAN OVER IT?
ASK HIM IF HE'LL SETTLE FOR THREE FOUR-INCH ONES
SCHULZ

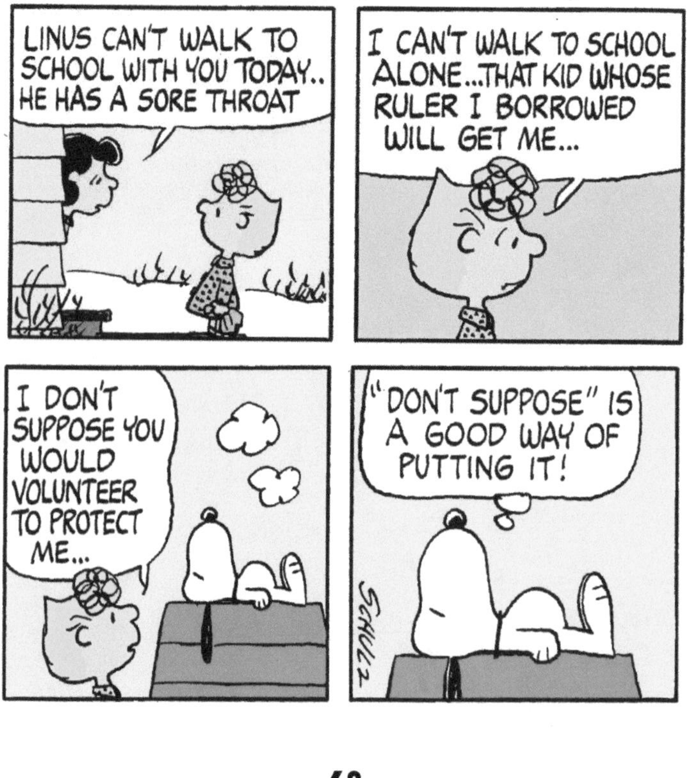
LINUS CAN'T WALK TO SCHOOL WITH YOU TODAY.. HE HAS A SORE THROAT
I CAN'T WALK TO SCHOOL ALONE...THAT KID WHOSE RULER I BORROWED WILL GET ME...
I DON'T SUPPOSE YOU WOULD VOLUNTEER TO PROTECT ME...
"DON'T SUPPOSE" IS A GOOD WAY OF PUTTING IT!
SCHULZ

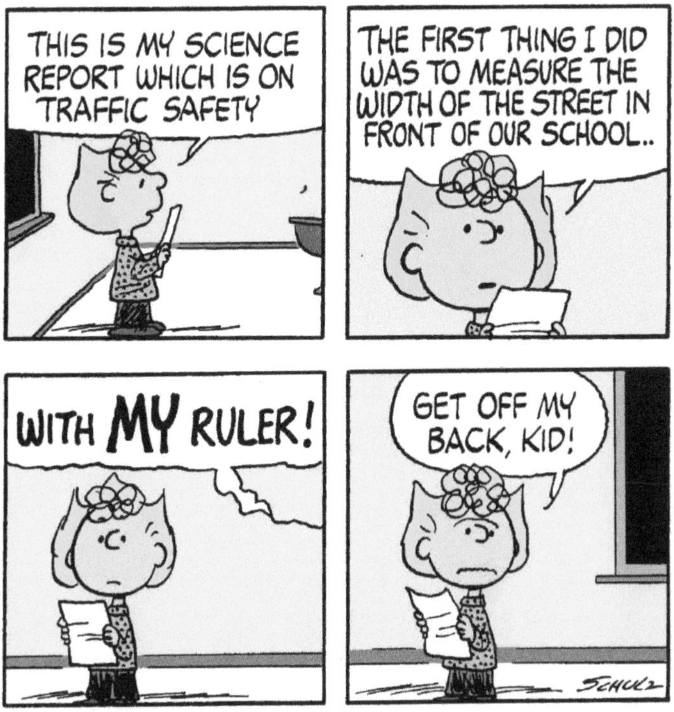
THIS IS MY SCIENCE REPORT WHICH IS ON TRAFFIC SAFETY
THE FIRST THING I DID WAS TO MEASURE THE WIDTH OF THE STREET IN FRONT OF OUR SCHOOL..
WITH MY RULER!
GET OFF MY BACK, KID!
SCHULZ

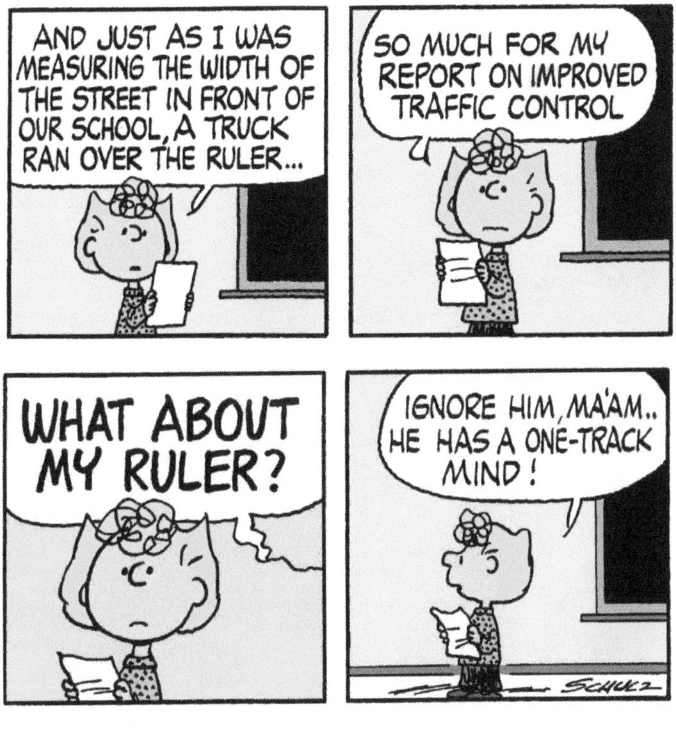
AND JUST AS I WAS MEASURING THE WIDTH OF THE STREET IN FRONT OF OUR SCHOOL, A TRUCK RAN OVER THE RULER...
SO MUCH FOR MY REPORT ON IMPROVED TRAFFIC CONTROL
WHAT ABOUT MY RULER?
IGNORE HIM, MA'AM.. HE HAS A ONE-TRACK MIND!
SCHULZ

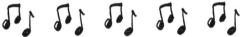

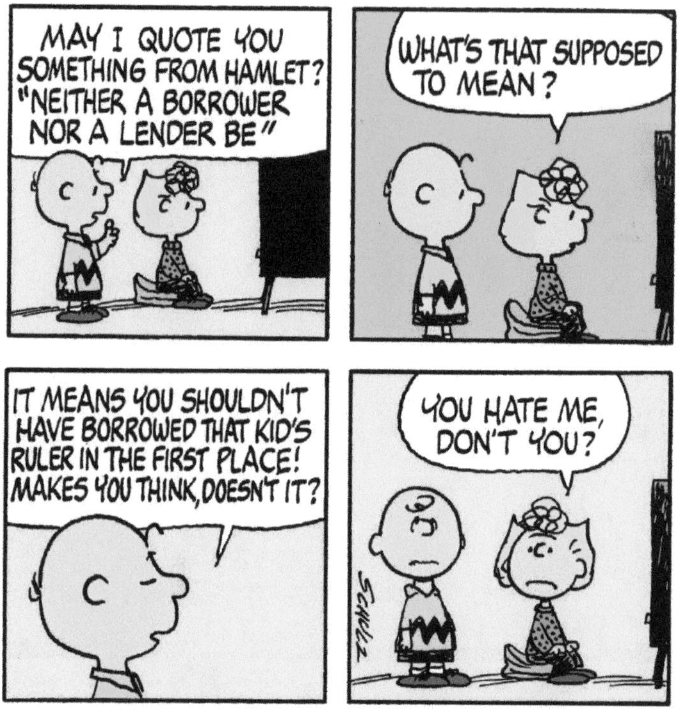
MAY I QUOTE YOU SOMETHING FROM HAMLET? "NEITHER A BORROWER NOR A LENDER BE"
WHAT'S THAT SUPPOSED TO MEAN?
IT MEANS YOU SHOULDN'T HAVE BORROWED THAT KID'S RULER IN THE FIRST PLACE! MAKES YOU THINK, DOESN'T IT?
YOU HATE ME, DON'T YOU?
SCHULZ

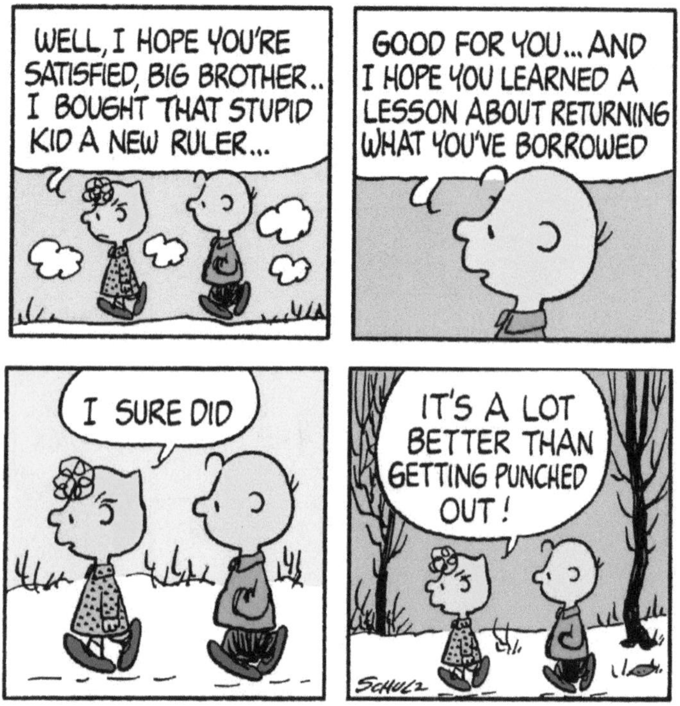
WELL, I HOPE YOU'RE SATISFIED, BIG BROTHER.. I BOUGHT THAT STUPID KID A NEW RULER...
GOOD FOR YOU... AND I HOPE YOU LEARNED A LESSON ABOUT RETURNING WHAT YOU'VE BORROWED
I SURE DID
IT'S A LOT BETTER THAN GETTING PUNCHED OUT!
SCHULZ

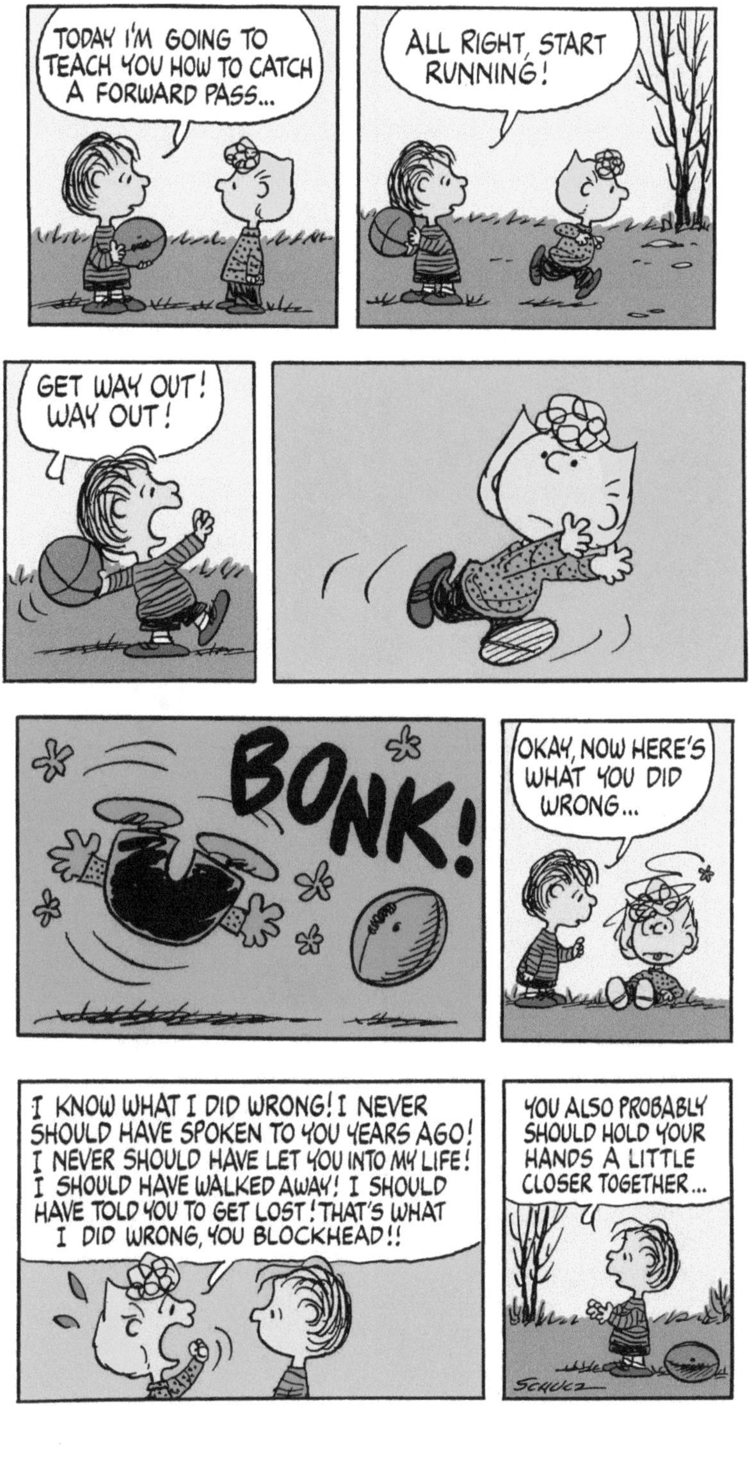
TODAY I'M GOING TO TEACH YOU HOW TO CATCH A FORWARD PASS...
ALL RIGHT, START RUNNING!
GET WAY OUT! WAY OUT!
BONK!
OKAY, NOW HERE'S WHAT YOU DID WRONG...
I KNOW WHAT I DID WRONG! I NEVER SHOULD HAVE SPOKEN TO YOU YEARS AGO! I NEVER SHOULD HAVE LET YOU INTO MY LIFE! I SHOULD HAVE WALKED AWAY! I SHOULD HAVE TOLD YOU TO GET LOST! THAT'S WHAT I DID WRONG, YOU BLOCKHEAD!!
YOU ALSO PROBABLY SHOULD HOLD YOUR HANDS A LITTLE CLOSER TOGETHER...
SCHULZ

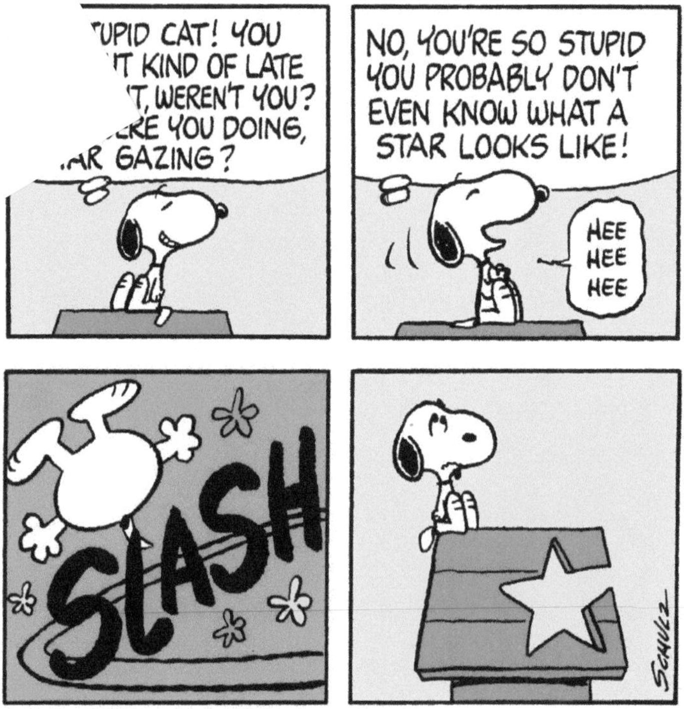
TUPID CAT! YOU
T KIND OF LATE
T, WEREN'T YOU?
ERE YOU DOING,
AR GAZING?
NO, YOU'RE SO STUPID YOU PROBABLY DON'T EVEN KNOW WHAT A STAR LOOKS LIKE!
HEE HEE HEE
SLASH
SCHULZ

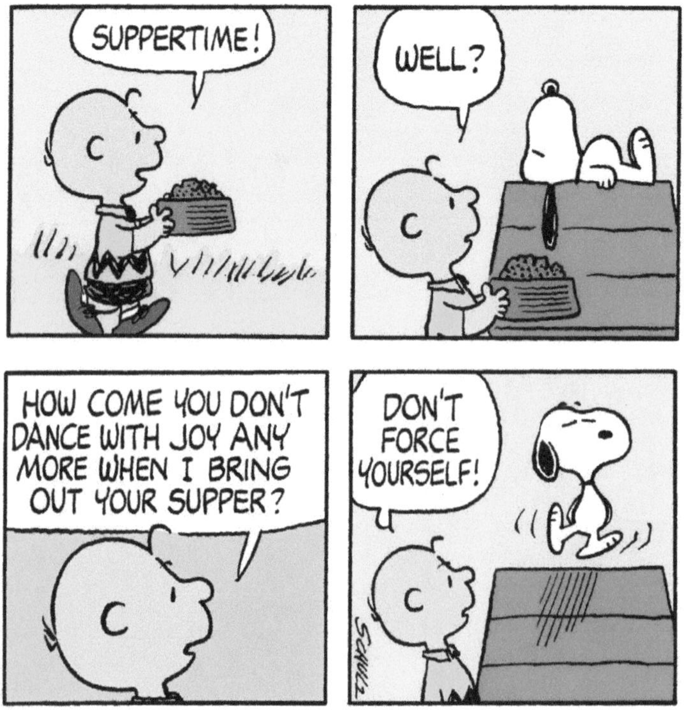
SUPPERTIME!
WELL?
HOW COME YOU DON'T DANCE WITH JOY ANY MORE WHEN I BRING OUT YOUR SUPPER?
DON'T FORCE YOURSELF!
SCHULZ

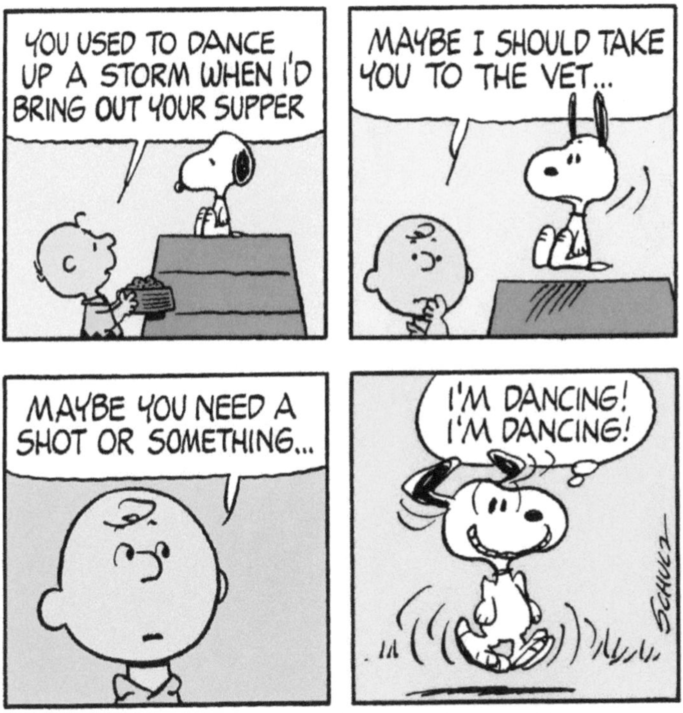
YOU USED TO DANCE UP A STORM WHEN I'D BRING OUT YOUR SUPPER
MAYBE I SHOULD TAKE YOU TO THE VET...
MAYBE YOU NEED A SHOT OR SOMETHING...
I'M DANCING! I'M DANCING!
SCHULZ

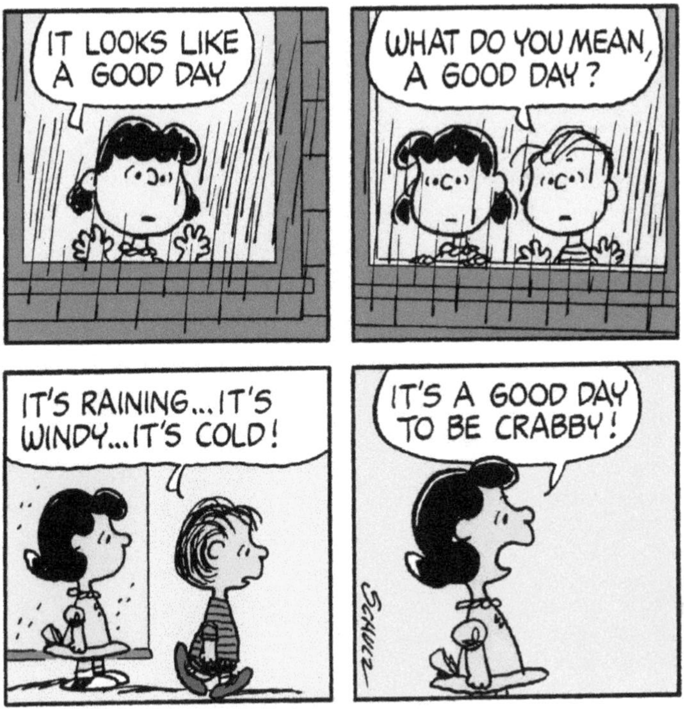
IT LOOKS LIKE A GOOD DAY
WHAT DO YOU MEAN, A GOOD DAY?
IT'S RAINING...IT'S WINDY...IT'S COLD!
IT'S A GOOD DAY TO BE CRABBY!
SCHULZ

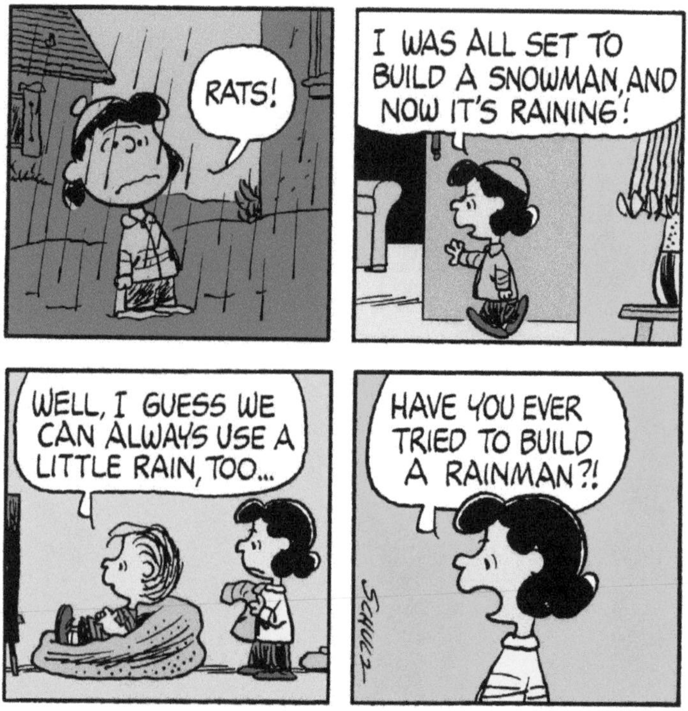
RATS!
I WAS ALL SET TO BUILD A SNOWMAN, AND NOW IT'S RAINING!
WELL, I GUESS WE CAN ALWAYS USE A LITTLE RAIN, TOO...
HAVE YOU EVER TRIED TO BUILD A RAINMAN?!
SCHULZ

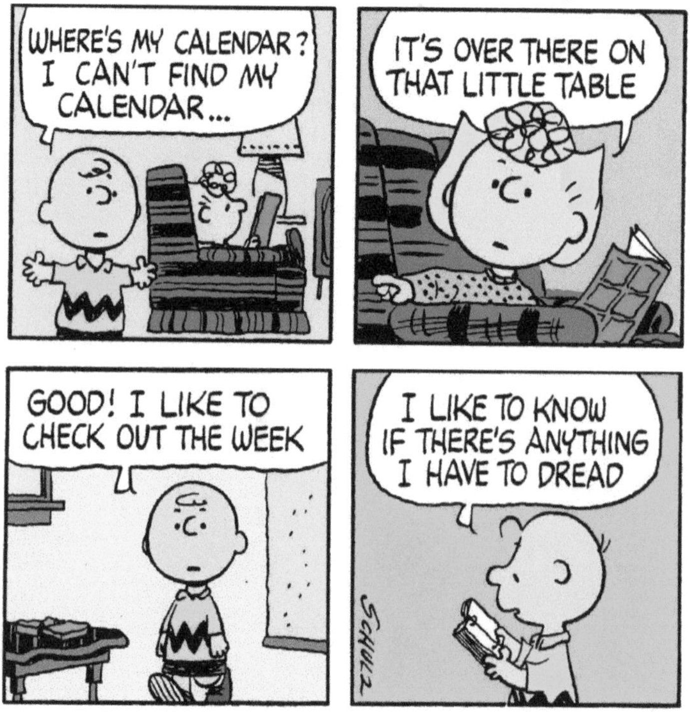
WHERE'S MY CALENDAR? I CAN'T FIND MY CALENDAR...
IT'S OVER THERE ON THAT LITTLE TABLE
GOOD! I LIKE TO CHECK OUT THE WEEK
I LIKE TO KNOW IF THERE'S ANYTHING I HAVE TO DREAD
SCHULZ

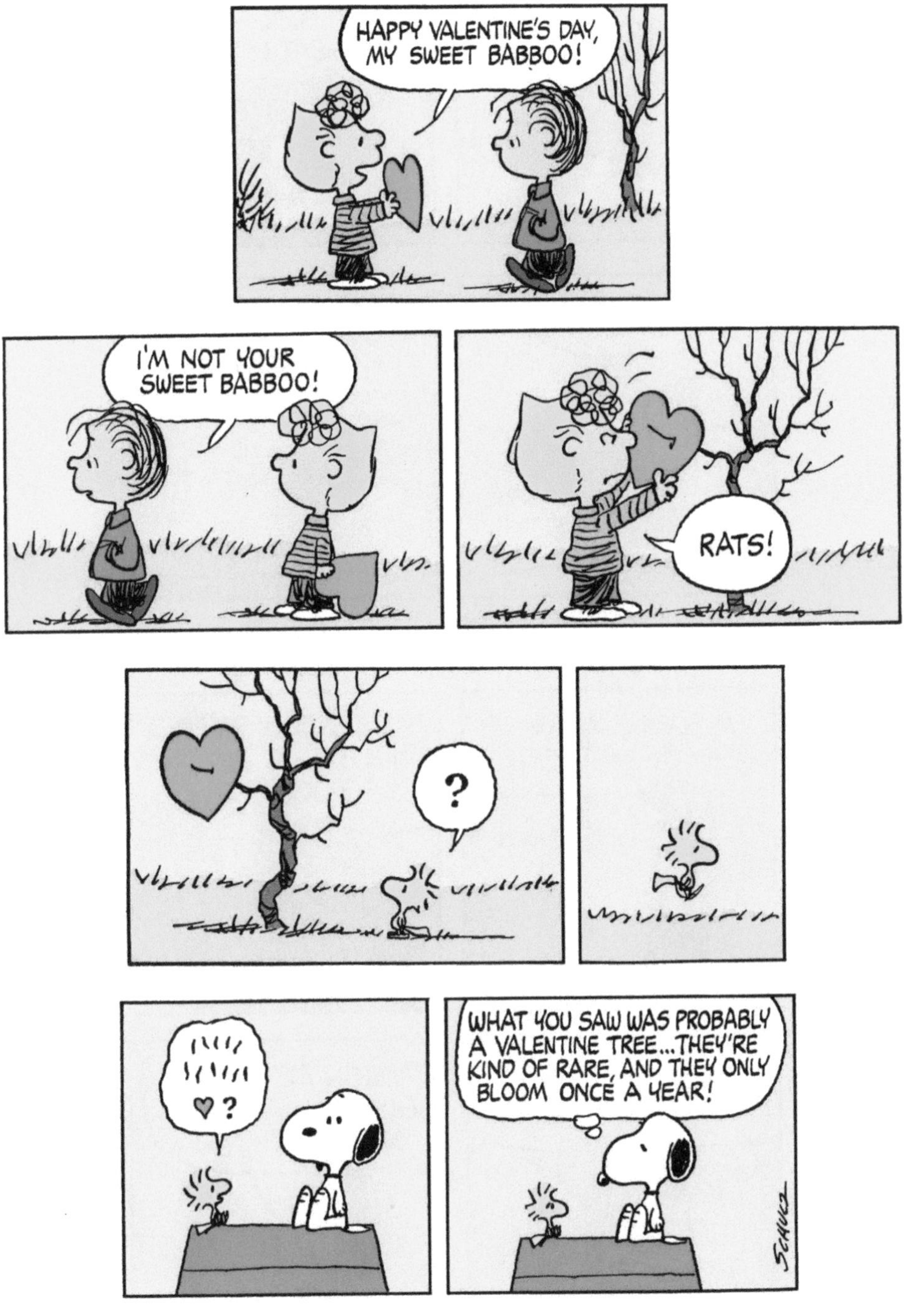
HAPPY VALENTINE'S DAY, MY SWEET BABBOO!
I'M NOT YOUR SWEET BABBOO!
RATS!
?
♥ ?
WHAT YOU SAW WAS PROBABLY A VALENTINE TREE...THEY'RE KIND OF RARE, AND THEY ONLY BLOOM ONCE A YEAR!
SCHULZ

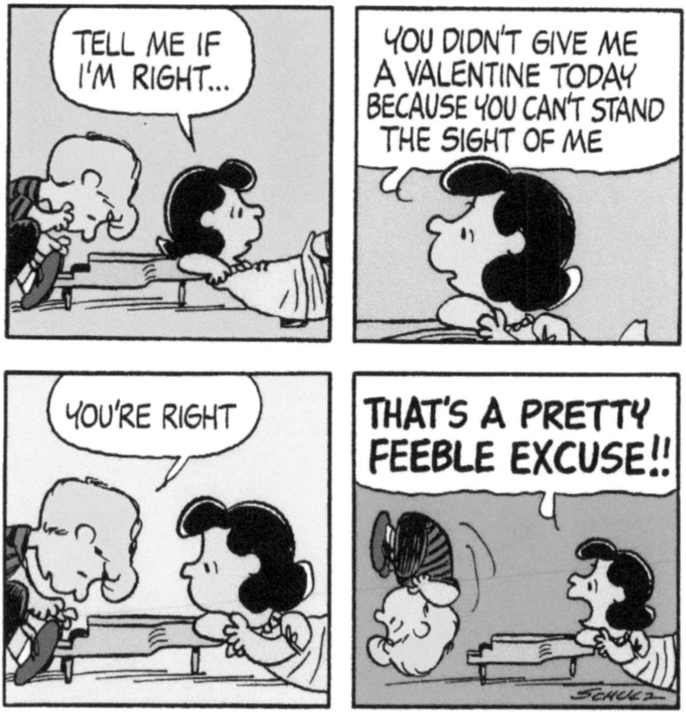
TELL ME IF I'M RIGHT...
YOU DIDN'T GIVE ME A VALENTINE TODAY BECAUSE YOU CAN'T STAND THE SIGHT OF ME
YOU'RE RIGHT
THAT'S A PRETTY FEEBLE EXCUSE!!

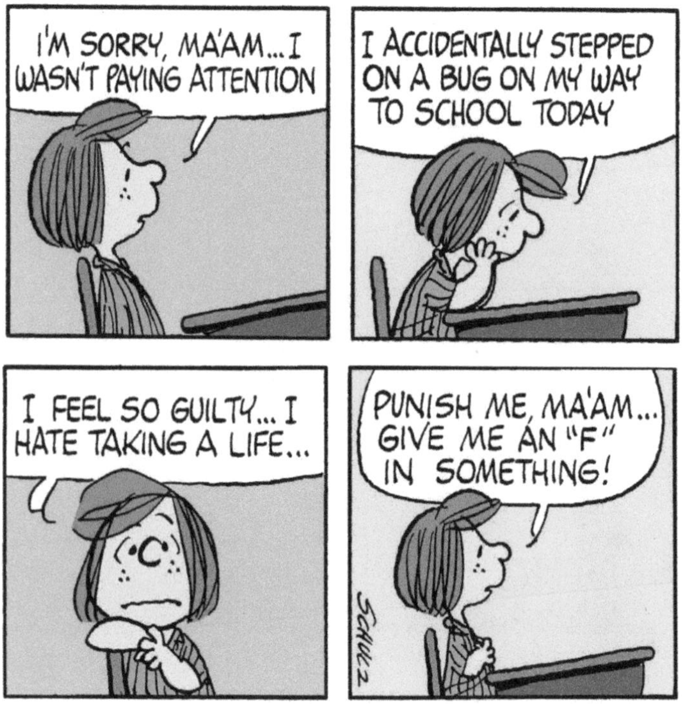
I'M SORRY, MA'AM...I WASN'T PAYING ATTENTION
I ACCIDENTALLY STEPPED ON A BUG ON MY WAY TO SCHOOL TODAY
I FEEL SO GUILTY... I HATE TAKING A LIFE...
PUNISH ME, MA'AM... GIVE ME AN "F" IN SOMETHING!

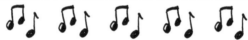

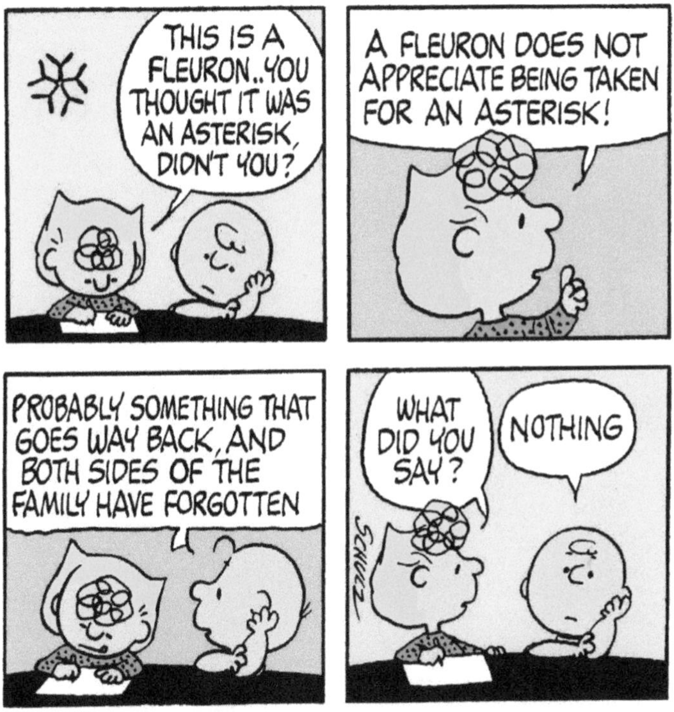
THIS IS A FLEURON..YOU THOUGHT IT WAS AN ASTERISK, DIDN'T YOU?
A FLEURON DOES NOT APPRECIATE BEING TAKEN FOR AN ASTERISK!
PROBABLY SOMETHING THAT GOES WAY BACK, AND BOTH SIDES OF THE FAMILY HAVE FORGOTTEN
WHAT DID YOU SAY?
NOTHING
SCHULZ

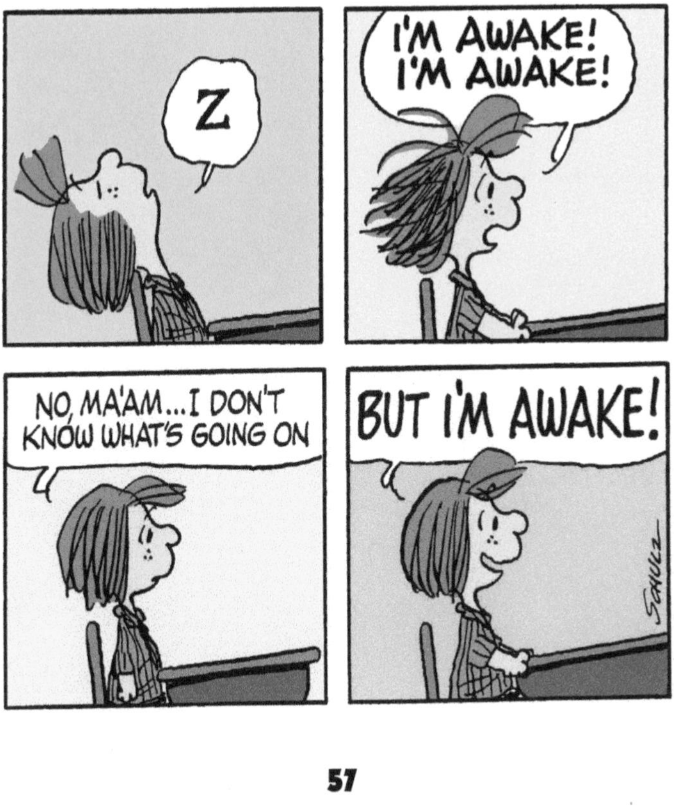
Z
I'M AWAKE! I'M AWAKE!
NO, MA'AM...I DON'T KNOW WHAT'S GOING ON
BUT I'M AWAKE!
SCHULZ

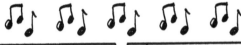

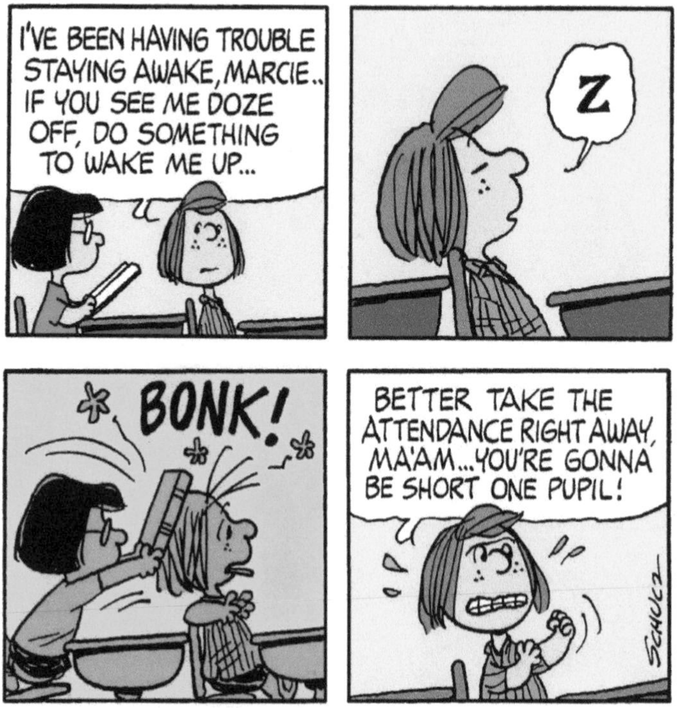
I'VE BEEN HAVING TROUBLE STAYING AWAKE, MARCIE.. IF YOU SEE ME DOZE OFF, DO SOMETHING TO WAKE ME UP...
Z
BONK!
BETTER TAKE THE ATTENDANCE RIGHT AWAY, MA'AM...YOU'RE GONNA BE SHORT ONE PUPIL!
SCHULZ

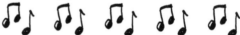

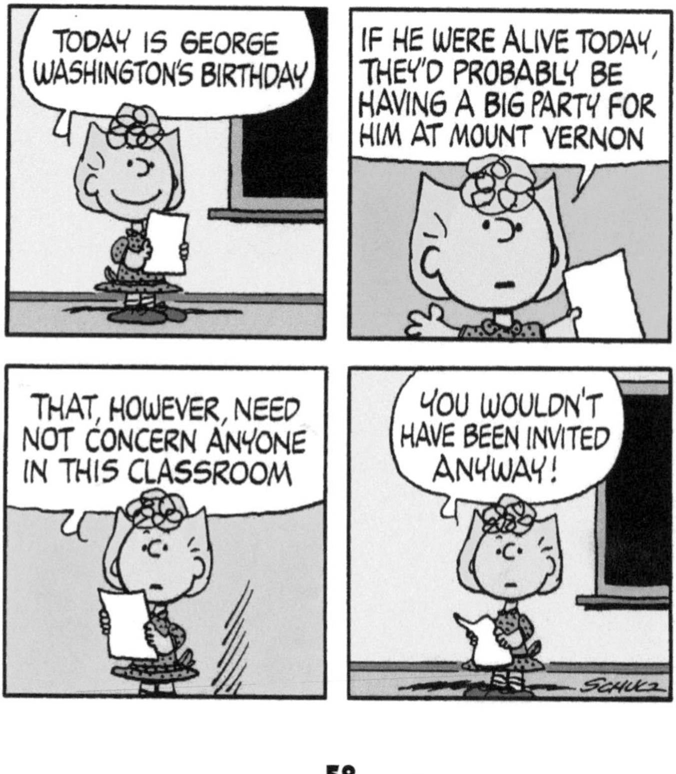
TODAY IS GEORGE WASHINGTON'S BIRTHDAY
IF HE WERE ALIVE TODAY, THEY'D PROBABLY BE HAVING A BIG PARTY FOR HIM AT MOUNT VERNON
THAT, HOWEVER, NEED NOT CONCERN ANYONE IN THIS CLASSROOM
YOU WOULDN'T HAVE BEEN INVITED ANYWAY!
SCHULZ

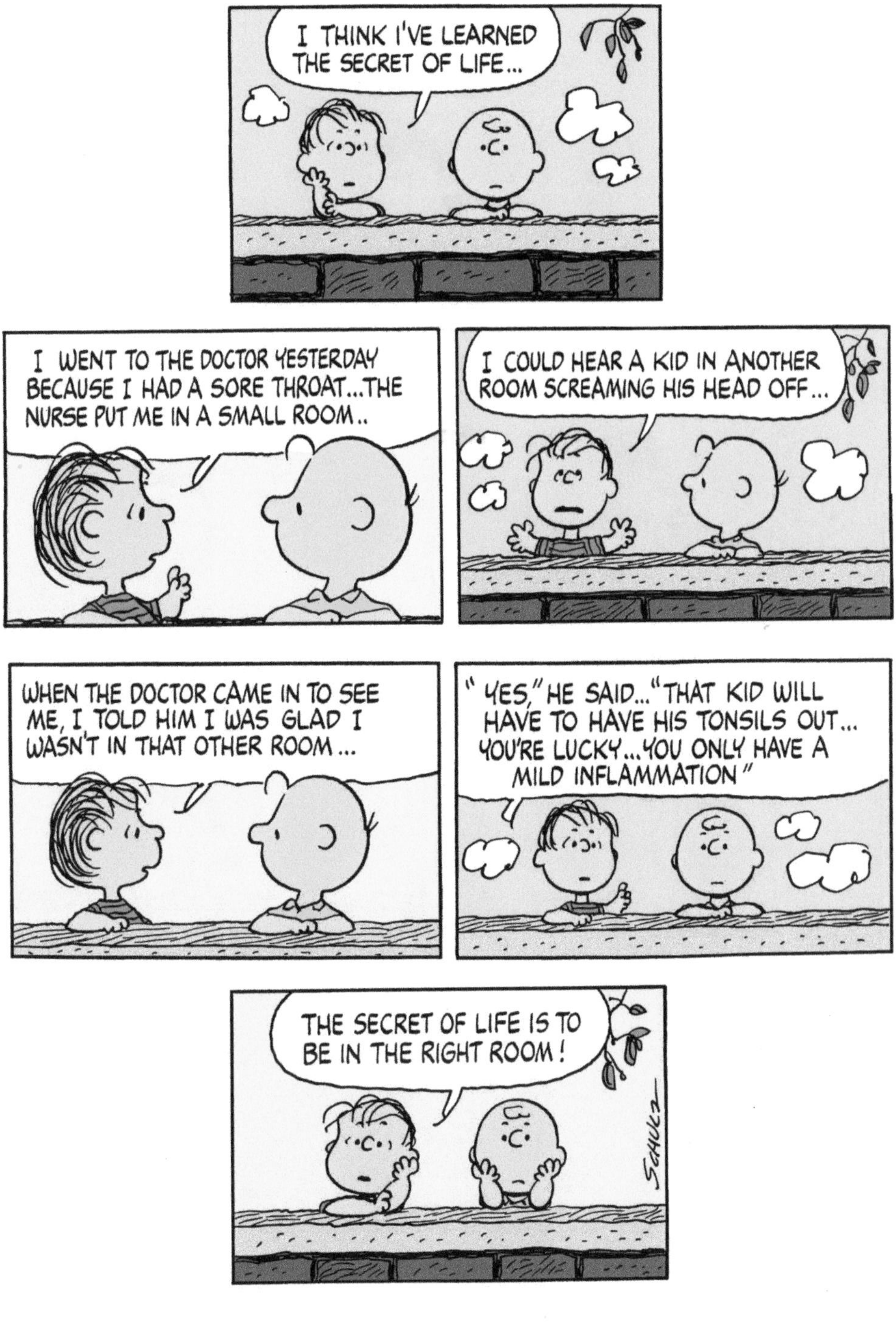
I THINK I'VE LEARNED THE SECRET OF LIFE...
I WENT TO THE DOCTOR YESTERDAY BECAUSE I HAD A SORE THROAT...THE NURSE PUT ME IN A SMALL ROOM..
I COULD HEAR A KID IN ANOTHER ROOM SCREAMING HIS HEAD OFF...
WHEN THE DOCTOR CAME IN TO SEE ME, I TOLD HIM I WAS GLAD I WASN'T IN THAT OTHER ROOM...
"YES," HE SAID..."THAT KID WILL HAVE TO HAVE HIS TONSILS OUT... YOU'RE LUCKY...YOU ONLY HAVE A MILD INFLAMMATION"
THE SECRET OF LIFE IS TO BE IN THE RIGHT ROOM!
SCHULZ

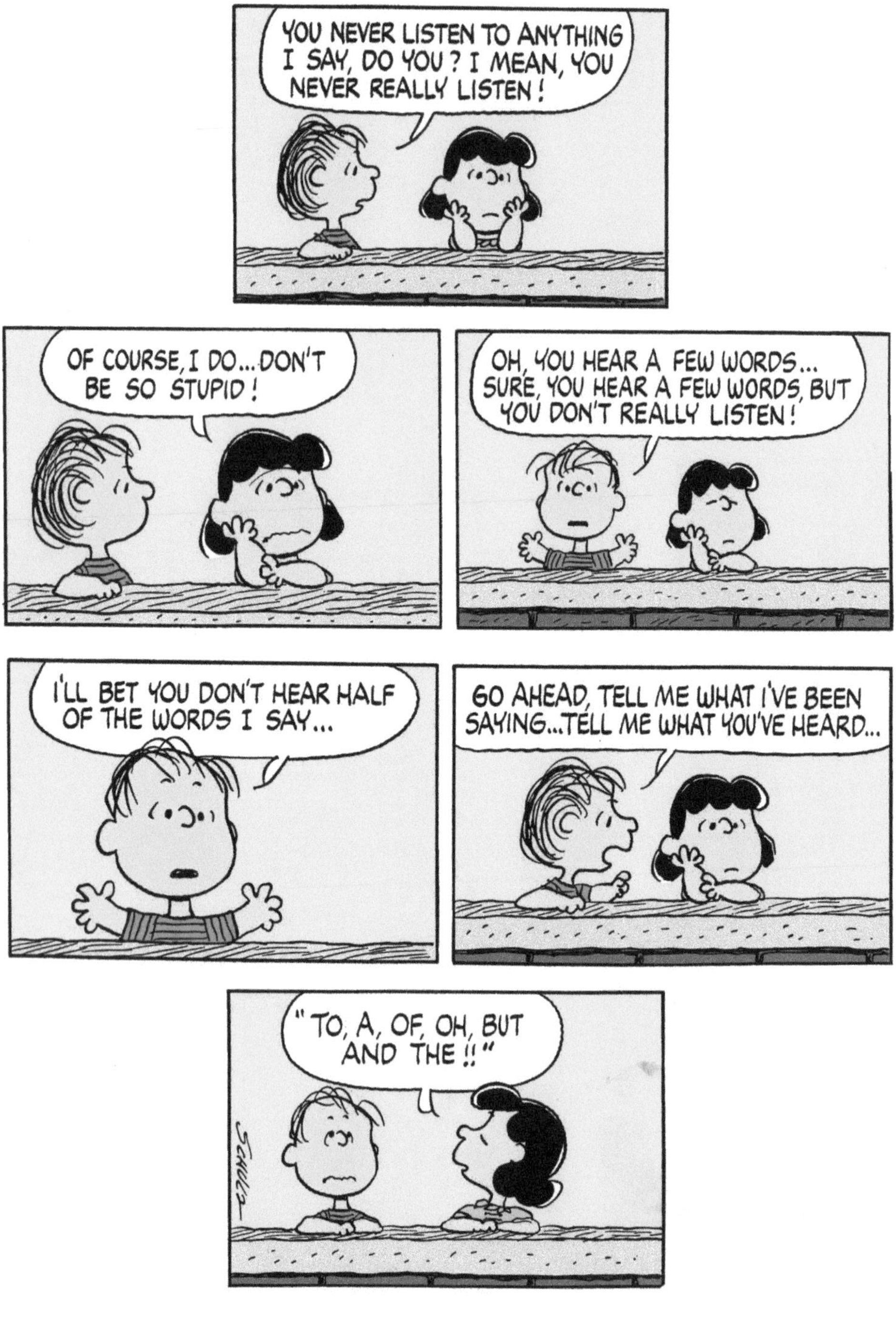
YOU NEVER LISTEN TO ANYTHING I SAY, DO YOU? I MEAN, YOU NEVER REALLY LISTEN!
OF COURSE, I DO...DON'T BE SO STUPID!
OH, YOU HEAR A FEW WORDS... SURE, YOU HEAR A FEW WORDS, BUT YOU DON'T REALLY LISTEN!
I'LL BET YOU DON'T HEAR HALF OF THE WORDS I SAY...
GO AHEAD, TELL ME WHAT I'VE BEEN SAYING...TELL ME WHAT YOU'VE HEARD...
"TO, A, OF, OH, BUT AND THE!!"
SCHULZ

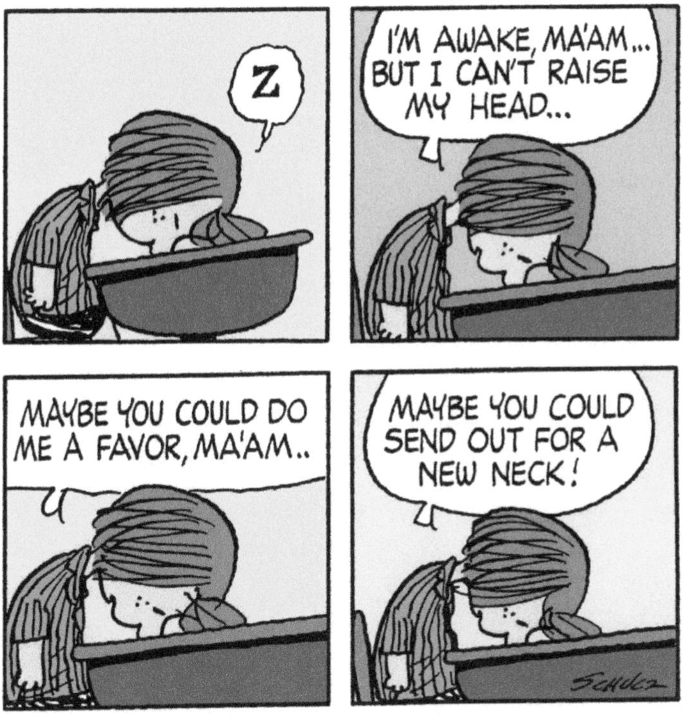
Z
I'M AWAKE, MA'AM... BUT I CAN'T RAISE MY HEAD...
MAYBE YOU COULD DO ME A FAVOR, MA'AM..
MAYBE YOU COULD SEND OUT FOR A NEW NECK!
SCHULZ

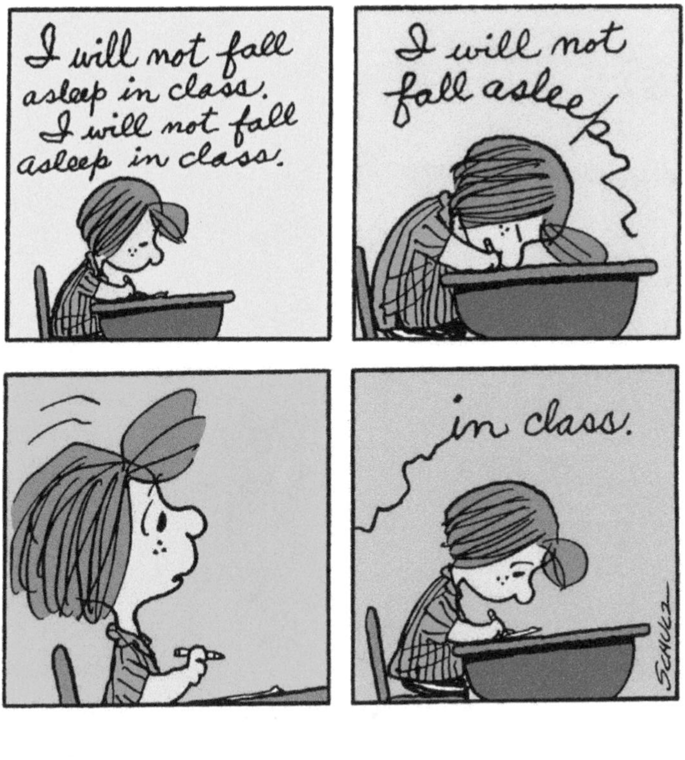
I will not fall asleep in class. I will not fall asleep in class.
I will not fall asleep
in class.
SCHULZ

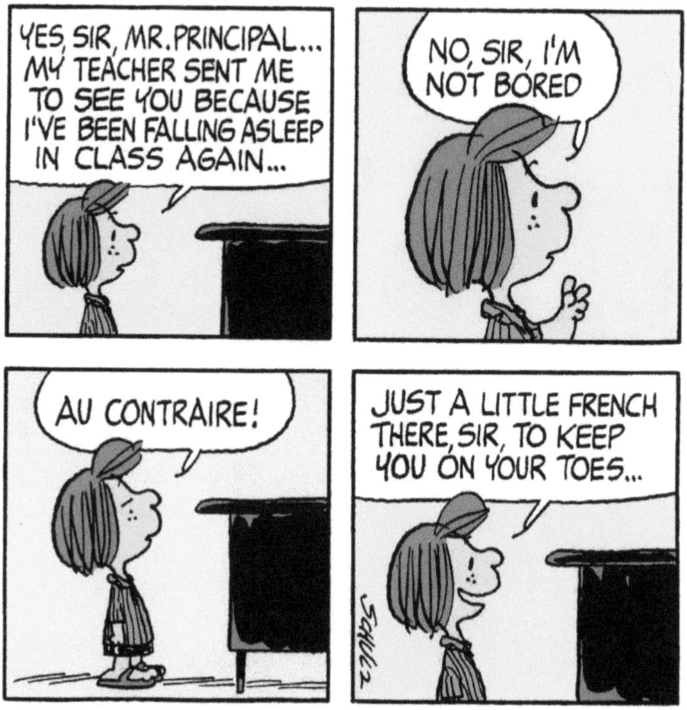
YES, SIR, MR. PRINCIPAL... MY TEACHER SENT ME TO SEE YOU BECAUSE I'VE BEEN FALLING ASLEEP IN CLASS AGAIN...
NO, SIR, I'M NOT BORED
AU CONTRAIRE!
JUST A LITTLE FRENCH THERE, SIR, TO KEEP YOU ON YOUR TOES...
SCHULZ

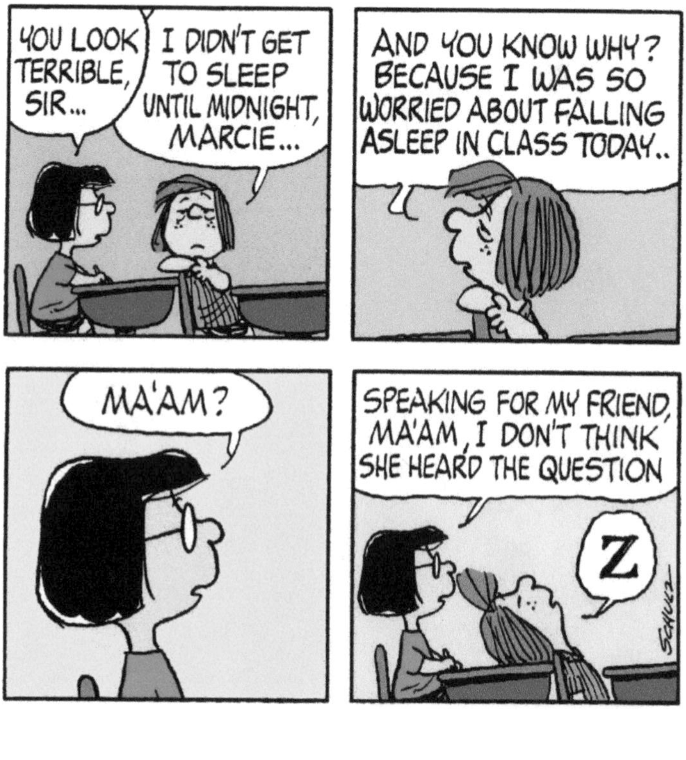
YOU LOOK TERRIBLE, SIR...
I DIDN'T GET TO SLEEP UNTIL MIDNIGHT, MARCIE...
AND YOU KNOW WHY? BECAUSE I WAS SO WORRIED ABOUT FALLING ASLEEP IN CLASS TODAY..
MA'AM?
SPEAKING FOR MY FRIEND, MA'AM, I DON'T THINK SHE HEARD THE QUESTION
Z
SCHULZ

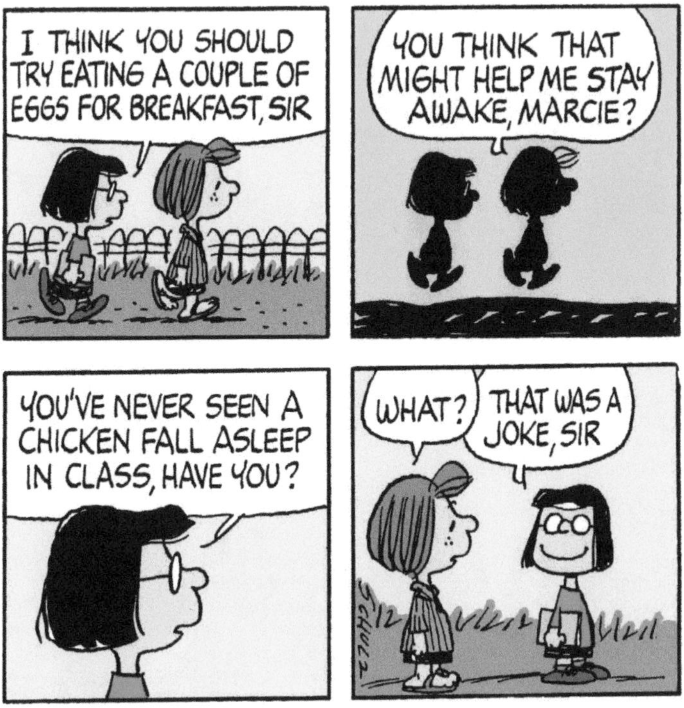
I THINK YOU SHOULD TRY EATING A COUPLE OF EGGS FOR BREAKFAST, SIR
YOU THINK THAT MIGHT HELP ME STAY AWAKE, MARCIE?
YOU'VE NEVER SEEN A CHICKEN FALL ASLEEP IN CLASS, HAVE YOU?
WHAT?
THAT WAS A JOKE, SIR

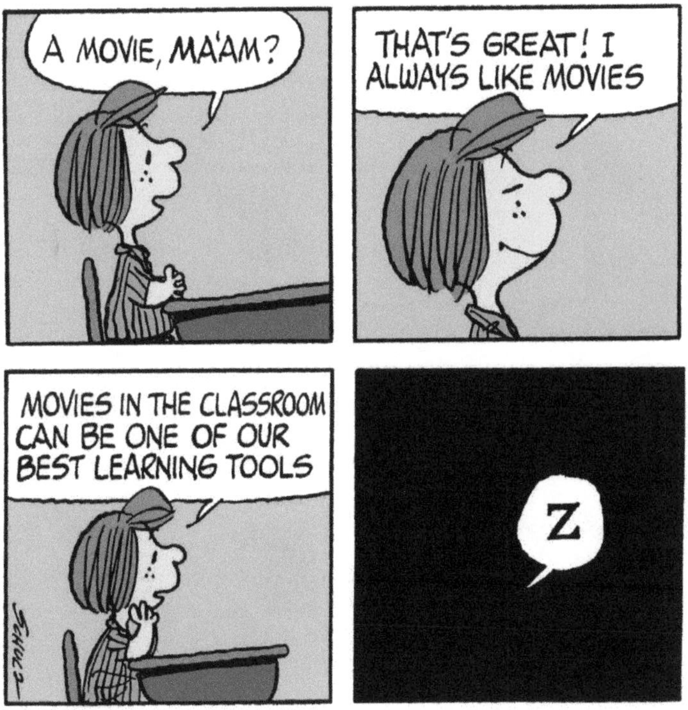
A MOVIE, MA'AM?
THAT'S GREAT! I ALWAYS LIKE MOVIES
MOVIES IN THE CLASSROOM CAN BE ONE OF OUR BEST LEARNING TOOLS
Z

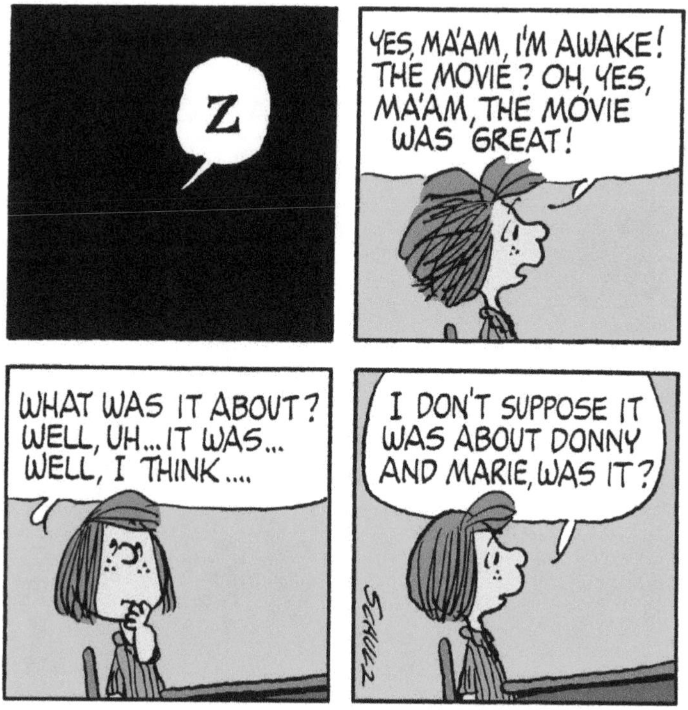
Z
YES, MA'AM, I'M AWAKE! THE MOVIE? OH, YES, MA'AM, THE MOVIE WAS GREAT!
WHAT WAS IT ABOUT? WELL, UH... IT WAS... WELL, I THINK....
I DON'T SUPPOSE IT WAS ABOUT DONNY AND MARIE, WAS IT?
SCHULZ

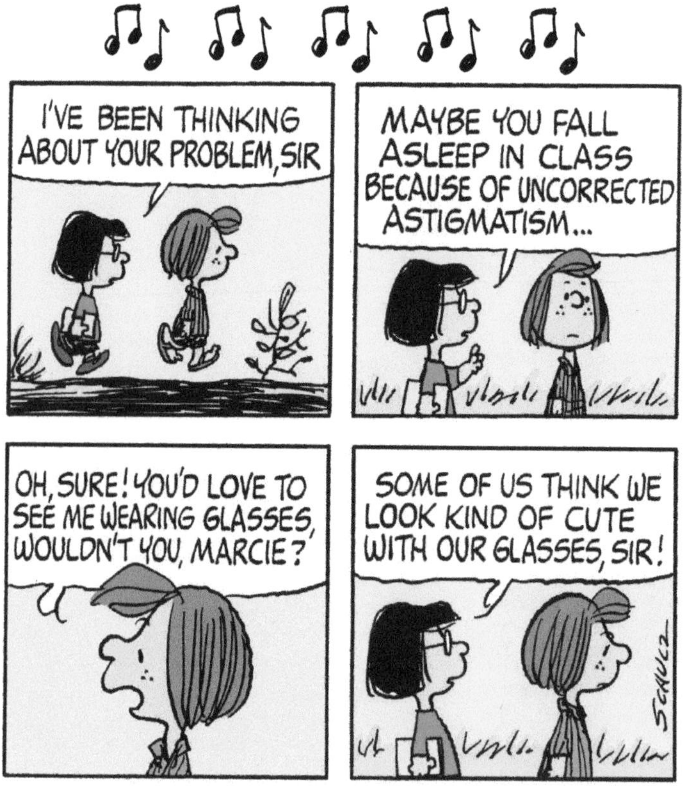
I'VE BEEN THINKING ABOUT YOUR PROBLEM, SIR
MAYBE YOU FALL ASLEEP IN CLASS BECAUSE OF UNCORRECTED ASTIGMATISM...
OH, SURE! YOU'D LOVE TO SEE ME WEARING GLASSES, WOULDN'T YOU, MARCIE?
SOME OF US THINK WE LOOK KIND OF CUTE WITH OUR GLASSES, SIR!
SCHULZ

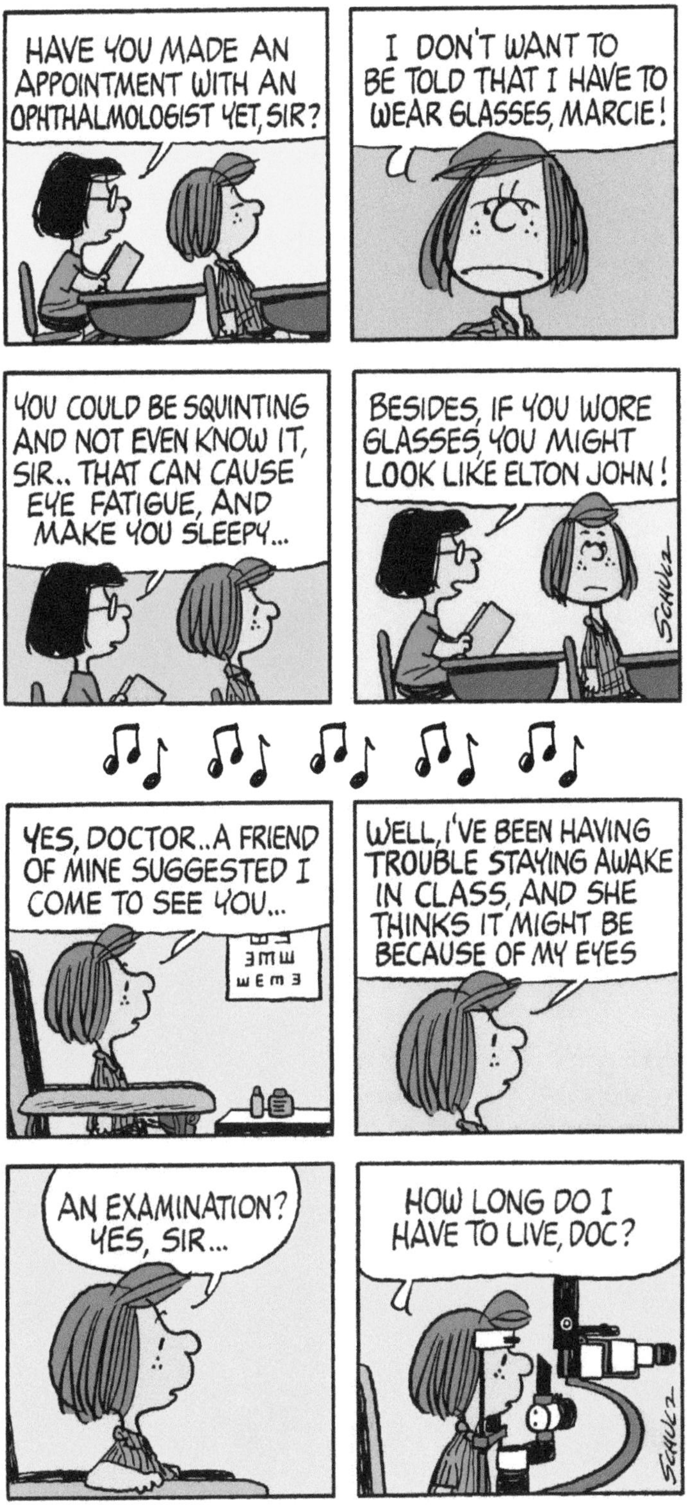
HAVE YOU MADE AN APPOINTMENT WITH AN OPHTHALMOLOGIST YET, SIR?
I DON'T WANT TO BE TOLD THAT I HAVE TO WEAR GLASSES, MARCIE!
YOU COULD BE SQUINTING AND NOT EVEN KNOW IT, SIR.. THAT CAN CAUSE EYE FATIGUE, AND MAKE YOU SLEEPY...
BESIDES, IF YOU WORE GLASSES, YOU MIGHT LOOK LIKE ELTON JOHN!
SCHULZ
YES, DOCTOR..A FRIEND OF MINE SUGGESTED I COME TO SEE YOU...
WELL, I'VE BEEN HAVING TROUBLE STAYING AWAKE IN CLASS, AND SHE THINKS IT MIGHT BE BECAUSE OF MY EYES
AN EXAMINATION? YES, SIR...
HOW LONG DO I HAVE TO LIVE, DOC?
SCHULZ

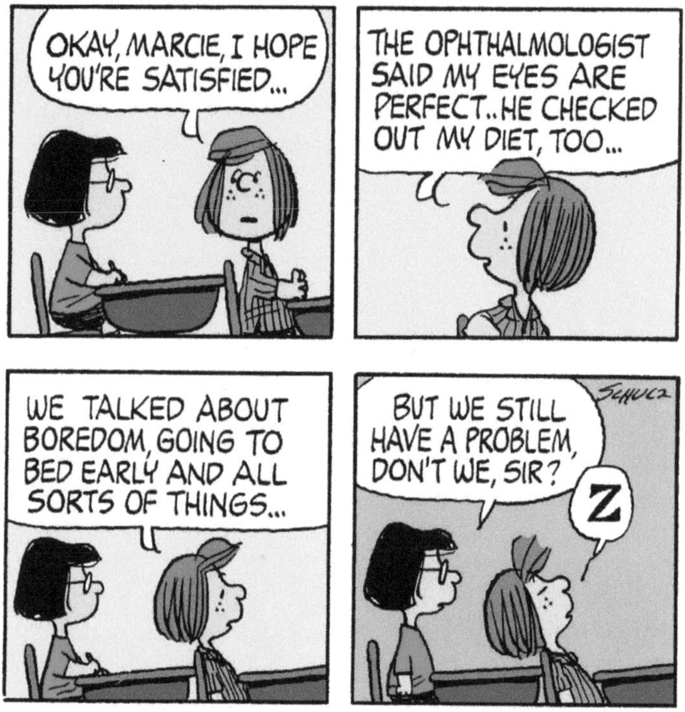
OKAY, MARCIE, I HOPE YOU'RE SATISFIED...
THE OPHTHALMOLOGIST SAID MY EYES ARE PERFECT..HE CHECKED OUT MY DIET, TOO...
WE TALKED ABOUT BOREDOM, GOING TO BED EARLY AND ALL SORTS OF THINGS...
SCHULZ
BUT WE STILL HAVE A PROBLEM, DON'T WE, SIR?
Z

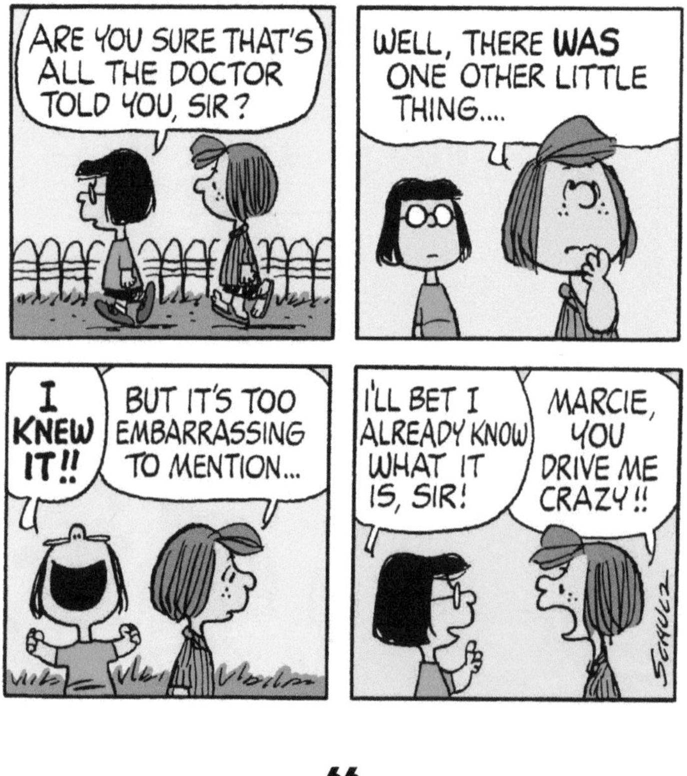
ARE YOU SURE THAT'S ALL THE DOCTOR TOLD YOU, SIR?
WELL, THERE **WAS** ONE OTHER LITTLE THING....
I KNEW IT!!
BUT IT'S TOO EMBARRASSING TO MENTION...
I'LL BET I ALREADY KNOW WHAT IT IS, SIR!
MARCIE, YOU DRIVE ME CRAZY!!
SCHULZ

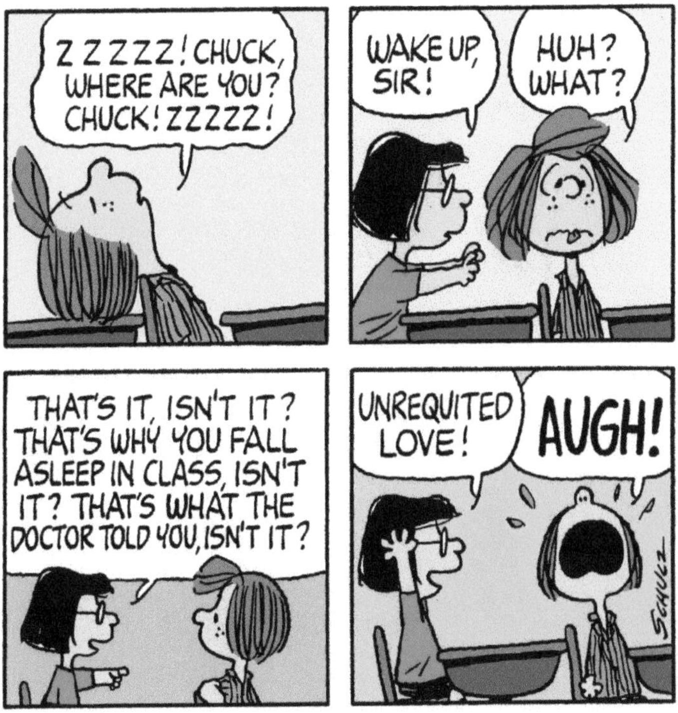
Z Z Z Z Z! CHUCK, WHERE ARE YOU? CHUCK! ZZZZZ!
WAKE UP, SIR!
HUH? WHAT?
THAT'S IT, ISN'T IT? THAT'S WHY YOU FALL ASLEEP IN CLASS, ISN'T IT? THAT'S WHAT THE DOCTOR TOLD YOU, ISN'T IT?
UNREQUITED LOVE!
AUGH!
SCHULZ

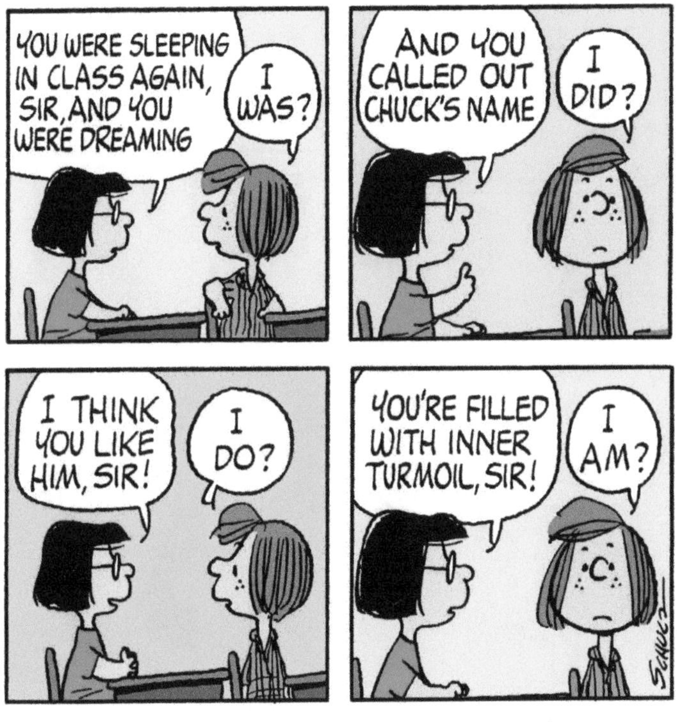
YOU WERE SLEEPING IN CLASS AGAIN, SIR, AND YOU WERE DREAMING
I WAS?
AND YOU CALLED OUT CHUCK'S NAME
I DID?
I THINK YOU LIKE HIM, SIR!
I DO?
YOU'RE FILLED WITH INNER TURMOIL, SIR!
I AM?
SCHULZ

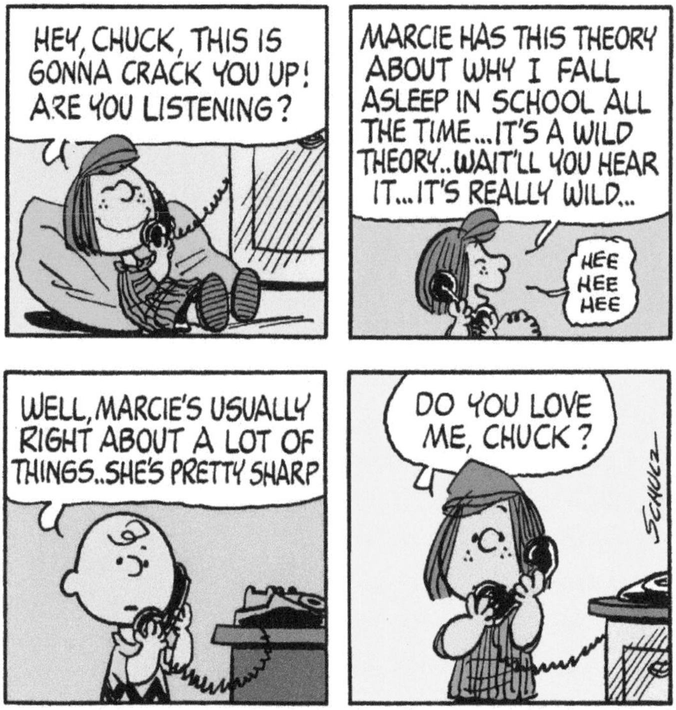
HEY, CHUCK, THIS IS GONNA CRACK YOU UP! ARE YOU LISTENING?
MARCIE HAS THIS THEORY ABOUT WHY I FALL ASLEEP IN SCHOOL ALL THE TIME...IT'S A WILD THEORY..WAIT'LL YOU HEAR IT...IT'S REALLY WILD...
HEE HEE HEE
WELL, MARCIE'S USUALLY RIGHT ABOUT A LOT OF THINGS..SHE'S PRETTY SHARP
DO YOU LOVE ME, CHUCK?
SCHULZ

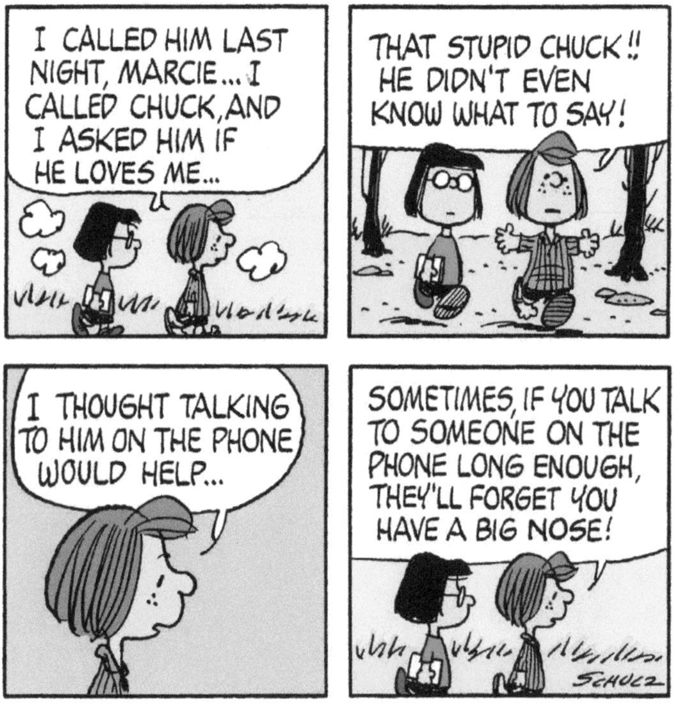
I CALLED HIM LAST NIGHT, MARCIE... I CALLED CHUCK, AND I ASKED HIM IF HE LOVES ME...
THAT STUPID CHUCK!! HE DIDN'T EVEN KNOW WHAT TO SAY!
I THOUGHT TALKING TO HIM ON THE PHONE WOULD HELP...
SOMETIMES, IF YOU TALK TO SOMEONE ON THE PHONE LONG ENOUGH, THEY'LL FORGET YOU HAVE A BIG NOSE!
SCHULZ

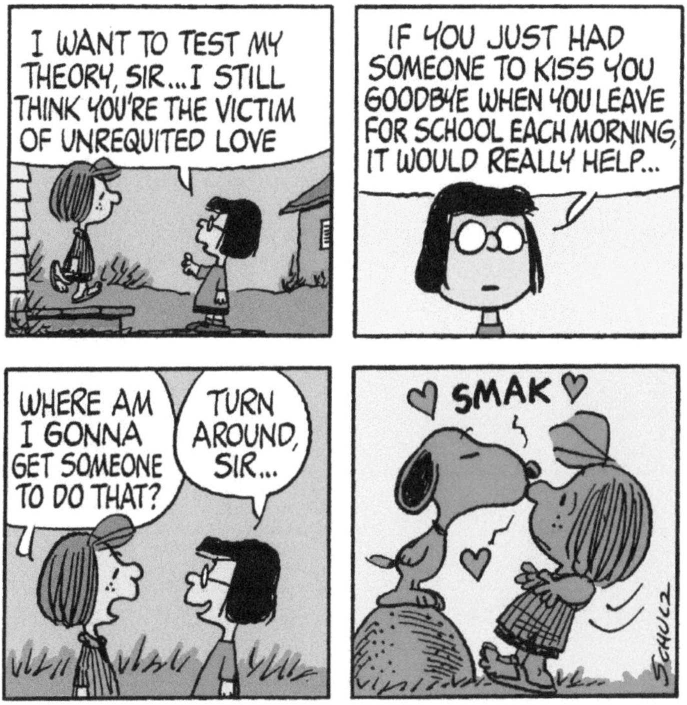
I WANT TO TEST MY THEORY, SIR...I STILL THINK YOU'RE THE VICTIM OF UNREQUITED LOVE
IF YOU JUST HAD SOMEONE TO KISS YOU GOODBYE WHEN YOU LEAVE FOR SCHOOL EACH MORNING, IT WOULD REALLY HELP...
WHERE AM I GONNA GET SOMEONE TO DO THAT?
TURN AROUND, SIR...
SMAK
SCHULZ

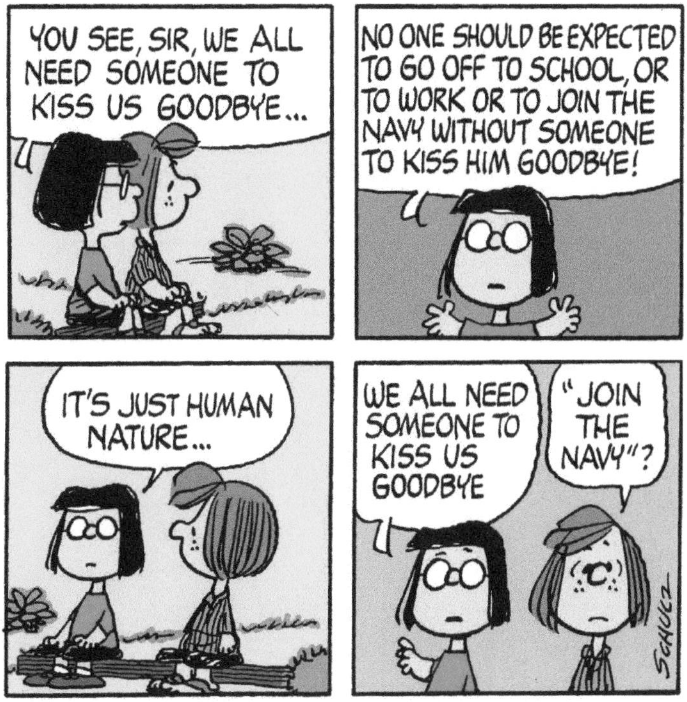
YOU SEE, SIR, WE ALL NEED SOMEONE TO KISS US GOODBYE...
NO ONE SHOULD BE EXPECTED TO GO OFF TO SCHOOL, OR TO WORK OR TO JOIN THE NAVY WITHOUT SOMEONE TO KISS HIM GOODBYE!
IT'S JUST HUMAN NATURE...
WE ALL NEED SOMEONE TO KISS US GOODBYE
"JOIN THE NAVY"?
SCHULZ

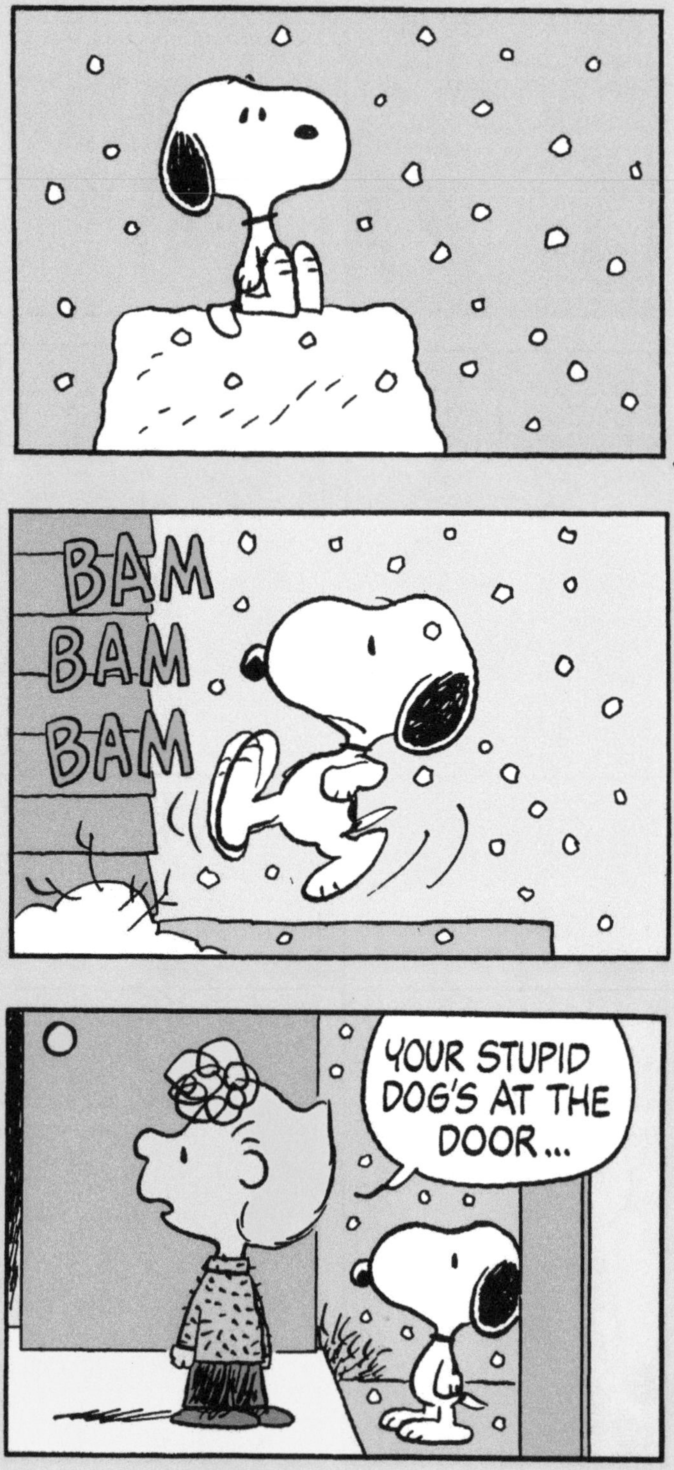
BAM
BAM
BAM
YOUR STUPID DOG'S AT THE DOOR...

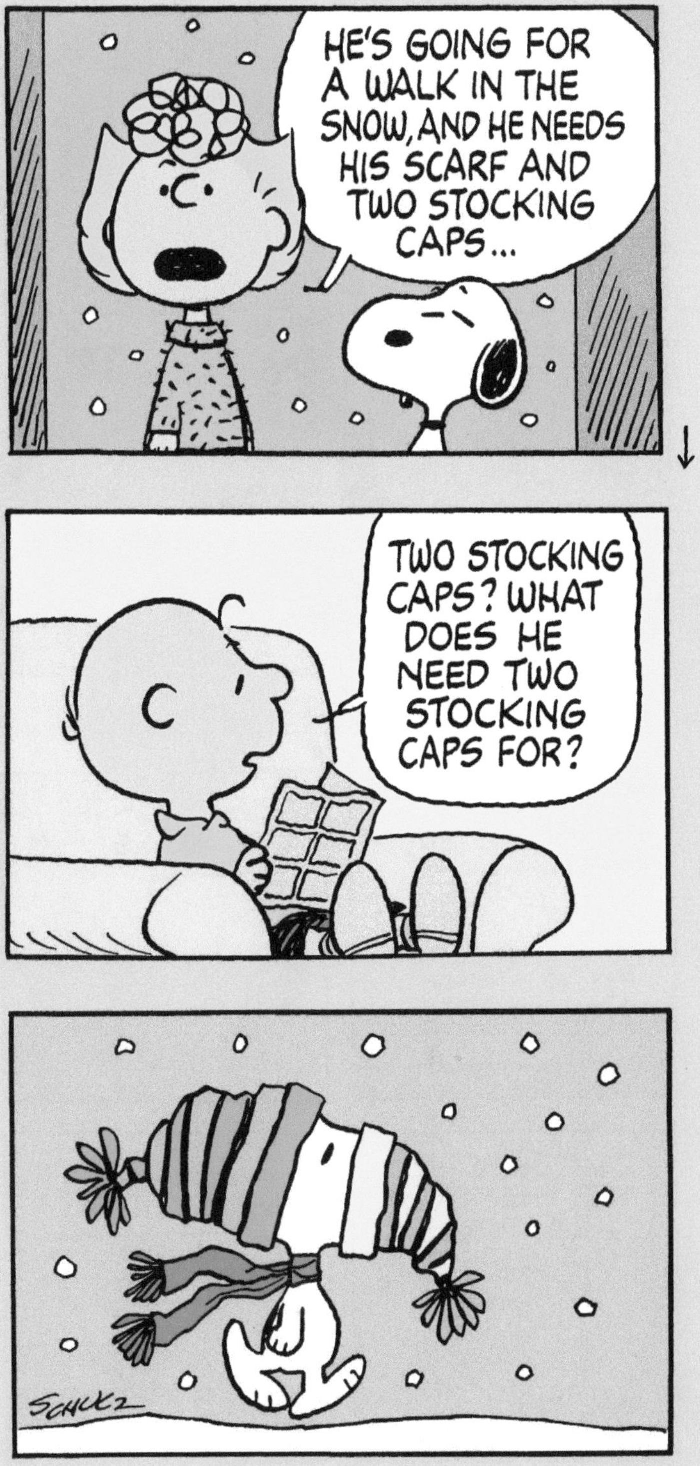
HE'S GOING FOR A WALK IN THE SNOW, AND HE NEEDS HIS SCARF AND TWO STOCKING CAPS...
TWO STOCKING CAPS? WHAT DOES HE NEED TWO STOCKING CAPS FOR?
SCHULZ

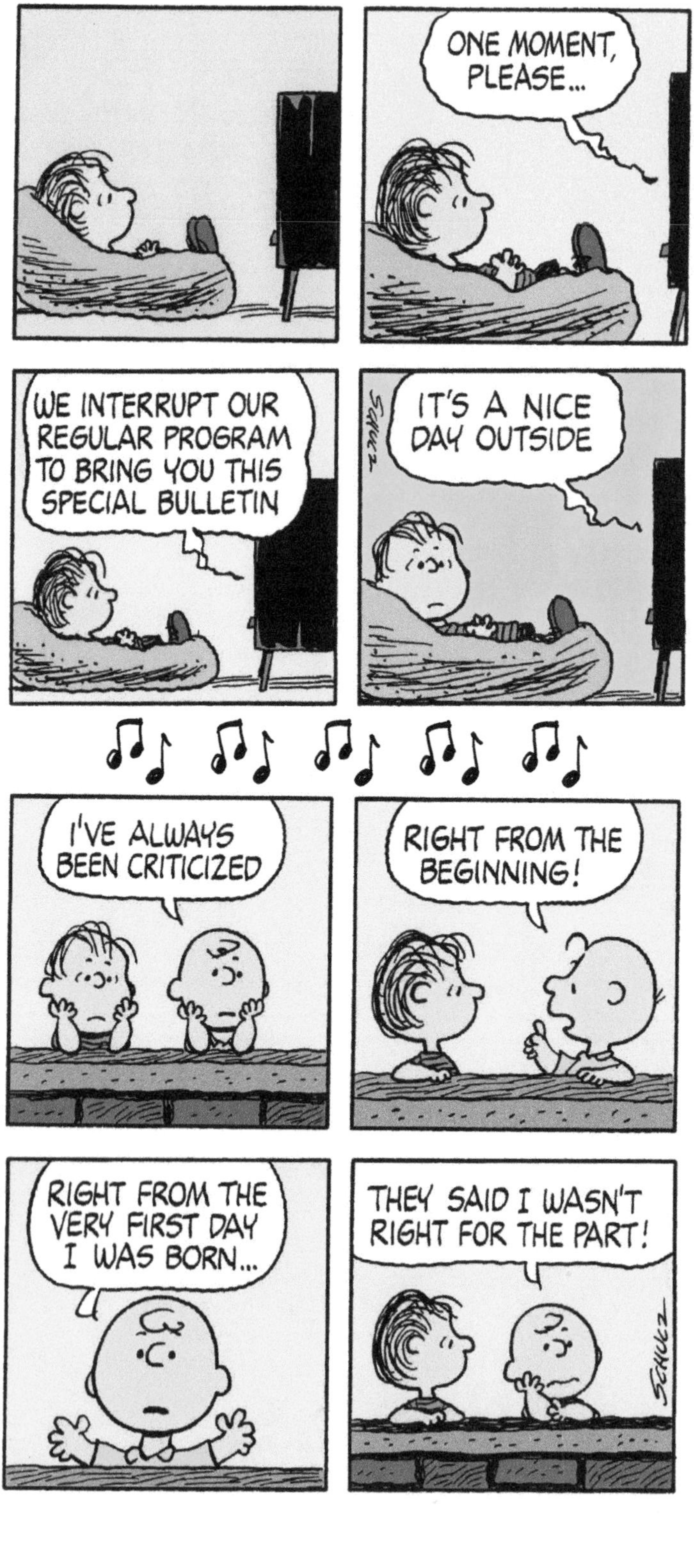
ONE MOMENT, PLEASE...
WE INTERRUPT OUR REGULAR PROGRAM TO BRING YOU THIS SPECIAL BULLETIN
IT'S A NICE DAY OUTSIDE
SCHULZ
I'VE ALWAYS BEEN CRITICIZED
RIGHT FROM THE BEGINNING!
RIGHT FROM THE VERY FIRST DAY I WAS BORN...
THEY SAID I WASN'T RIGHT FOR THE PART!
SCHULZ

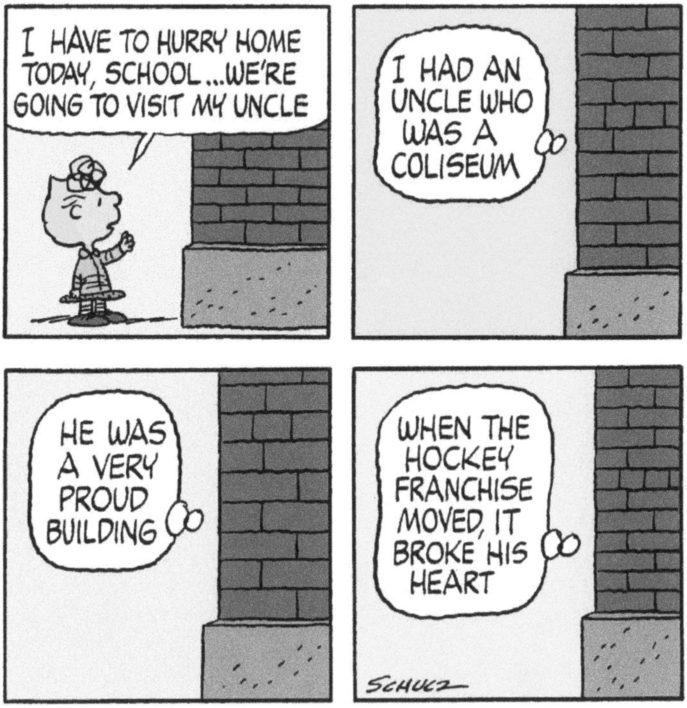
I HAVE TO HURRY HOME TODAY, SCHOOL...WE'RE GOING TO VISIT MY UNCLE
I HAD AN UNCLE WHO WAS A COLISEUM
HE WAS A VERY PROUD BUILDING
WHEN THE HOCKEY FRANCHISE MOVED, IT BROKE HIS HEART
SCHULZ

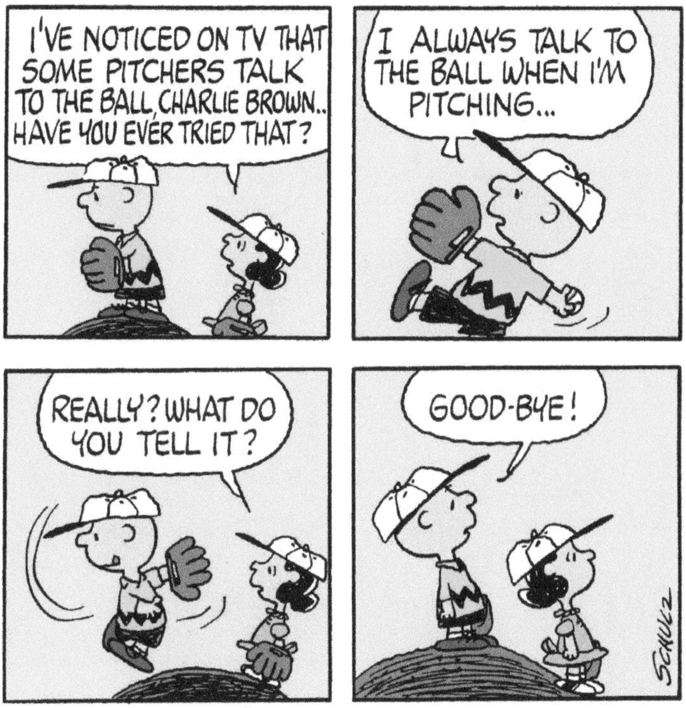
I'VE NOTICED ON TV THAT SOME PITCHERS TALK TO THE BALL, CHARLIE BROWN.. HAVE YOU EVER TRIED THAT?
I ALWAYS TALK TO THE BALL WHEN I'M PITCHING...
REALLY? WHAT DO YOU TELL IT?
GOOD-BYE!
SCHULZ

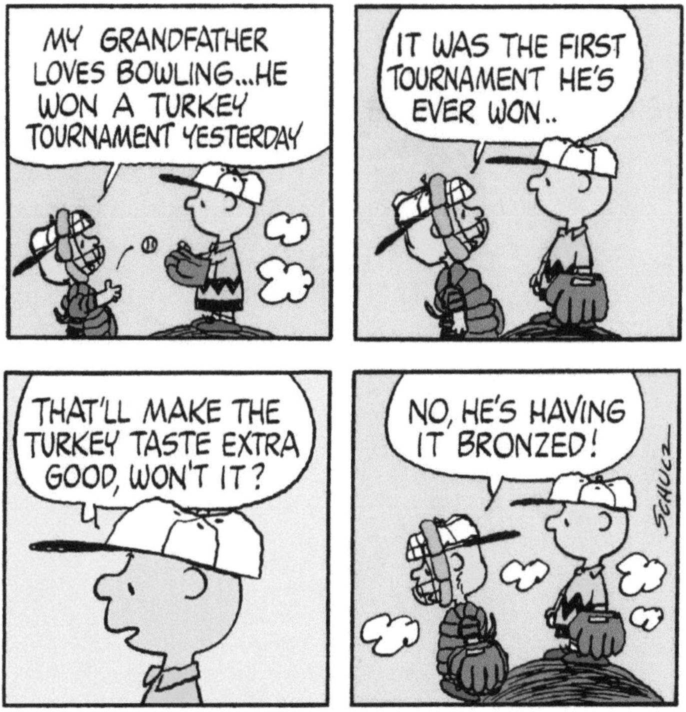
MY GRANDFATHER LOVES BOWLING...HE WON A TURKEY TOURNAMENT YESTERDAY
IT WAS THE FIRST TOURNAMENT HE'S EVER WON..
THAT'LL MAKE THE TURKEY TASTE EXTRA GOOD, WON'T IT?
NO, HE'S HAVING IT BRONZED!

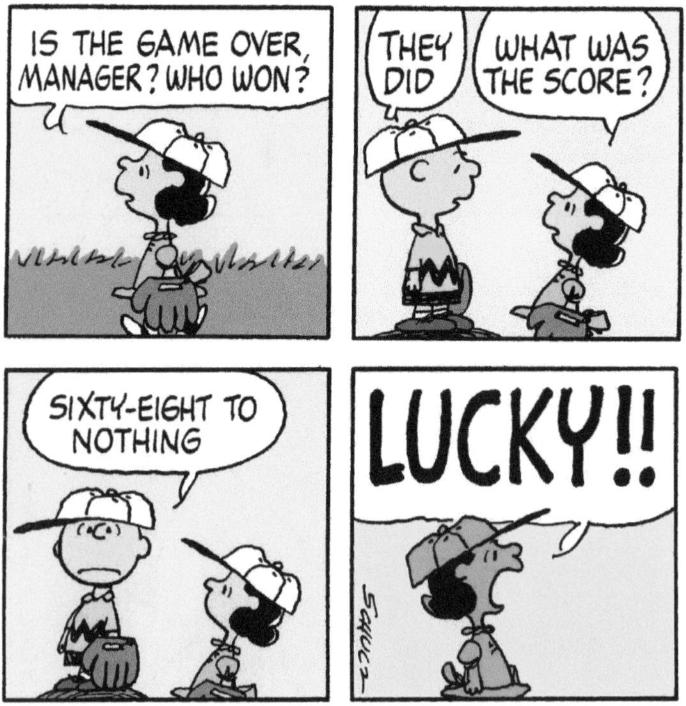
IS THE GAME OVER, MANAGER? WHO WON?
THEY DID
WHAT WAS THE SCORE?
SIXTY-EIGHT TO NOTHING
LUCKY!!

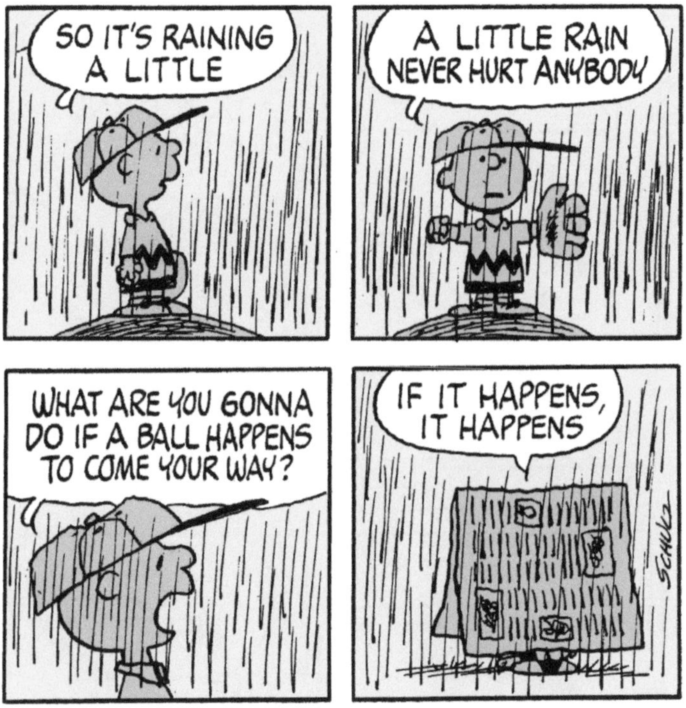
SO IT'S RAINING A LITTLE
A LITTLE RAIN NEVER HURT ANYBODY
WHAT ARE YOU GONNA DO IF A BALL HAPPENS TO COME YOUR WAY?
IF IT HAPPENS, IT HAPPENS
SCHULZ

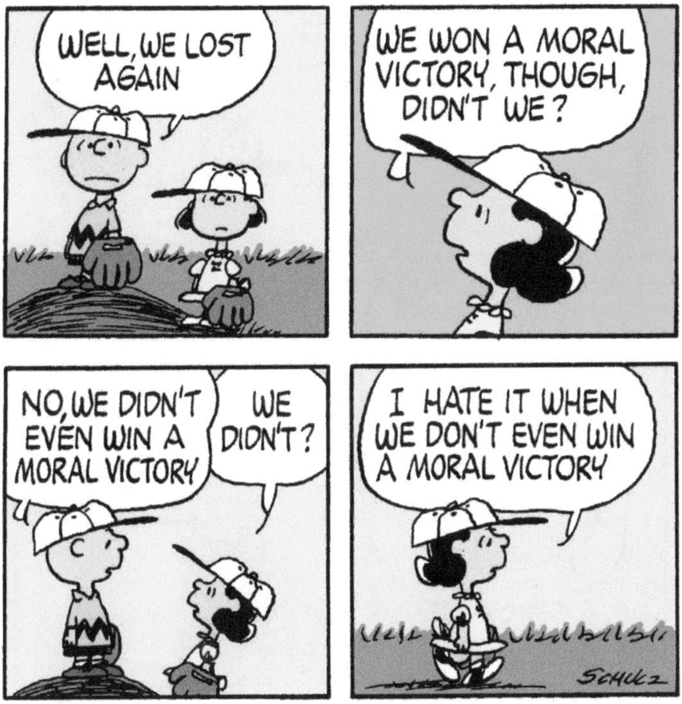
WELL, WE LOST AGAIN
WE WON A MORAL VICTORY, THOUGH, DIDN'T WE?
NO, WE DIDN'T EVEN WIN A MORAL VICTORY
WE DIDN'T?
I HATE IT WHEN WE DON'T EVEN WIN A MORAL VICTORY
SCHULZ

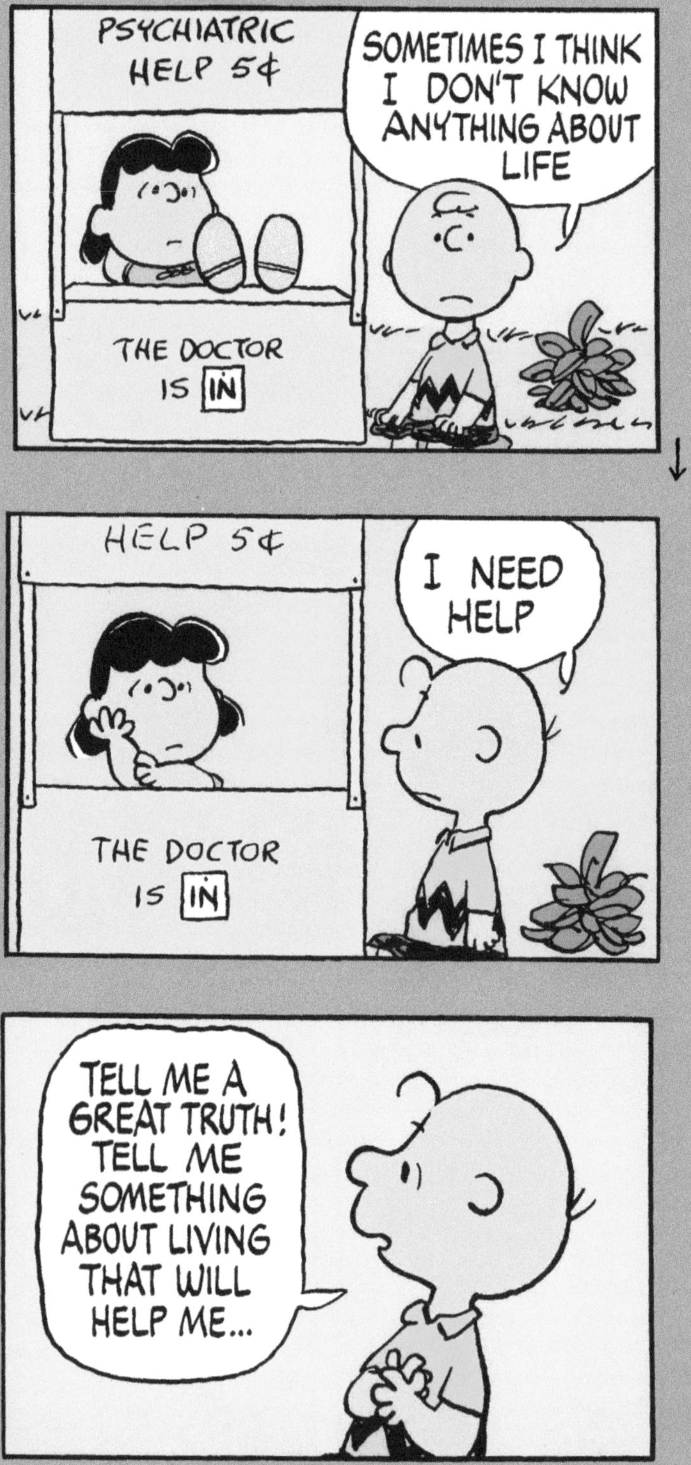
PSYCHIATRIC HELP 5¢
SOMETIMES I THINK I DON'T KNOW ANYTHING ABOUT LIFE
THE DOCTOR IS IN
HELP 5¢
I NEED HELP
THE DOCTOR IS IN
TELL ME A GREAT TRUTH! TELL ME SOMETHING ABOUT LIVING THAT WILL HELP ME...

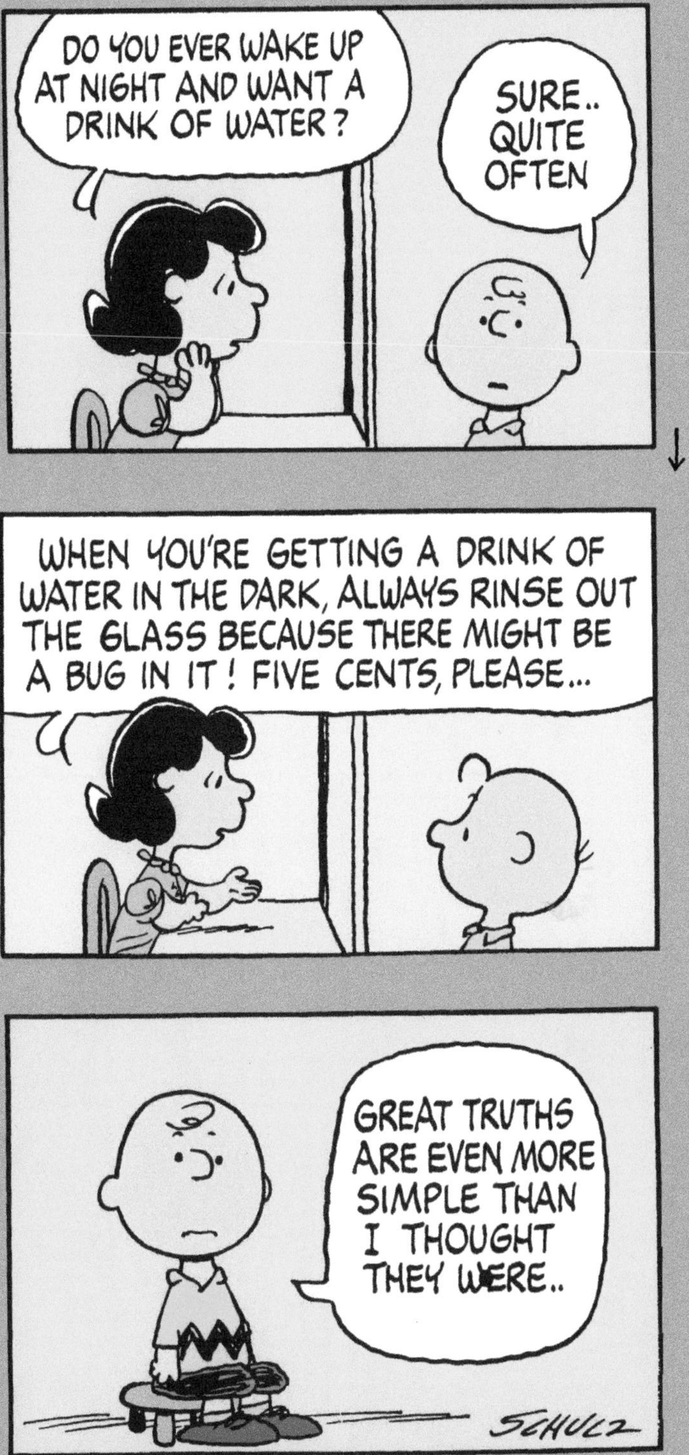
DO YOU EVER WAKE UP AT NIGHT AND WANT A DRINK OF WATER?
SURE.. QUITE OFTEN
WHEN YOU'RE GETTING A DRINK OF WATER IN THE DARK, ALWAYS RINSE OUT THE GLASS BECAUSE THERE MIGHT BE A BUG IN IT! FIVE CENTS, PLEASE...
GREAT TRUTHS ARE EVEN MORE SIMPLE THAN I THOUGHT THEY WERE..
SCHULZ

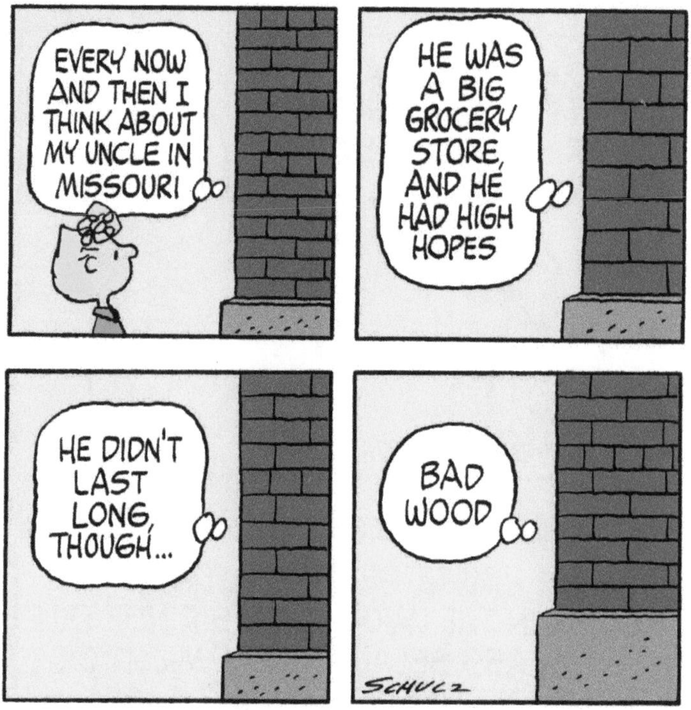
EVERY NOW AND THEN I THINK ABOUT MY UNCLE IN MISSOURI
HE WAS A BIG GROCERY STORE, AND HE HAD HIGH HOPES
HE DIDN'T LAST LONG, THOUGH...
BAD WOOD
SCHULZ

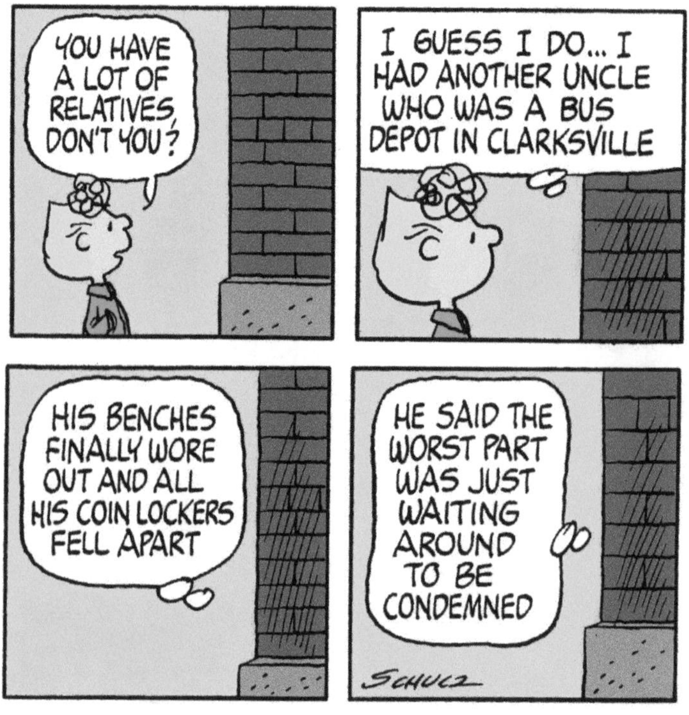
YOU HAVE A LOT OF RELATIVES, DON'T YOU?
I GUESS I DO... I HAD ANOTHER UNCLE WHO WAS A BUS DEPOT IN CLARKSVILLE
HIS BENCHES FINALLY WORE OUT AND ALL HIS COIN LOCKERS FELL APART
HE SAID THE WORST PART WAS JUST WAITING AROUND TO BE CONDEMNED
SCHULZ

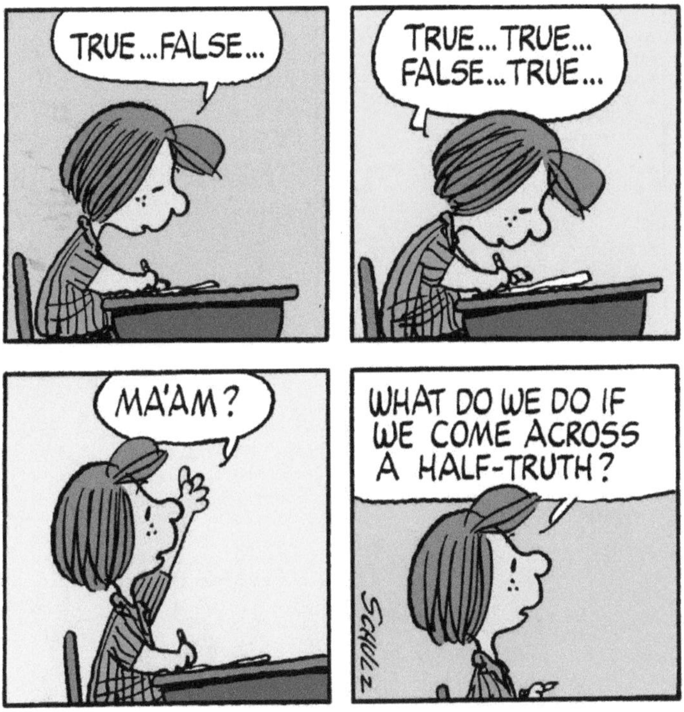
TRUE...FALSE...
TRUE...TRUE...
FALSE...TRUE...
MA'AM?
WHAT DO WE DO IF
WE COME ACROSS
A HALF-TRUTH?
SCHULZ

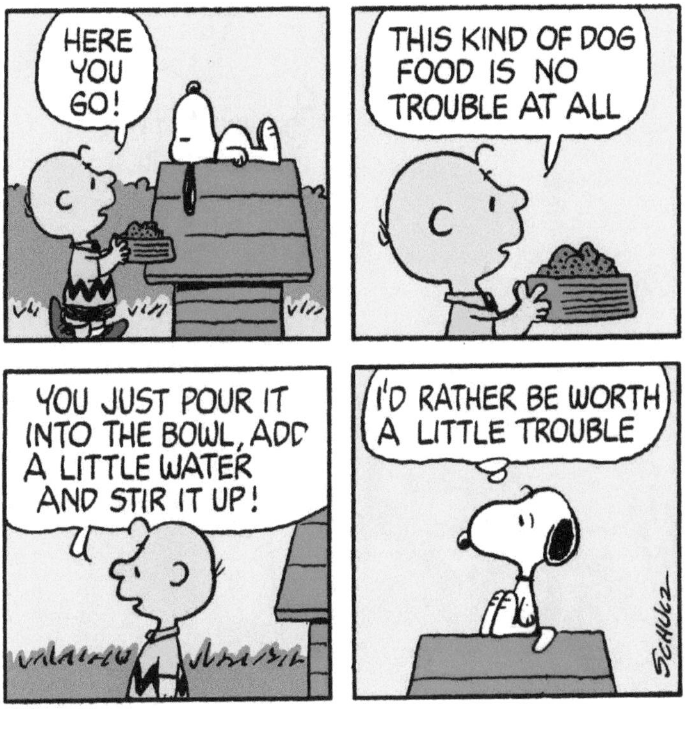
HERE
YOU
GO!
THIS KIND OF DOG
FOOD IS NO
TROUBLE AT ALL
YOU JUST POUR IT
INTO THE BOWL, ADD
A LITTLE WATER
AND STIR IT UP!
I'D RATHER BE WORTH
A LITTLE TROUBLE
SCHULZ

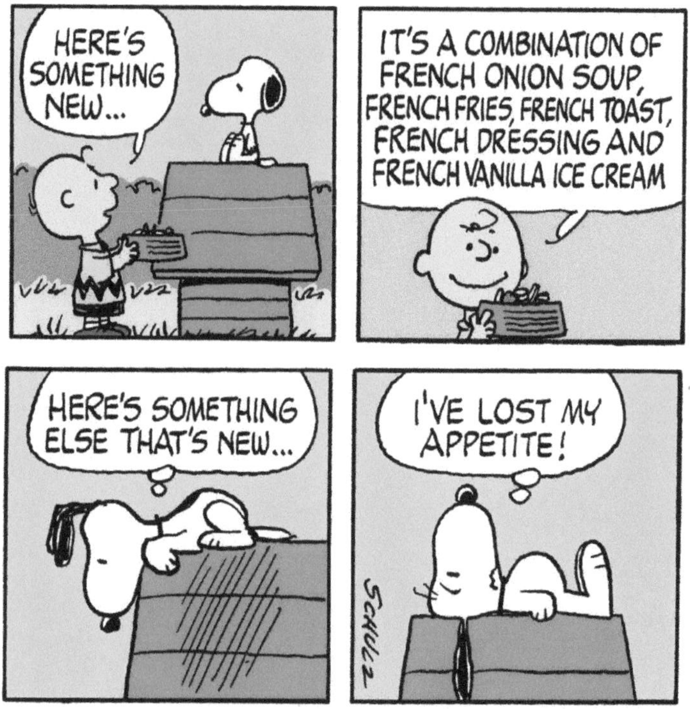
HERE'S SOMETHING NEW...
IT'S A COMBINATION OF FRENCH ONION SOUP, FRENCH FRIES, FRENCH TOAST, FRENCH DRESSING AND FRENCH VANILLA ICE CREAM
HERE'S SOMETHING ELSE THAT'S NEW...
I'VE LOST MY APPETITE!
SCHULZ

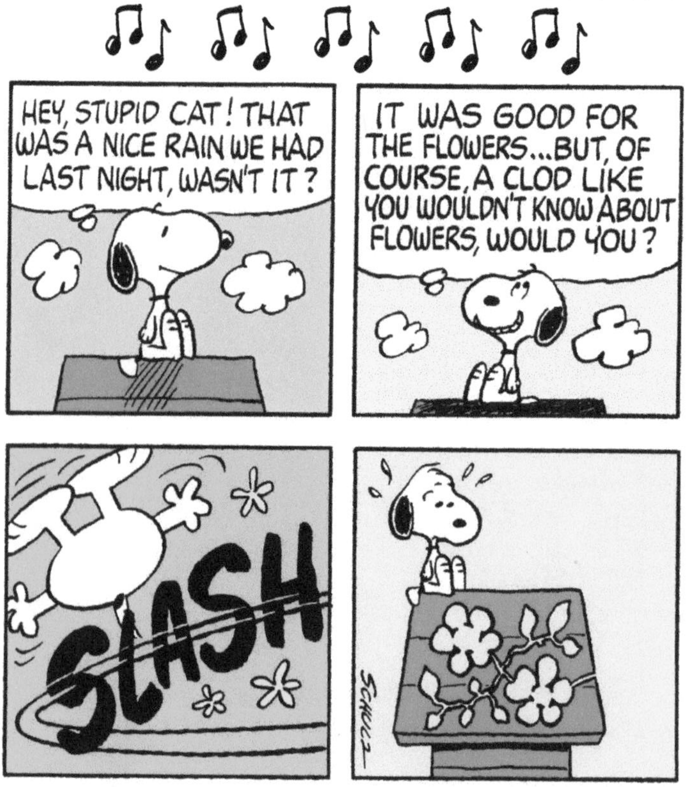
HEY, STUPID CAT! THAT WAS A NICE RAIN WE HAD LAST NIGHT, WASN'T IT?
IT WAS GOOD FOR THE FLOWERS...BUT, OF COURSE, A CLOD LIKE YOU WOULDN'T KNOW ABOUT FLOWERS, WOULD YOU?
SLASH
SCHULZ

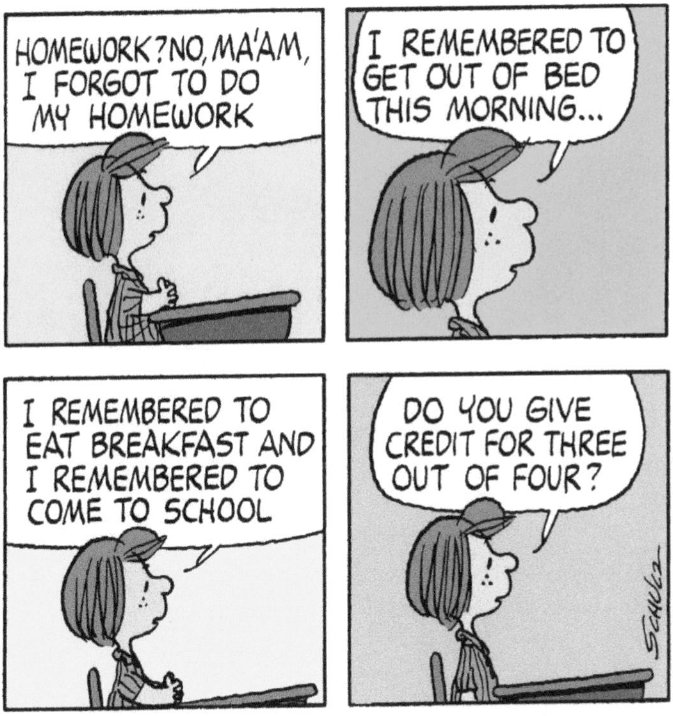
HOMEWORK? NO, MA'AM, I FORGOT TO DO MY HOMEWORK
I REMEMBERED TO GET OUT OF BED THIS MORNING...
I REMEMBERED TO EAT BREAKFAST AND I REMEMBERED TO COME TO SCHOOL
DO YOU GIVE CREDIT FOR THREE OUT OF FOUR?
SCHULZ

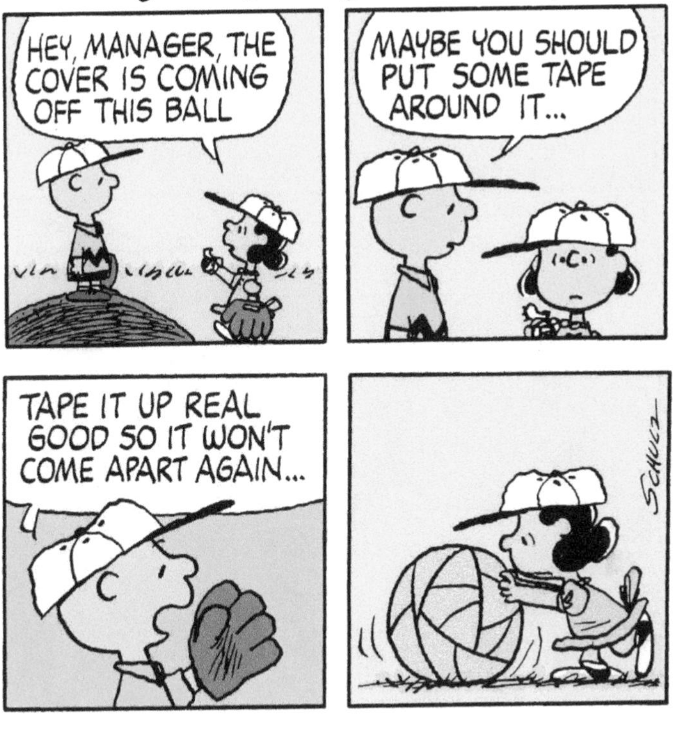
HEY, MANAGER, THE COVER IS COMING OFF THIS BALL
MAYBE YOU SHOULD PUT SOME TAPE AROUND IT...
TAPE IT UP REAL GOOD SO IT WON'T COME APART AGAIN...
SCHULZ

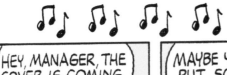

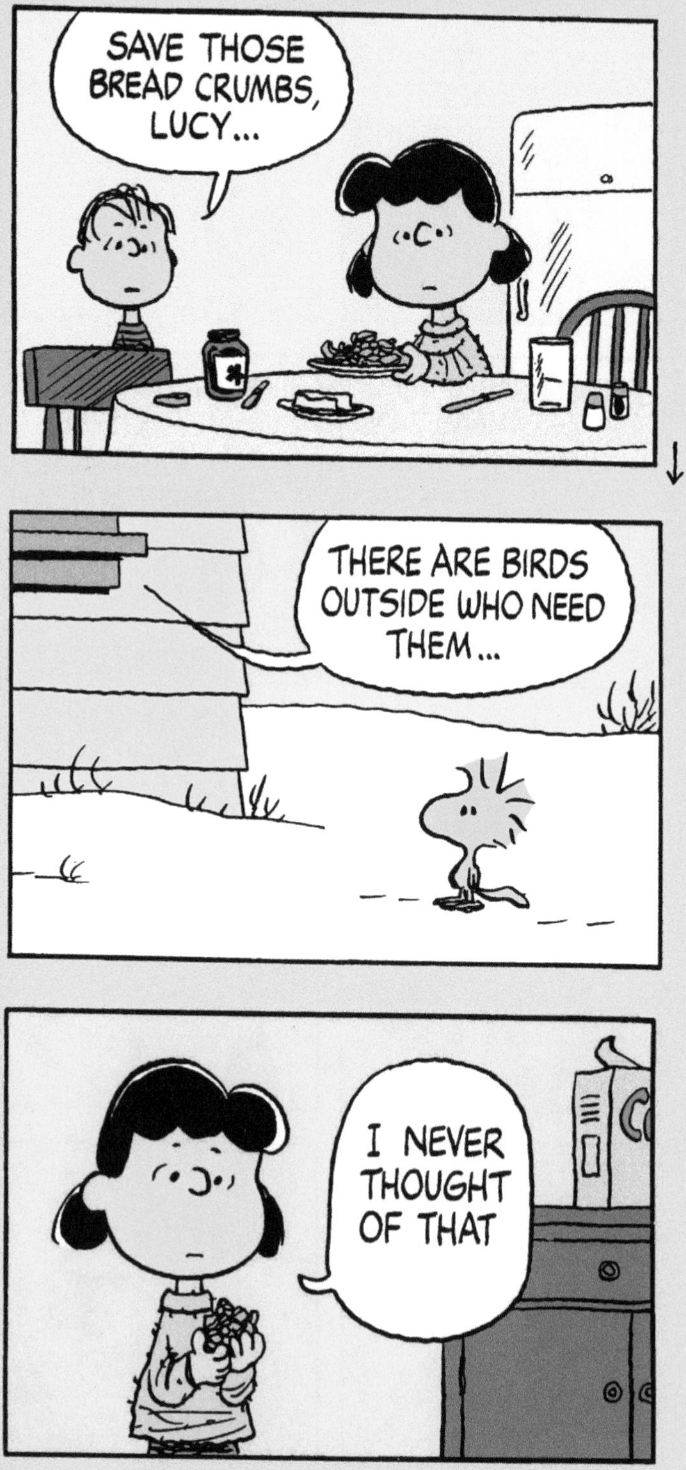
SAVE THOSE BREAD CRUMBS, LUCY...
THERE ARE BIRDS OUTSIDE WHO NEED THEM...
I NEVER THOUGHT OF THAT

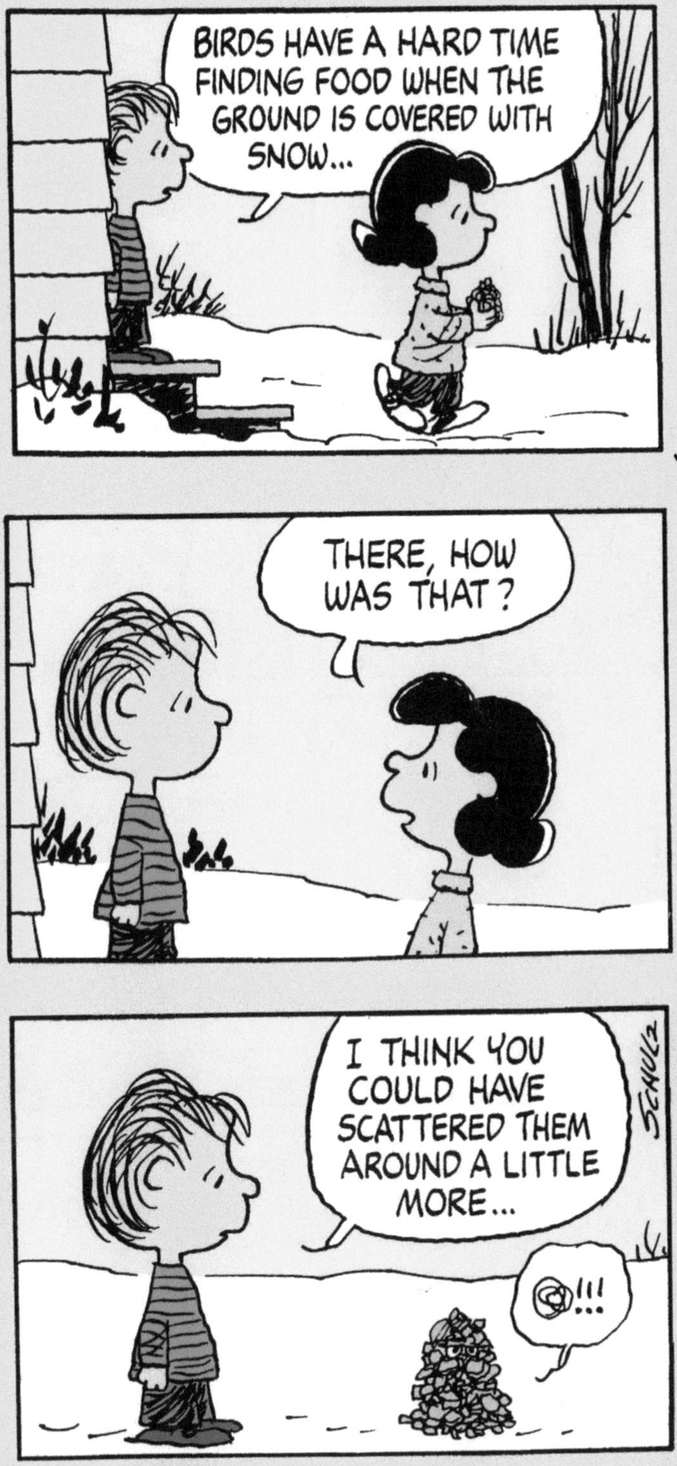
BIRDS HAVE A HARD TIME FINDING FOOD WHEN THE GROUND IS COVERED WITH SNOW...
THERE, HOW WAS THAT?
I THINK YOU COULD HAVE SCATTERED THEM AROUND A LITTLE MORE...
!!!
SCHULZ

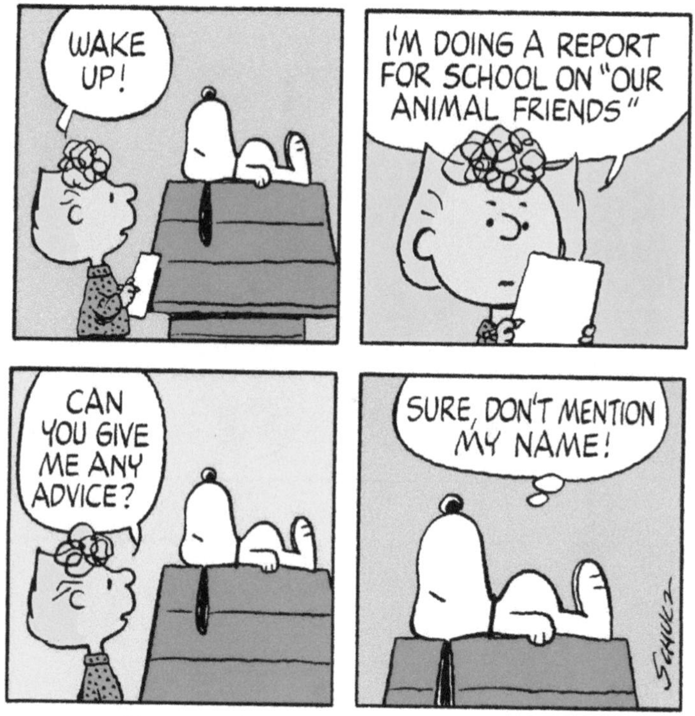
WAKE UP!
I'M DOING A REPORT FOR SCHOOL ON "OUR ANIMAL FRIENDS"
CAN YOU GIVE ME ANY ADVICE?
SURE, DON'T MENTION MY NAME!
SCHULZ

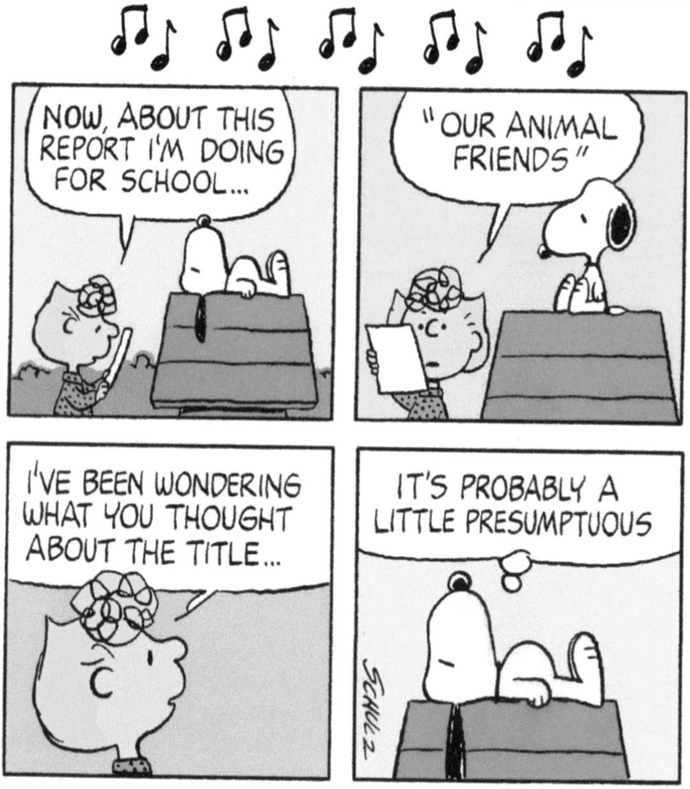
NOW, ABOUT THIS REPORT I'M DOING FOR SCHOOL...
"OUR ANIMAL FRIENDS"
I'VE BEEN WONDERING WHAT YOU THOUGHT ABOUT THE TITLE...
IT'S PROBABLY A LITTLE PRESUMPTUOUS
SCHULZ

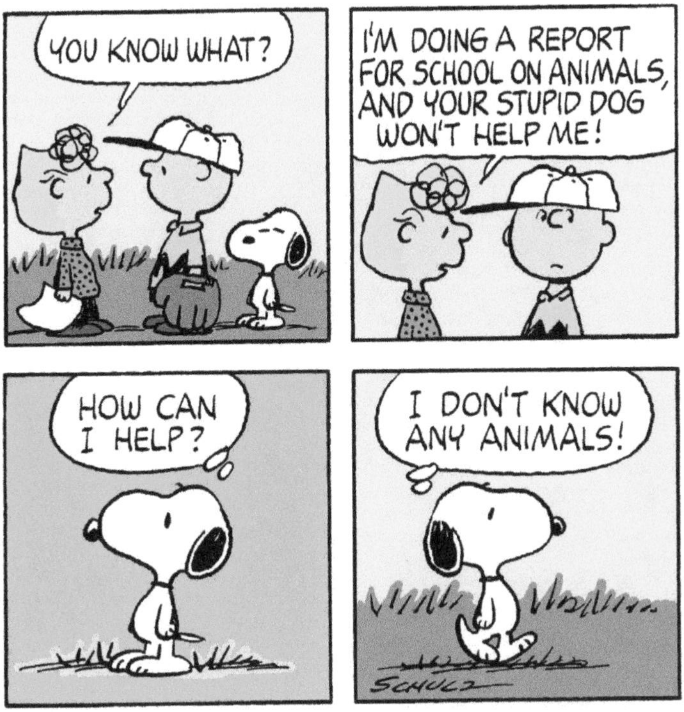
YOU KNOW WHAT?
I'M DOING A REPORT FOR SCHOOL ON ANIMALS, AND YOUR STUPID DOG WON'T HELP ME!
HOW CAN I HELP?
I DON'T KNOW ANY ANIMALS!
SCHULZ

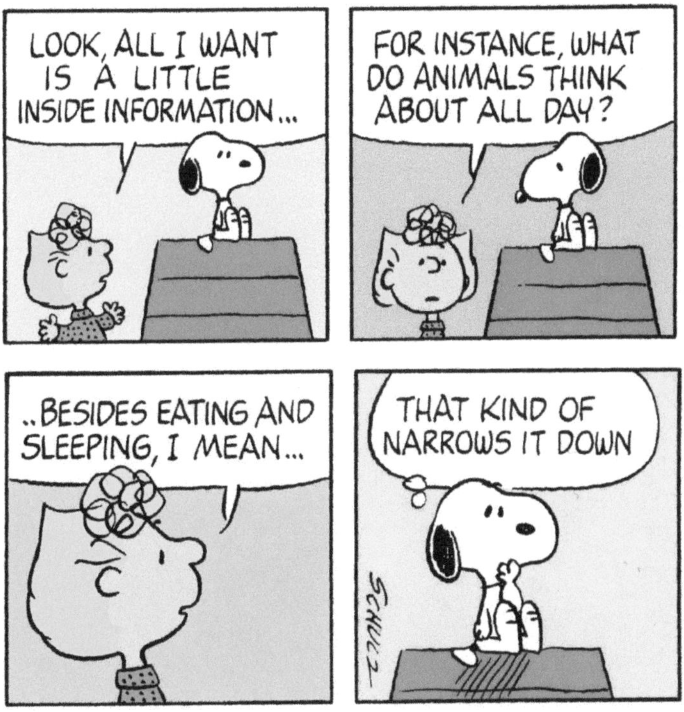
LOOK, ALL I WANT IS A LITTLE INSIDE INFORMATION...
FOR INSTANCE, WHAT DO ANIMALS THINK ABOUT ALL DAY?
..BESIDES EATING AND SLEEPING, I MEAN...
THAT KIND OF NARROWS IT DOWN
SCHULZ

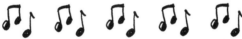

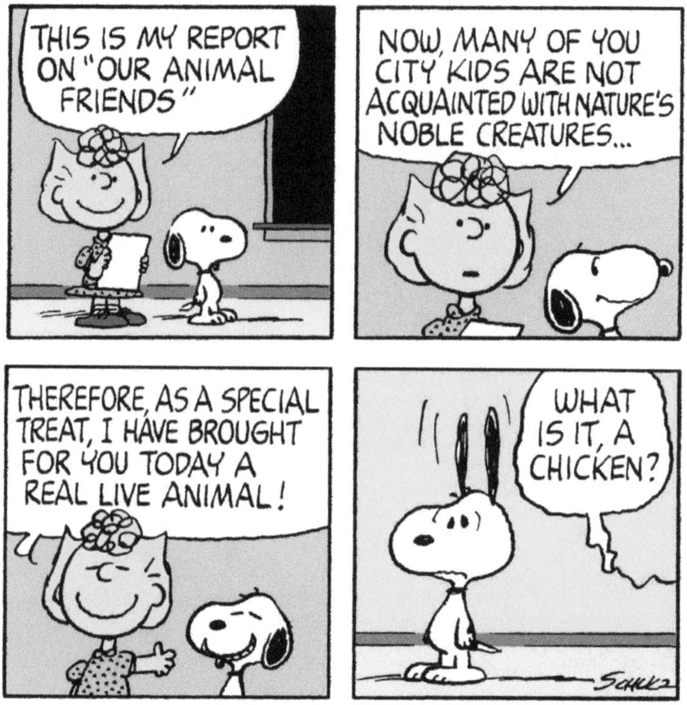
THIS IS MY REPORT ON "OUR ANIMAL FRIENDS"
NOW, MANY OF YOU CITY KIDS ARE NOT ACQUAINTED WITH NATURE'S NOBLE CREATURES...
THEREFORE, AS A SPECIAL TREAT, I HAVE BROUGHT FOR YOU TODAY A REAL LIVE ANIMAL!
WHAT IS IT, A CHICKEN?
SCHULZ

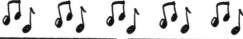

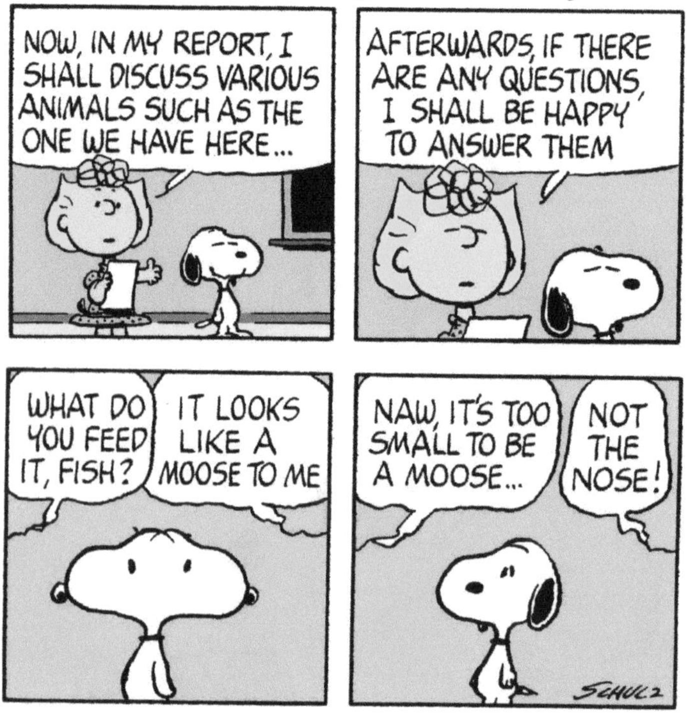
NOW, IN MY REPORT, I SHALL DISCUSS VARIOUS ANIMALS SUCH AS THE ONE WE HAVE HERE...
AFTERWARDS, IF THERE ARE ANY QUESTIONS, I SHALL BE HAPPY TO ANSWER THEM
WHAT DO YOU FEED IT, FISH?
IT LOOKS LIKE A MOOSE TO ME
NAW, IT'S TOO SMALL TO BE A MOOSE...
NOT THE NOSE!
SCHULZ

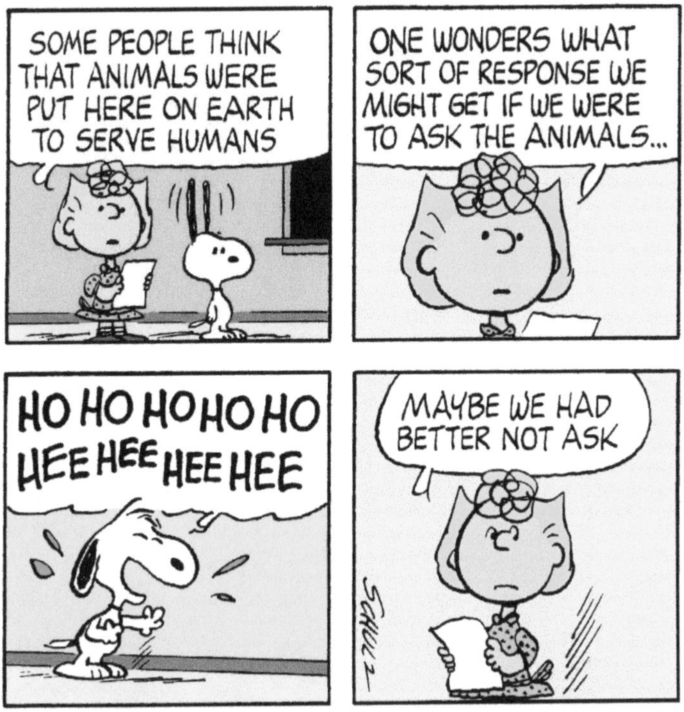
SOME PEOPLE THINK THAT ANIMALS WERE PUT HERE ON EARTH TO SERVE HUMANS
ONE WONDERS WHAT SORT OF RESPONSE WE MIGHT GET IF WE WERE TO ASK THE ANIMALS...
HO HO HO HO HO HEE HEE HEE HEE
MAYBE WE HAD BETTER NOT ASK
SCHULZ

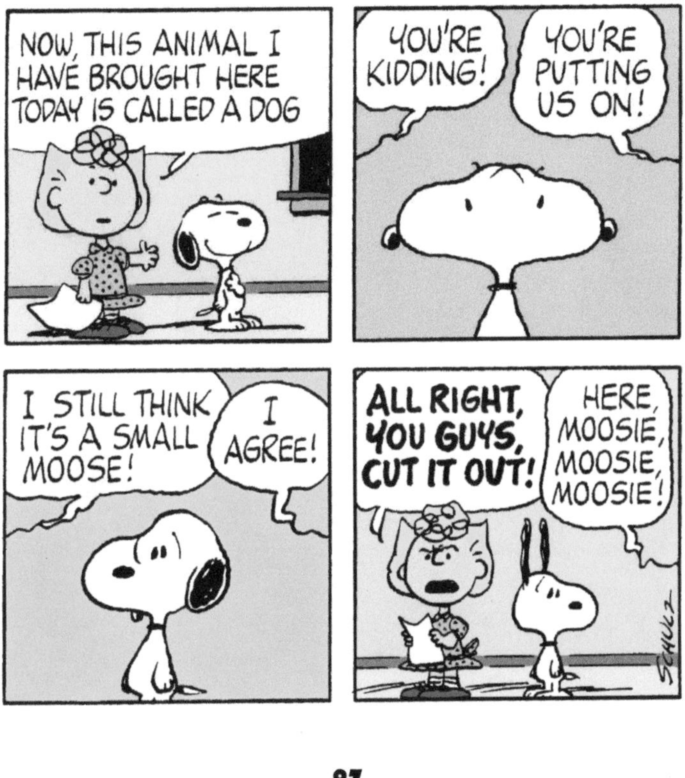
NOW, THIS ANIMAL I HAVE BROUGHT HERE TODAY IS CALLED A DOG
YOU'RE KIDDING!
YOU'RE PUTTING US ON!
I STILL THINK IT'S A SMALL MOOSE!
I AGREE!
ALL RIGHT, YOU GUYS, CUT IT OUT!
HERE, MOOSIE, MOOSIE, MOOSIE!
SCHULZ

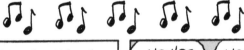

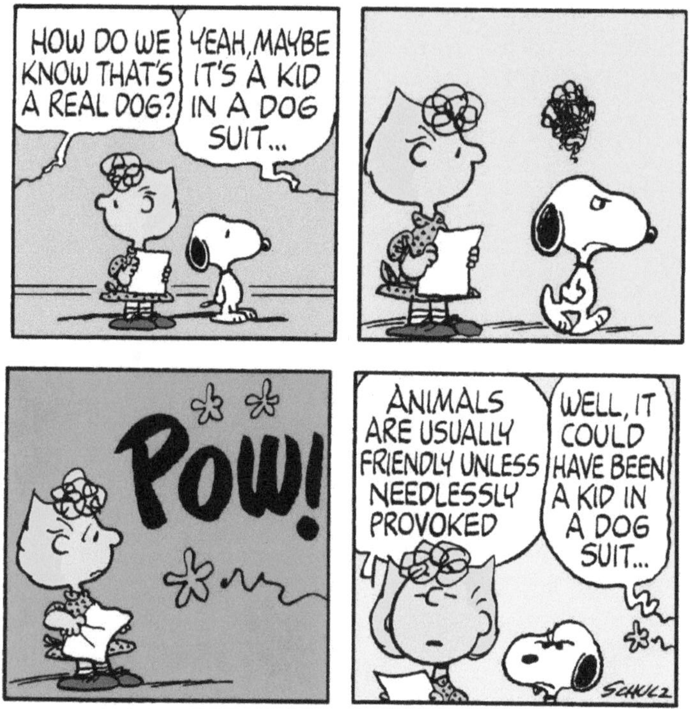
HOW DO WE KNOW THAT'S A REAL DOG?
YEAH, MAYBE IT'S A KID IN A DOG SUIT...
POW!
ANIMALS ARE USUALLY FRIENDLY UNLESS NEEDLESSLY PROVOKED
WELL, IT COULD HAVE BEEN A KID IN A DOG SUIT...
SCHULZ

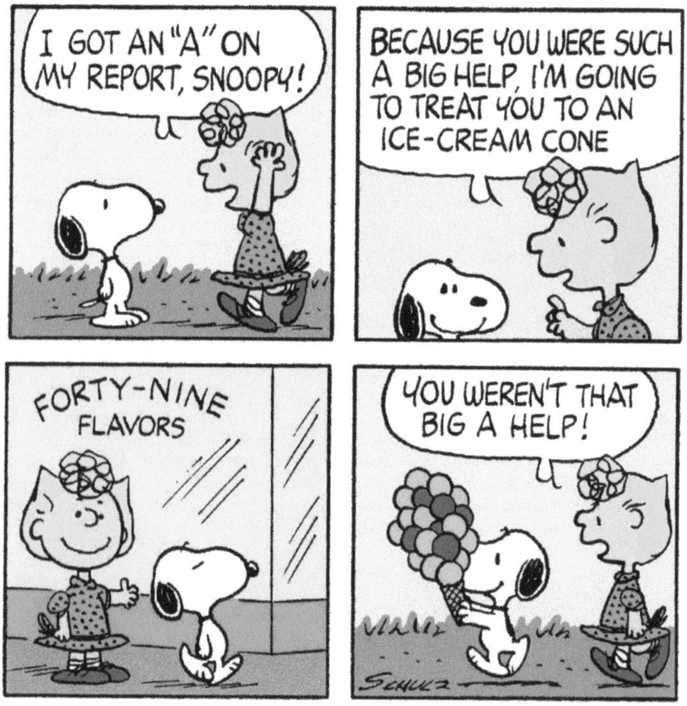
I GOT AN "A" ON MY REPORT, SNOOPY!
BECAUSE YOU WERE SUCH A BIG HELP, I'M GOING TO TREAT YOU TO AN ICE-CREAM CONE
FORTY-NINE FLAVORS
YOU WEREN'T THAT BIG A HELP!
SCHULZ

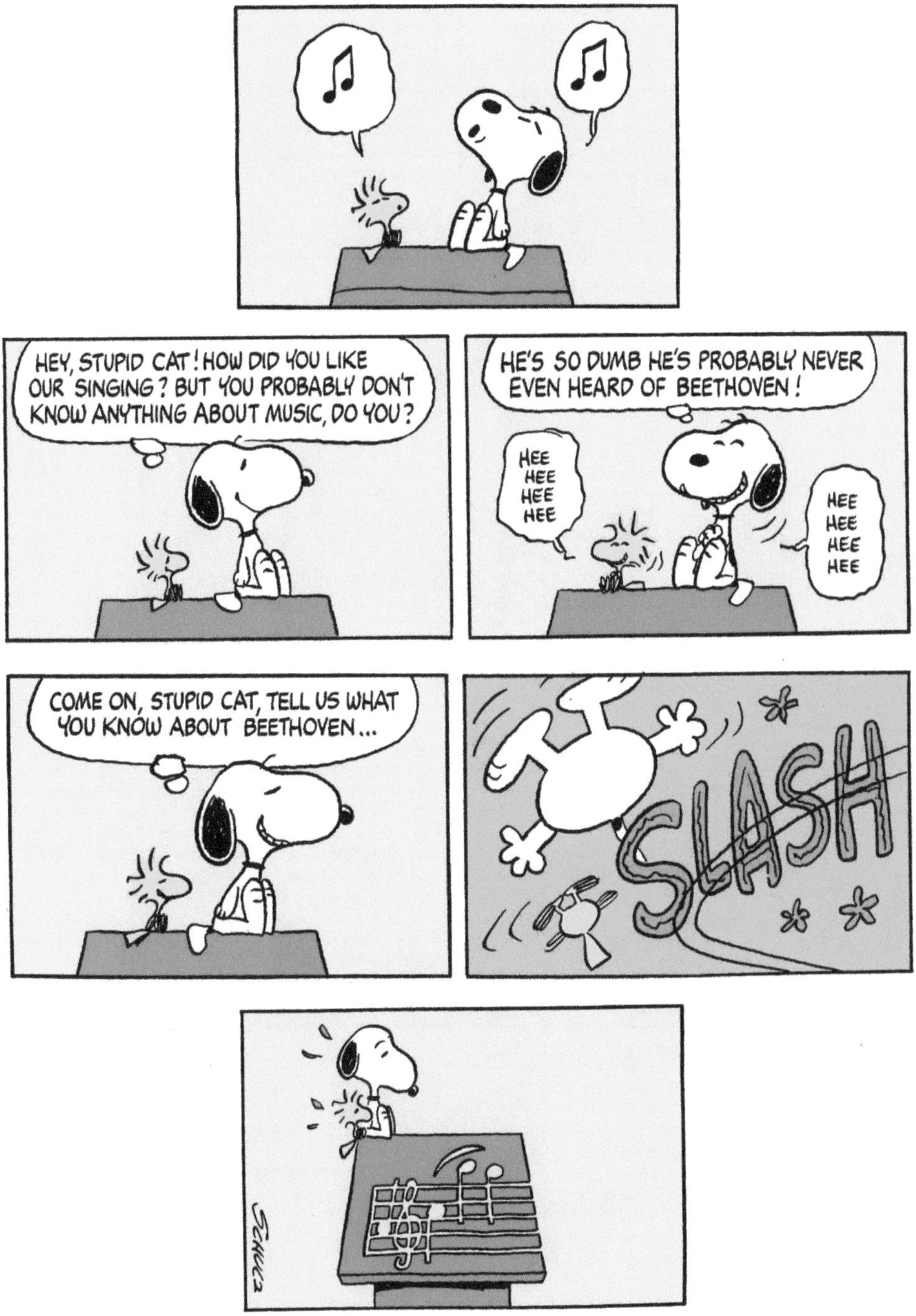
HEY, STUPID CAT! HOW DID YOU LIKE OUR SINGING? BUT YOU PROBABLY DON'T KNOW ANYTHING ABOUT MUSIC, DO YOU?
HE'S SO DUMB HE'S PROBABLY NEVER EVEN HEARD OF BEETHOVEN!
HEE HEE HEE HEE
HEE HEE HEE HEE
COME ON, STUPID CAT, TELL US WHAT YOU KNOW ABOUT BEETHOVEN...
SLASH
SCHULZ

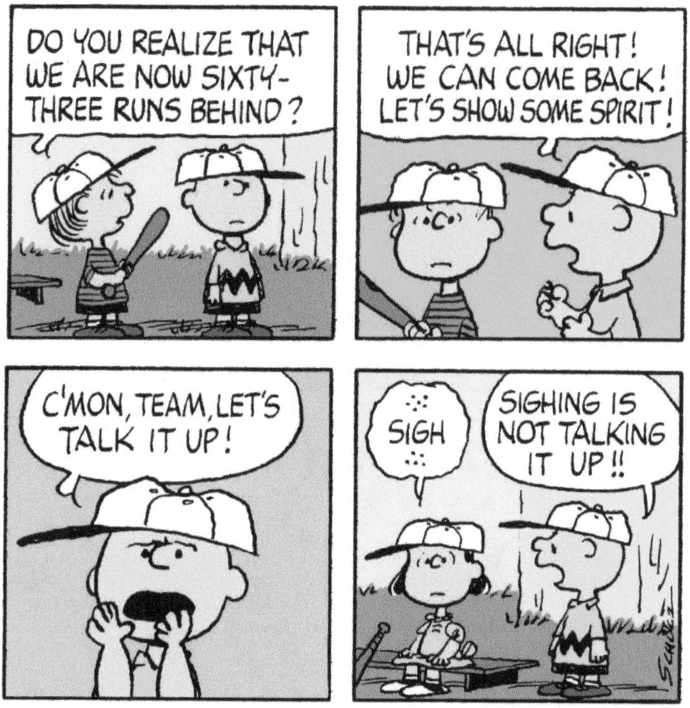
DO YOU REALIZE THAT WE ARE NOW SIXTY-THREE RUNS BEHIND?
THAT'S ALL RIGHT! WE CAN COME BACK! LET'S SHOW SOME SPIRIT!
C'MON, TEAM, LET'S TALK IT UP!
SIGH
SIGHING IS NOT TALKING IT UP!!
SCHULZ

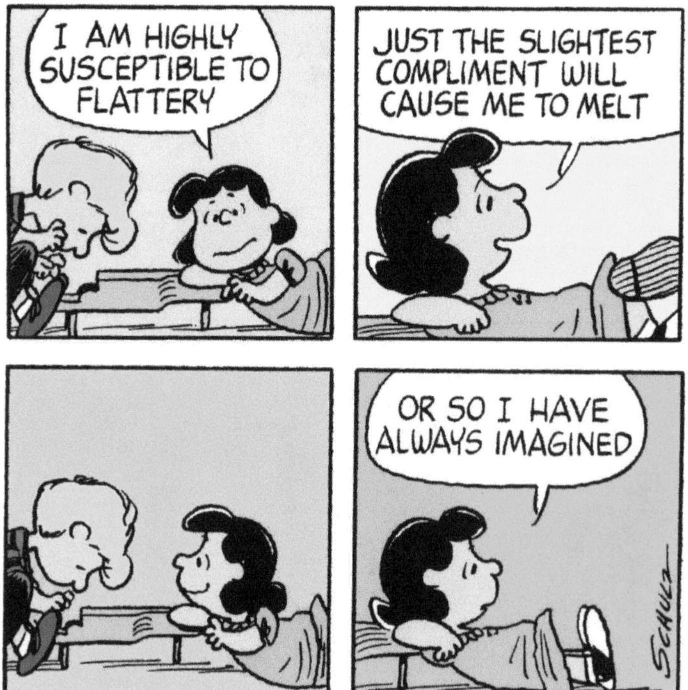
I AM HIGHLY SUSCEPTIBLE TO FLATTERY
JUST THE SLIGHTEST COMPLIMENT WILL CAUSE ME TO MELT
OR SO I HAVE ALWAYS IMAGINED
SCHULZ

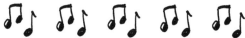

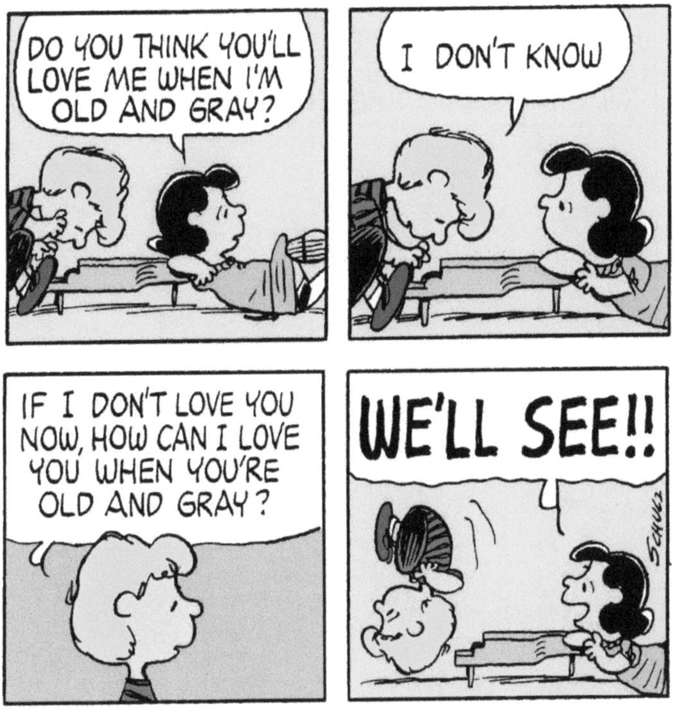
DO YOU THINK YOU'LL LOVE ME WHEN I'M OLD AND GRAY?
I DON'T KNOW
IF I DON'T LOVE YOU NOW, HOW CAN I LOVE YOU WHEN YOU'RE OLD AND GRAY?
WE'LL SEE!!
SCHULZ

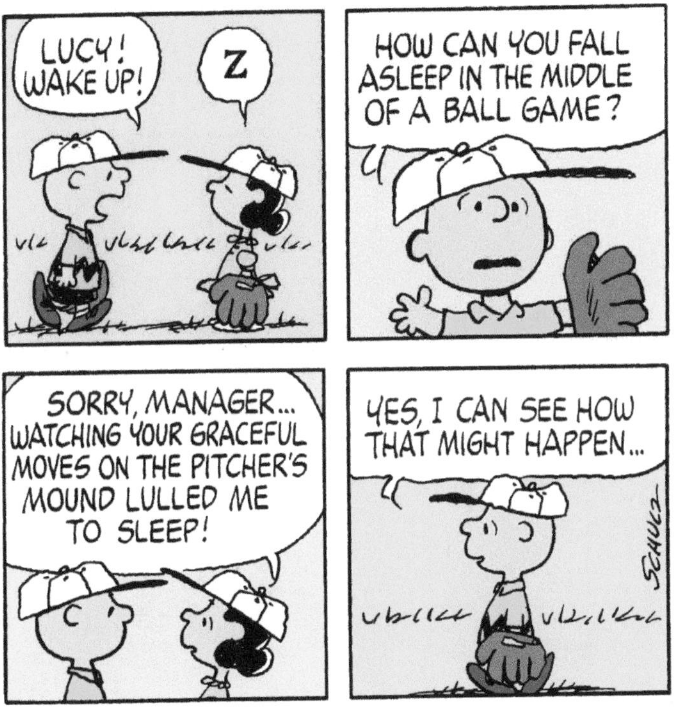
LUCY! WAKE UP!
Z
HOW CAN YOU FALL ASLEEP IN THE MIDDLE OF A BALL GAME?
SORRY, MANAGER... WATCHING YOUR GRACEFUL MOVES ON THE PITCHER'S MOUND LULLED ME TO SLEEP!
YES, I CAN SEE HOW THAT MIGHT HAPPEN...
SCHULZ

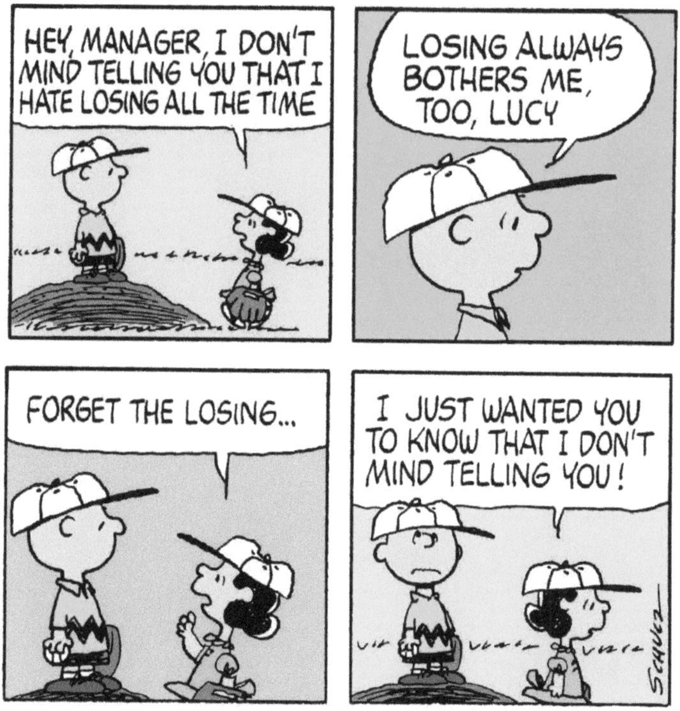
HEY, MANAGER, I DON'T MIND TELLING YOU THAT I HATE LOSING ALL THE TIME
LOSING ALWAYS BOTHERS ME, TOO, LUCY
FORGET THE LOSING...
I JUST WANTED YOU TO KNOW THAT I DON'T MIND TELLING YOU!
SCHULZ

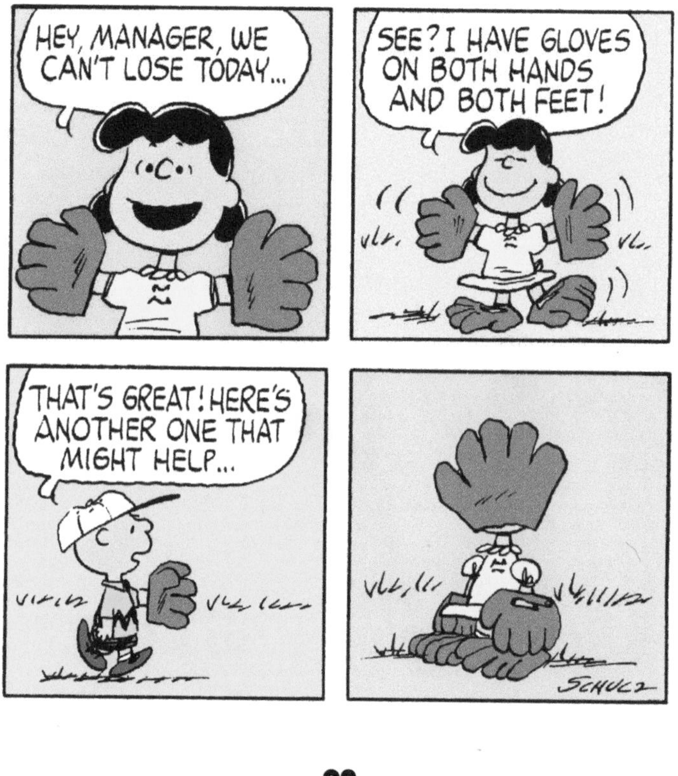
HEY, MANAGER, WE CAN'T LOSE TODAY...
SEE? I HAVE GLOVES ON BOTH HANDS AND BOTH FEET!
THAT'S GREAT! HERE'S ANOTHER ONE THAT MIGHT HELP...
SCHULZ

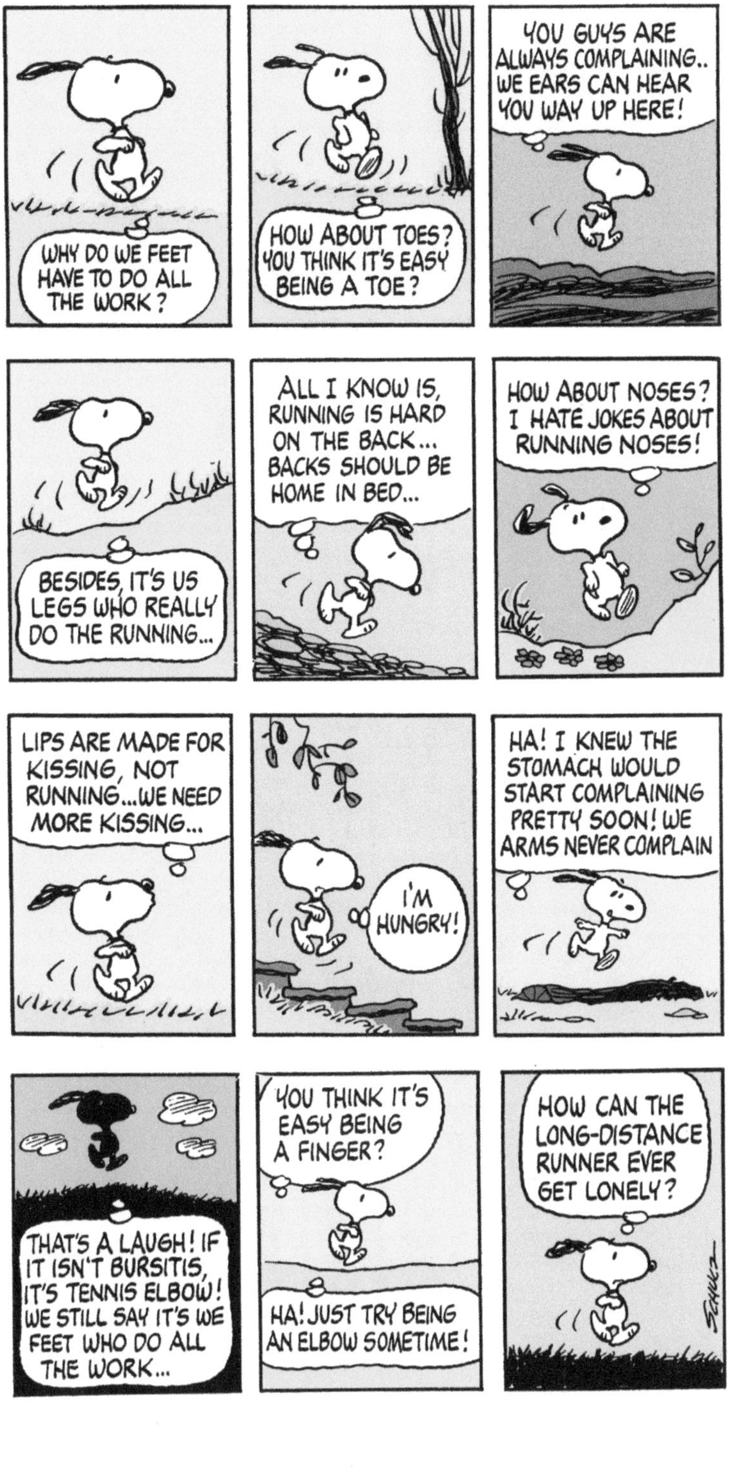
WHY DO WE FEET HAVE TO DO ALL THE WORK?
HOW ABOUT TOES? YOU THINK IT'S EASY BEING A TOE?
YOU GUYS ARE ALWAYS COMPLAINING.. WE EARS CAN HEAR YOU WAY UP HERE!
BESIDES, IT'S US LEGS WHO REALLY DO THE RUNNING...
ALL I KNOW IS, RUNNING IS HARD ON THE BACK... BACKS SHOULD BE HOME IN BED...
HOW ABOUT NOSES? I HATE JOKES ABOUT RUNNING NOSES!
LIPS ARE MADE FOR KISSING, NOT RUNNING...WE NEED MORE KISSING...
I'M HUNGRY!
HA! I KNEW THE STOMACH WOULD START COMPLAINING PRETTY SOON! WE ARMS NEVER COMPLAIN
THAT'S A LAUGH! IF IT ISN'T BURSITIS, IT'S TENNIS ELBOW! WE STILL SAY IT'S WE FEET WHO DO ALL THE WORK...
YOU THINK IT'S EASY BEING A FINGER?
HA! JUST TRY BEING AN ELBOW SOMETIME!
HOW CAN THE LONG-DISTANCE RUNNER EVER GET LONELY?
SCHULZ

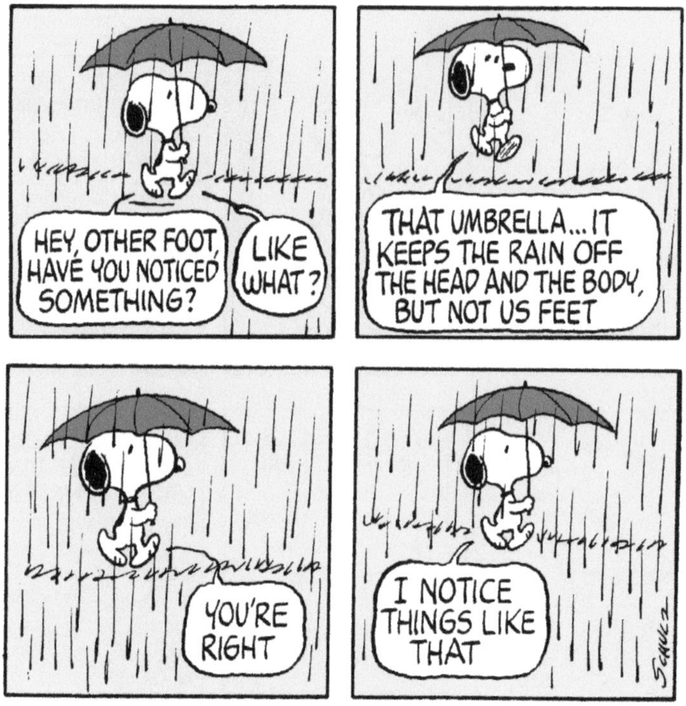
HEY, OTHER FOOT, HAVE YOU NOTICED SOMETHING?
LIKE WHAT?
THAT UMBRELLA... IT KEEPS THE RAIN OFF THE HEAD AND THE BODY, BUT NOT US FEET
YOU'RE RIGHT
I NOTICE THINGS LIKE THAT

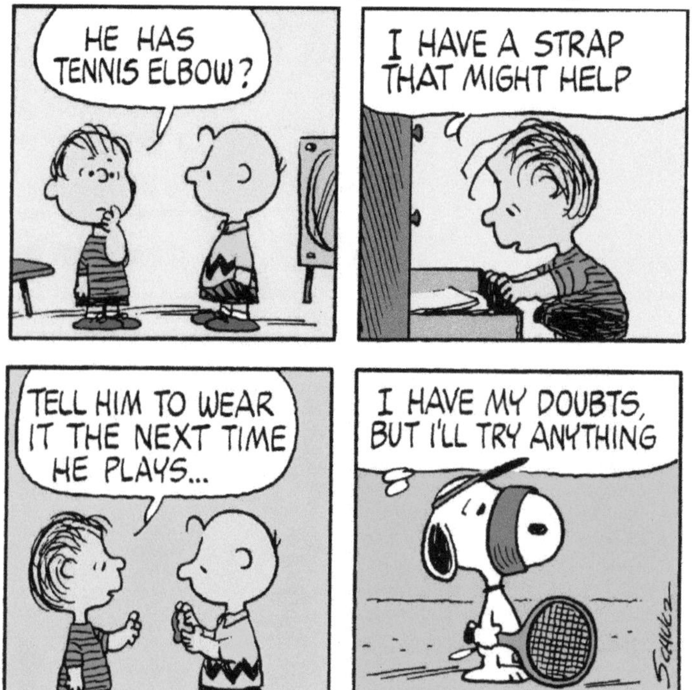
HE HAS TENNIS ELBOW?
I HAVE A STRAP THAT MIGHT HELP
TELL HIM TO WEAR IT THE NEXT TIME HE PLAYS...
I HAVE MY DOUBTS, BUT I'LL TRY ANYTHING

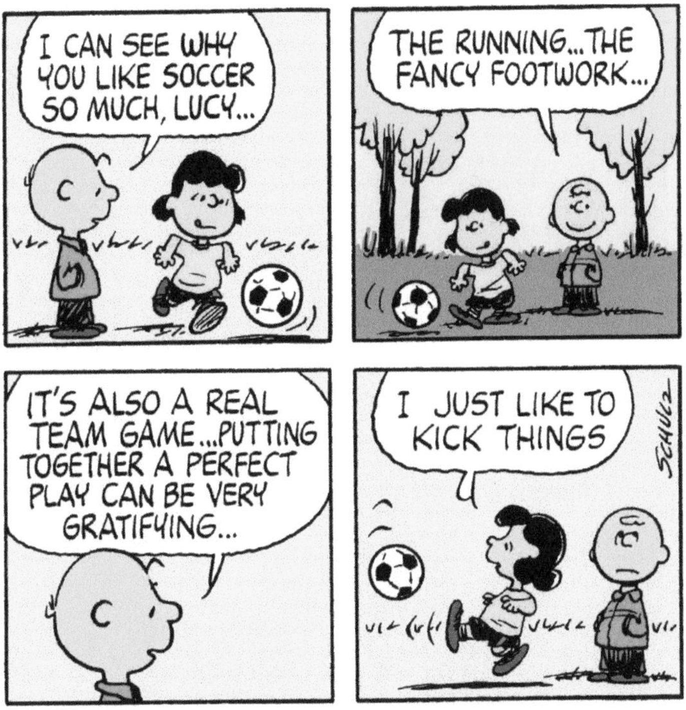
I CAN SEE WHY YOU LIKE SOCCER SO MUCH, LUCY...
THE RUNNING...THE FANCY FOOTWORK...
IT'S ALSO A REAL TEAM GAME...PUTTING TOGETHER A PERFECT PLAY CAN BE VERY GRATIFYING...
I JUST LIKE TO KICK THINGS
SCHULZ

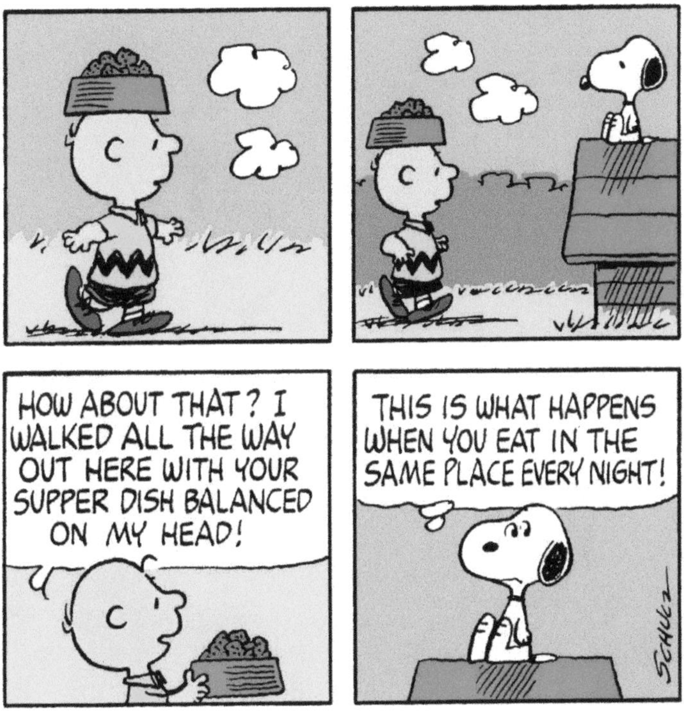
HOW ABOUT THAT? I WALKED ALL THE WAY OUT HERE WITH YOUR SUPPER DISH BALANCED ON MY HEAD!
THIS IS WHAT HAPPENS WHEN YOU EAT IN THE SAME PLACE EVERY NIGHT!
SCHULZ

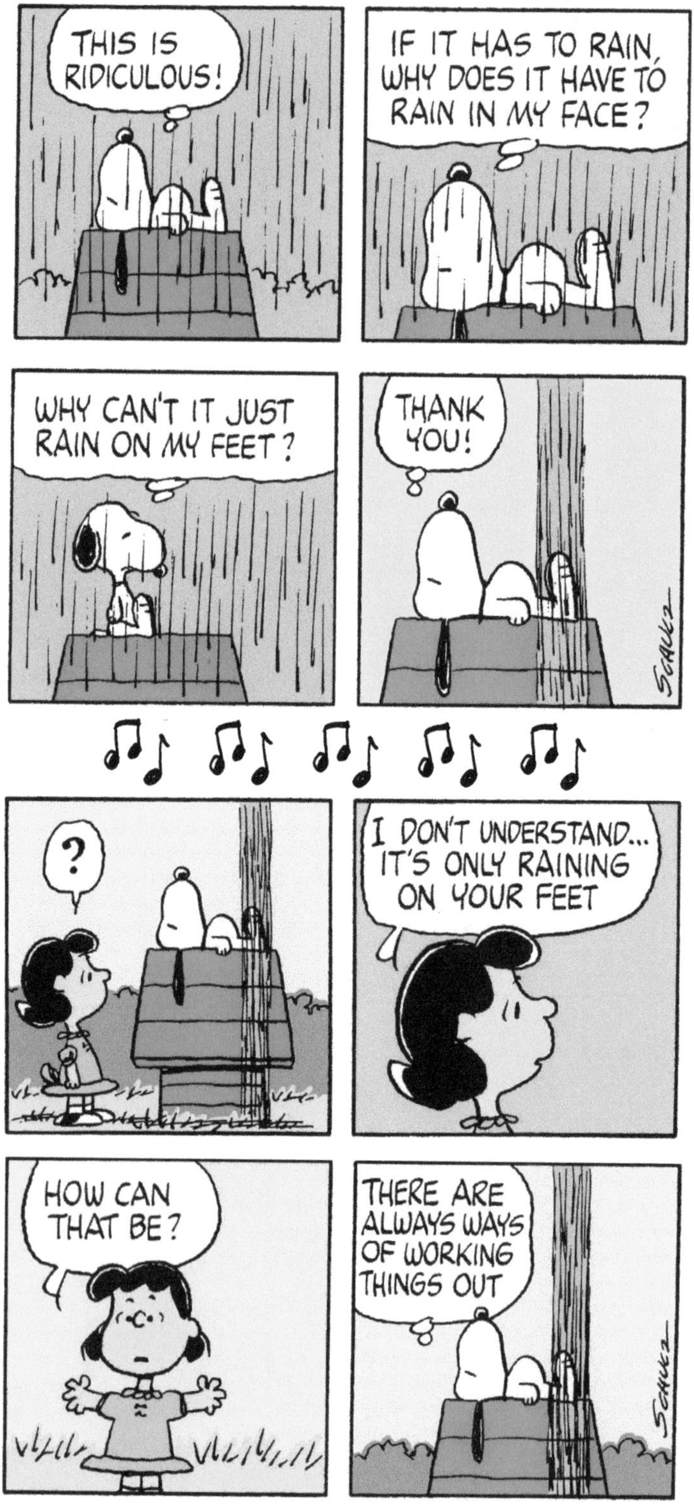
THIS IS RIDICULOUS!
IF IT HAS TO RAIN, WHY DOES IT HAVE TO RAIN IN MY FACE?
WHY CAN'T IT JUST RAIN ON MY FEET?
THANK YOU!
?
I DON'T UNDERSTAND... IT'S ONLY RAINING ON YOUR FEET
HOW CAN THAT BE?
THERE ARE ALWAYS WAYS OF WORKING THINGS OUT

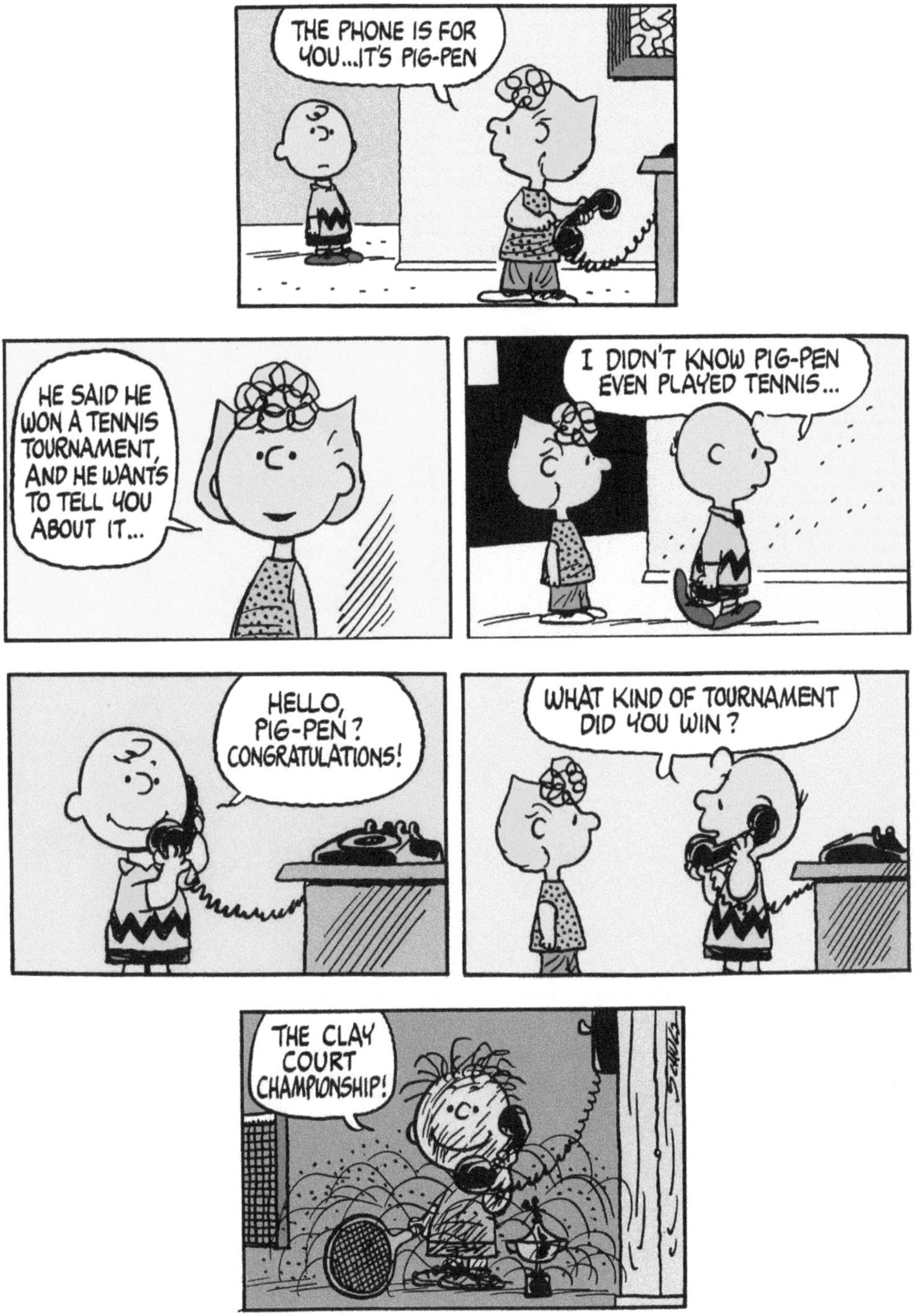
THE PHONE IS FOR YOU...IT'S PIG-PEN
HE SAID HE WON A TENNIS TOURNAMENT, AND HE WANTS TO TELL YOU ABOUT IT...
I DIDN'T KNOW PIG-PEN EVEN PLAYED TENNIS...
HELLO, PIG-PEN? CONGRATULATIONS!
WHAT KIND OF TOURNAMENT DID YOU WIN?
THE CLAY COURT CHAMPIONSHIP!
SCHULZ

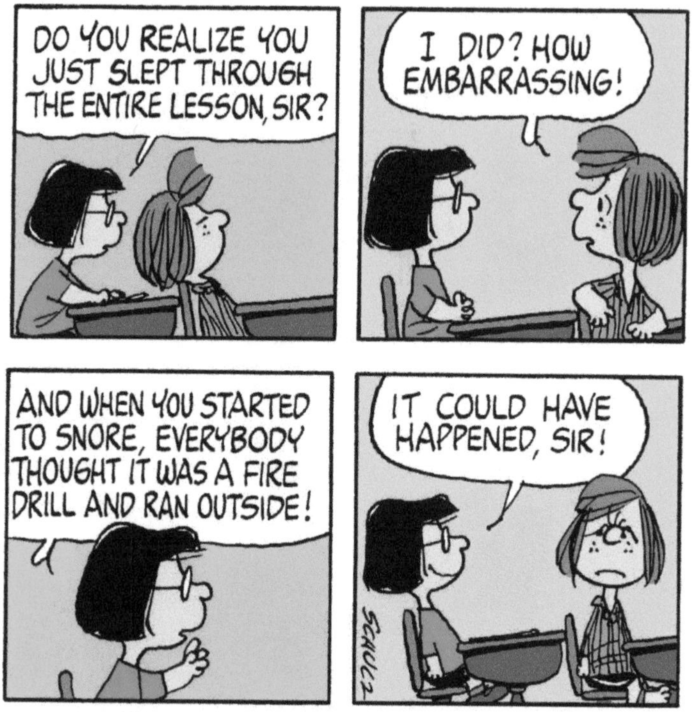
DO YOU REALIZE YOU JUST SLEPT THROUGH THE ENTIRE LESSON, SIR?
I DID? HOW EMBARRASSING!
AND WHEN YOU STARTED TO SNORE, EVERYBODY THOUGHT IT WAS A FIRE DRILL AND RAN OUTSIDE!
IT COULD HAVE HAPPENED, SIR!
SCHULZ

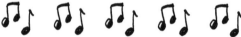

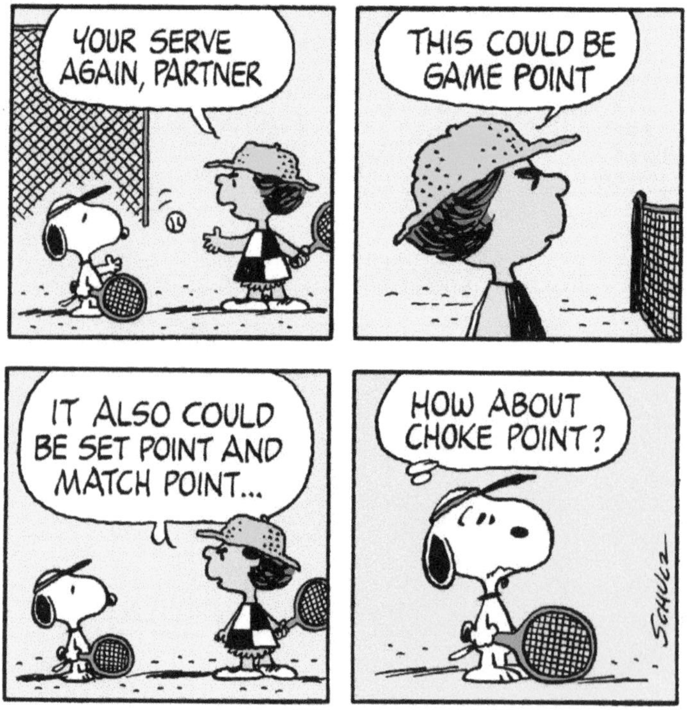
YOUR SERVE AGAIN, PARTNER
THIS COULD BE GAME POINT
IT ALSO COULD BE SET POINT AND MATCH POINT...
HOW ABOUT CHOKE POINT?
SCHULZ

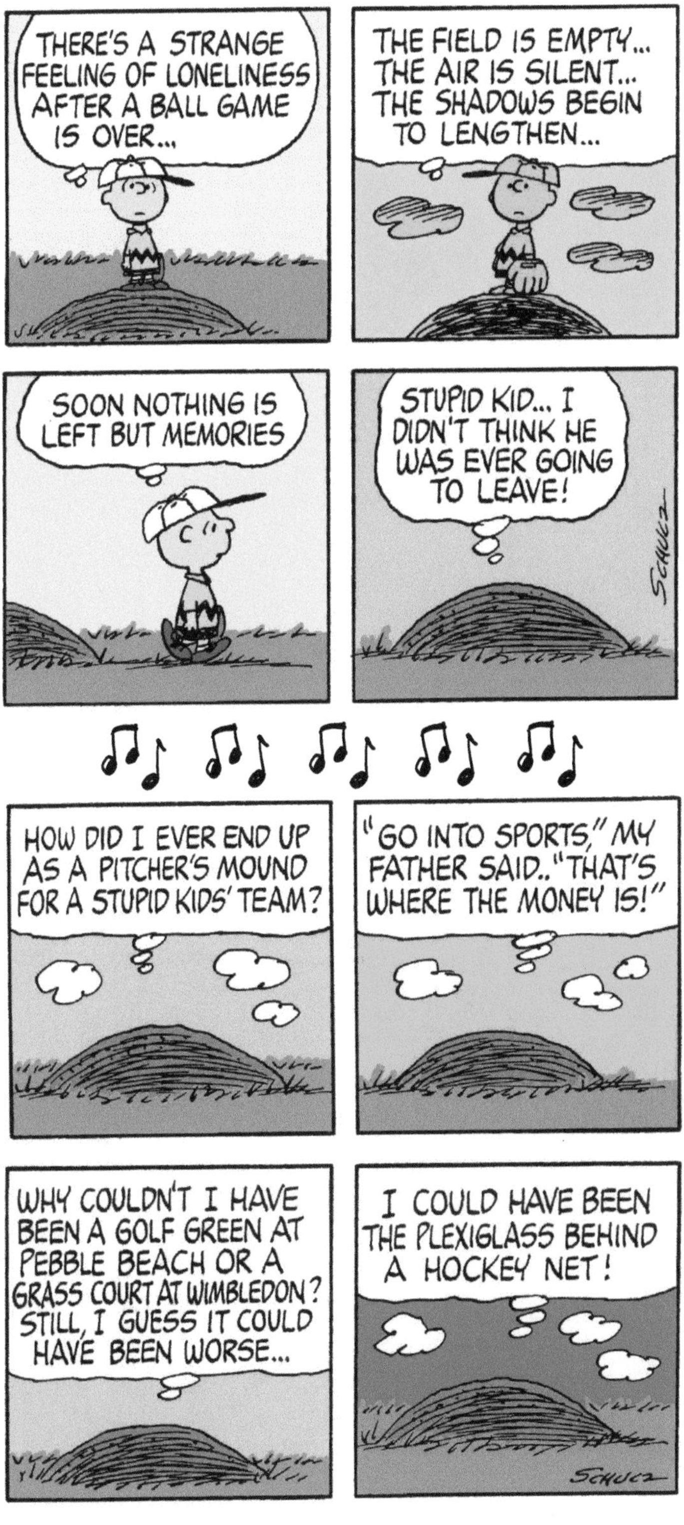
THERE'S A STRANGE FEELING OF LONELINESS AFTER A BALL GAME IS OVER...
THE FIELD IS EMPTY... THE AIR IS SILENT... THE SHADOWS BEGIN TO LENGTHEN...
SOON NOTHING IS LEFT BUT MEMORIES
STUPID KID... I DIDN'T THINK HE WAS EVER GOING TO LEAVE!
SCHULZ
HOW DID I EVER END UP AS A PITCHER'S MOUND FOR A STUPID KIDS' TEAM?
"GO INTO SPORTS," MY FATHER SAID.. "THAT'S WHERE THE MONEY IS!"
WHY COULDN'T I HAVE BEEN A GOLF GREEN AT PEBBLE BEACH OR A GRASS COURT AT WIMBLEDON? STILL, I GUESS IT COULD HAVE BEEN WORSE...
I COULD HAVE BEEN THE PLEXIGLASS BEHIND A HOCKEY NET!
SCHULZ

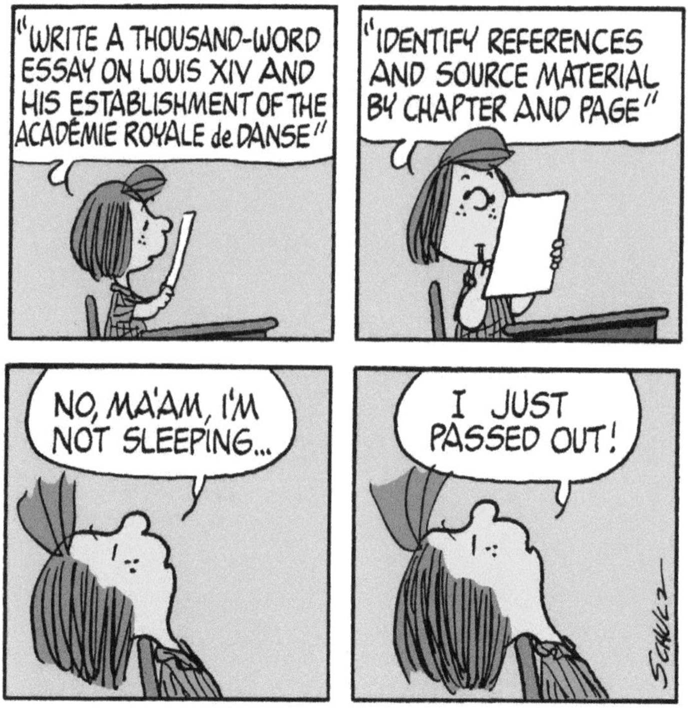
"WRITE A THOUSAND-WORD ESSAY ON LOUIS XIV AND HIS ESTABLISHMENT OF THE ACADÉMIE ROYALE de DANSE"
"IDENTIFY REFERENCES AND SOURCE MATERIAL BY CHAPTER AND PAGE"
NO, MA'AM, I'M NOT SLEEPING...
I JUST PASSED OUT!
SCHULZ

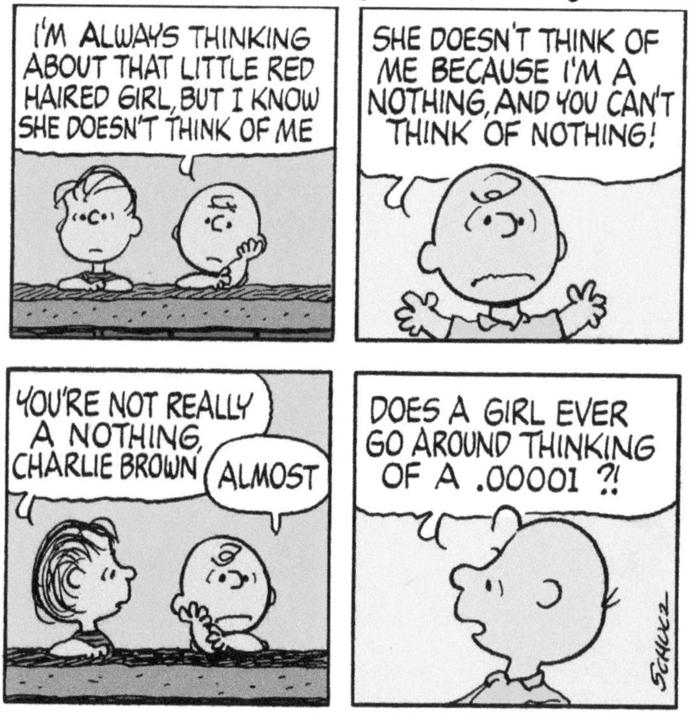
I'M ALWAYS THINKING ABOUT THAT LITTLE RED HAIRED GIRL, BUT I KNOW SHE DOESN'T THINK OF ME
SHE DOESN'T THINK OF ME BECAUSE I'M A NOTHING, AND YOU CAN'T THINK OF NOTHING!
YOU'RE NOT REALLY A NOTHING, CHARLIE BROWN
ALMOST
DOES A GIRL EVER GO AROUND THINKING OF A .00001 ?!
SCHULZ

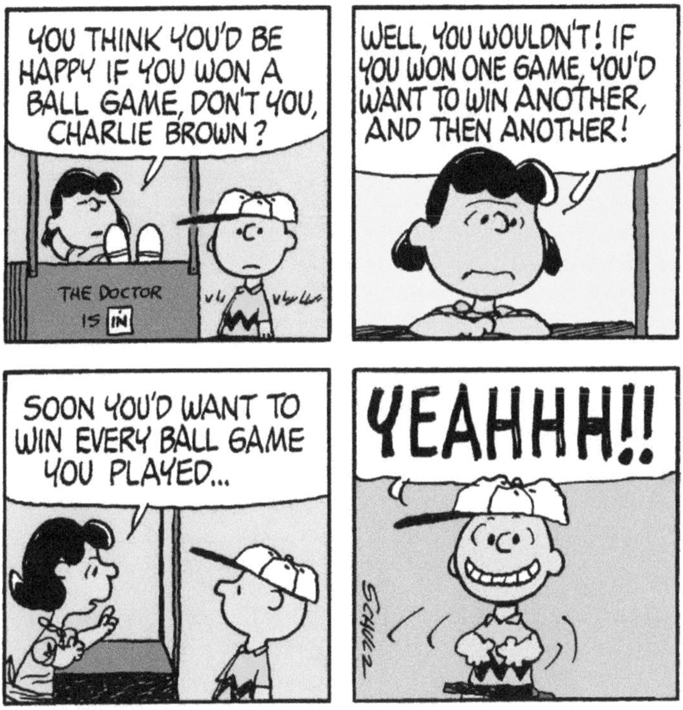
YOU THINK YOU'D BE HAPPY IF YOU WON A BALL GAME, DON'T YOU, CHARLIE BROWN?
THE DOCTOR IS IN
WELL, YOU WOULDN'T! IF YOU WON ONE GAME, YOU'D WANT TO WIN ANOTHER, AND THEN ANOTHER!
SOON YOU'D WANT TO WIN EVERY BALL GAME YOU PLAYED...
YEAHHH!!
SCHULZ

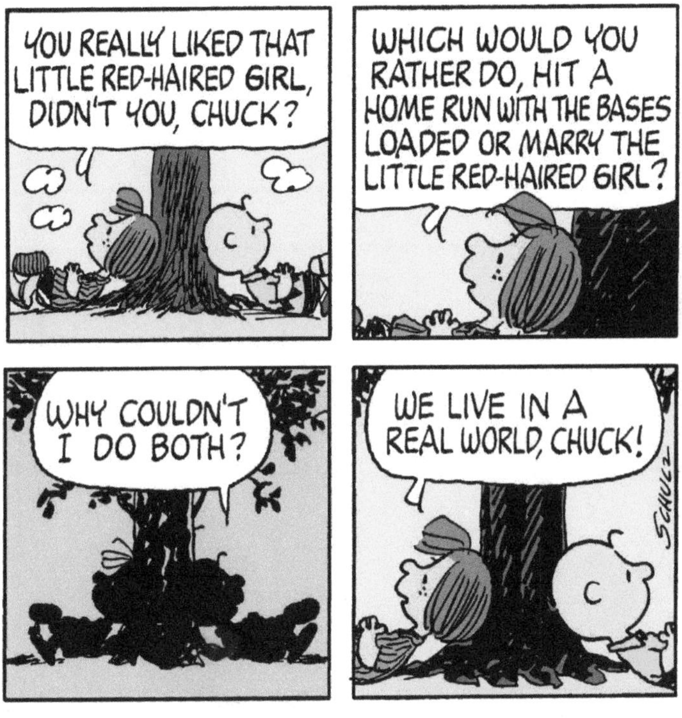
YOU REALLY LIKED THAT LITTLE RED-HAIRED GIRL, DIDN'T YOU, CHUCK?
WHICH WOULD YOU RATHER DO, HIT A HOME RUN WITH THE BASES LOADED OR MARRY THE LITTLE RED-HAIRED GIRL?
WHY COULDN'T I DO BOTH?
WE LIVE IN A REAL WORLD, CHUCK!
SCHULZ

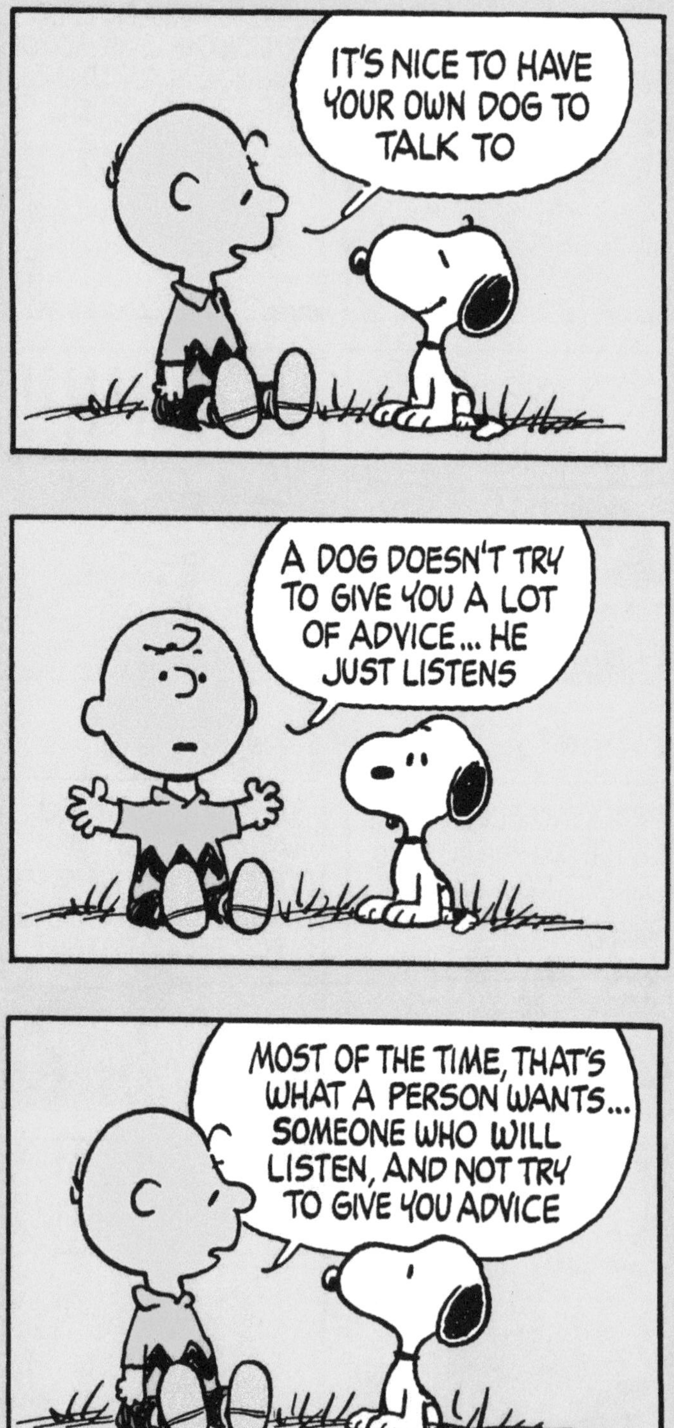
IT'S NICE TO HAVE YOUR OWN DOG TO TALK TO
A DOG DOESN'T TRY TO GIVE YOU A LOT OF ADVICE... HE JUST LISTENS
MOST OF THE TIME, THAT'S WHAT A PERSON WANTS... SOMEONE WHO WILL LISTEN, AND NOT TRY TO GIVE YOU ADVICE

MOST OF THE TIME, YOU JUST WANT TO TALK... WHICH IS WHY A DOG IS THE PERFECT ONE TO..
YAWN
ON THE OTHER HAND... SIGH
SCHULZ

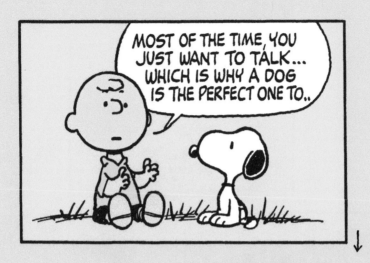

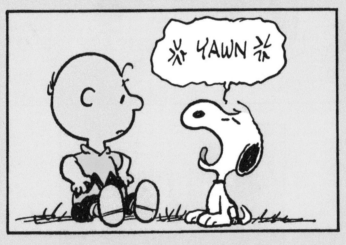

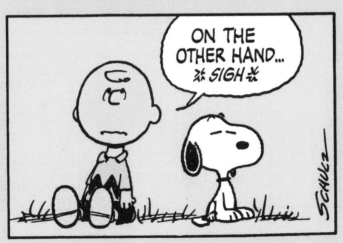

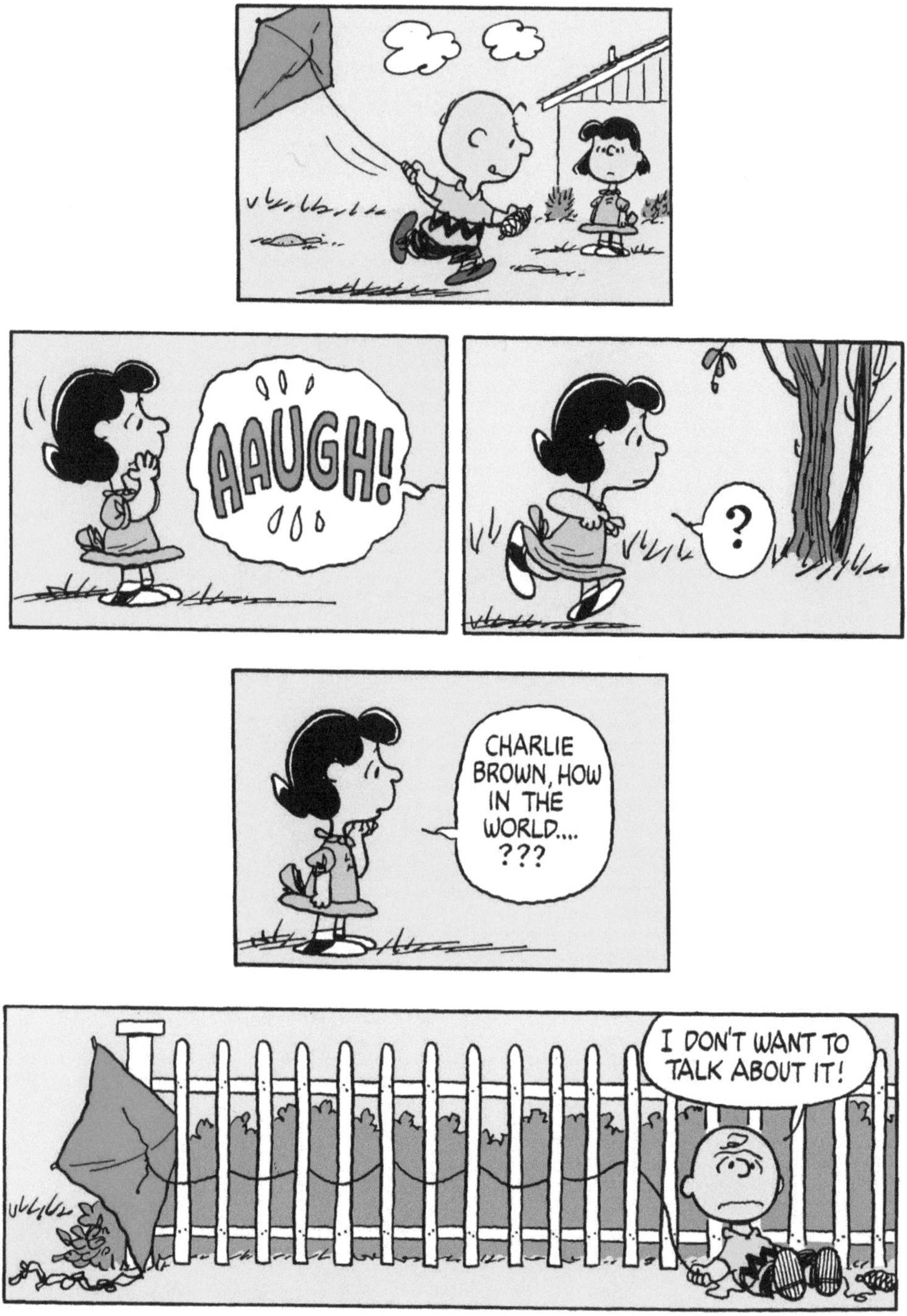
AAUGH!
?
CHARLIE BROWN, HOW IN THE WORLD.... ???
I DON'T WANT TO TALK ABOUT IT!

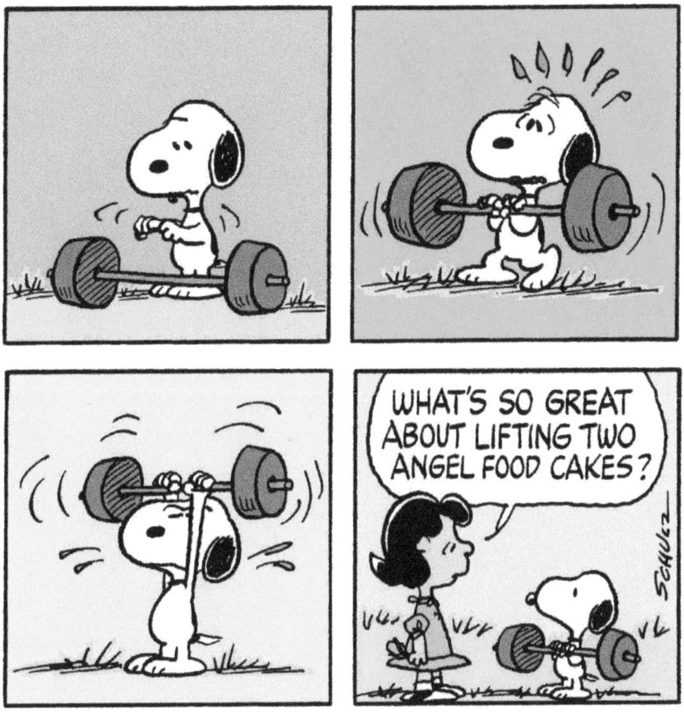
WHAT'S SO GREAT ABOUT LIFTING TWO ANGEL FOOD CAKES?
SCHULZ

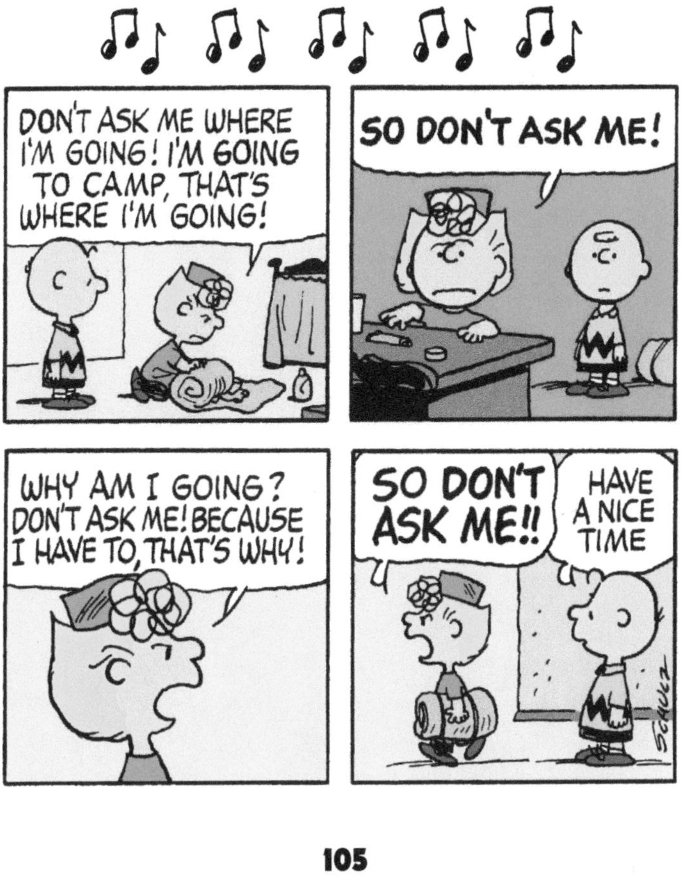
DON'T ASK ME WHERE I'M GOING! I'M GOING TO CAMP, THAT'S WHERE I'M GOING!
SO DON'T ASK ME!
WHY AM I GOING? DON'T ASK ME! BECAUSE I HAVE TO, THAT'S WHY!
SO DON'T ASK ME!!
HAVE A NICE TIME
SCHULZ

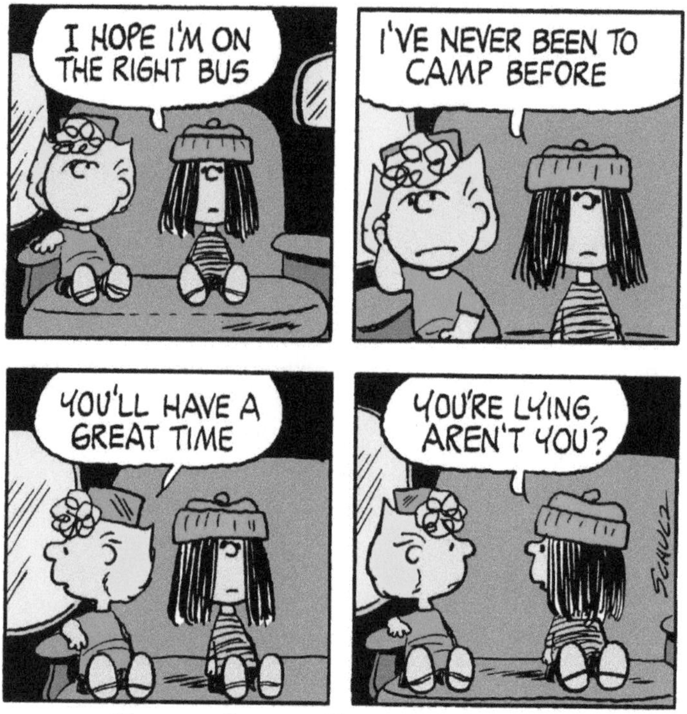
I HOPE I'M ON THE RIGHT BUS
I'VE NEVER BEEN TO CAMP BEFORE
YOU'LL HAVE A GREAT TIME
YOU'RE LYING, AREN'T YOU?
SCHULZ

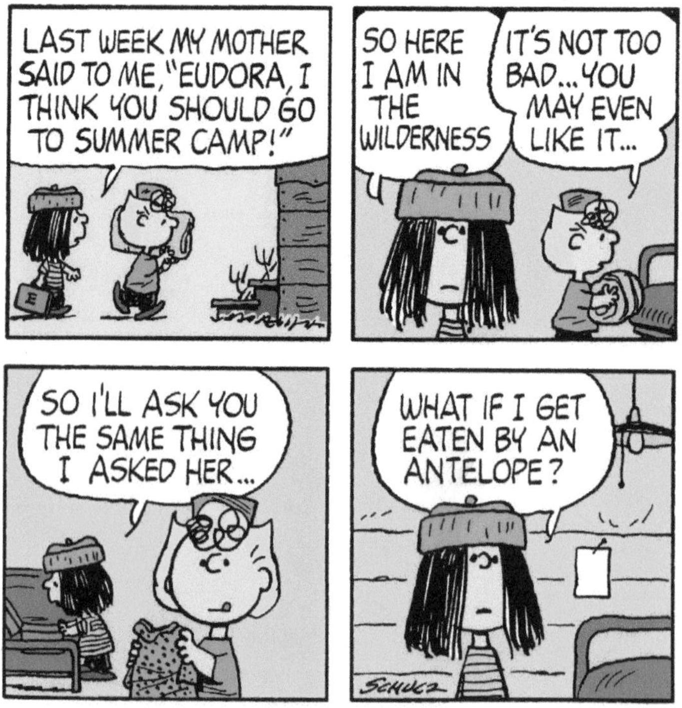
LAST WEEK MY MOTHER SAID TO ME, "EUDORA, I THINK YOU SHOULD GO TO SUMMER CAMP!"
SO HERE I AM IN THE WILDERNESS
IT'S NOT TOO BAD...YOU MAY EVEN LIKE IT...
SO I'LL ASK YOU THE SAME THING I ASKED HER...
WHAT IF I GET EATEN BY AN ANTELOPE?
SCHULZ

HEY, EUDORA, WE HAVE TO GO TO THE MAIN HALL FOR ORIENTATION!
IF THEY TRY TO SHIP US TO THE ORIENT, FORGET IT!
HOW DO YOU FEEL ABOUT WASHING DISHES AND SETTING TABLES?
I'D RATHER GO TO THE ORIENT!
SCHULZ

I DIDN'T UNDERSTAND WHAT THEY SAID IN THAT MEETING
THEY SAID THAT OUR GROUP IS GOING TO CAMP OUT TONIGHT
YOU MEAN SLEEP OUTSIDE?
THAT'S RIGHT
ON PURPOSE?
SCHULZ

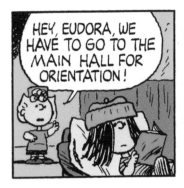

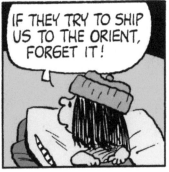

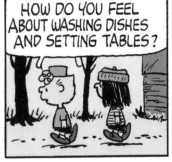

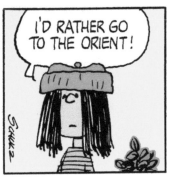

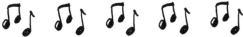

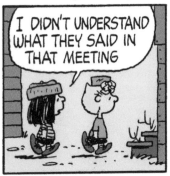

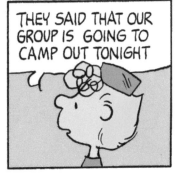

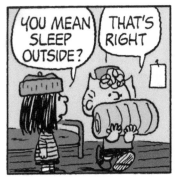

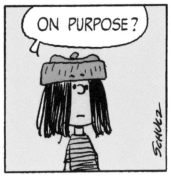

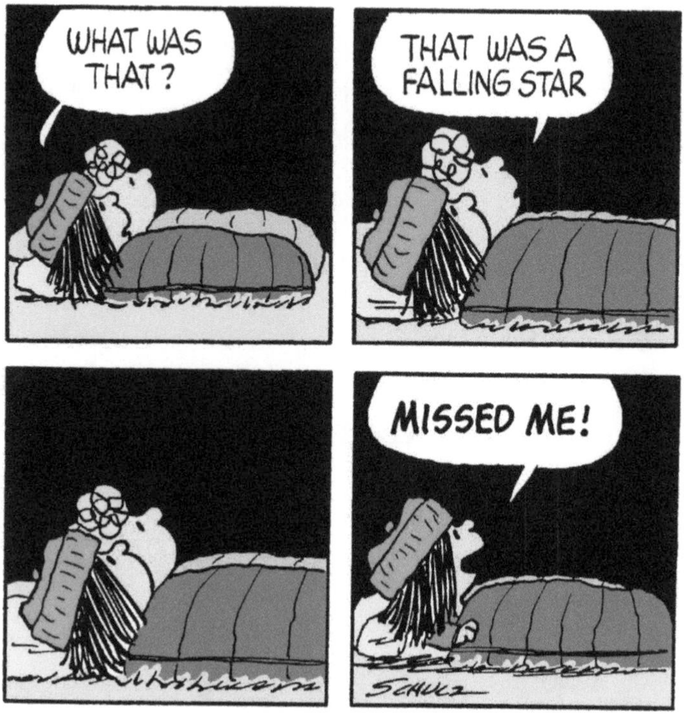
WHAT WAS THAT?
THAT WAS A FALLING STAR
MISSED ME!
SCHULZ

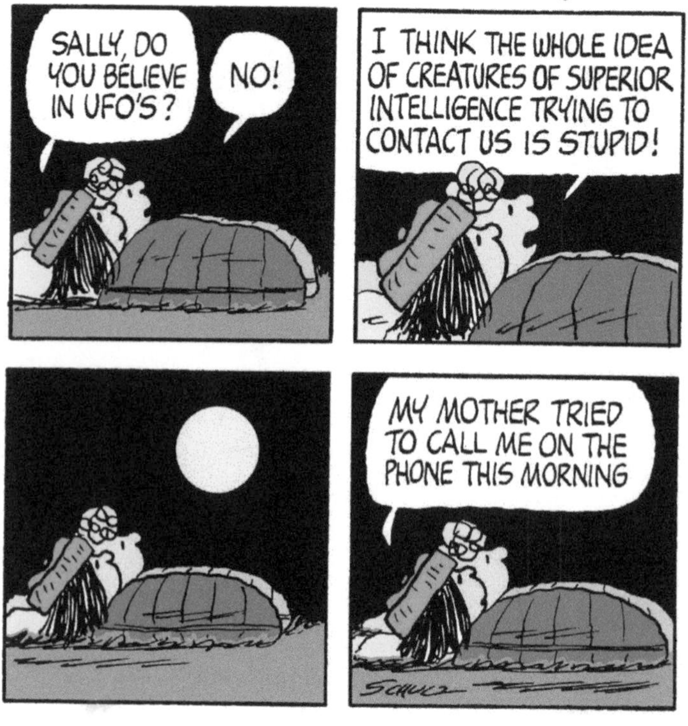
SALLY, DO YOU BELIEVE IN UFO'S?
NO!
I THINK THE WHOLE IDEA OF CREATURES OF SUPERIOR INTELLIGENCE TRYING TO CONTACT US IS STUPID!
MY MOTHER TRIED TO CALL ME ON THE PHONE THIS MORNING
SCHULZ

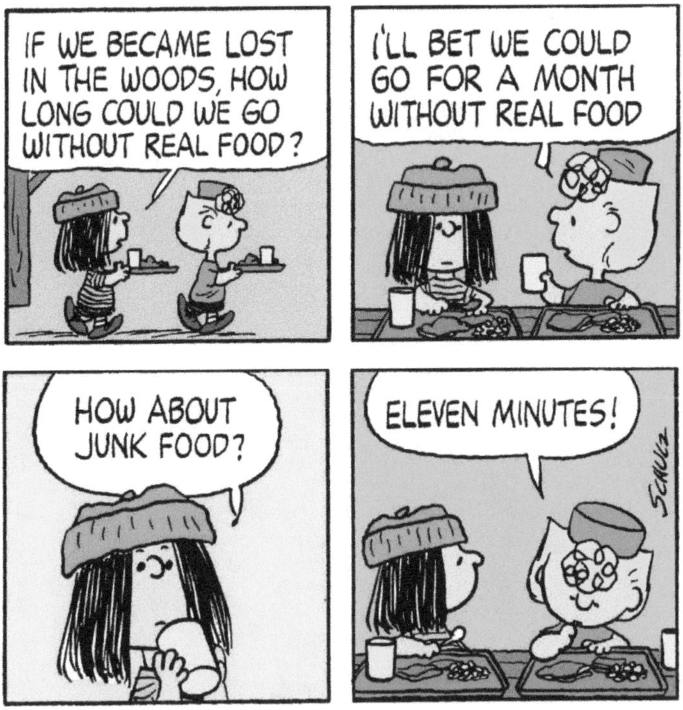
IF WE BECAME LOST IN THE WOODS, HOW LONG COULD WE GO WITHOUT REAL FOOD?
I'LL BET WE COULD GO FOR A MONTH WITHOUT REAL FOOD
HOW ABOUT JUNK FOOD?
ELEVEN MINUTES!
SCHULZ

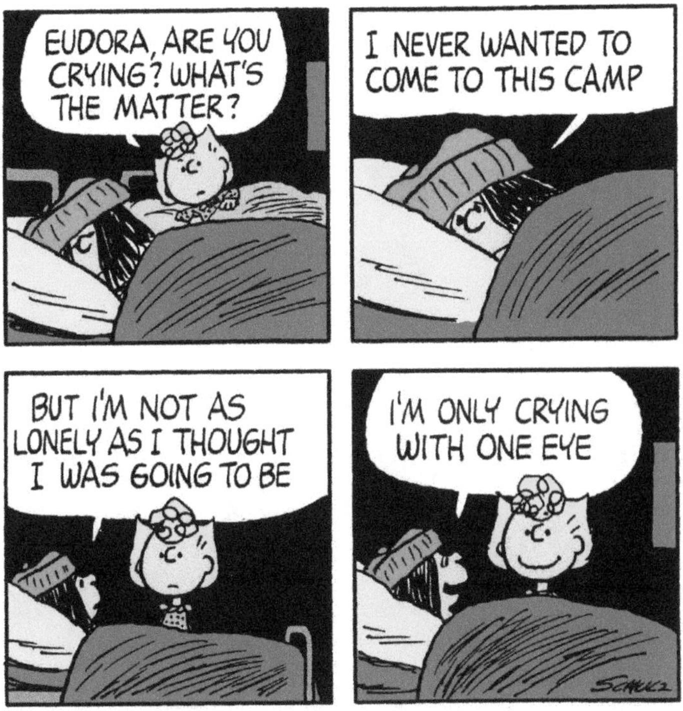
EUDORA, ARE YOU CRYING? WHAT'S THE MATTER?
I NEVER WANTED TO COME TO THIS CAMP
BUT I'M NOT AS LONELY AS I THOUGHT I WAS GOING TO BE
I'M ONLY CRYING WITH ONE EYE
SCHULZ

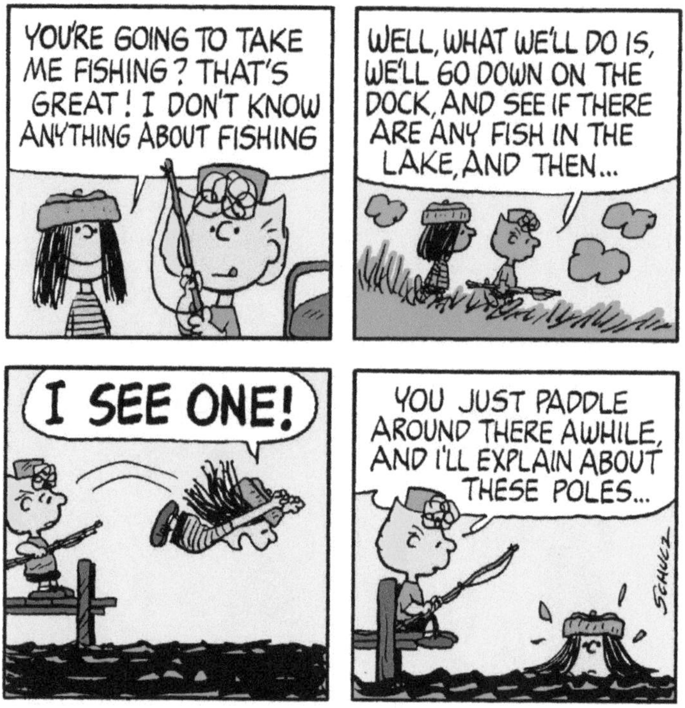
YOU'RE GOING TO TAKE ME FISHING? THAT'S GREAT! I DON'T KNOW ANYTHING ABOUT FISHING
WELL, WHAT WE'LL DO IS, WE'LL GO DOWN ON THE DOCK, AND SEE IF THERE ARE ANY FISH IN THE LAKE, AND THEN...
I SEE ONE!
YOU JUST PADDLE AROUND THERE AWHILE, AND I'LL EXPLAIN ABOUT THESE POLES...
SCHULZ

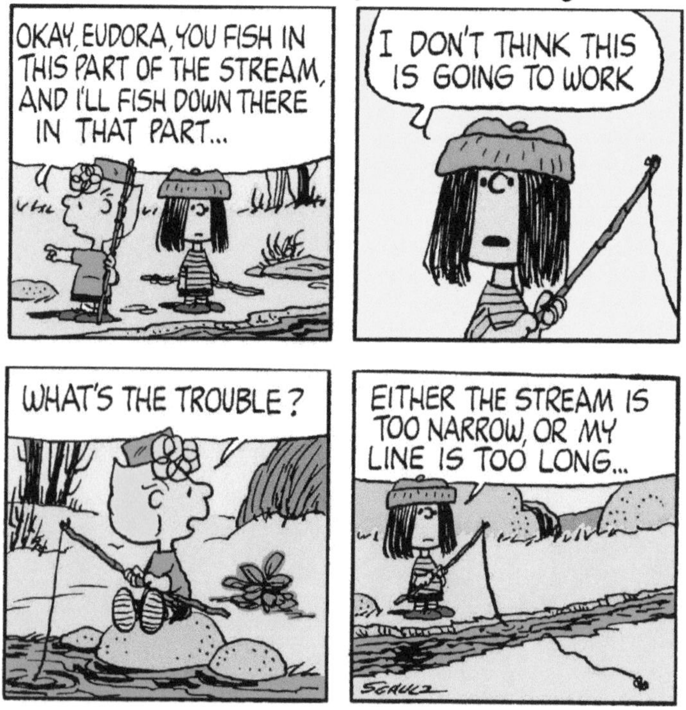
OKAY, EUDORA, YOU FISH IN THIS PART OF THE STREAM, AND I'LL FISH DOWN THERE IN THAT PART...
I DON'T THINK THIS IS GOING TO WORK
WHAT'S THE TROUBLE?
EITHER THE STREAM IS TOO NARROW, OR MY LINE IS TOO LONG...
SCHULZ

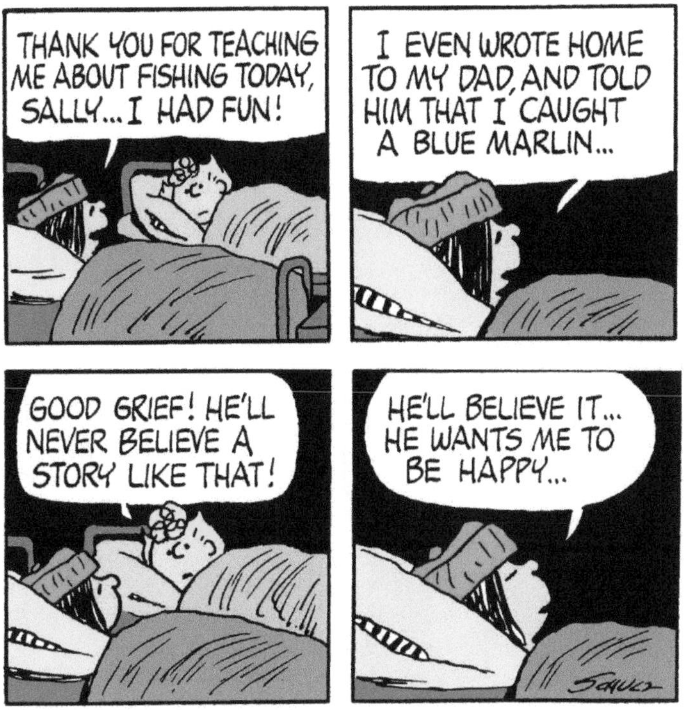
THANK YOU FOR TEACHING ME ABOUT FISHING TODAY, SALLY... I HAD FUN!
I EVEN WROTE HOME TO MY DAD, AND TOLD HIM THAT I CAUGHT A BLUE MARLIN...
GOOD GRIEF! HE'LL NEVER BELIEVE A STORY LIKE THAT!
HE'LL BELIEVE IT... HE WANTS ME TO BE HAPPY...
SCHULZ

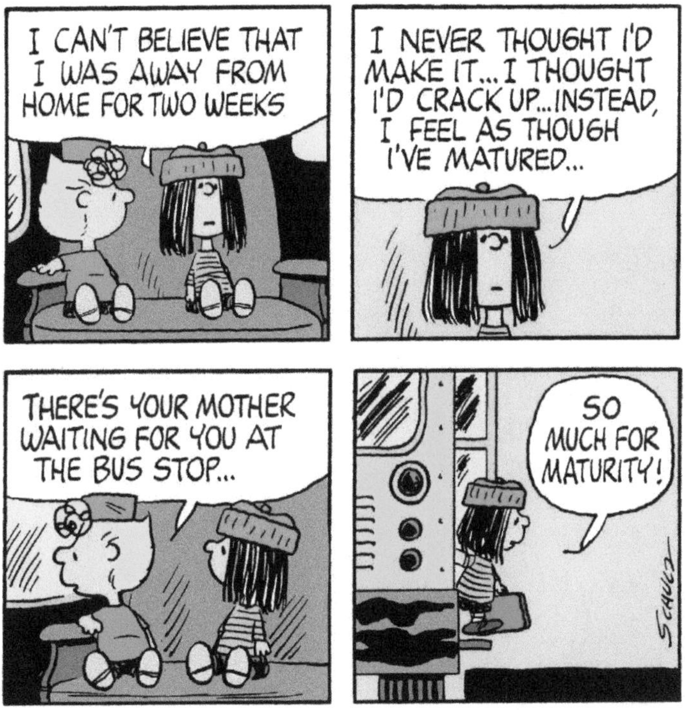
I CAN'T BELIEVE THAT I WAS AWAY FROM HOME FOR TWO WEEKS
I NEVER THOUGHT I'D MAKE IT... I THOUGHT I'D CRACK UP... INSTEAD, I FEEL AS THOUGH I'VE MATURED...
THERE'S YOUR MOTHER WAITING FOR YOU AT THE BUS STOP...
SO MUCH FOR MATURITY!
SCHULZ

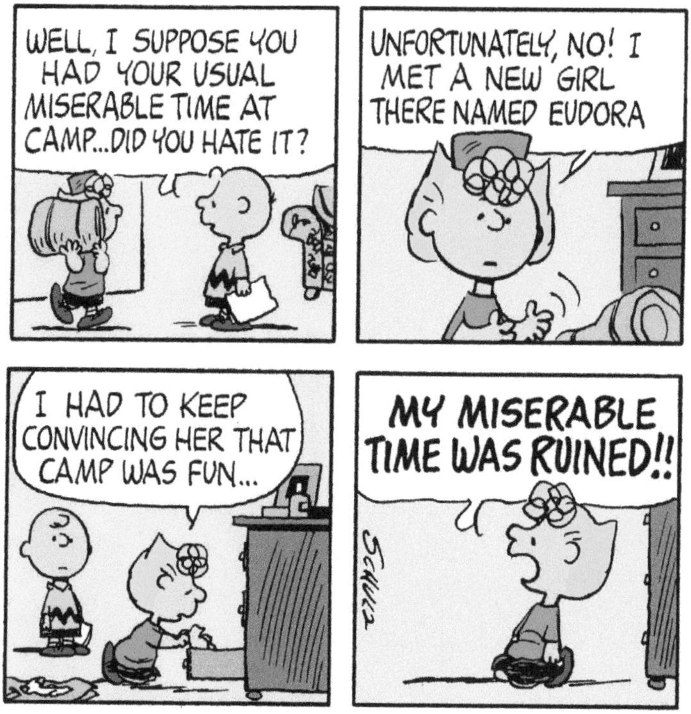
WELL, I SUPPOSE YOU HAD YOUR USUAL MISERABLE TIME AT CAMP...DID YOU HATE IT?
UNFORTUNATELY, NO! I MET A NEW GIRL THERE NAMED EUDORA
I HAD TO KEEP CONVINCING HER THAT CAMP WAS FUN...
MY MISERABLE TIME WAS RUINED!!
SCHULZ

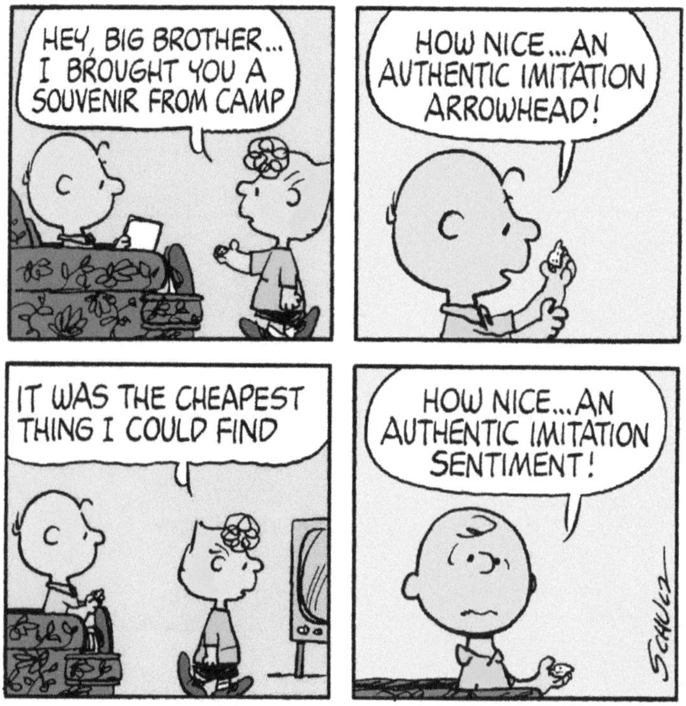
HEY, BIG BROTHER... I BROUGHT YOU A SOUVENIR FROM CAMP
HOW NICE...AN AUTHENTIC IMITATION ARROWHEAD!
IT WAS THE CHEAPEST THING I COULD FIND
HOW NICE...AN AUTHENTIC IMITATION SENTIMENT!
SCHULZ

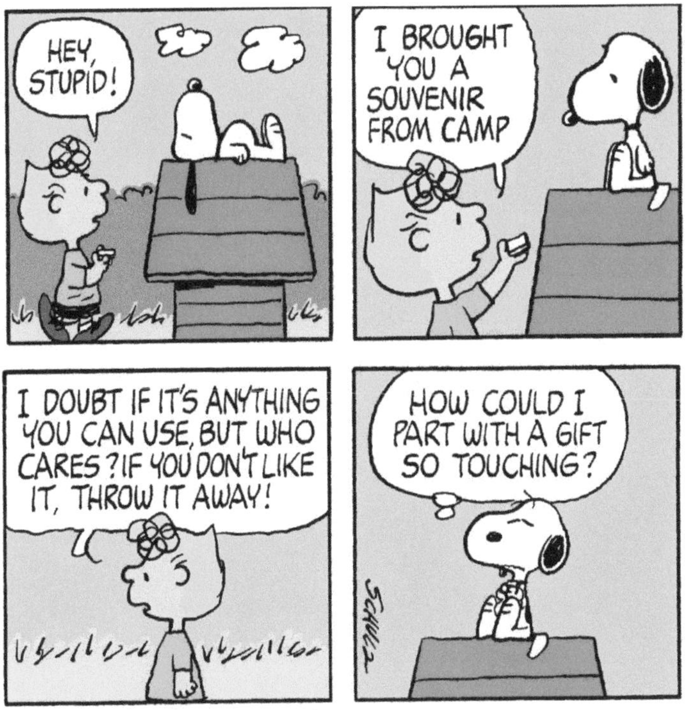
HEY, STUPID!
I BROUGHT YOU A SOUVENIR FROM CAMP
I DOUBT IF IT'S ANYTHING YOU CAN USE, BUT WHO CARES? IF YOU DON'T LIKE IT, THROW IT AWAY!
HOW COULD I PART WITH A GIFT SO TOUCHING?

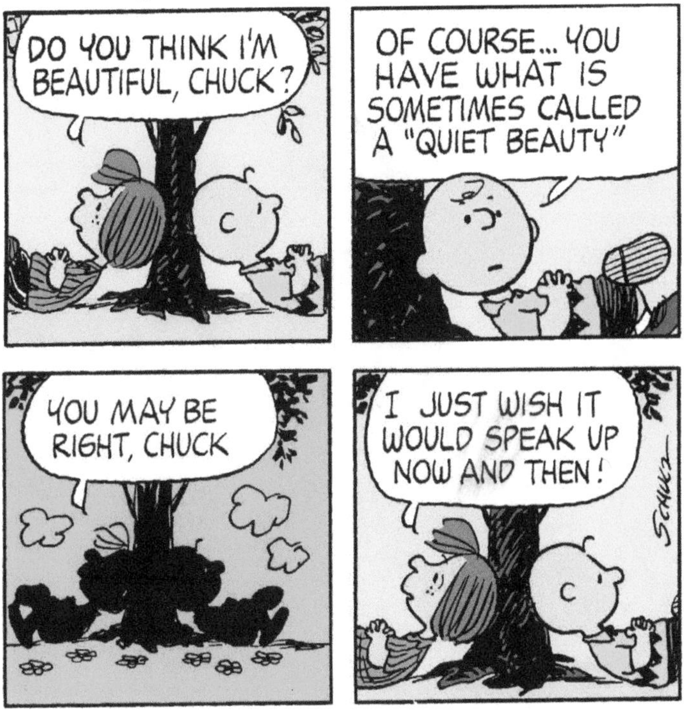
DO YOU THINK I'M BEAUTIFUL, CHUCK?
OF COURSE... YOU HAVE WHAT IS SOMETIMES CALLED A "QUIET BEAUTY"
YOU MAY BE RIGHT, CHUCK
I JUST WISH IT WOULD SPEAK UP NOW AND THEN!

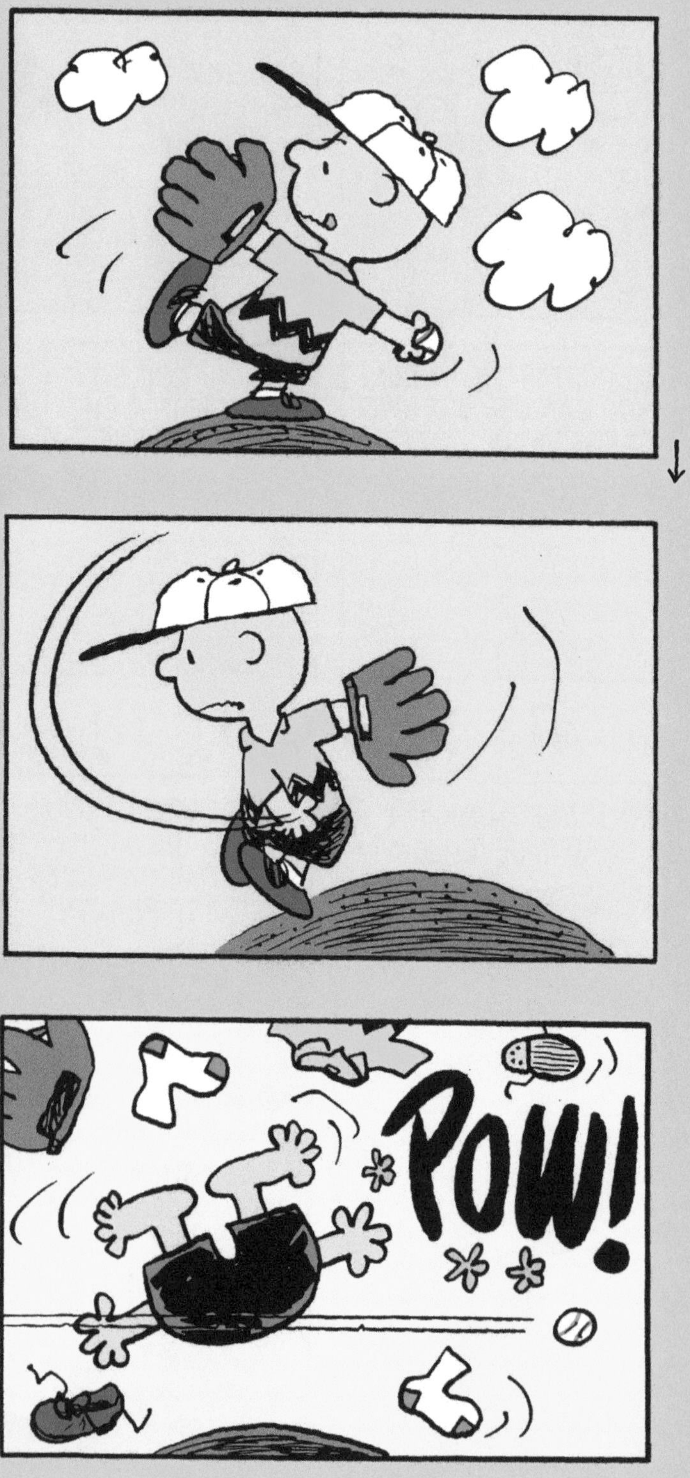
POW!

OOOO! YOU LOOK SO CUTE LYING THERE, CHARLIE BROWN, WITH YOUR LITTLE EASTER TOES SPARKLING IN THE SUN
GET BACK IN CENTER FIELD WHERE YOU BELONG!
HOW CAN A PITCHER BE SO CRABBY ON EASTER?
SCHULZ

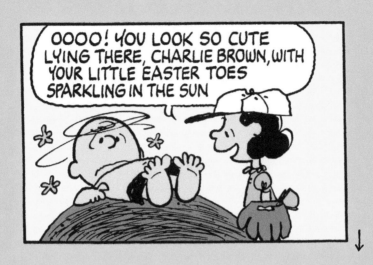

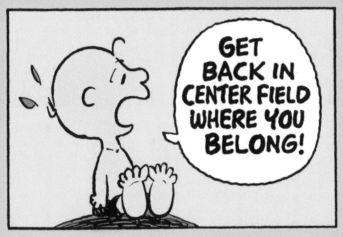

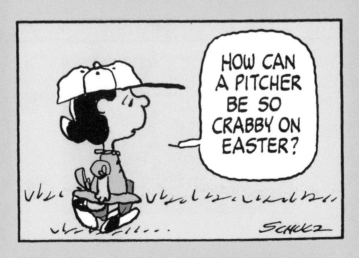

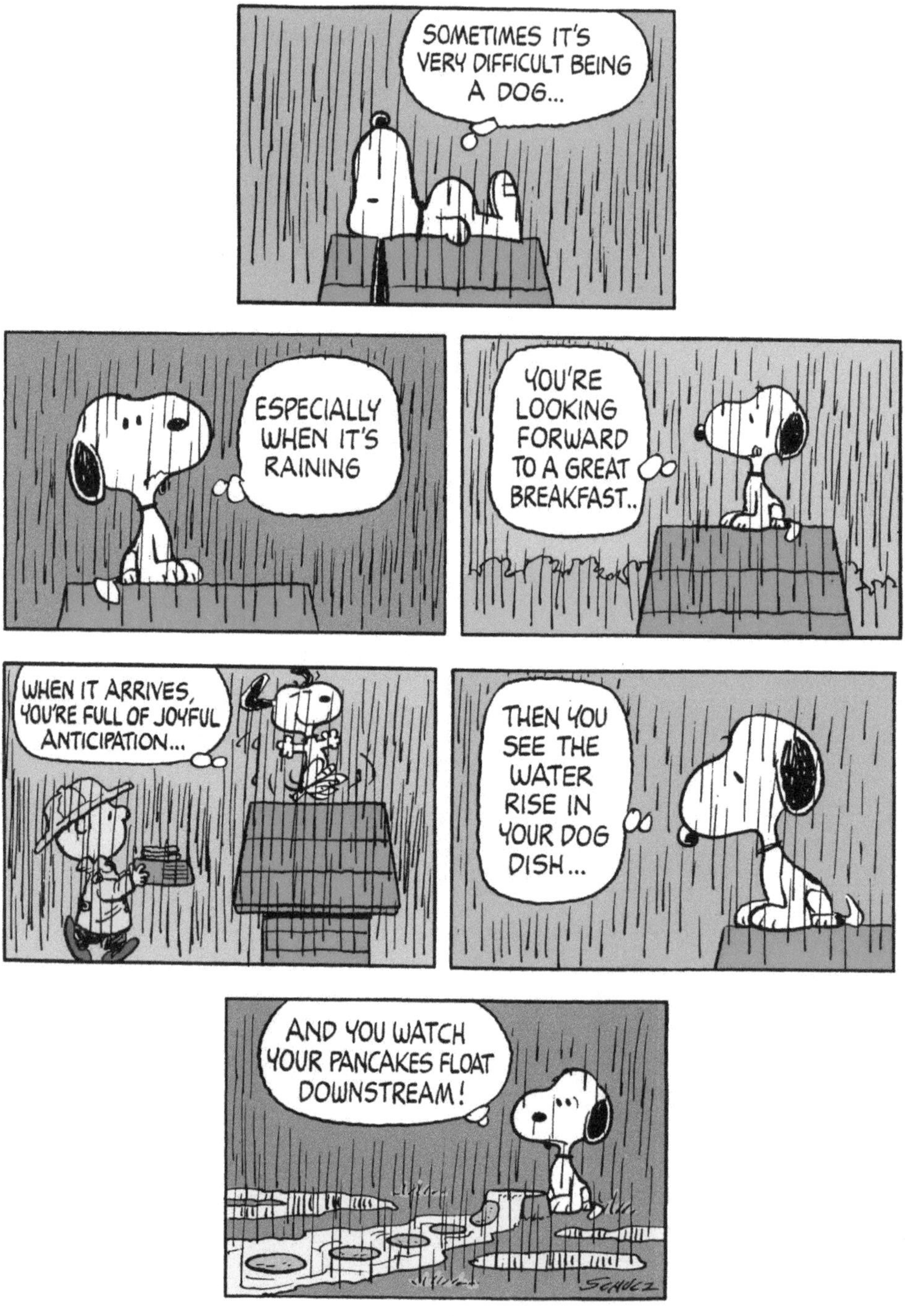
SOMETIMES IT'S VERY DIFFICULT BEING A DOG...
ESPECIALLY WHEN IT'S RAINING
YOU'RE LOOKING FORWARD TO A GREAT BREAKFAST..
WHEN IT ARRIVES, YOU'RE FULL OF JOYFUL ANTICIPATION...
THEN YOU SEE THE WATER RISE IN YOUR DOG DISH...
AND YOU WATCH YOUR PANCAKES FLOAT DOWNSTREAM!
SCHULZ

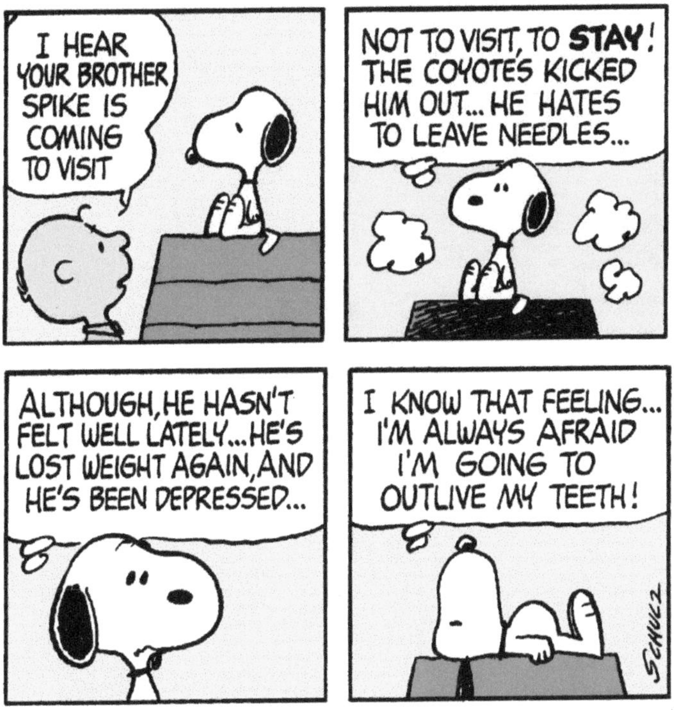
I HEAR YOUR BROTHER SPIKE IS COMING TO VISIT
NOT TO VISIT, TO **STAY**! THE COYOTES KICKED HIM OUT... HE HATES TO LEAVE NEEDLES...
ALTHOUGH, HE HASN'T FELT WELL LATELY...HE'S LOST WEIGHT AGAIN, AND HE'S BEEN DEPRESSED...
I KNOW THAT FEELING... I'M ALWAYS AFRAID I'M GOING TO OUTLIVE MY TEETH!
SCHULZ

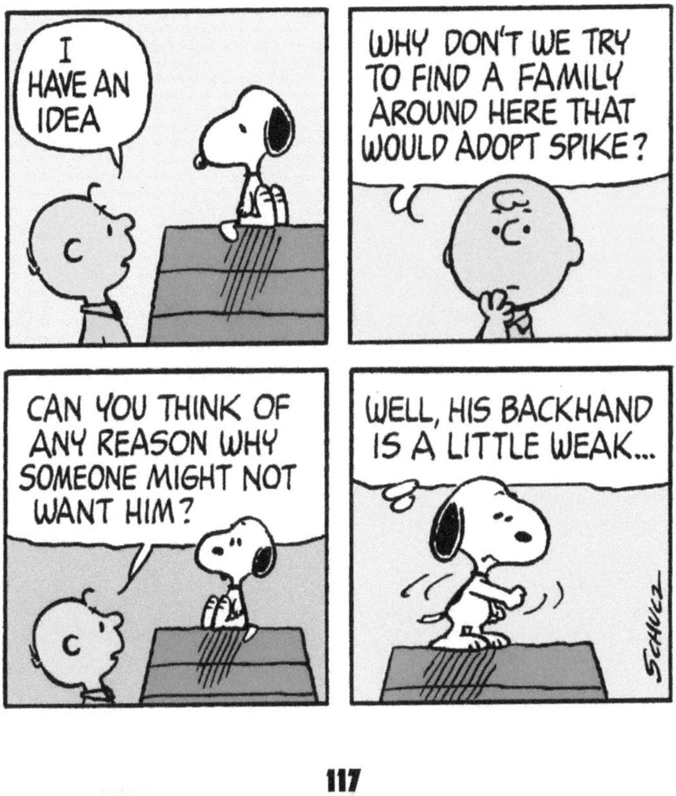
I HAVE AN IDEA
WHY DON'T WE TRY TO FIND A FAMILY AROUND HERE THAT WOULD ADOPT SPIKE?
CAN YOU THINK OF ANY REASON WHY SOMEONE MIGHT NOT WANT HIM?
WELL, HIS BACKHAND IS A LITTLE WEAK...
SCHULZ

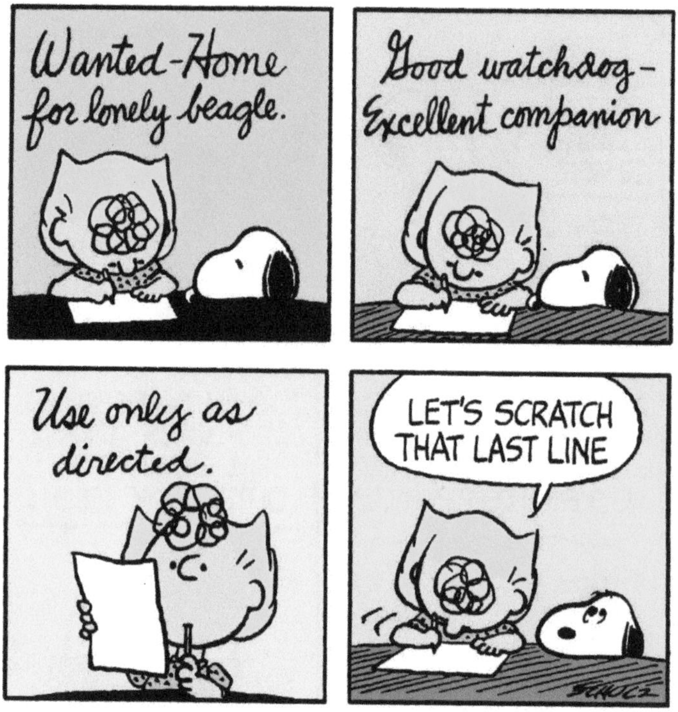
Wanted-Home for lonely beagle.
Good watchdog-Excellent companion
Use only as directed.
LET'S SCRATCH THAT LAST LINE
SCHULZ

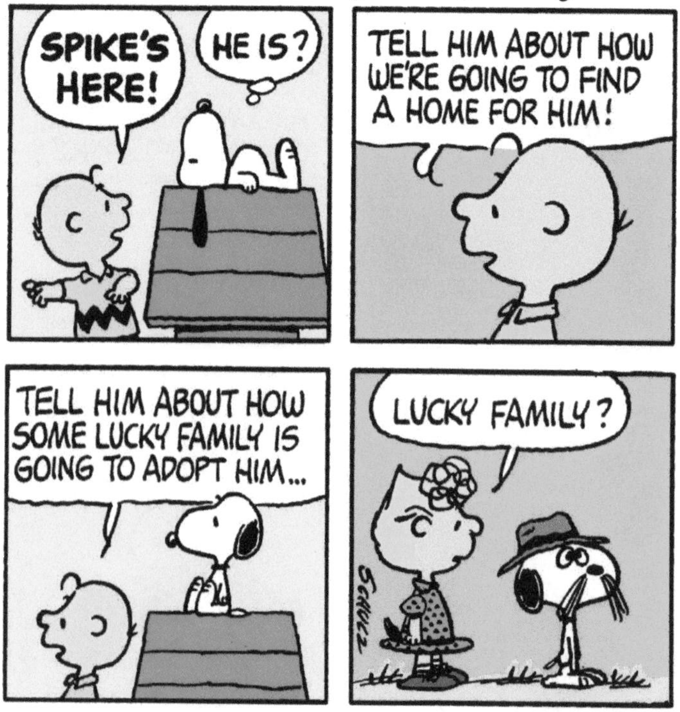
SPIKE'S HERE!
HE IS?
TELL HIM ABOUT HOW WE'RE GOING TO FIND A HOME FOR HIM!
TELL HIM ABOUT HOW SOME LUCKY FAMILY IS GOING TO ADOPT HIM...
LUCKY FAMILY?
SCHULZ

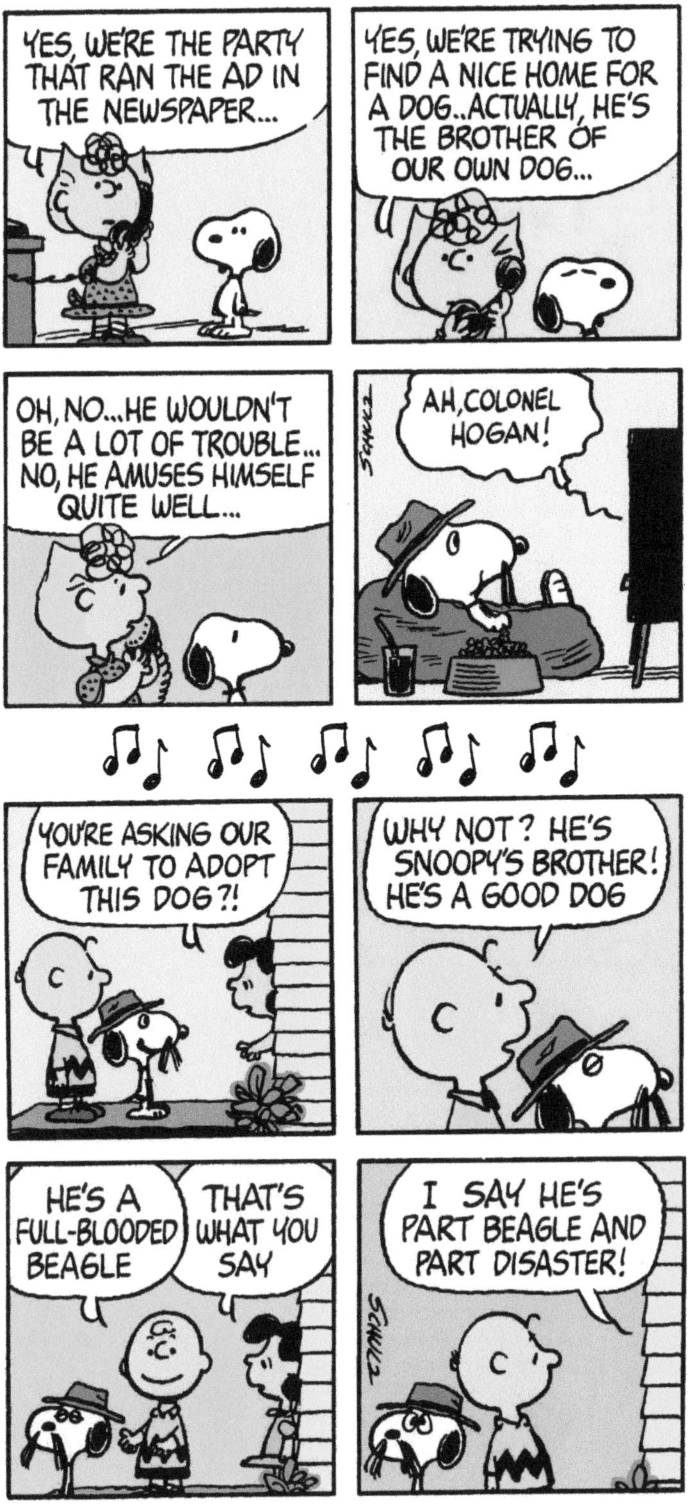
YES, WE'RE THE PARTY THAT RAN THE AD IN THE NEWSPAPER...
YES, WE'RE TRYING TO FIND A NICE HOME FOR A DOG..ACTUALLY, HE'S THE BROTHER OF OUR OWN DOG...
OH, NO...HE WOULDN'T BE A LOT OF TROUBLE... NO, HE AMUSES HIMSELF QUITE WELL...
AH, COLONEL HOGAN!
YOU'RE ASKING OUR FAMILY TO ADOPT THIS DOG?!
WHY NOT? HE'S SNOOPY'S BROTHER! HE'S A GOOD DOG
HE'S A FULL-BLOODED BEAGLE
THAT'S WHAT YOU SAY
I SAY HE'S PART BEAGLE AND PART DISASTER!

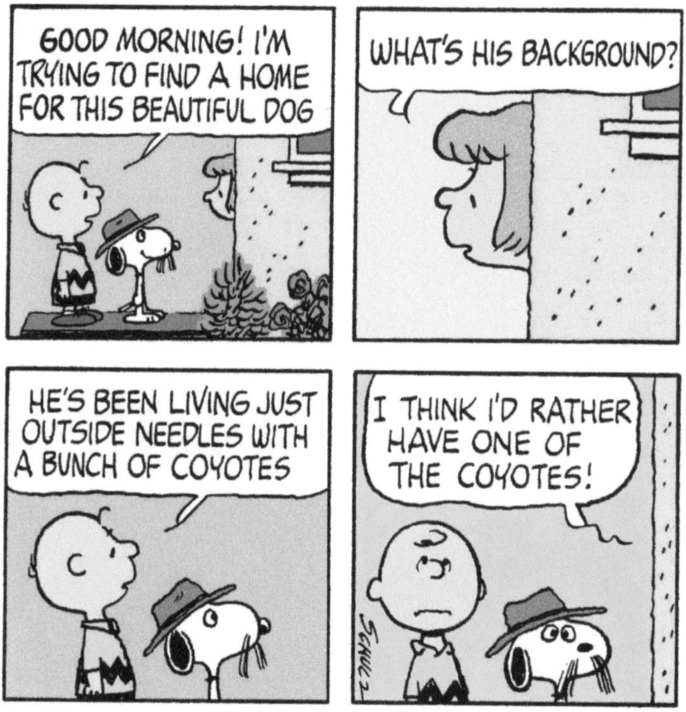
GOOD MORNING! I'M TRYING TO FIND A HOME FOR THIS BEAUTIFUL DOG
WHAT'S HIS BACKGROUND?
HE'S BEEN LIVING JUST OUTSIDE NEEDLES WITH A BUNCH OF COYOTES
I THINK I'D RATHER HAVE ONE OF THE COYOTES!
SCHULZ

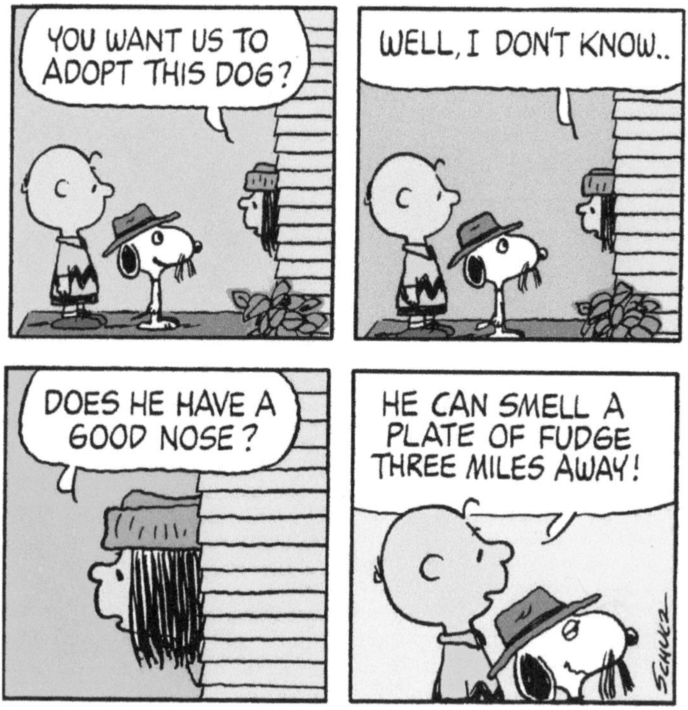
YOU WANT US TO ADOPT THIS DOG?
WELL, I DON'T KNOW..
DOES HE HAVE A GOOD NOSE?
HE CAN SMELL A PLATE OF FUDGE THREE MILES AWAY!
SCHULZ

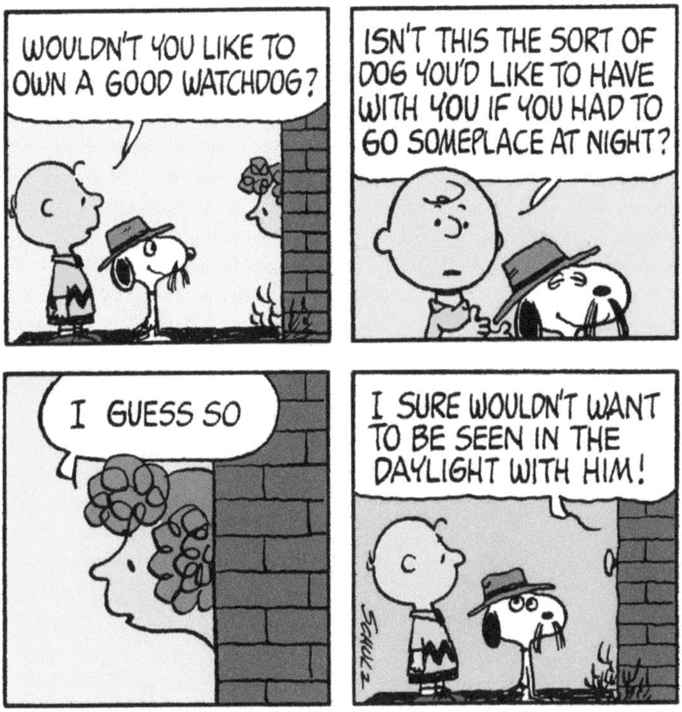
WOULDN'T YOU LIKE TO OWN A GOOD WATCHDOG?
ISN'T THIS THE SORT OF DOG YOU'D LIKE TO HAVE WITH YOU IF YOU HAD TO GO SOMEPLACE AT NIGHT?
I GUESS SO
I SURE WOULDN'T WANT TO BE SEEN IN THE DAYLIGHT WITH HIM!
SCHULZ

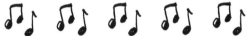

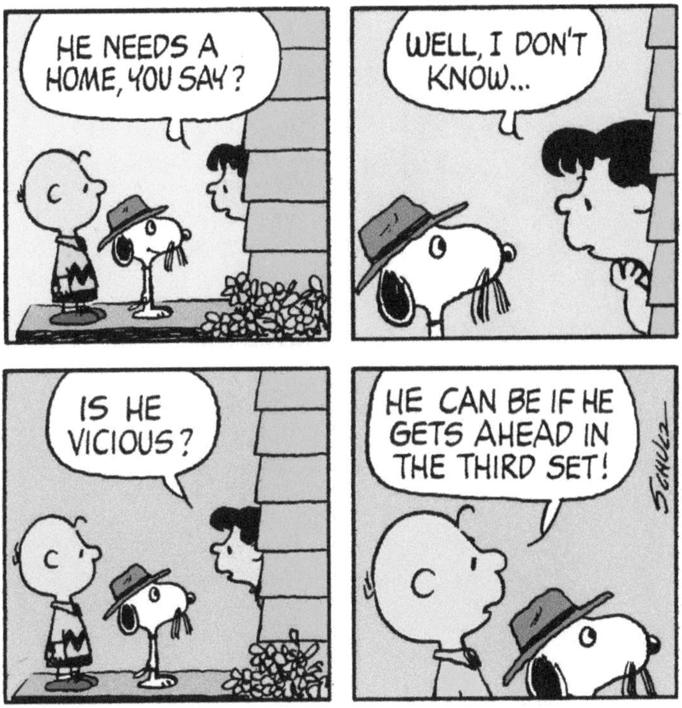
HE NEEDS A HOME, YOU SAY?
WELL, I DON'T KNOW...
IS HE VICIOUS?
HE CAN BE IF HE GETS AHEAD IN THE THIRD SET!
SCHULZ

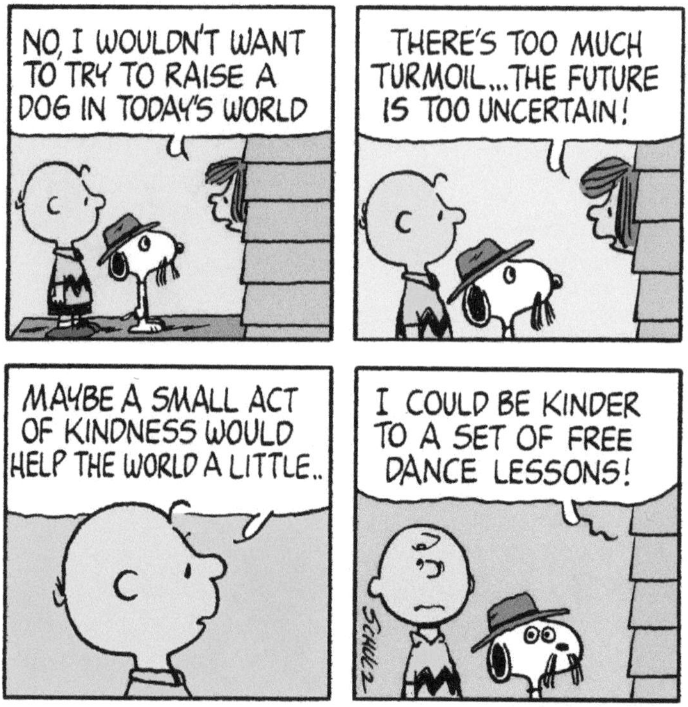
NO, I WOULDN'T WANT TO TRY TO RAISE A DOG IN TODAY'S WORLD
THERE'S TOO MUCH TURMOIL...THE FUTURE IS TOO UNCERTAIN!
MAYBE A SMALL ACT OF KINDNESS WOULD HELP THE WORLD A LITTLE..
I COULD BE KINDER TO A SET OF FREE DANCE LESSONS!
SCHULZ

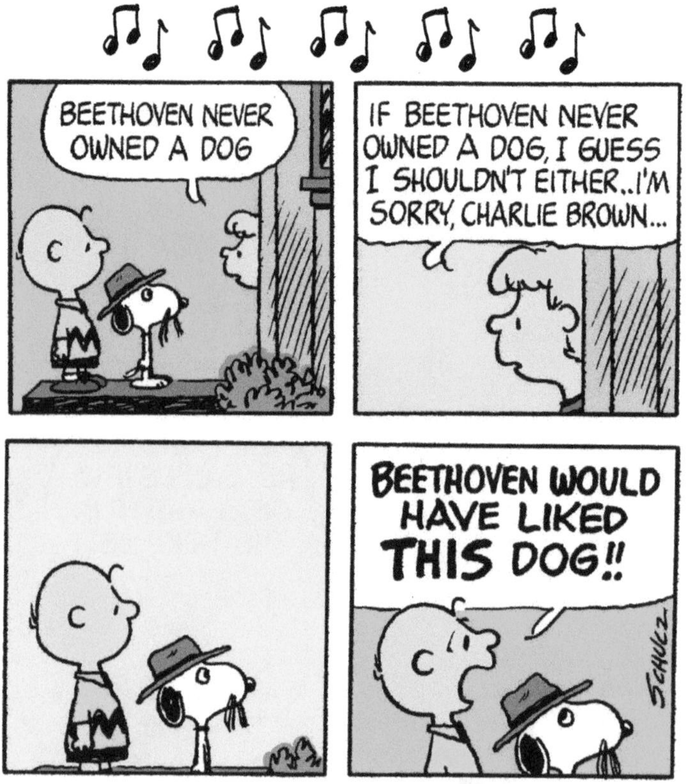
BEETHOVEN NEVER OWNED A DOG
IF BEETHOVEN NEVER OWNED A DOG, I GUESS I SHOULDN'T EITHER..I'M SORRY, CHARLIE BROWN...
BEETHOVEN WOULD HAVE LIKED THIS DOG!!
SCHULZ

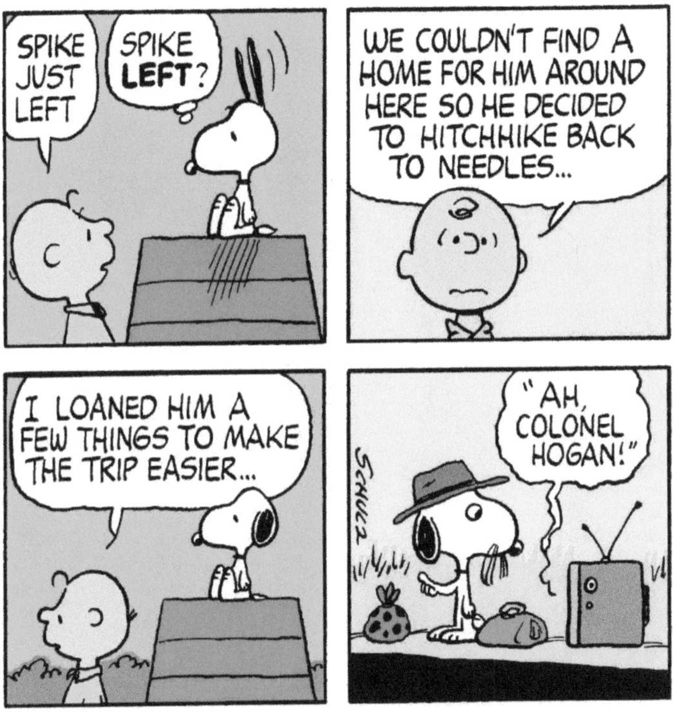
SPIKE JUST LEFT
SPIKE **LEFT**?
WE COULDN'T FIND A HOME FOR HIM AROUND HERE SO HE DECIDED TO HITCHHIKE BACK TO NEEDLES...
I LOANED HIM A FEW THINGS TO MAKE THE TRIP EASIER...
"AH, COLONEL HOGAN!"
SCHULZ

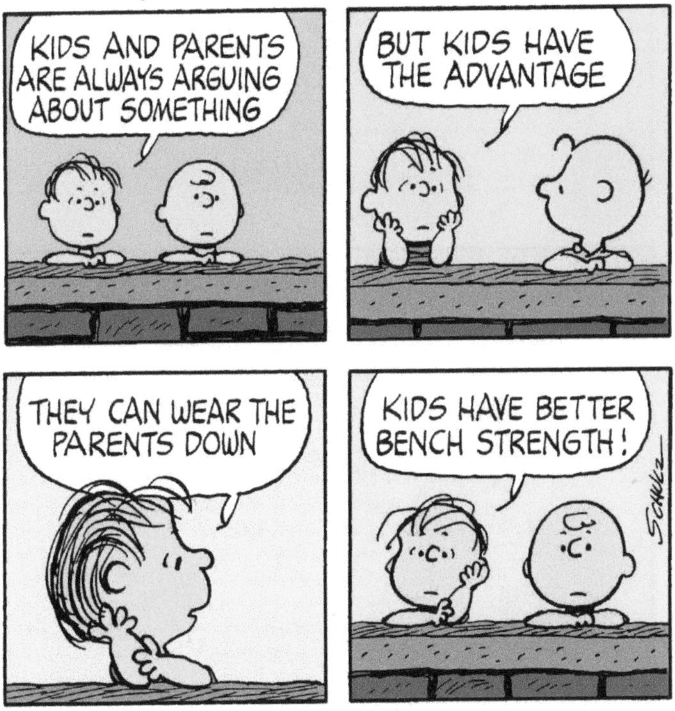
KIDS AND PARENTS ARE ALWAYS ARGUING ABOUT SOMETHING
BUT KIDS HAVE THE ADVANTAGE
THEY CAN WEAR THE PARENTS DOWN
KIDS HAVE BETTER BENCH STRENGTH!
SCHULZ

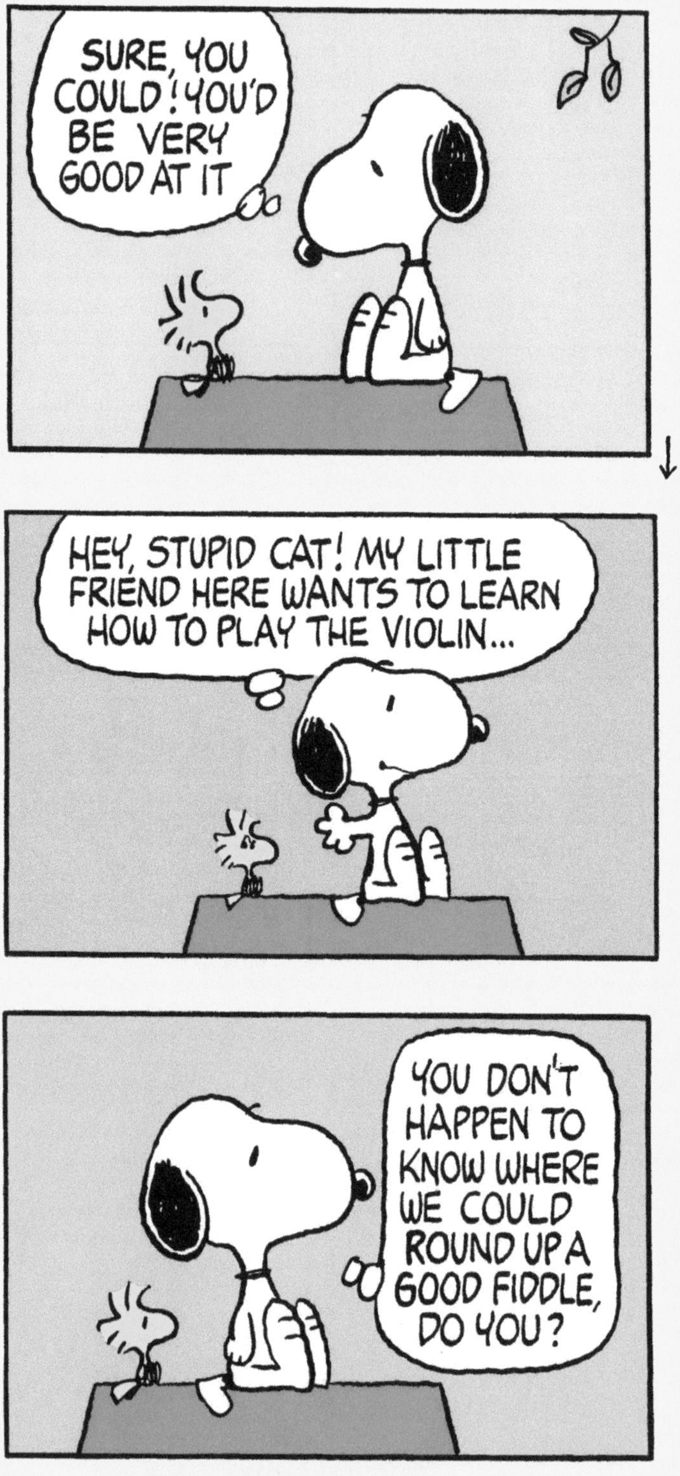
SURE, YOU COULD! YOU'D BE VERY GOOD AT IT
HEY, STUPID CAT! MY LITTLE FRIEND HERE WANTS TO LEARN HOW TO PLAY THE VIOLIN...
YOU DON'T HAPPEN TO KNOW WHERE WE COULD ROUND UP A GOOD FIDDLE, DO YOU?

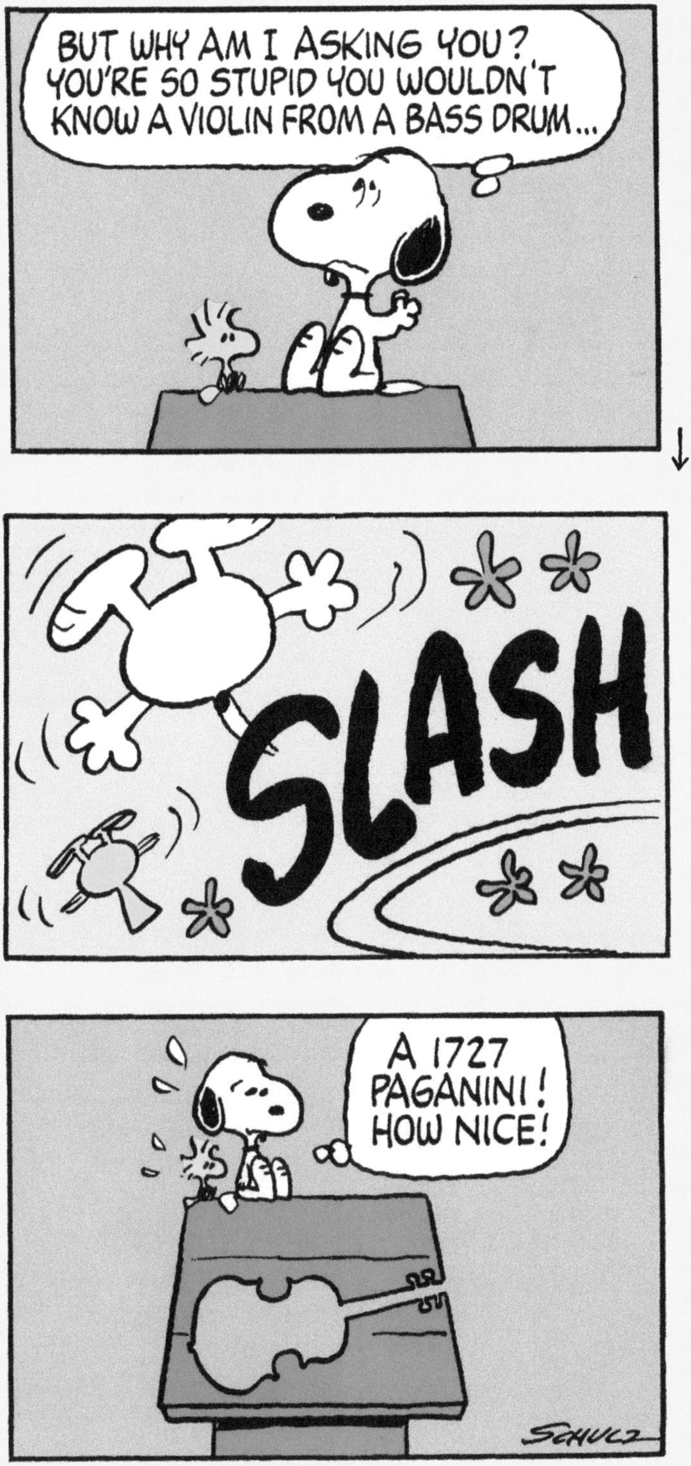
BUT WHY AM I ASKING YOU? YOU'RE SO STUPID YOU WOULDN'T KNOW A VIOLIN FROM A BASS DRUM...
SLASH
A 1727 PAGANINI! HOW NICE!
SCHULZ

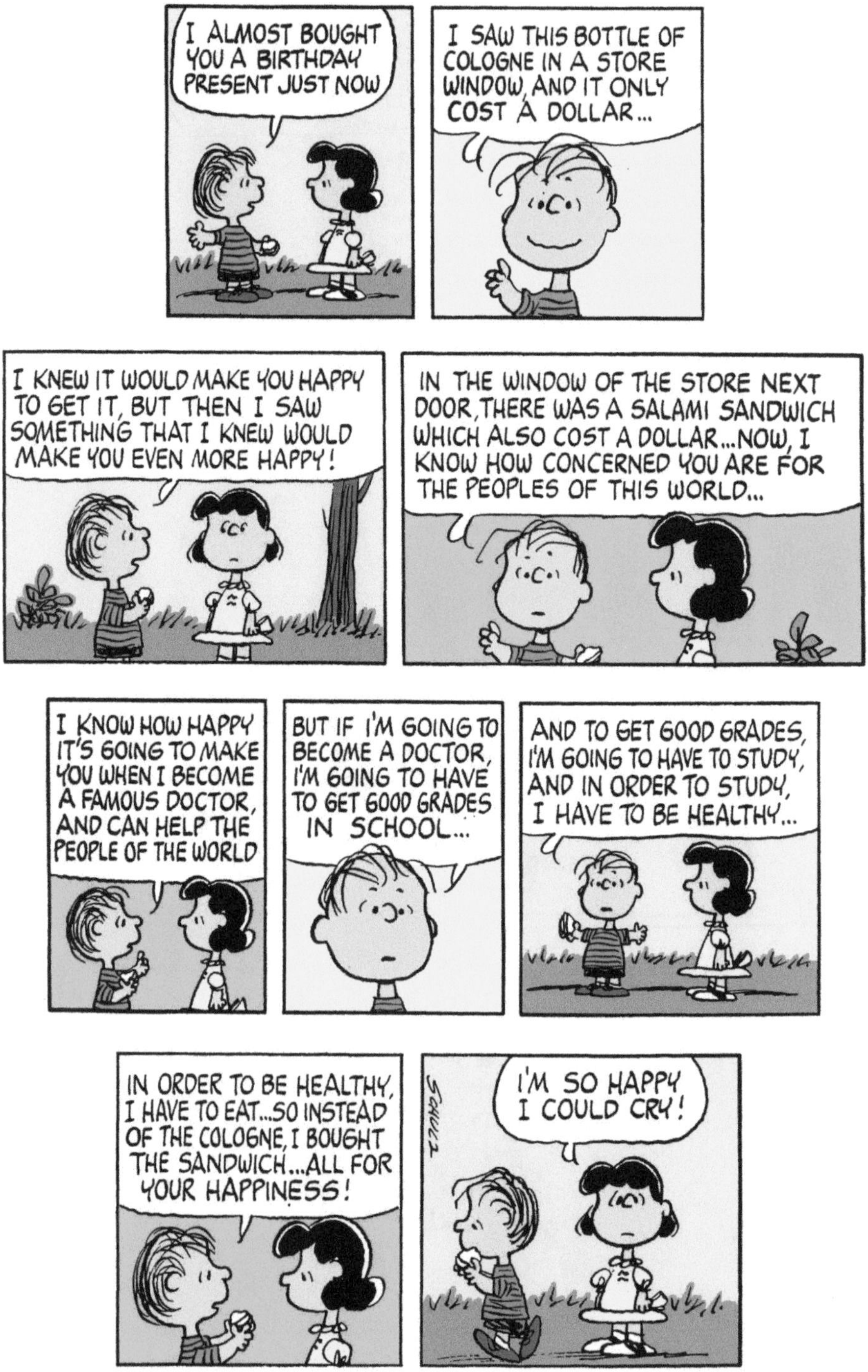
I ALMOST BOUGHT YOU A BIRTHDAY PRESENT JUST NOW
I SAW THIS BOTTLE OF COLOGNE IN A STORE WINDOW, AND IT ONLY COST A DOLLAR...
I KNEW IT WOULD MAKE YOU HAPPY TO GET IT, BUT THEN I SAW SOMETHING THAT I KNEW WOULD MAKE YOU EVEN MORE HAPPY!
IN THE WINDOW OF THE STORE NEXT DOOR, THERE WAS A SALAMI SANDWICH WHICH ALSO COST A DOLLAR...NOW, I KNOW HOW CONCERNED YOU ARE FOR THE PEOPLES OF THIS WORLD...
I KNOW HOW HAPPY IT'S GOING TO MAKE YOU WHEN I BECOME A FAMOUS DOCTOR, AND CAN HELP THE PEOPLE OF THE WORLD
BUT IF I'M GOING TO BECOME A DOCTOR, I'M GOING TO HAVE TO GET GOOD GRADES IN SCHOOL...
AND TO GET GOOD GRADES, I'M GOING TO HAVE TO STUDY, AND IN ORDER TO STUDY, I HAVE TO BE HEALTHY...
IN ORDER TO BE HEALTHY, I HAVE TO EAT...SO INSTEAD OF THE COLOGNE, I BOUGHT THE SANDWICH...ALL FOR YOUR HAPPINESS!
SCHULZ
I'M SO HAPPY I COULD CRY!

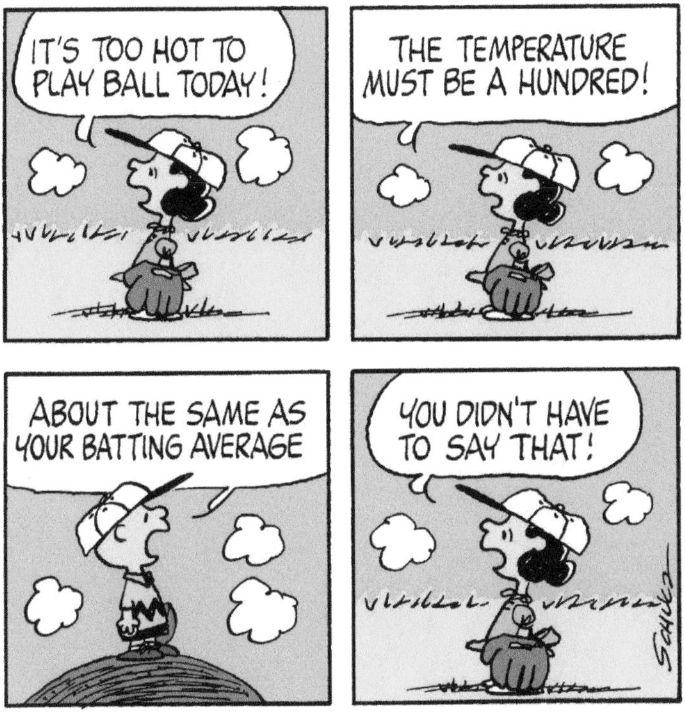
IT'S TOO HOT TO PLAY BALL TODAY!
THE TEMPERATURE MUST BE A HUNDRED!
ABOUT THE SAME AS YOUR BATTING AVERAGE
YOU DIDN'T HAVE TO SAY THAT!

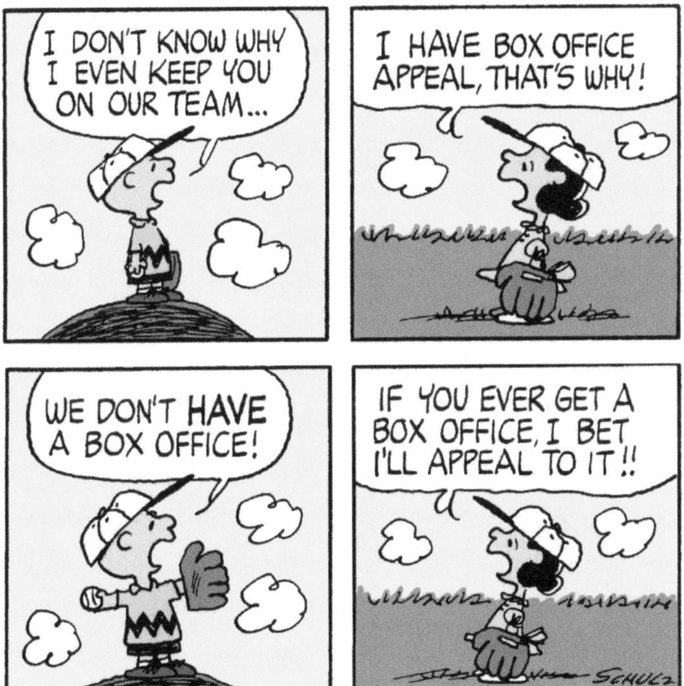
I DON'T KNOW WHY I EVEN KEEP YOU ON OUR TEAM...
I HAVE BOX OFFICE APPEAL, THAT'S WHY!
WE DON'T **HAVE** A BOX OFFICE!
IF YOU EVER GET A BOX OFFICE, I BET I'LL APPEAL TO IT!!

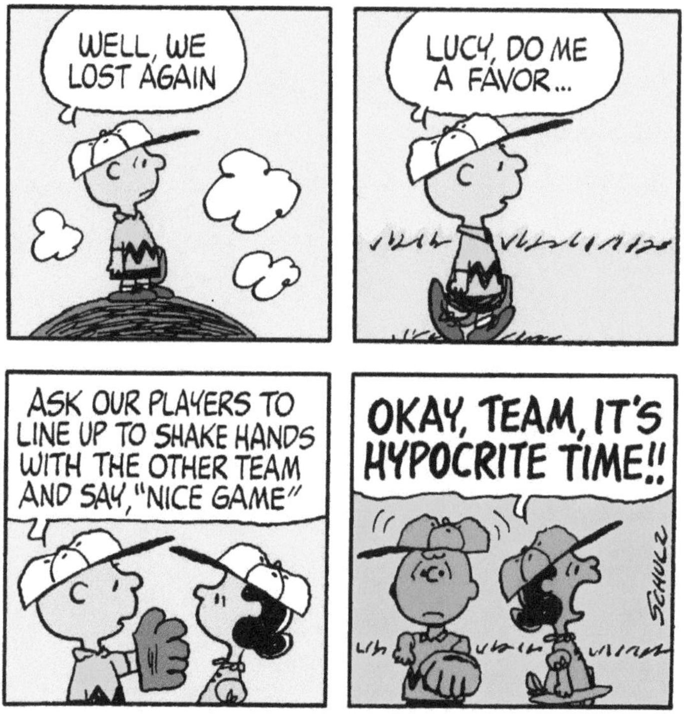
WELL, WE LOST AGAIN
LUCY, DO ME A FAVOR...
ASK OUR PLAYERS TO LINE UP TO SHAKE HANDS WITH THE OTHER TEAM AND SAY, "NICE GAME"
OKAY, TEAM, IT'S HYPOCRITE TIME!!
SCHULZ

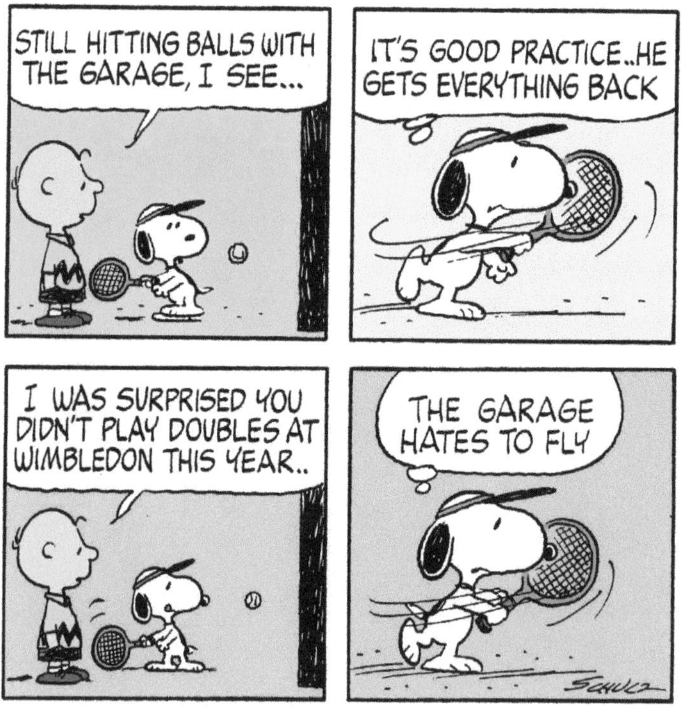
STILL HITTING BALLS WITH THE GARAGE, I SEE...
IT'S GOOD PRACTICE..HE GETS EVERYTHING BACK
I WAS SURPRISED YOU DIDN'T PLAY DOUBLES AT WIMBLEDON THIS YEAR..
THE GARAGE HATES TO FLY
SCHULZ

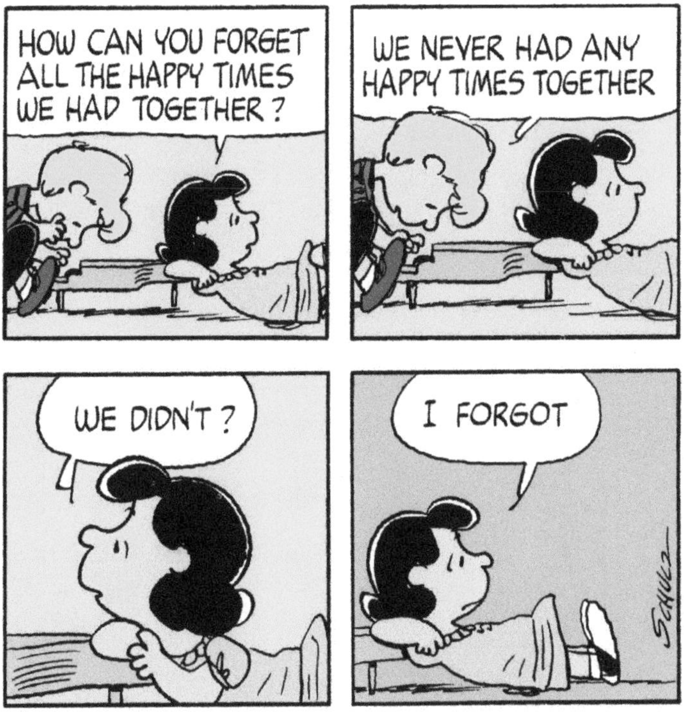
HOW CAN YOU FORGET ALL THE HAPPY TIMES WE HAD TOGETHER?
WE NEVER HAD ANY HAPPY TIMES TOGETHER
WE DIDN'T?
I FORGOT
SCHULZ

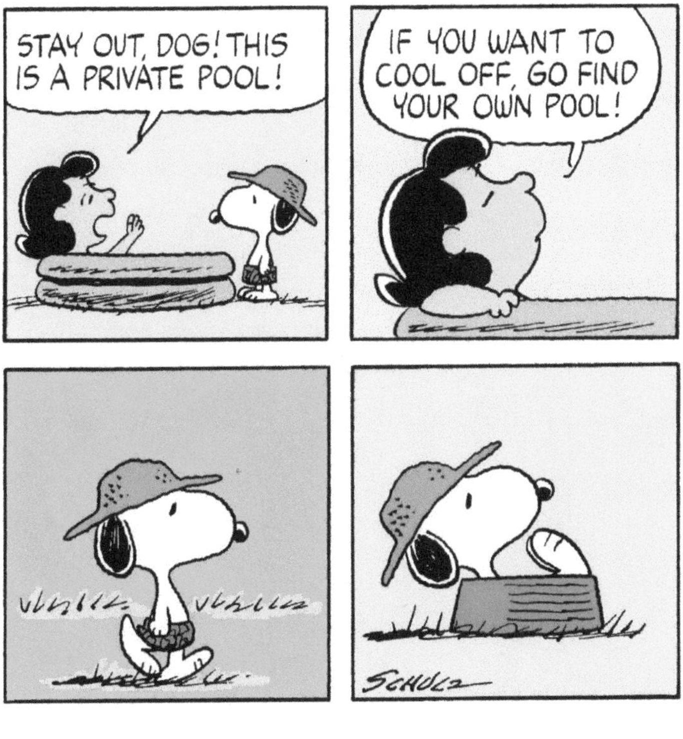
STAY OUT, DOG! THIS IS A PRIVATE POOL!
IF YOU WANT TO COOL OFF, GO FIND YOUR OWN POOL!
SCHULZ

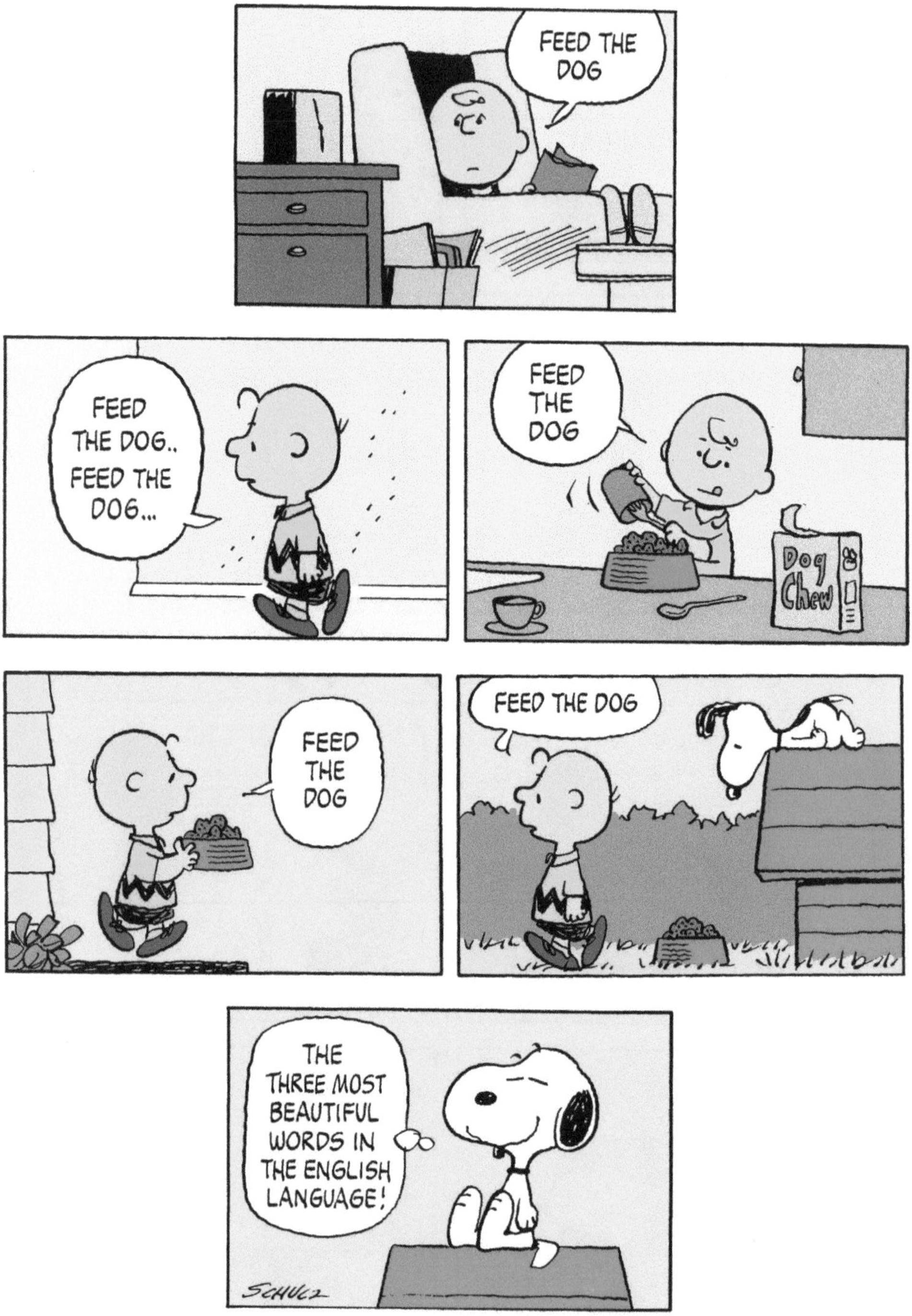
FEED THE DOG
FEED THE DOG.. FEED THE DOG...
FEED THE DOG
Dog Chew
FEED THE DOG
FEED THE DOG
THE THREE MOST BEAUTIFUL WORDS IN THE ENGLISH LANGUAGE!
SCHULZ

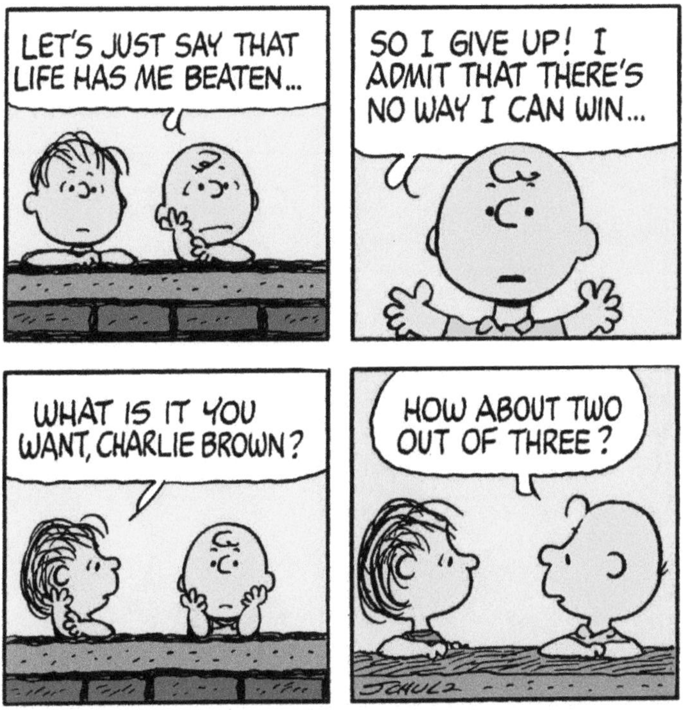
LET'S JUST SAY THAT LIFE HAS ME BEATEN...
SO I GIVE UP! I ADMIT THAT THERE'S NO WAY I CAN WIN...
WHAT IS IT YOU WANT, CHARLIE BROWN?
HOW ABOUT TWO OUT OF THREE?

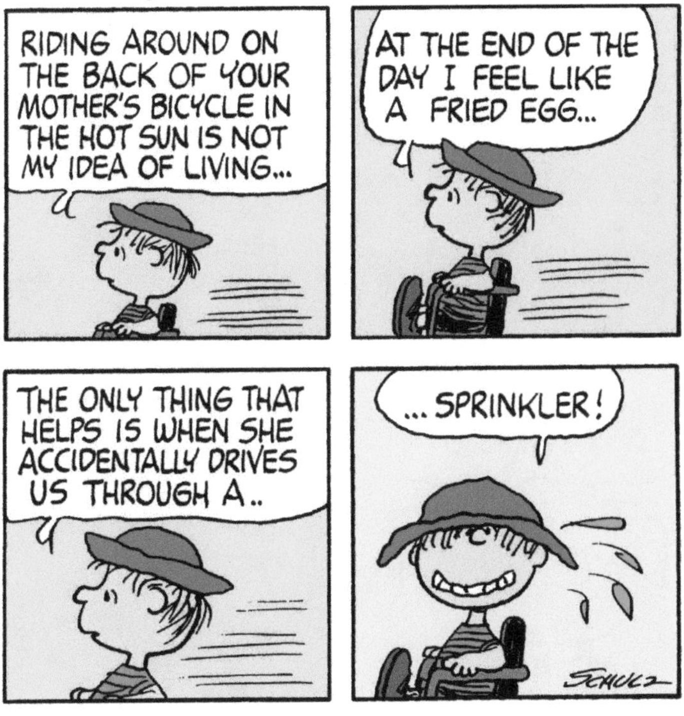
RIDING AROUND ON THE BACK OF YOUR MOTHER'S BICYCLE IN THE HOT SUN IS NOT MY IDEA OF LIVING...
AT THE END OF THE DAY I FEEL LIKE A FRIED EGG...
THE ONLY THING THAT HELPS IS WHEN SHE ACCIDENTALLY DRIVES US THROUGH A..
...SPRINKLER!

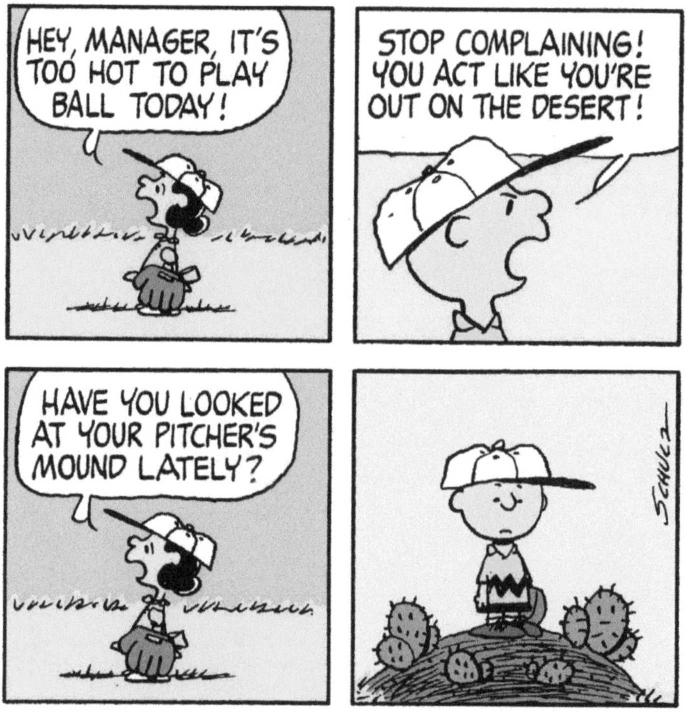
HEY, MANAGER, IT'S TOO HOT TO PLAY BALL TODAY!
STOP COMPLAINING! YOU ACT LIKE YOU'RE OUT ON THE DESERT!
HAVE YOU LOOKED AT YOUR PITCHER'S MOUND LATELY?
SCHULZ

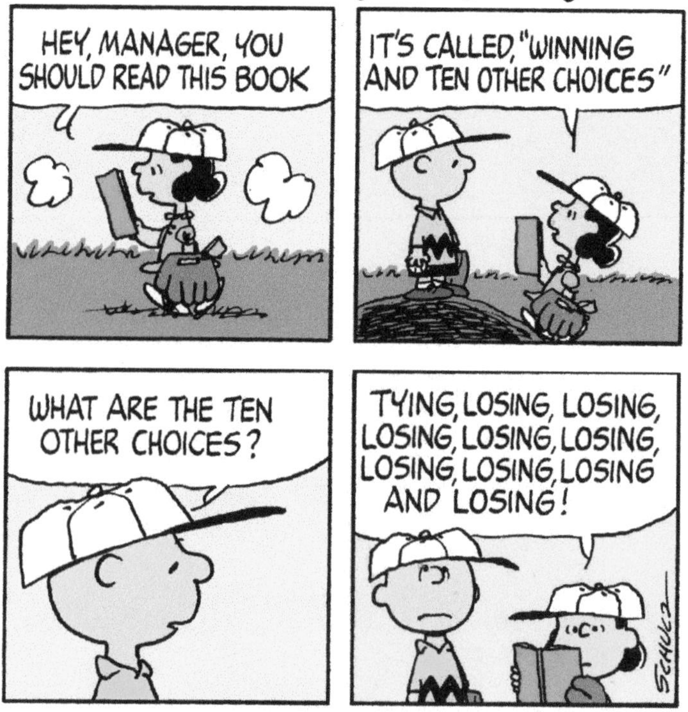
HEY, MANAGER, YOU SHOULD READ THIS BOOK
IT'S CALLED, "WINNING AND TEN OTHER CHOICES"
WHAT ARE THE TEN OTHER CHOICES?
TYING, LOSING, LOSING, LOSING, LOSING, LOSING, LOSING, LOSING, LOSING AND LOSING!
SCHULZ

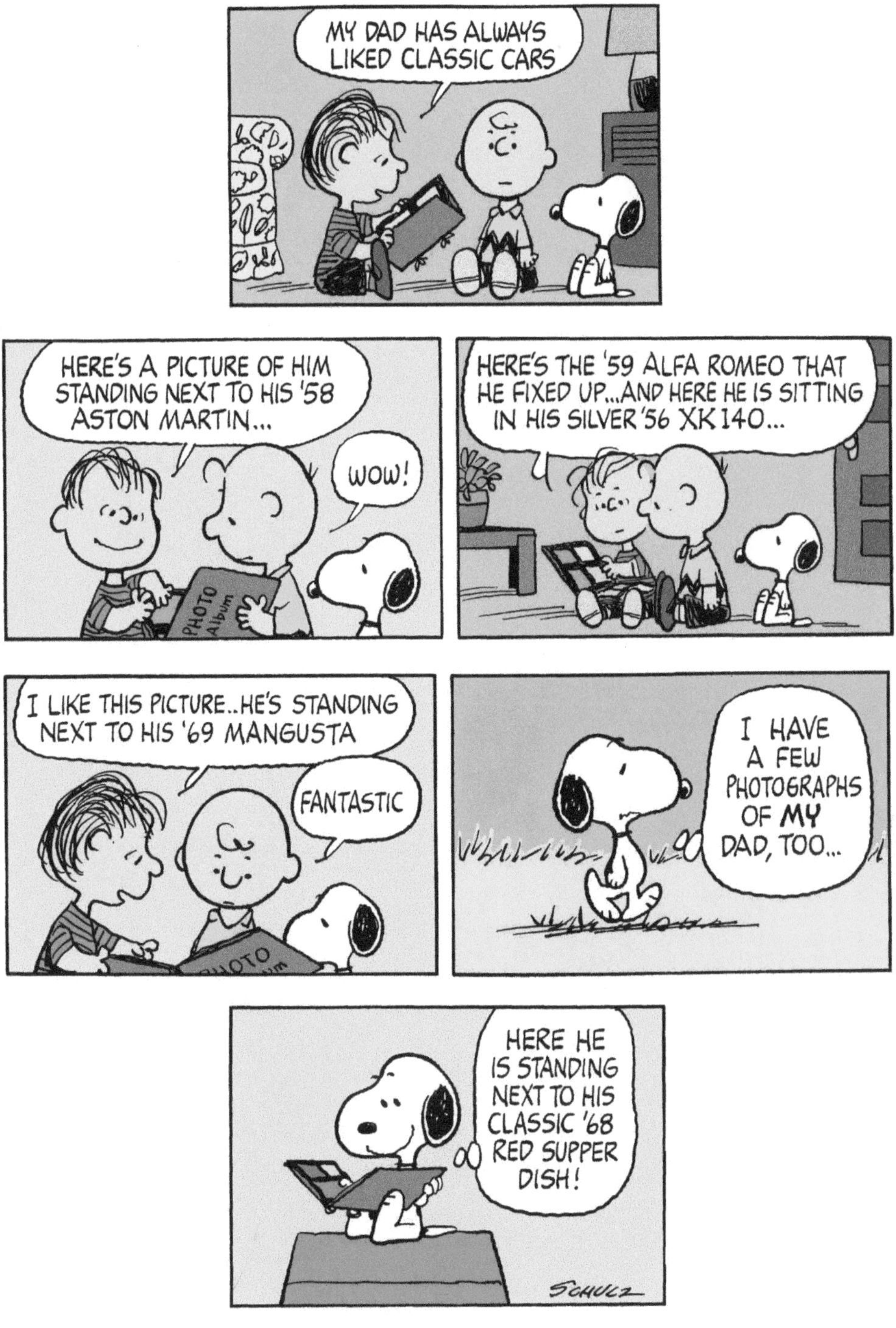
MY DAD HAS ALWAYS LIKED CLASSIC CARS
HERE'S A PICTURE OF HIM STANDING NEXT TO HIS '58 ASTON MARTIN...
WOW!
PHOTO Album
HERE'S THE '59 ALFA ROMEO THAT HE FIXED UP...AND HERE HE IS SITTING IN HIS SILVER '56 XK140...
I LIKE THIS PICTURE..HE'S STANDING NEXT TO HIS '69 MANGUSTA
FANTASTIC
I HAVE A FEW PHOTOGRAPHS OF MY DAD, TOO...
HERE HE IS STANDING NEXT TO HIS CLASSIC '68 RED SUPPER DISH!
SCHULZ

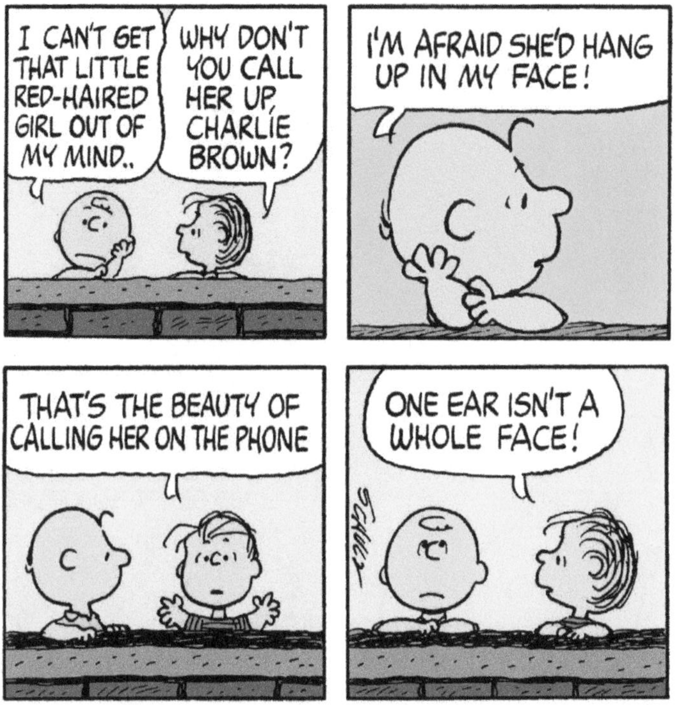
I CAN'T GET THAT LITTLE RED-HAIRED GIRL OUT OF MY MIND..
WHY DON'T YOU CALL HER UP, CHARLIE BROWN?
I'M AFRAID SHE'D HANG UP IN MY FACE!
THAT'S THE BEAUTY OF CALLING HER ON THE PHONE
ONE EAR ISN'T A WHOLE FACE!
SCHULZ

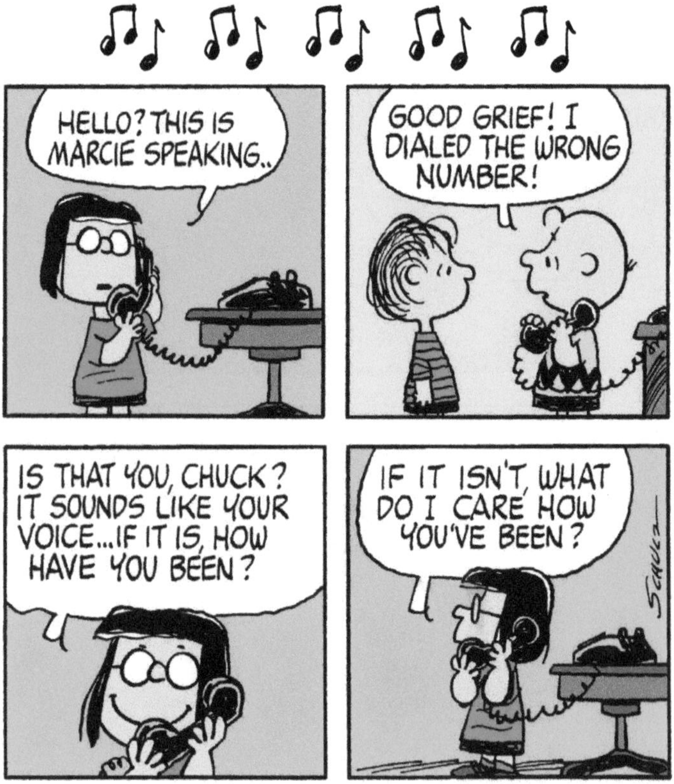
HELLO? THIS IS MARCIE SPEAKING..
GOOD GRIEF! I DIALED THE WRONG NUMBER!
IS THAT YOU, CHUCK? IT SOUNDS LIKE YOUR VOICE...IF IT IS, HOW HAVE YOU BEEN?
IF IT ISN'T, WHAT DO I CARE HOW YOU'VE BEEN?
SCHULZ

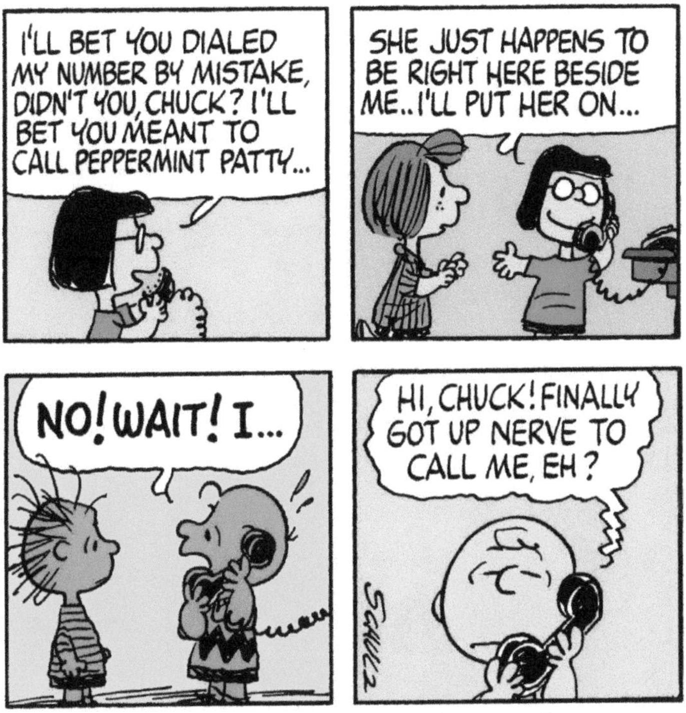

I'LL BET YOU DIALED MY NUMBER BY MISTAKE, DIDN'T YOU, CHUCK? I'LL BET YOU MEANT TO CALL PEPPERMINT PATTY...
SHE JUST HAPPENS TO BE RIGHT HERE BESIDE ME..I'LL PUT HER ON...
NO! WAIT! I...
HI, CHUCK! FINALLY GOT UP NERVE TO CALL ME, EH?
SCHULZ

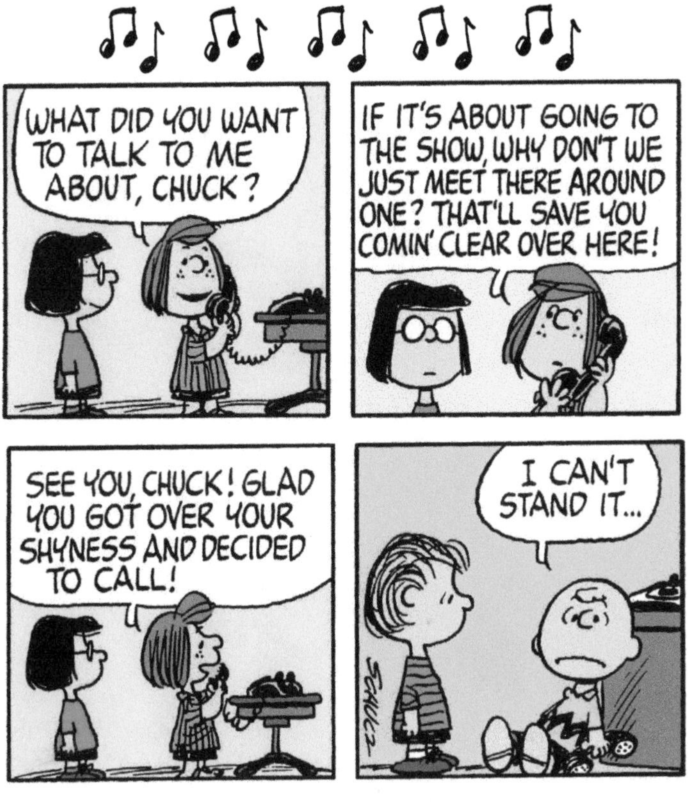

WHAT DID YOU WANT TO TALK TO ME ABOUT, CHUCK?
IF IT'S ABOUT GOING TO THE SHOW, WHY DON'T WE JUST MEET THERE AROUND ONE? THAT'LL SAVE YOU COMIN' CLEAR OVER HERE!
SEE YOU, CHUCK! GLAD YOU GOT OVER YOUR SHYNESS AND DECIDED TO CALL!
I CAN'T STAND IT...
SCHULZ

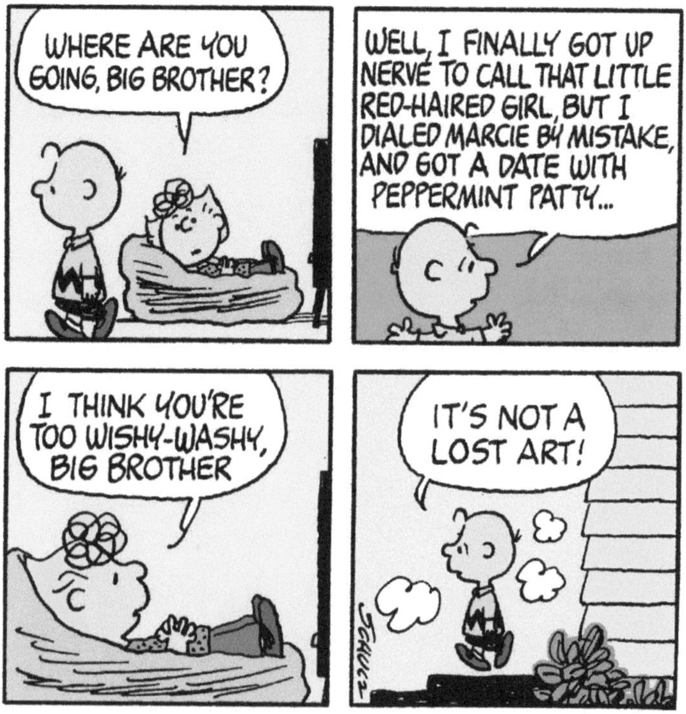
WHERE ARE YOU GOING, BIG BROTHER?
WELL, I FINALLY GOT UP NERVE TO CALL THAT LITTLE RED-HAIRED GIRL, BUT I DIALED MARCIE BY MISTAKE, AND GOT A DATE WITH PEPPERMINT PATTY...
I THINK YOU'RE TOO WISHY-WASHY, BIG BROTHER
IT'S NOT A LOST ART!
SCHULZ

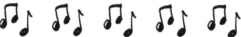

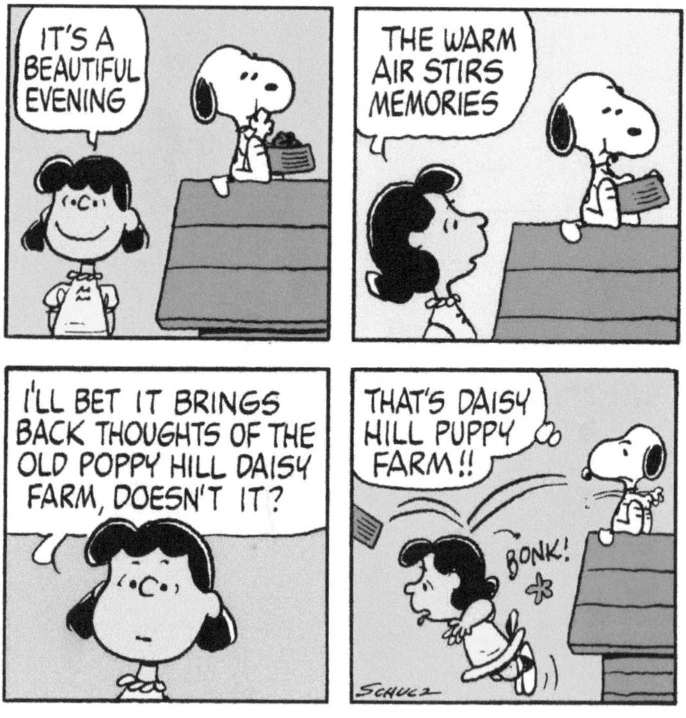
IT'S A BEAUTIFUL EVENING
THE WARM AIR STIRS MEMORIES
I'LL BET IT BRINGS BACK THOUGHTS OF THE OLD POPPY HILL DAISY FARM, DOESN'T IT?
THAT'S DAISY HILL PUPPY FARM!!
BONK!
SCHULZ

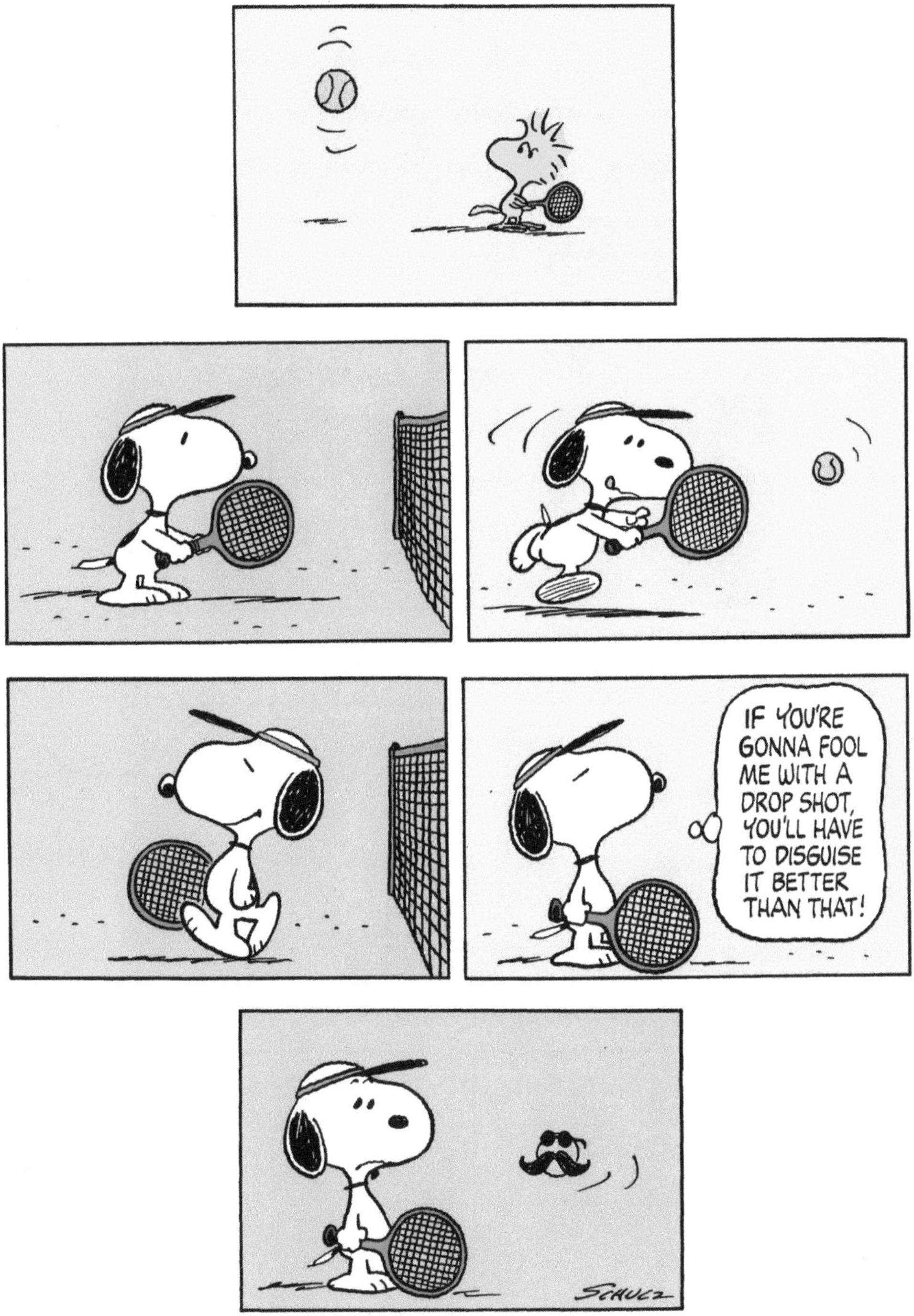
IF YOU'RE GONNA FOOL ME WITH A DROP SHOT, YOU'LL HAVE TO DISGUISE IT BETTER THAN THAT!
SCHULZ

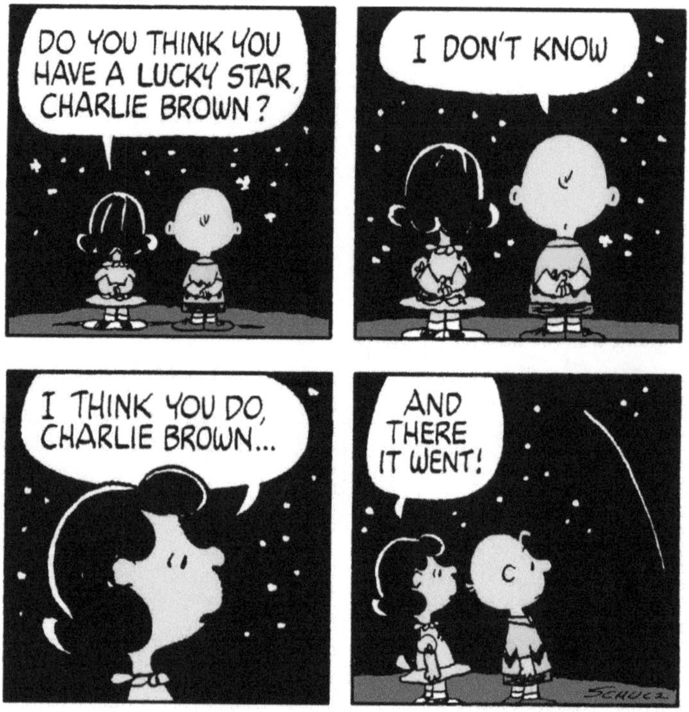
DO YOU THINK YOU HAVE A LUCKY STAR, CHARLIE BROWN?
I DON'T KNOW
I THINK YOU DO, CHARLIE BROWN...
AND THERE IT WENT!

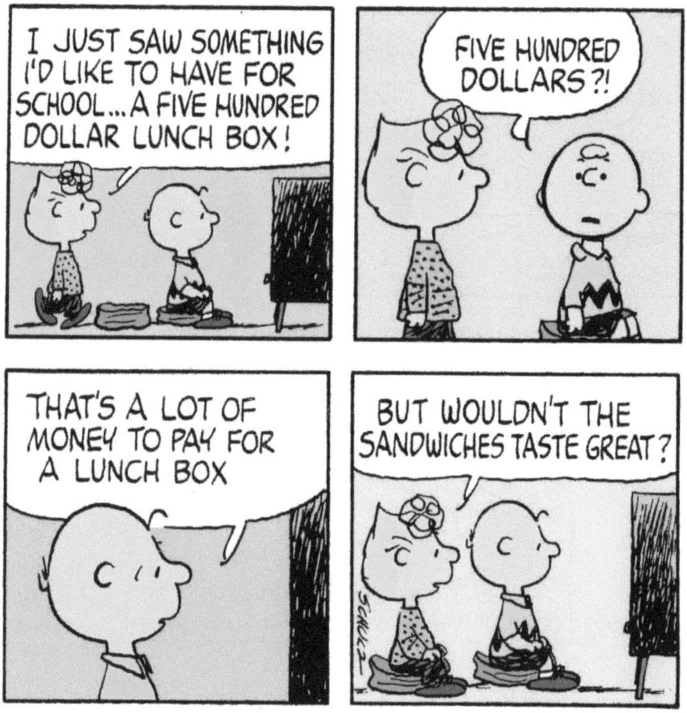
I JUST SAW SOMETHING I'D LIKE TO HAVE FOR SCHOOL...A FIVE HUNDRED DOLLAR LUNCH BOX!
FIVE HUNDRED DOLLARS?!
THAT'S A LOT OF MONEY TO PAY FOR A LUNCH BOX
BUT WOULDN'T THE SANDWICHES TASTE GREAT?

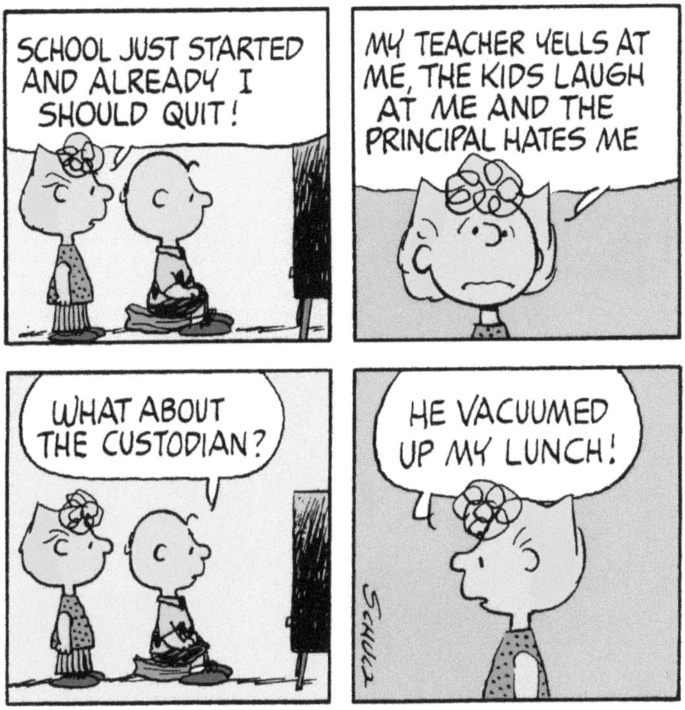
SCHOOL JUST STARTED AND ALREADY I SHOULD QUIT!
MY TEACHER YELLS AT ME, THE KIDS LAUGH AT ME AND THE PRINCIPAL HATES ME
WHAT ABOUT THE CUSTODIAN?
HE VACUUMED UP MY LUNCH!
SCHULZ

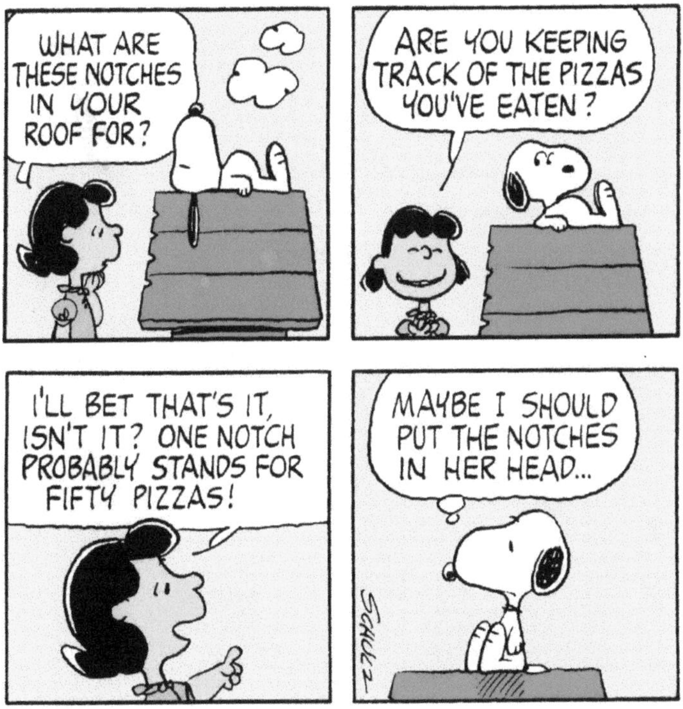
WHAT ARE THESE NOTCHES IN YOUR ROOF FOR?
ARE YOU KEEPING TRACK OF THE PIZZAS YOU'VE EATEN?
I'LL BET THAT'S IT, ISN'T IT? ONE NOTCH PROBABLY STANDS FOR FIFTY PIZZAS!
MAYBE I SHOULD PUT THE NOTCHES IN HER HEAD...
SCHULZ

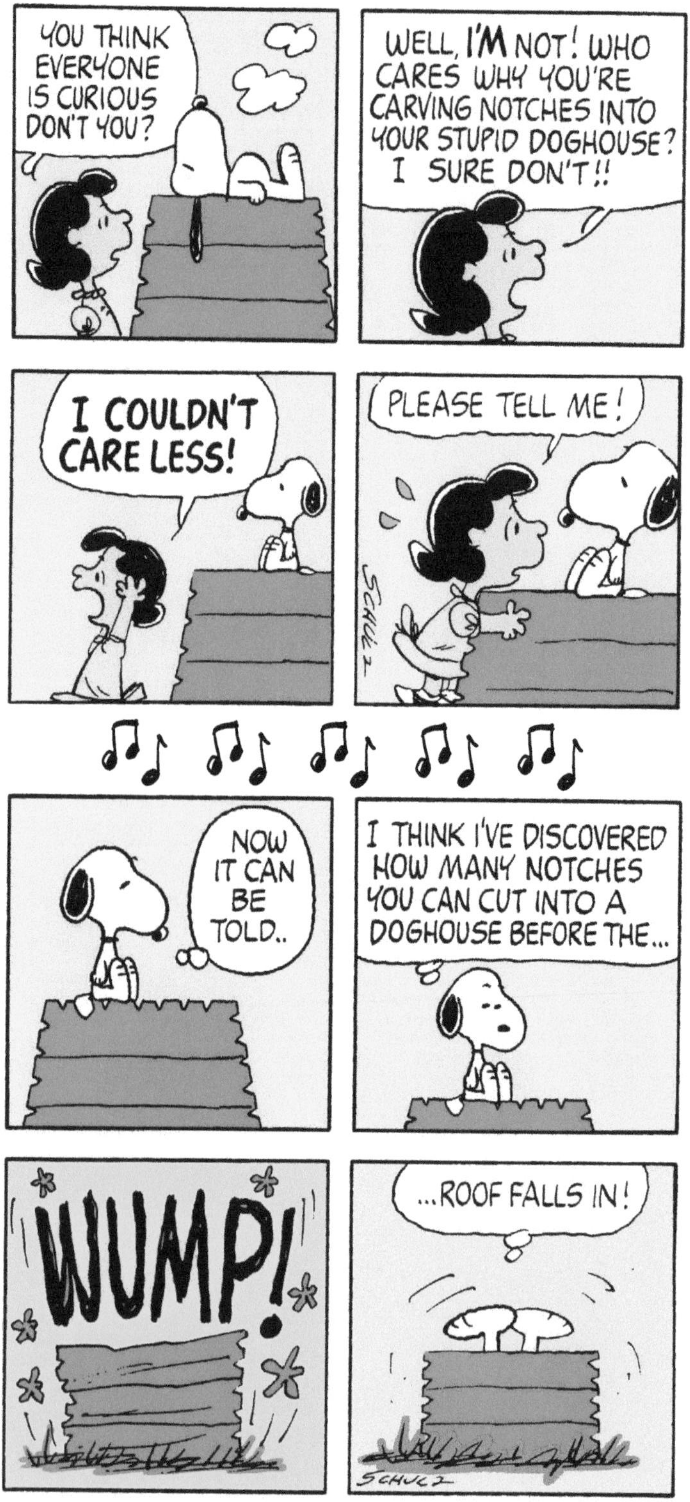
YOU THINK EVERYONE IS CURIOUS DON'T YOU?
WELL, I'M NOT! WHO CARES WHY YOU'RE CARVING NOTCHES INTO YOUR STUPID DOGHOUSE? I SURE DON'T!!
I COULDN'T CARE LESS!
PLEASE TELL ME!
SCHULZ
NOW IT CAN BE TOLD..
I THINK I'VE DISCOVERED HOW MANY NOTCHES YOU CAN CUT INTO A DOGHOUSE BEFORE THE...
WUMP!
...ROOF FALLS IN!
SCHULZ

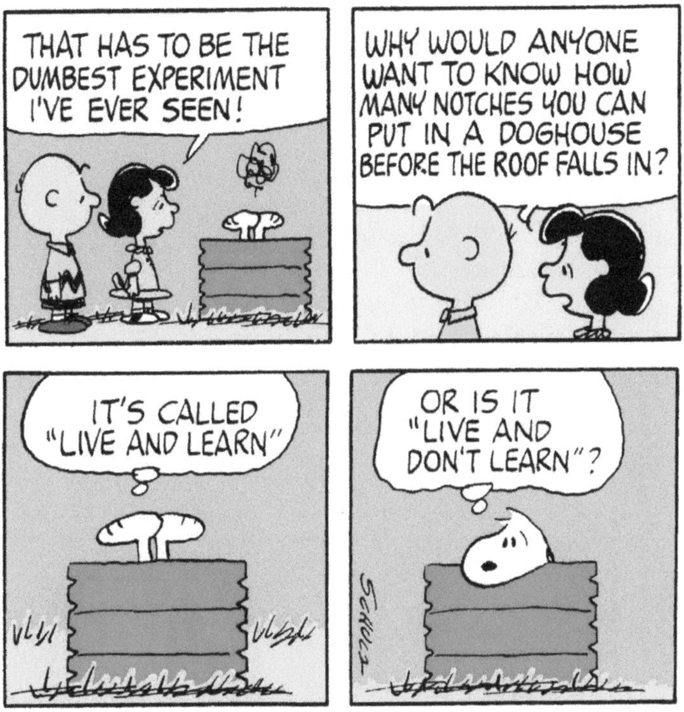
THAT HAS TO BE THE DUMBEST EXPERIMENT I'VE EVER SEEN!
WHY WOULD ANYONE WANT TO KNOW HOW MANY NOTCHES YOU CAN PUT IN A DOGHOUSE BEFORE THE ROOF FALLS IN?
IT'S CALLED "LIVE AND LEARN"
OR IS IT "LIVE AND DON'T LEARN"?
SCHULZ

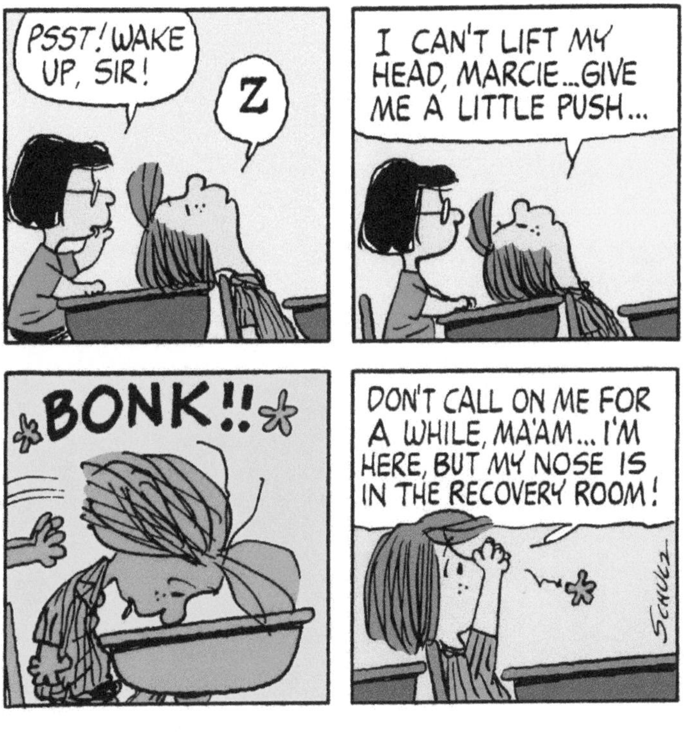
PSST! WAKE UP, SIR!
Z
I CAN'T LIFT MY HEAD, MARCIE...GIVE ME A LITTLE PUSH...
BONK!!
DON'T CALL ON ME FOR A WHILE, MA'AM... I'M HERE, BUT MY NOSE IS IN THE RECOVERY ROOM!
SCHULZ

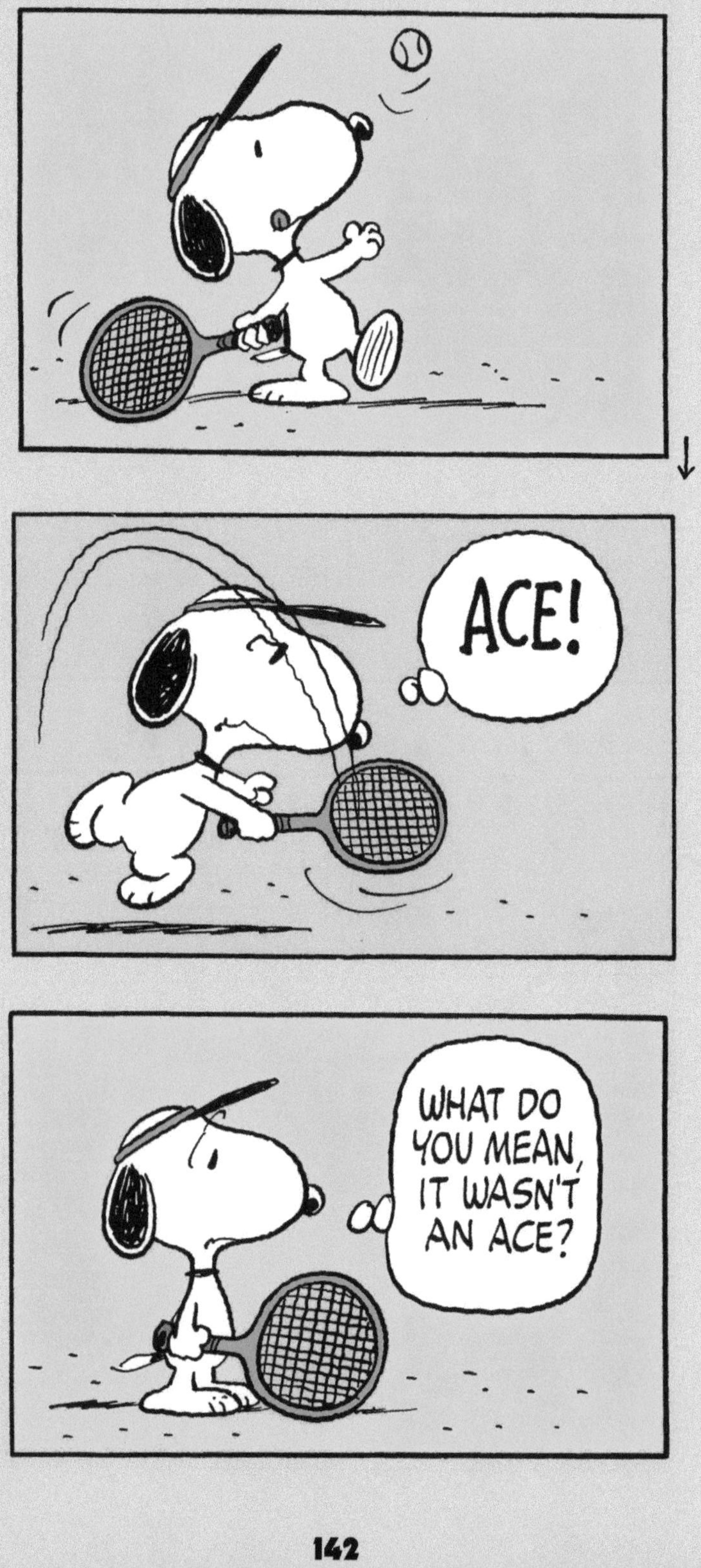
ACE!
WHAT DO YOU MEAN, IT WASN'T AN ACE?

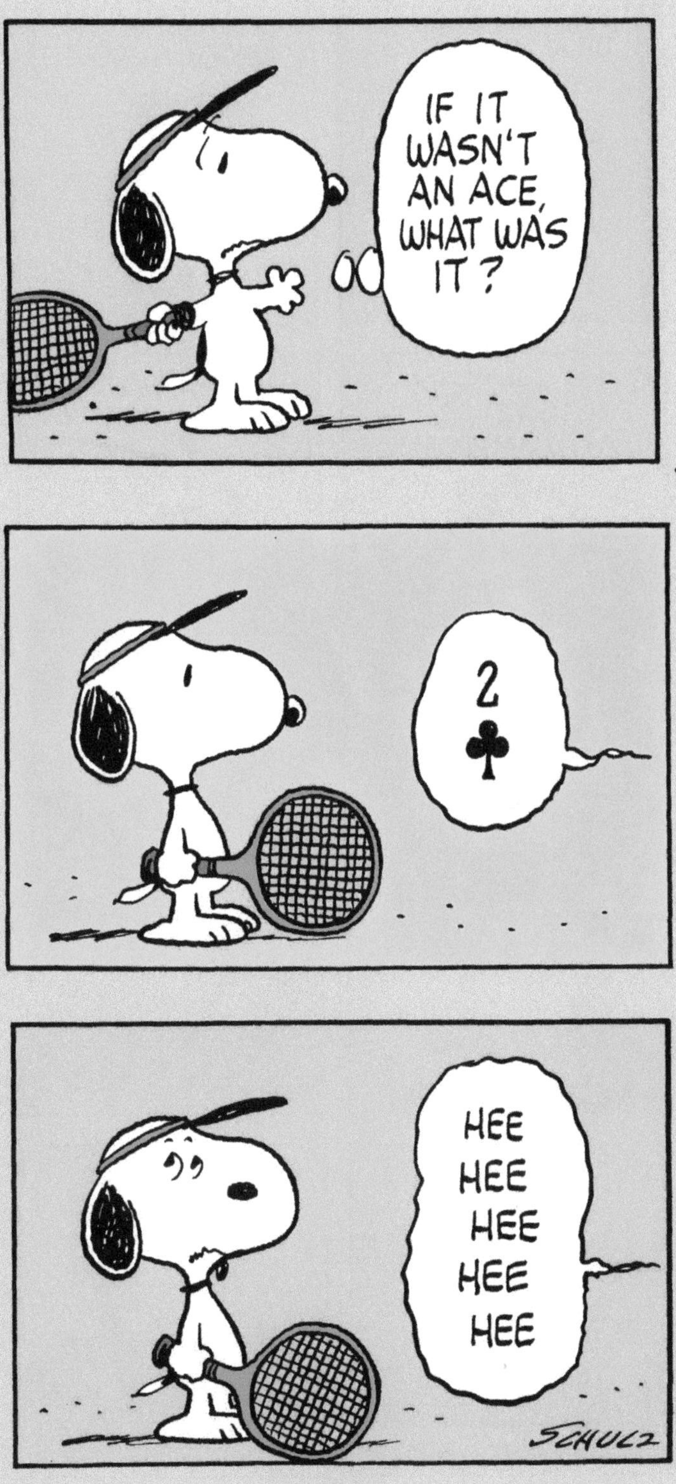
IF IT WASN'T AN ACE, WHAT WAS IT ?
2 ♣
HEE HEE HEE HEE HEE
SCHULZ

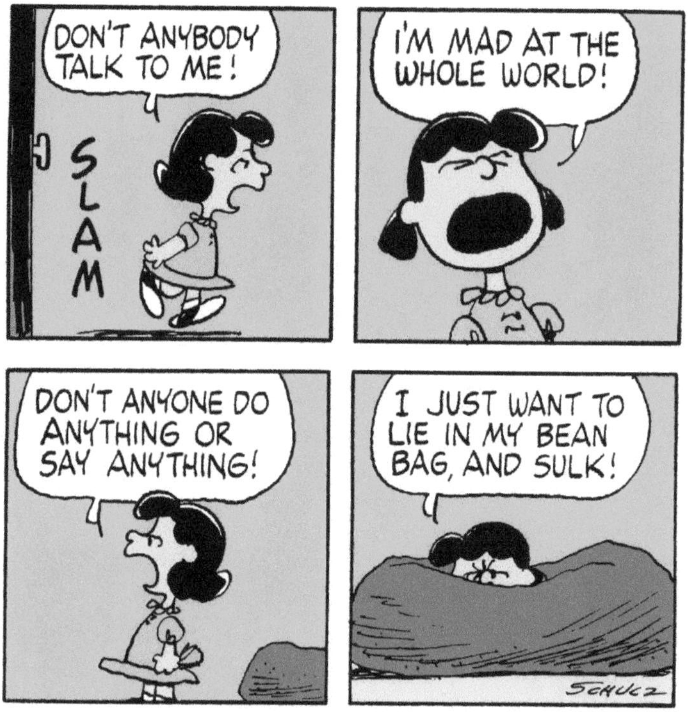
DON'T ANYBODY TALK TO ME!
SLAM
I'M MAD AT THE WHOLE WORLD!
DON'T ANYONE DO ANYTHING OR SAY ANYTHING!
I JUST WANT TO LIE IN MY BEAN BAG, AND SULK!
SCHULZ

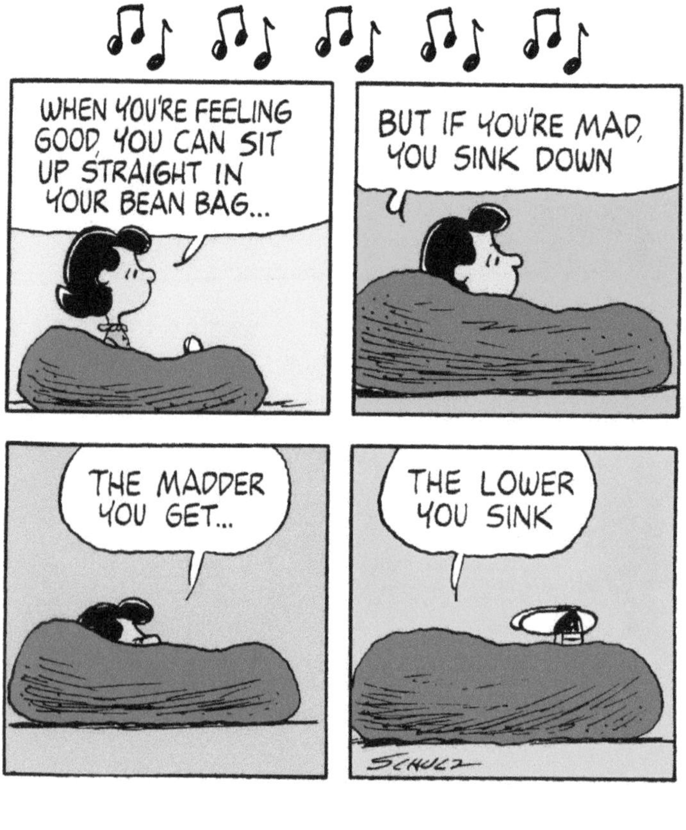
WHEN YOU'RE FEELING GOOD, YOU CAN SIT UP STRAIGHT IN YOUR BEAN BAG...
BUT IF YOU'RE MAD, YOU SINK DOWN
THE MADDER YOU GET...
THE LOWER YOU SINK
SCHULZ

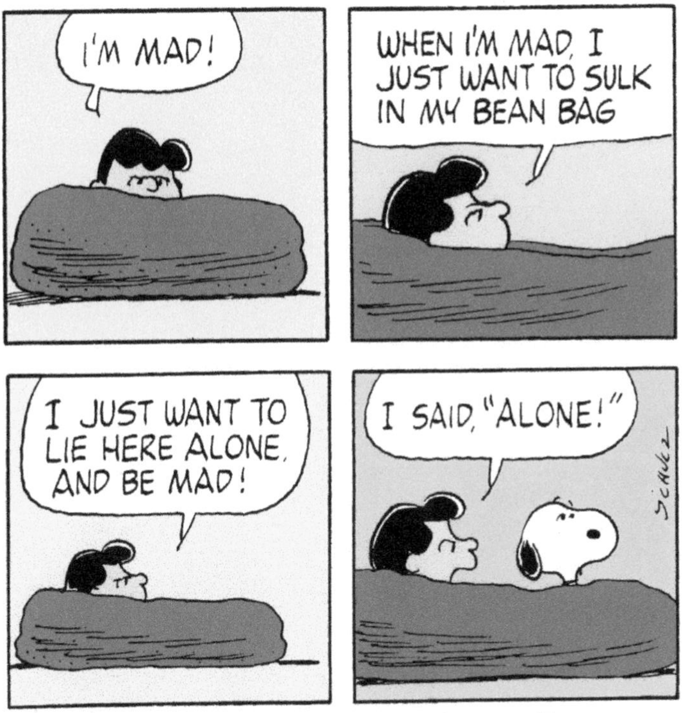
I'M MAD!
WHEN I'M MAD, I JUST WANT TO SULK IN MY BEAN BAG
I JUST WANT TO LIE HERE ALONE AND BE MAD!
I SAID, "ALONE!"
SCHULZ

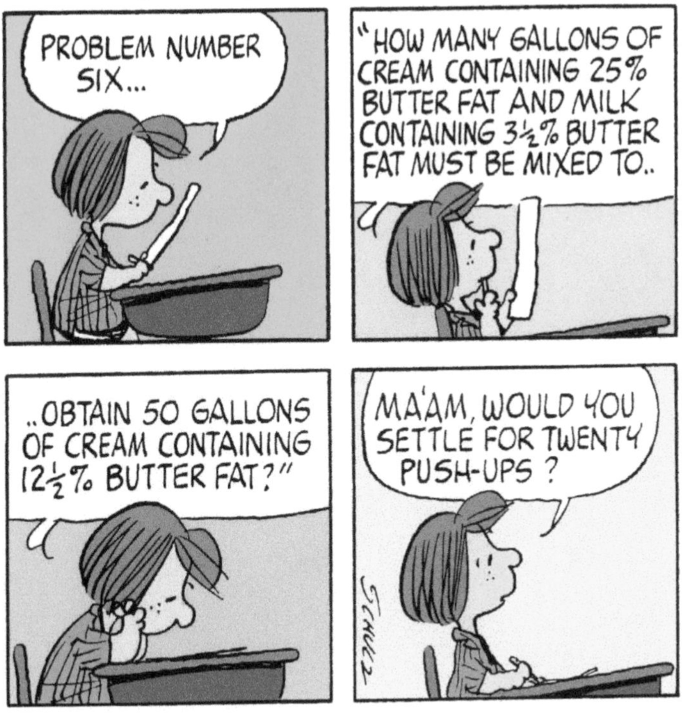
PROBLEM NUMBER SIX...
"HOW MANY GALLONS OF CREAM CONTAINING 25% BUTTER FAT AND MILK CONTAINING 3½% BUTTER FAT MUST BE MIXED TO..
..OBTAIN 50 GALLONS OF CREAM CONTAINING 12½% BUTTER FAT?"
MA'AM, WOULD YOU SETTLE FOR TWENTY PUSH-UPS?
SCHULZ

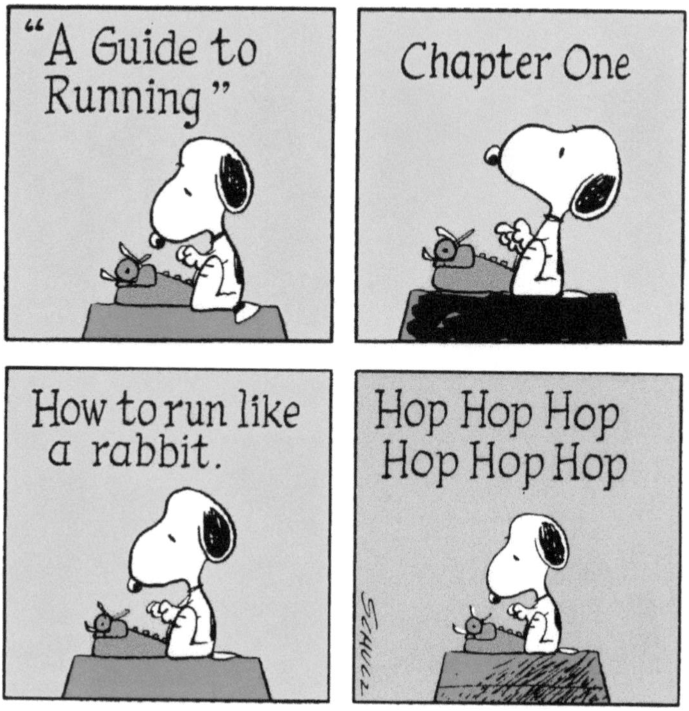
"A Guide to Running"
Chapter One
How to run like a rabbit.
Hop Hop Hop Hop Hop Hop
SCHULZ

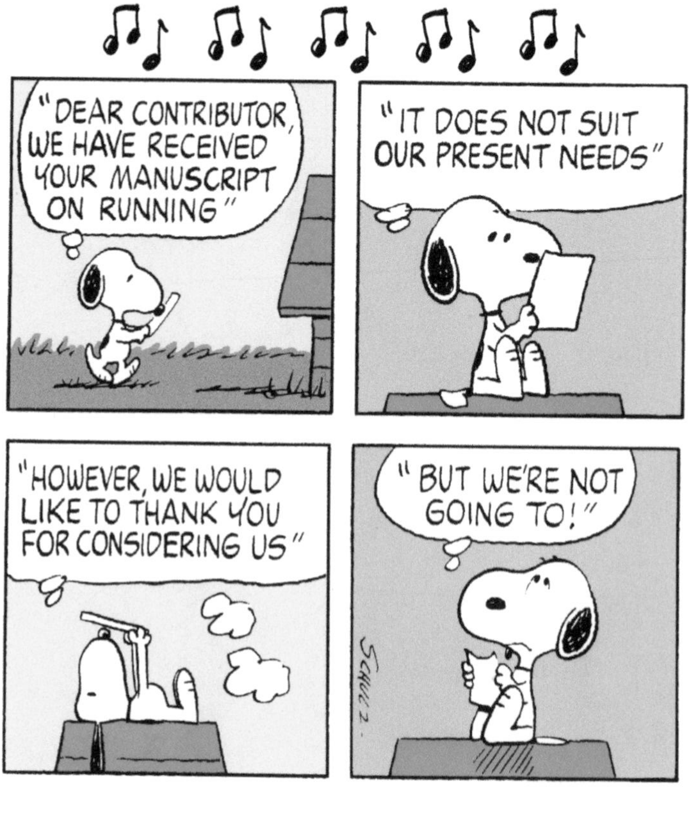
"DEAR CONTRIBUTOR, WE HAVE RECEIVED YOUR MANUSCRIPT ON RUNNING"
"IT DOES NOT SUIT OUR PRESENT NEEDS"
"HOWEVER, WE WOULD LIKE TO THANK YOU FOR CONSIDERING US"
"BUT WE'RE NOT GOING TO!"
SCHULZ

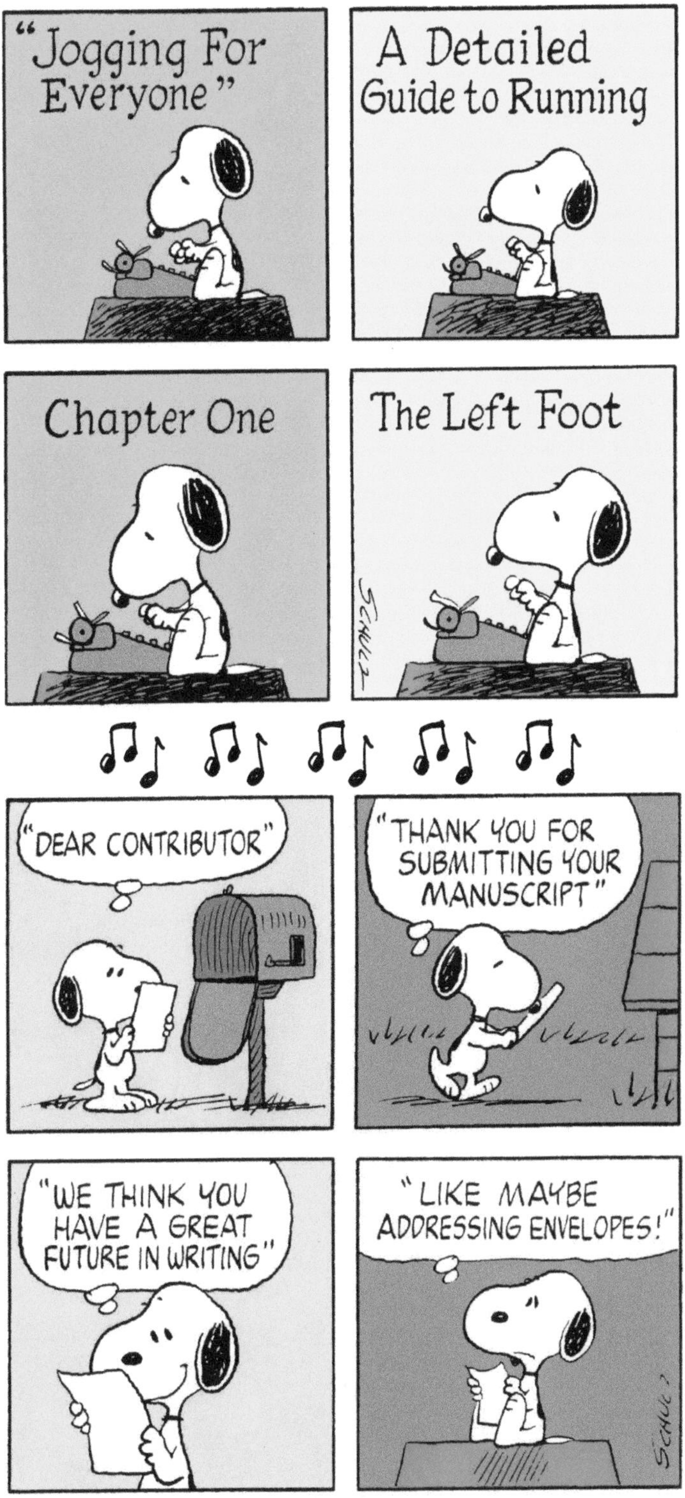
"Jogging For Everyone"
A Detailed Guide to Running
Chapter One
The Left Foot
"DEAR CONTRIBUTOR"
"THANK YOU FOR SUBMITTING YOUR MANUSCRIPT"
"WE THINK YOU HAVE A GREAT FUTURE IN WRITING"
"LIKE MAYBE ADDRESSING ENVELOPES!"

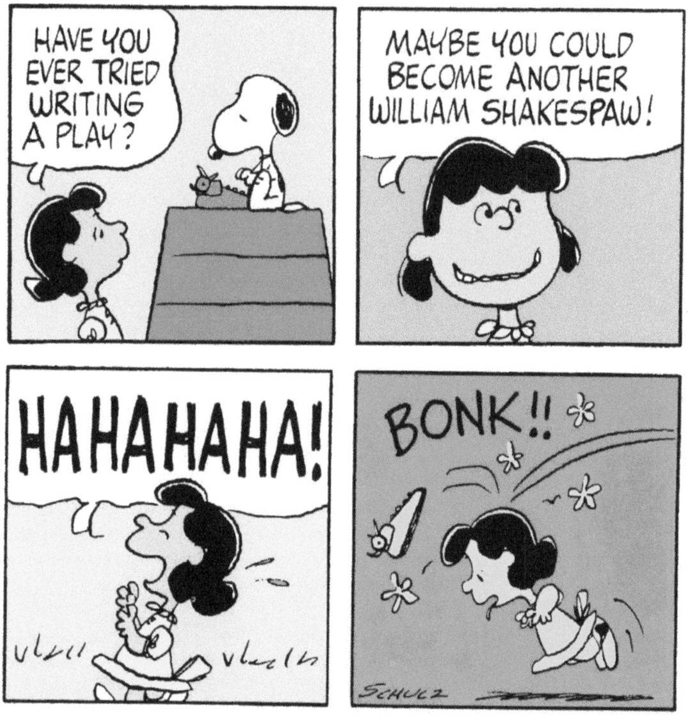
HAVE YOU EVER TRIED WRITING A PLAY?
MAYBE YOU COULD BECOME ANOTHER WILLIAM SHAKESPAW!
HAHAHAHA!
BONK!!
SCHULZ

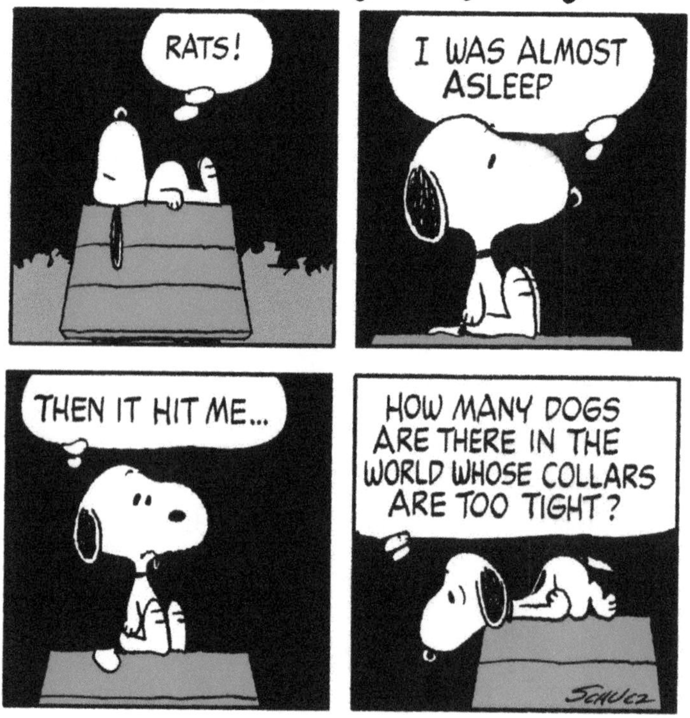
RATS!
I WAS ALMOST ASLEEP
THEN IT HIT ME...
HOW MANY DOGS ARE THERE IN THE WORLD WHOSE COLLARS ARE TOO TIGHT?
SCHULZ

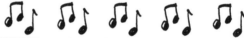

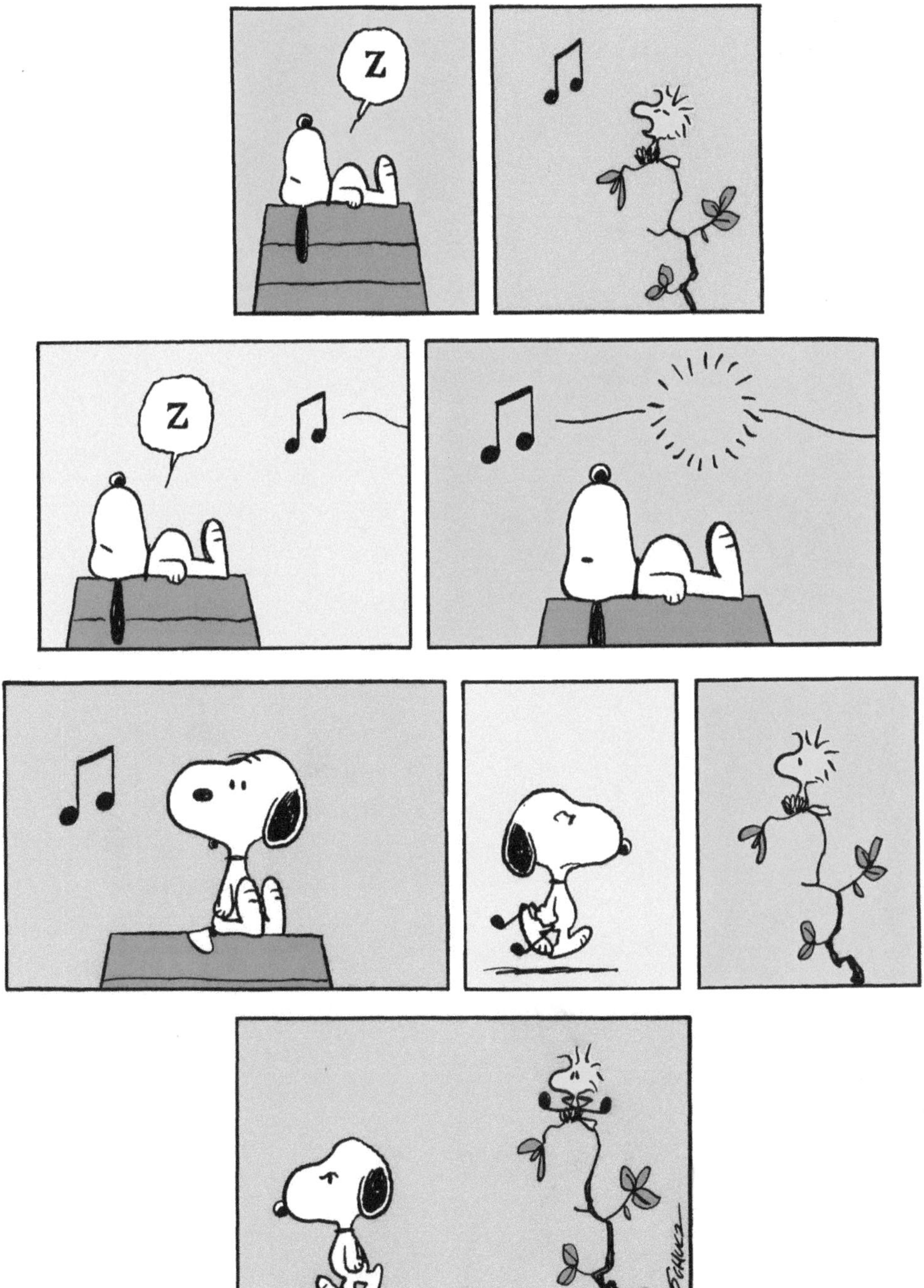
Z
Z

Z
Z

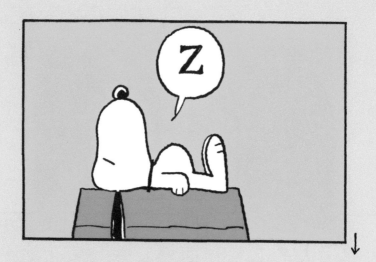

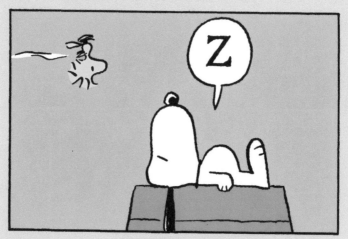

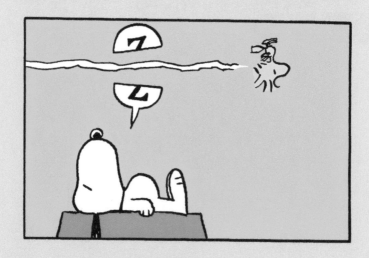

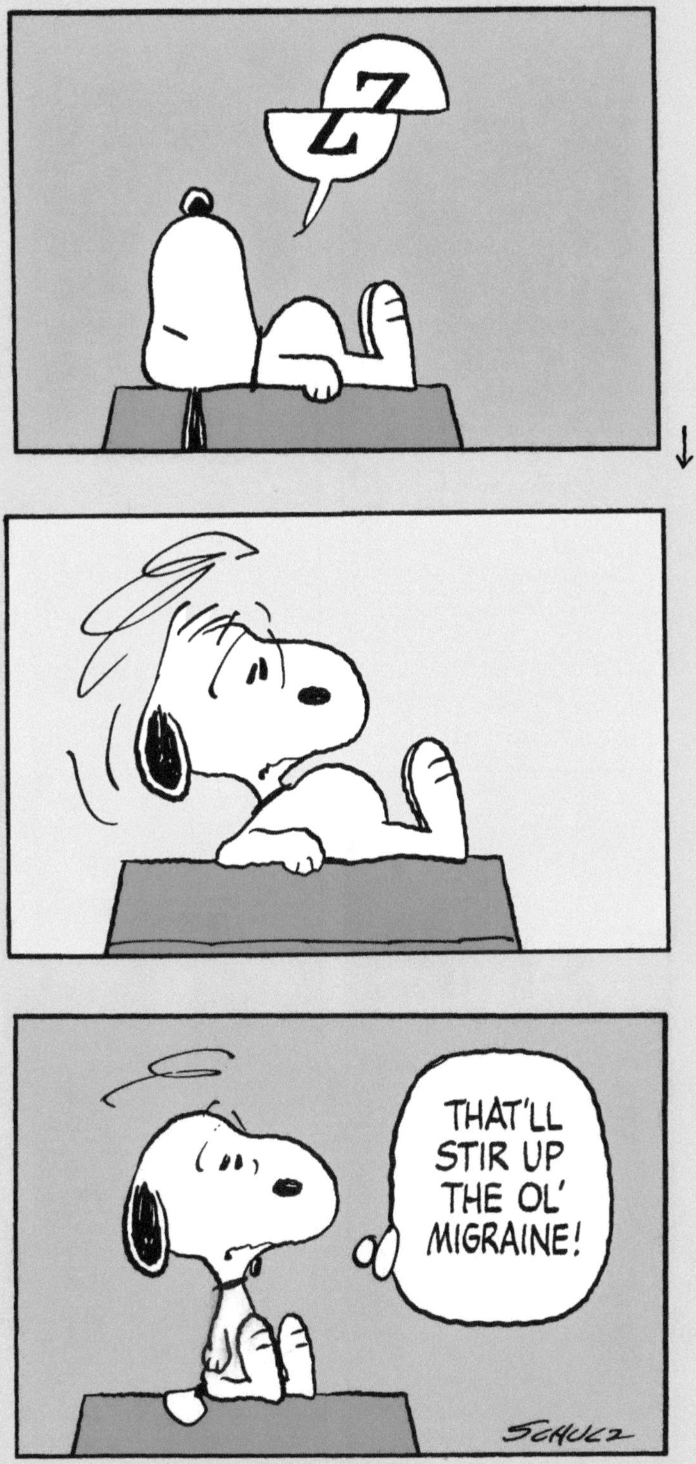
Z
Z
THAT'LL STIR UP THE OL' MIGRAINE!
SCHULZ

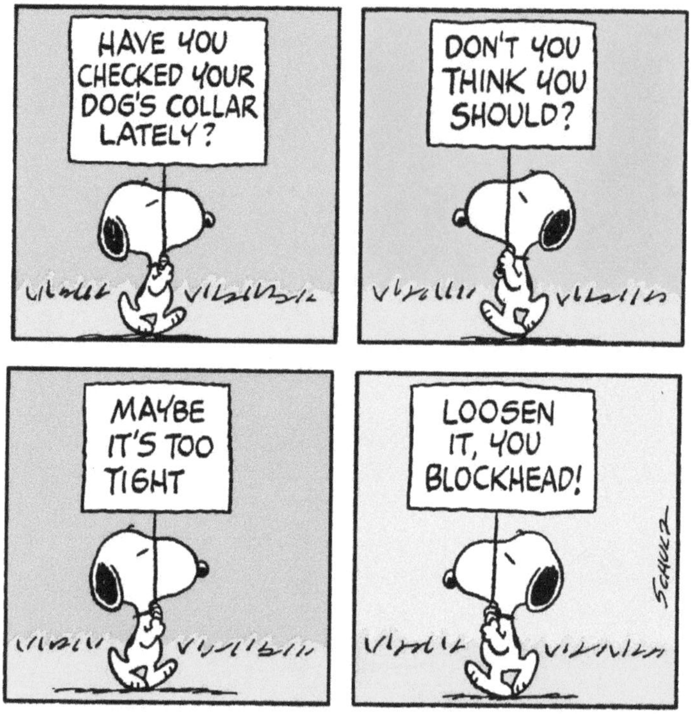
HAVE YOU CHECKED YOUR DOG'S COLLAR LATELY?
DON'T YOU THINK YOU SHOULD?
MAYBE IT'S TOO TIGHT
LOOSEN IT, YOU BLOCKHEAD!
SCHULZ

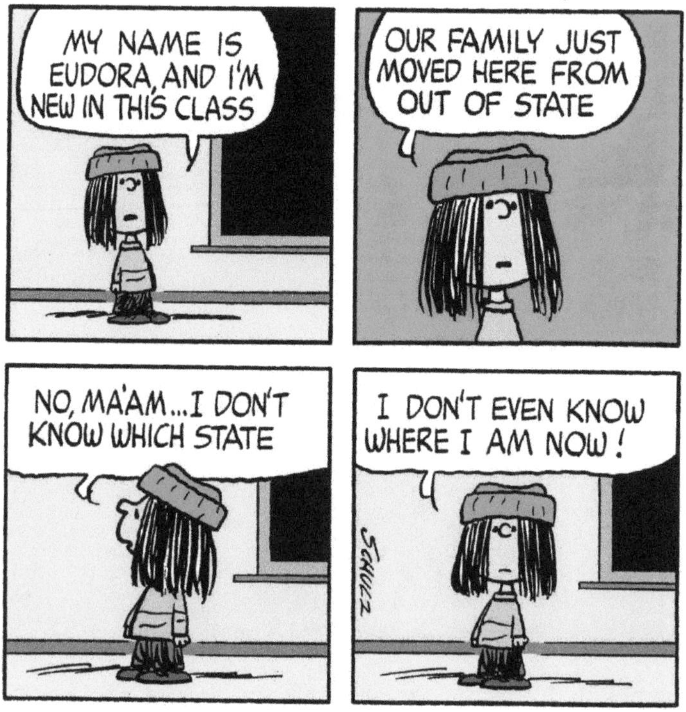
MY NAME IS EUDORA, AND I'M NEW IN THIS CLASS
OUR FAMILY JUST MOVED HERE FROM OUT OF STATE
NO, MA'AM...I DON'T KNOW WHICH STATE
I DON'T EVEN KNOW WHERE I AM NOW!
SCHULZ

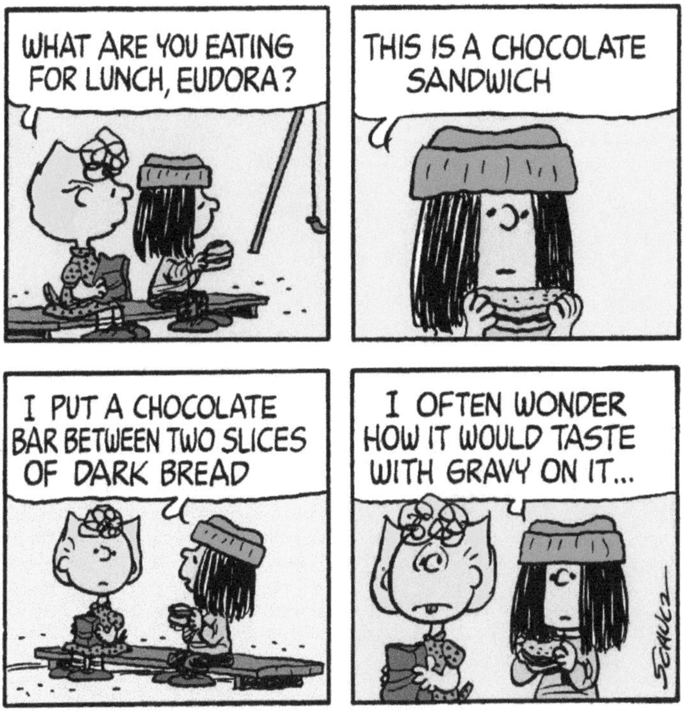
WHAT ARE YOU EATING FOR LUNCH, EUDORA?
THIS IS A CHOCOLATE SANDWICH
I PUT A CHOCOLATE BAR BETWEEN TWO SLICES OF DARK BREAD
I OFTEN WONDER HOW IT WOULD TASTE WITH GRAVY ON IT...
SCHULZ

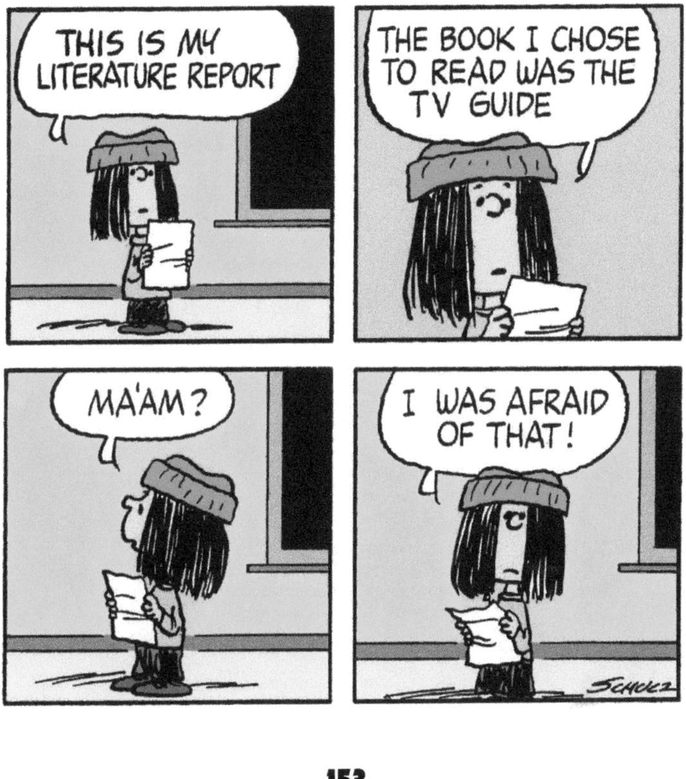
THIS IS MY LITERATURE REPORT
THE BOOK I CHOSE TO READ WAS THE TV GUIDE
MA'AM?
I WAS AFRAID OF THAT!
SCHULZ

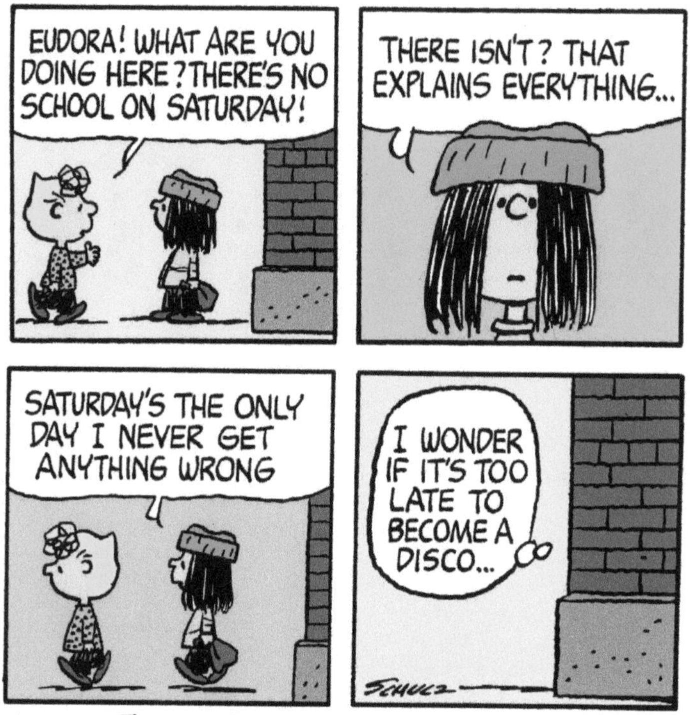
EUDORA! WHAT ARE YOU DOING HERE? THERE'S NO SCHOOL ON SATURDAY!
THERE ISN'T? THAT EXPLAINS EVERYTHING...
SATURDAY'S THE ONLY DAY I NEVER GET ANYTHING WRONG
I WONDER IF IT'S TOO LATE TO BECOME A DISCO...
SCHULZ

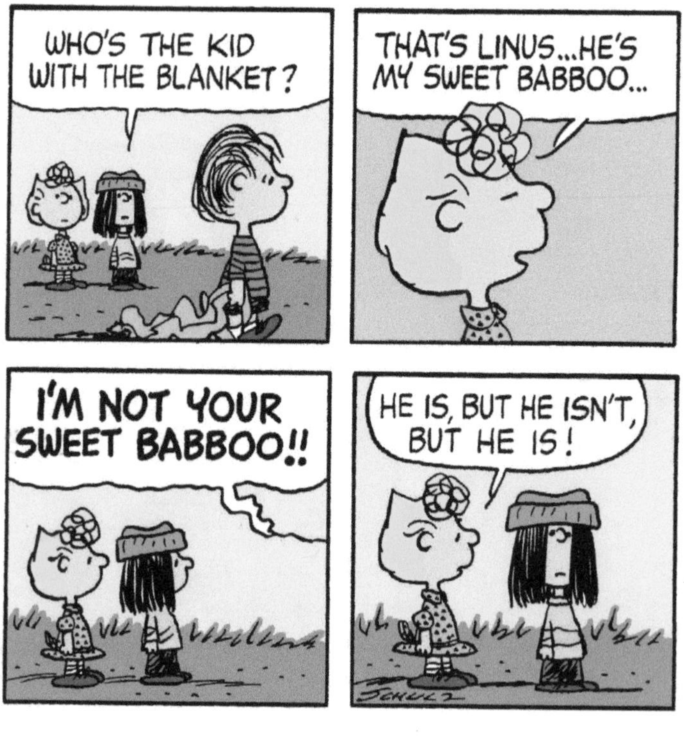
WHO'S THE KID WITH THE BLANKET?
THAT'S LINUS...HE'S MY SWEET BABBOO...
I'M NOT YOUR SWEET BABBOO!!
HE IS, BUT HE ISN'T, BUT HE IS!
SCHULZ

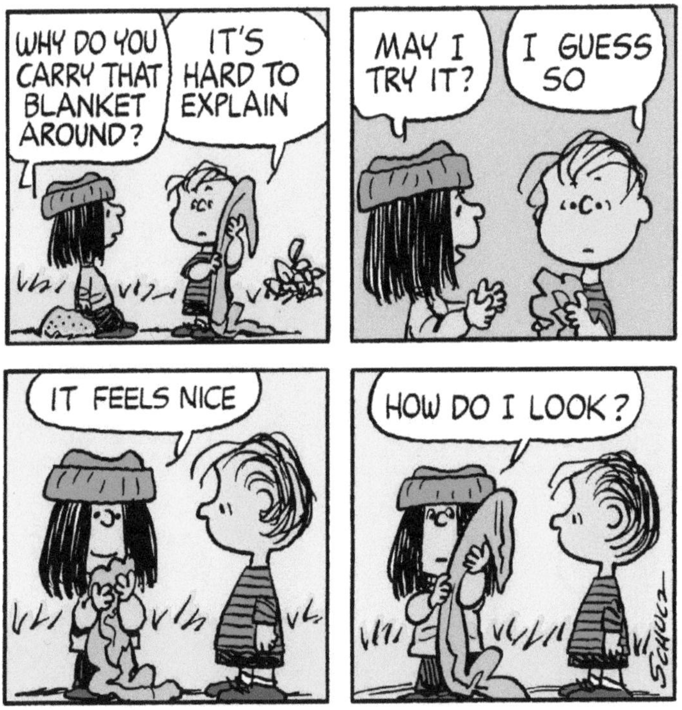
WHY DO YOU CARRY THAT BLANKET AROUND?
IT'S HARD TO EXPLAIN
MAY I TRY IT?
I GUESS SO
IT FEELS NICE
HOW DO I LOOK?
SCHULZ

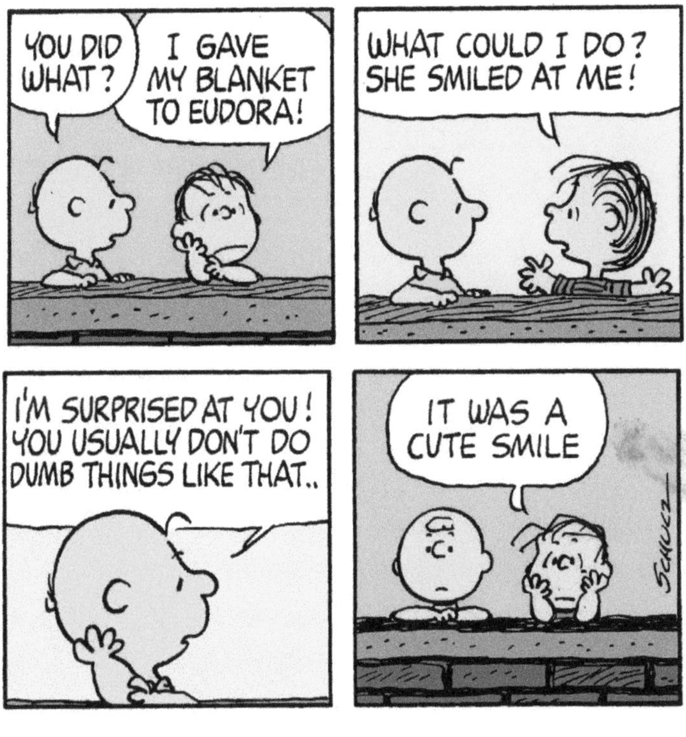
YOU DID WHAT?
I GAVE MY BLANKET TO EUDORA!
WHAT COULD I DO? SHE SMILED AT ME!
I'M SURPRISED AT YOU! YOU USUALLY DON'T DO DUMB THINGS LIKE THAT..
IT WAS A CUTE SMILE
SCHULZ

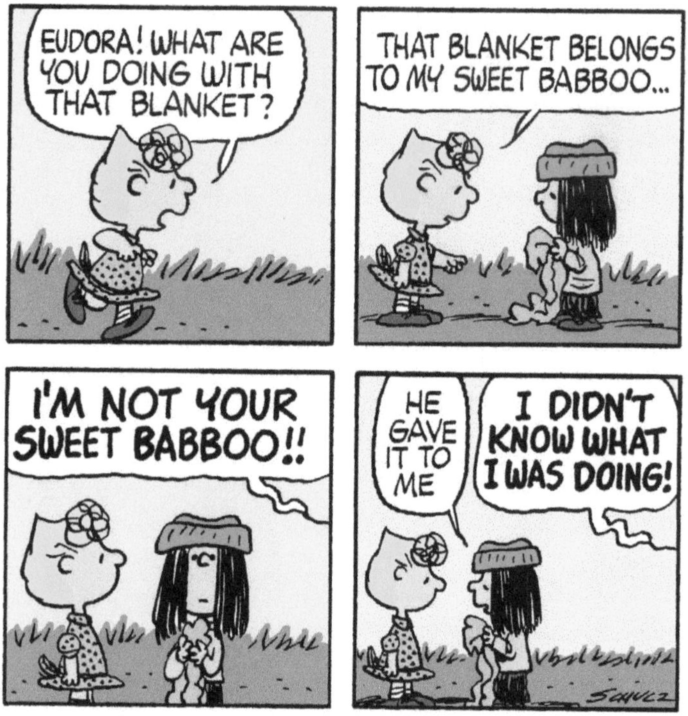
EUDORA! WHAT ARE YOU DOING WITH THAT BLANKET?
THAT BLANKET BELONGS TO MY SWEET BABBOO...
I'M NOT YOUR SWEET BABBOO!!
HE GAVE IT TO ME
I DIDN'T KNOW WHAT I WAS DOING!
SCHULZ

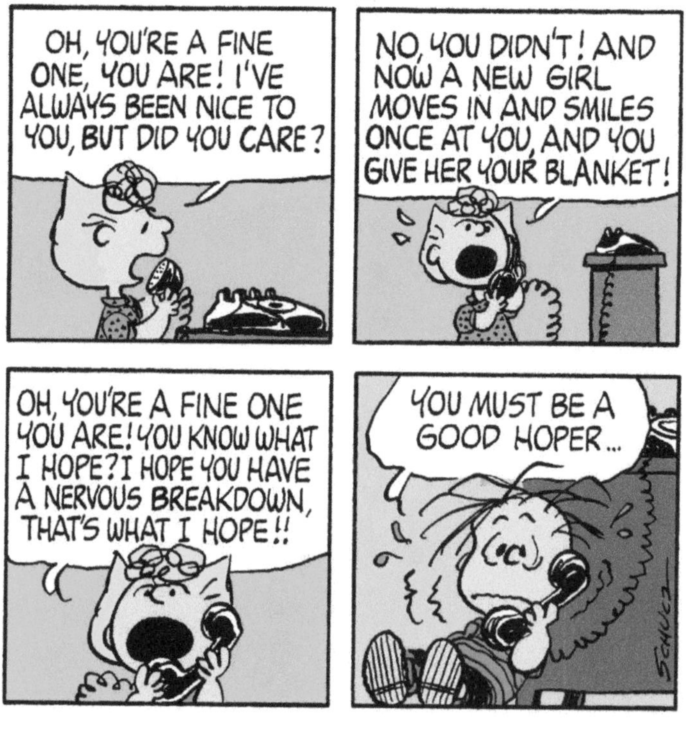
OH, YOU'RE A FINE ONE, YOU ARE! I'VE ALWAYS BEEN NICE TO YOU, BUT DID YOU CARE?
NO, YOU DIDN'T! AND NOW A NEW GIRL MOVES IN AND SMILES ONCE AT YOU, AND YOU GIVE HER YOUR BLANKET!
OH, YOU'RE A FINE ONE YOU ARE! YOU KNOW WHAT I HOPE? I HOPE YOU HAVE A NERVOUS BREAKDOWN, THAT'S WHAT I HOPE!!
YOU MUST BE A GOOD HOPER...
SCHULZ

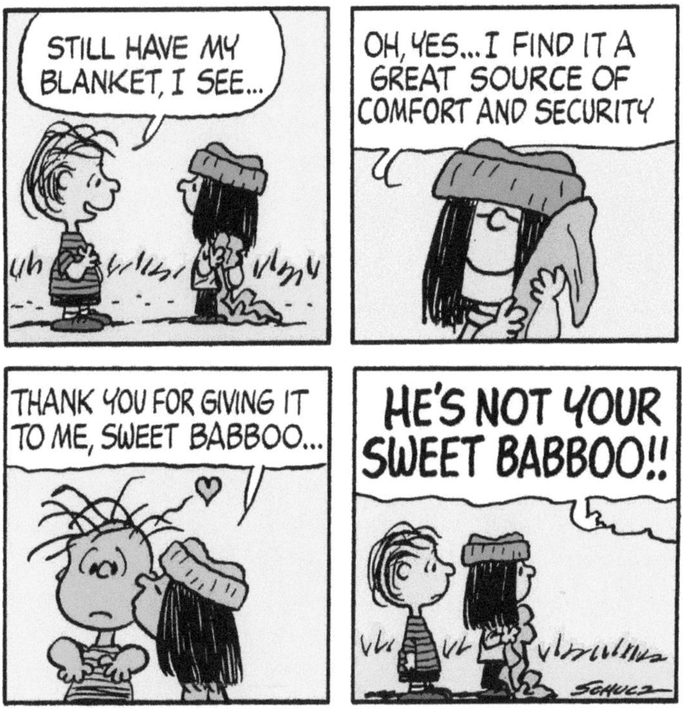
STILL HAVE MY BLANKET, I SEE...
OH, YES...I FIND IT A GREAT SOURCE OF COMFORT AND SECURITY
THANK YOU FOR GIVING IT TO ME, SWEET BABBOO...
HE'S NOT YOUR SWEET BABBOO!!
SCHULZ

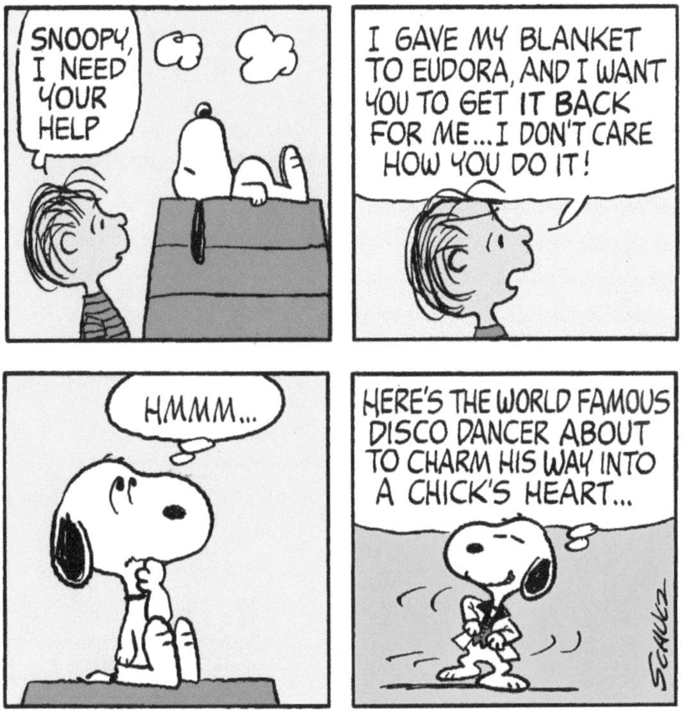
SNOOPY, I NEED YOUR HELP
I GAVE MY BLANKET TO EUDORA, AND I WANT YOU TO GET IT BACK FOR ME...I DON'T CARE HOW YOU DO IT!
HMMM...
HERE'S THE WORLD FAMOUS DISCO DANCER ABOUT TO CHARM HIS WAY INTO A CHICK'S HEART...
SCHULZ

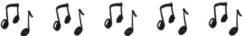

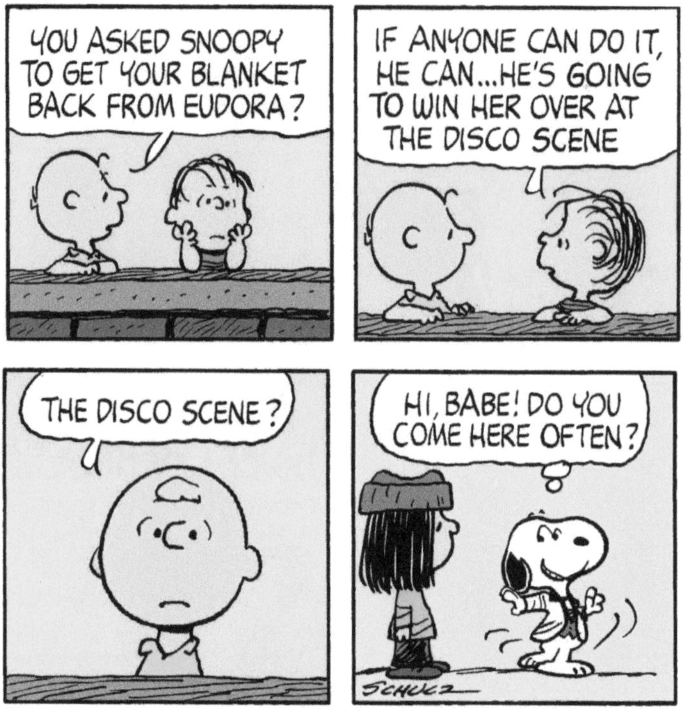
YOU ASKED SNOOPY TO GET YOUR BLANKET BACK FROM EUDORA?
IF ANYONE CAN DO IT, HE CAN...HE'S GOING TO WIN HER OVER AT THE DISCO SCENE
THE DISCO SCENE?
HI, BABE! DO YOU COME HERE OFTEN?

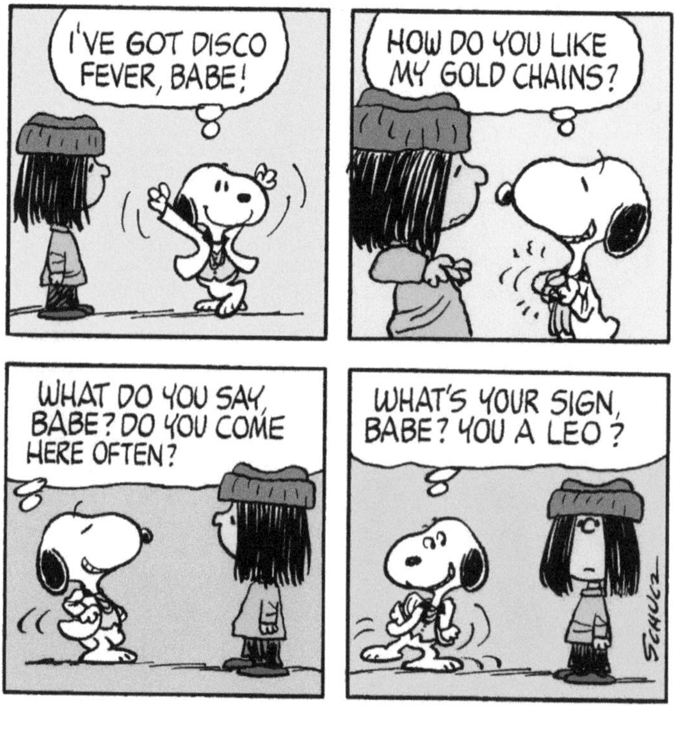
I'VE GOT DISCO FEVER, BABE!
HOW DO YOU LIKE MY GOLD CHAINS?
WHAT DO YOU SAY, BABE? DO YOU COME HERE OFTEN?
WHAT'S YOUR SIGN, BABE? YOU A LEO?

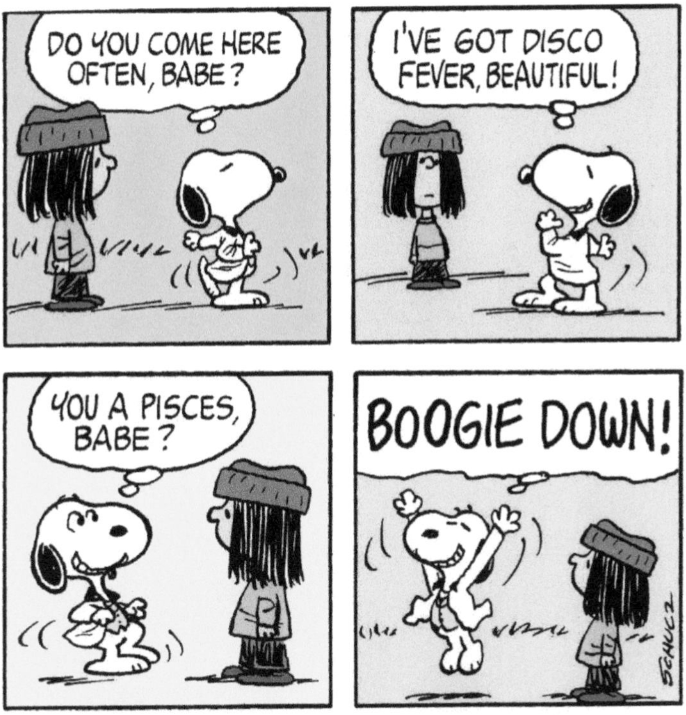
DO YOU COME HERE OFTEN, BABE?
I'VE GOT DISCO FEVER, BEAUTIFUL!
YOU A PISCES, BABE?
BOOGIE DOWN!
SCHULZ

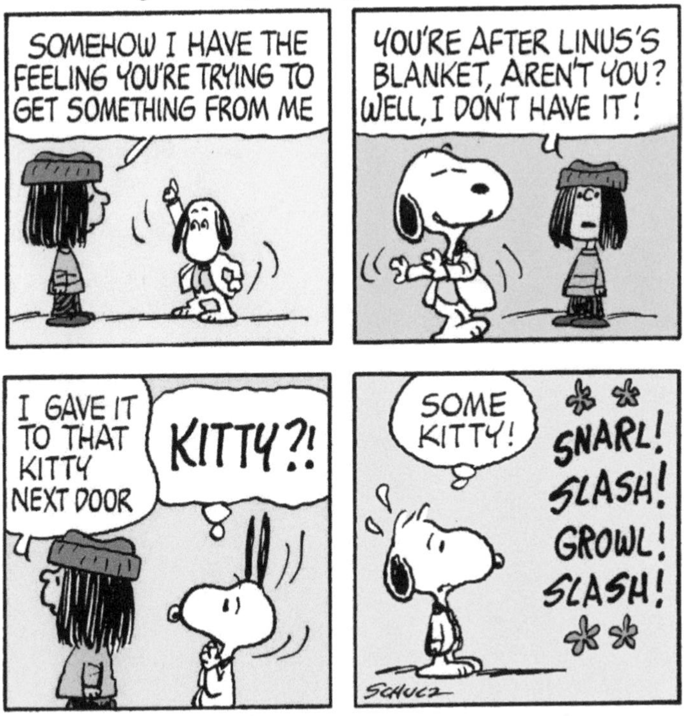
SOMEHOW I HAVE THE FEELING YOU'RE TRYING TO GET SOMETHING FROM ME
YOU'RE AFTER LINUS'S BLANKET, AREN'T YOU? WELL, I DON'T HAVE IT!
I GAVE IT TO THAT KITTY NEXT DOOR
KITTY?!
SOME KITTY!
SNARL! SLASH! GROWL! SLASH!
SCHULZ

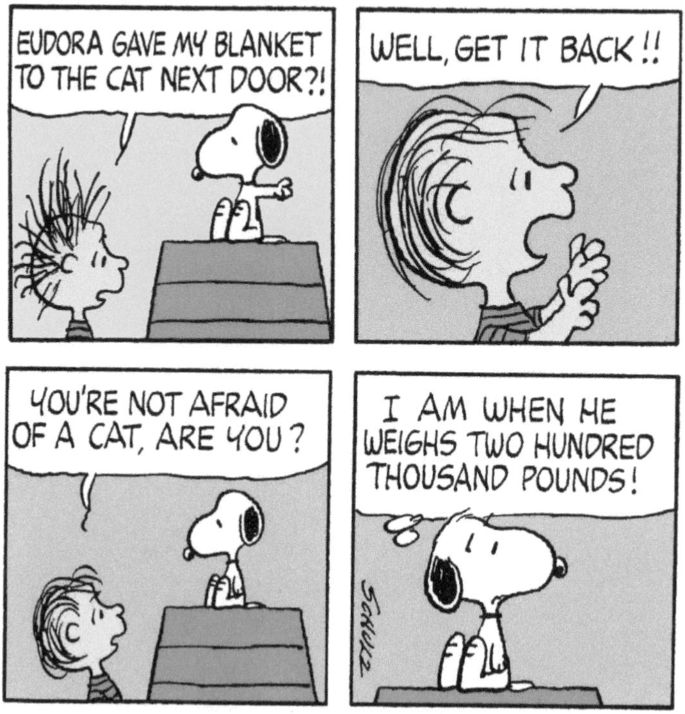
EUDORA GAVE MY BLANKET TO THE CAT NEXT DOOR?!
WELL, GET IT BACK!!
YOU'RE NOT AFRAID OF A CAT, ARE YOU?
I AM WHEN HE WEIGHS TWO HUNDRED THOUSAND POUNDS!

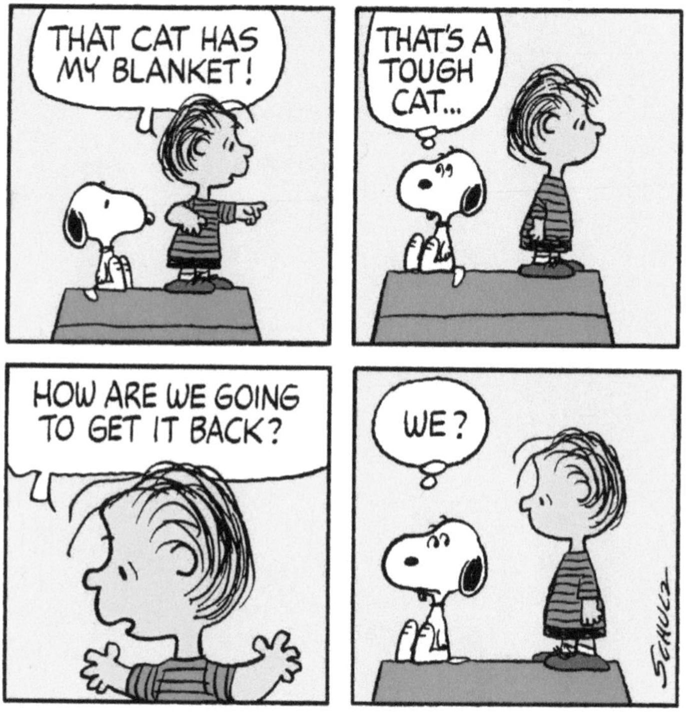
THAT CAT HAS MY BLANKET!
THAT'S A TOUGH CAT...
HOW ARE WE GOING TO GET IT BACK?
WE?

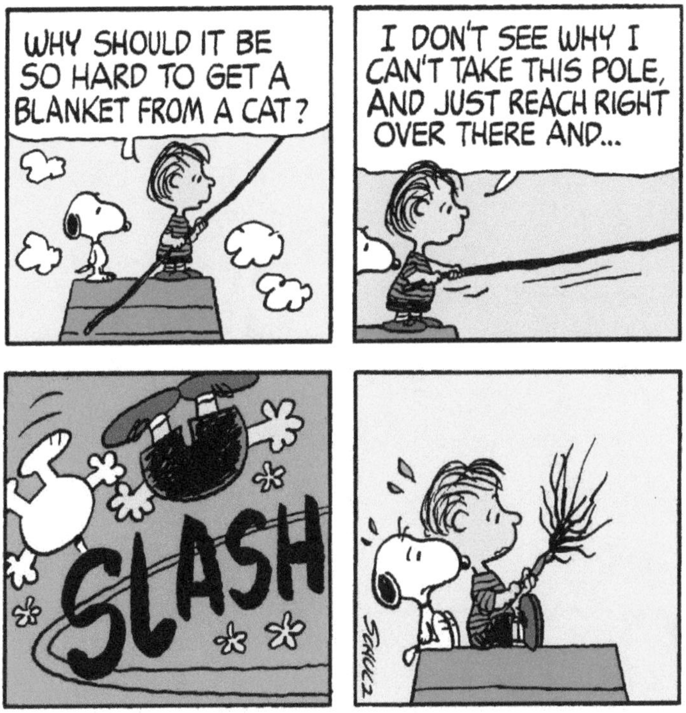
WHY SHOULD IT BE SO HARD TO GET A BLANKET FROM A CAT?
I DON'T SEE WHY I CAN'T TAKE THIS POLE, AND JUST REACH RIGHT OVER THERE AND...
SLASH
SCHULZ

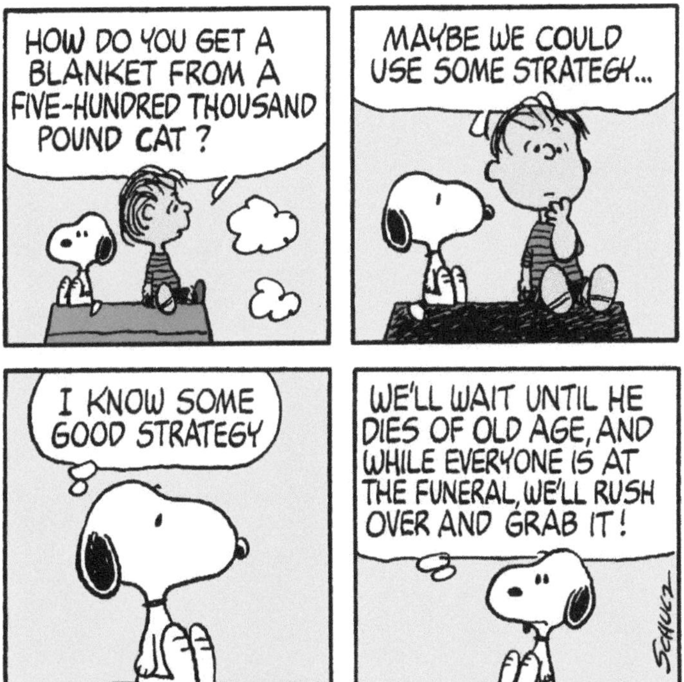
HOW DO YOU GET A BLANKET FROM A FIVE-HUNDRED THOUSAND POUND CAT?
MAYBE WE COULD USE SOME STRATEGY...
I KNOW SOME GOOD STRATEGY
WE'LL WAIT UNTIL HE DIES OF OLD AGE, AND WHILE EVERYONE IS AT THE FUNERAL, WE'LL RUSH OVER AND GRAB IT!
SCHULZ

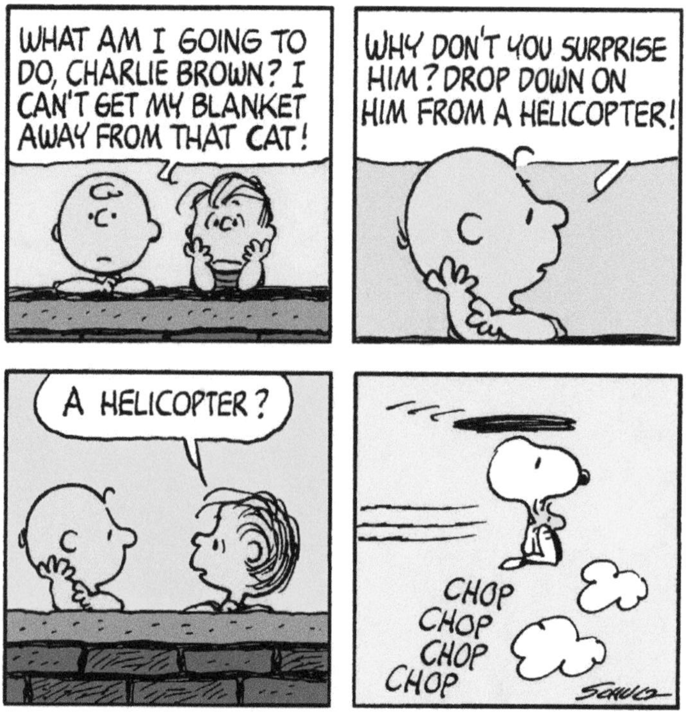
WHAT AM I GOING TO DO, CHARLIE BROWN? I CAN'T GET MY BLANKET AWAY FROM THAT CAT!
WHY DON'T YOU SURPRISE HIM? DROP DOWN ON HIM FROM A HELICOPTER!
A HELICOPTER?
CHOP
CHOP
CHOP
CHOP
SCHULZ

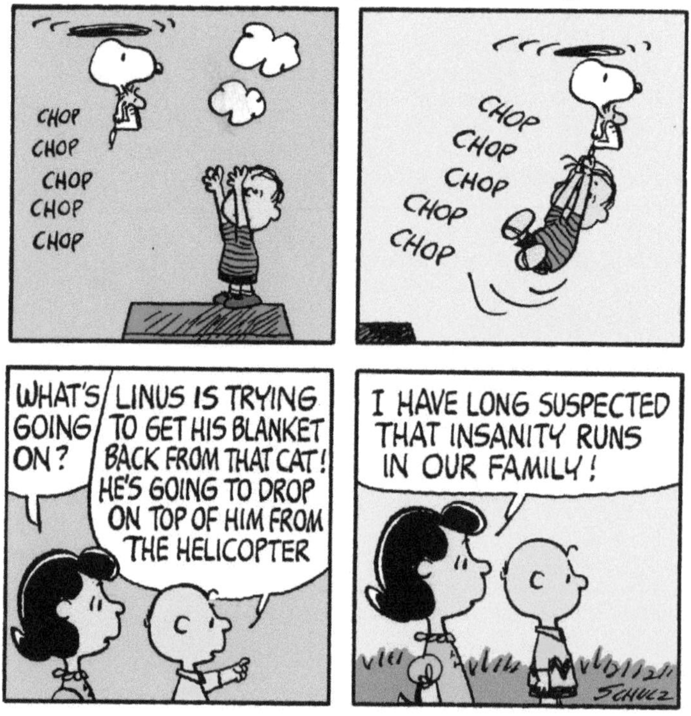
CHOP
CHOP
CHOP
CHOP
CHOP
CHOP
CHOP
CHOP
CHOP
CHOP
WHAT'S GOING ON?
LINUS IS TRYING TO GET HIS BLANKET BACK FROM THAT CAT! HE'S GOING TO DROP ON TOP OF HIM FROM THE HELICOPTER
I HAVE LONG SUSPECTED THAT INSANITY RUNS IN OUR FAMILY!
SCHULZ

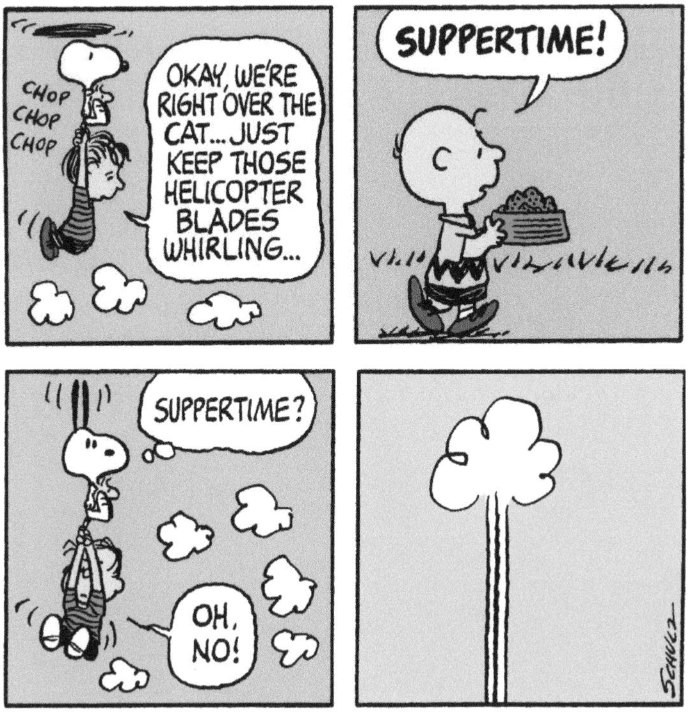
CHOP
CHOP
CHOP
OKAY, WE'RE RIGHT OVER THE CAT... JUST KEEP THOSE HELICOPTER BLADES WHIRLING...
SUPPERTIME!
SUPPERTIME?
OH, NO!
SCHULZ

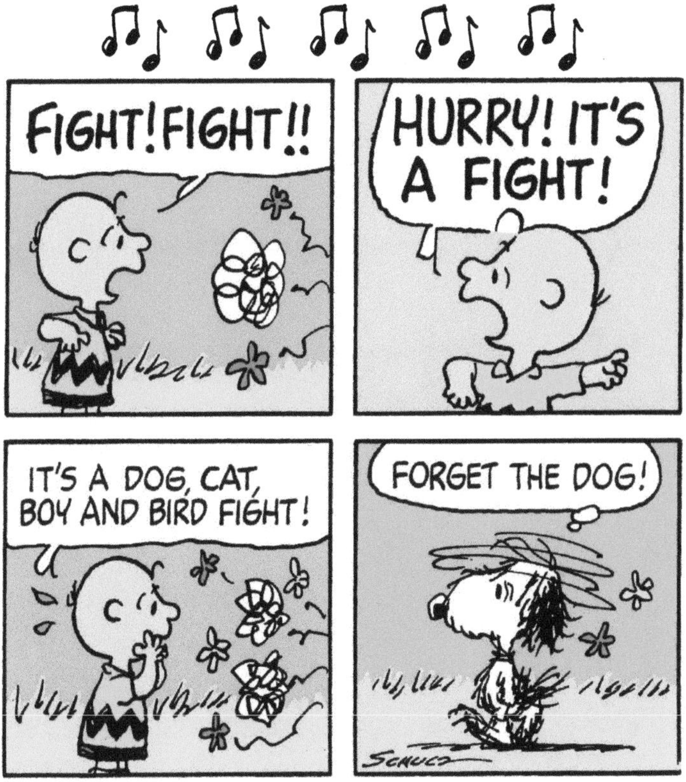
FIGHT! FIGHT!!
HURRY! IT'S A FIGHT!
IT'S A DOG, CAT, BOY AND BIRD FIGHT!
FORGET THE DOG!
SCHULZ

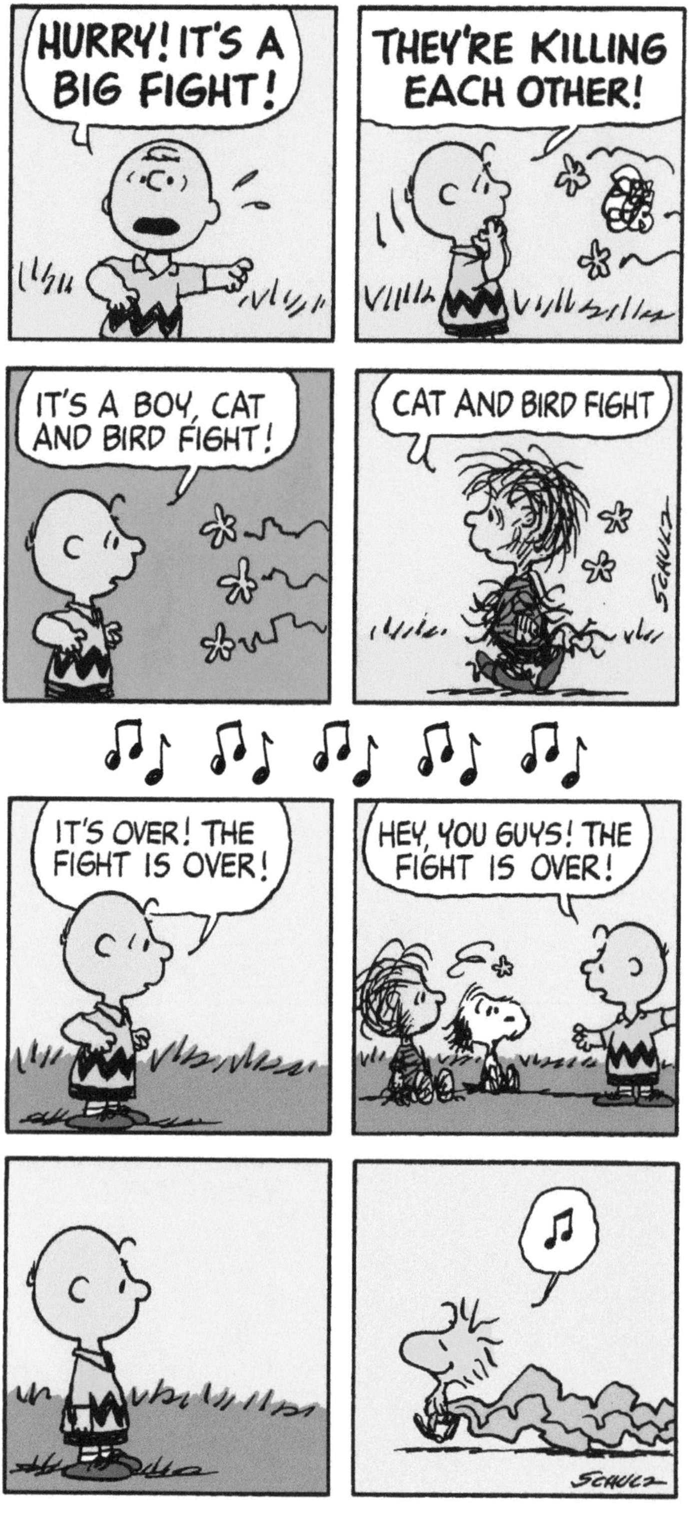
HURRY! IT'S A BIG FIGHT!
THEY'RE KILLING EACH OTHER!
IT'S A BOY, CAT AND BIRD FIGHT!
CAT AND BIRD FIGHT
SCHULZ
IT'S OVER! THE FIGHT IS OVER!
HEY, YOU GUYS! THE FIGHT IS OVER!
SCHULZ

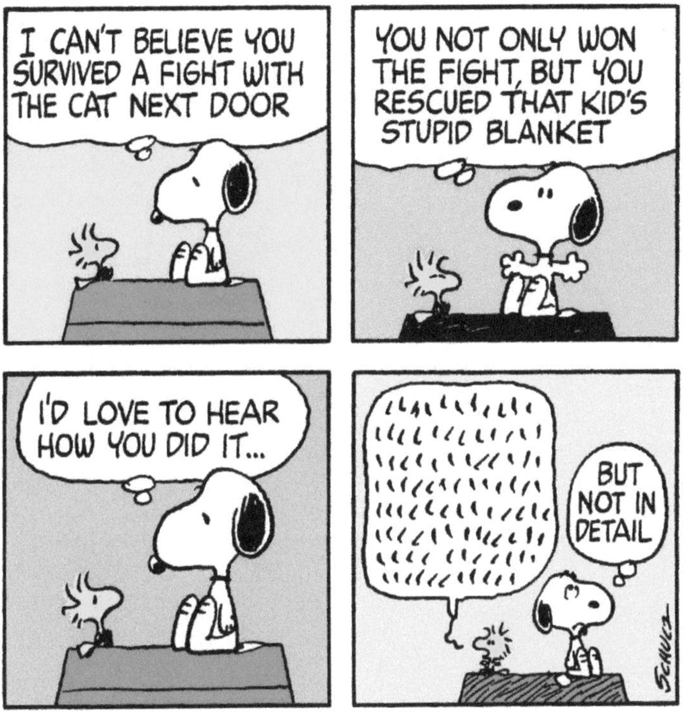
I CAN'T BELIEVE YOU SURVIVED A FIGHT WITH THE CAT NEXT DOOR
YOU NOT ONLY WON THE FIGHT, BUT YOU RESCUED THAT KID'S STUPID BLANKET
I'D LOVE TO HEAR HOW YOU DID IT...
BUT NOT IN DETAIL
SCHULZ

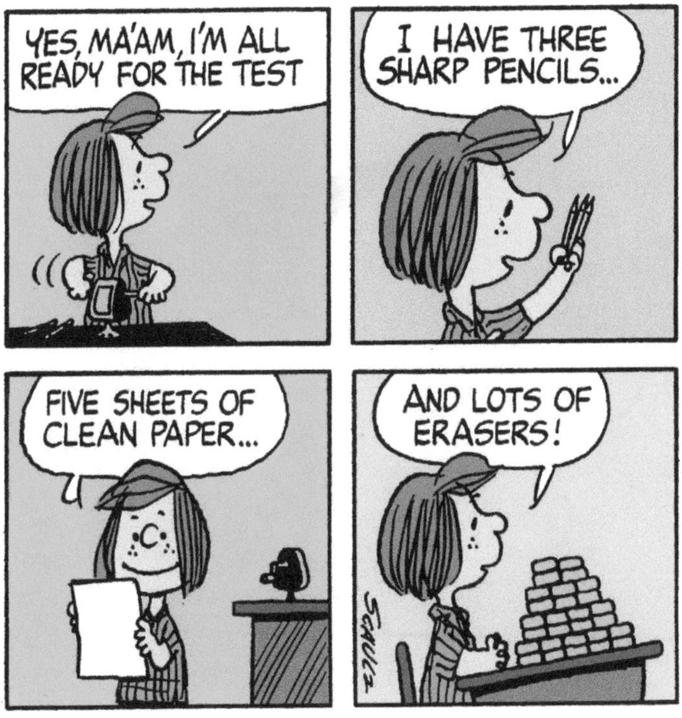
YES, MA'AM, I'M ALL READY FOR THE TEST
I HAVE THREE SHARP PENCILS...
FIVE SHEETS OF CLEAN PAPER...
AND LOTS OF ERASERS!
SCHULZ

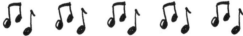

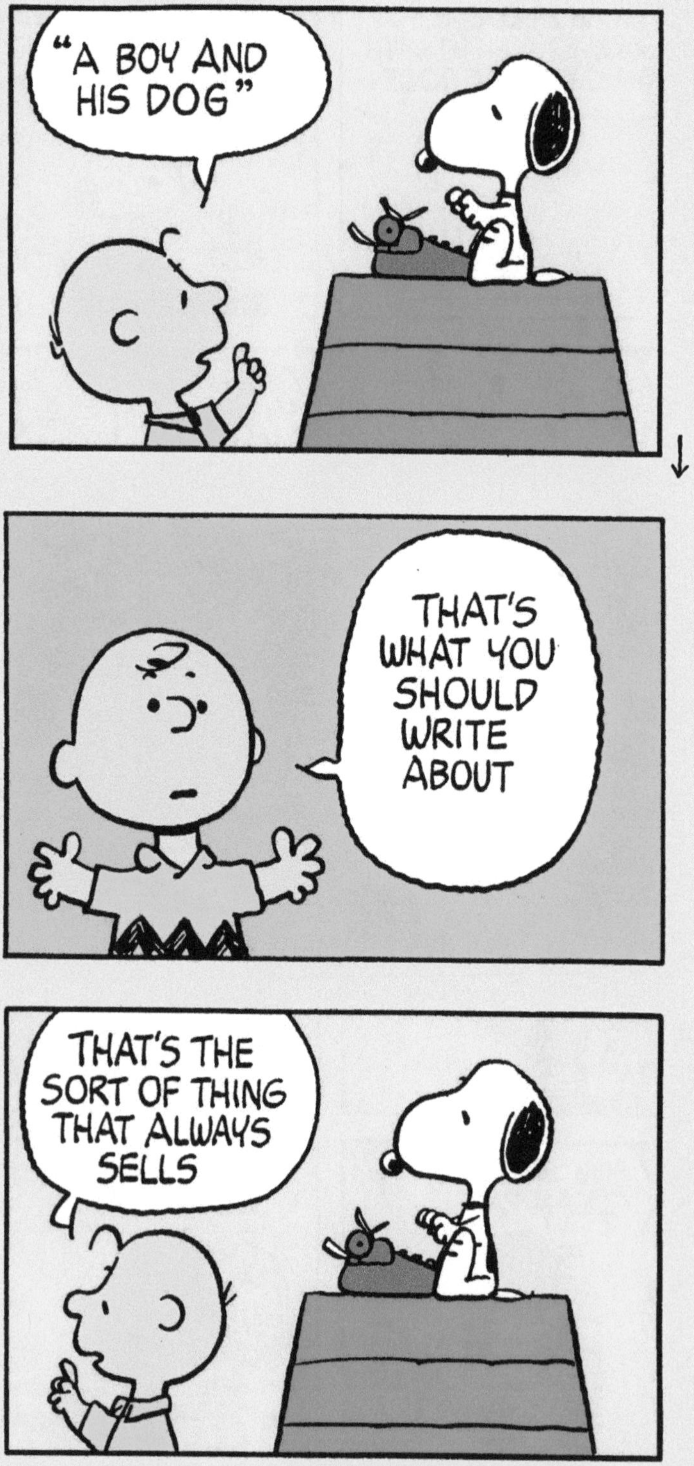
"A BOY AND HIS DOG"
THAT'S WHAT YOU SHOULD WRITE ABOUT
THAT'S THE SORT OF THING THAT ALWAYS SELLS

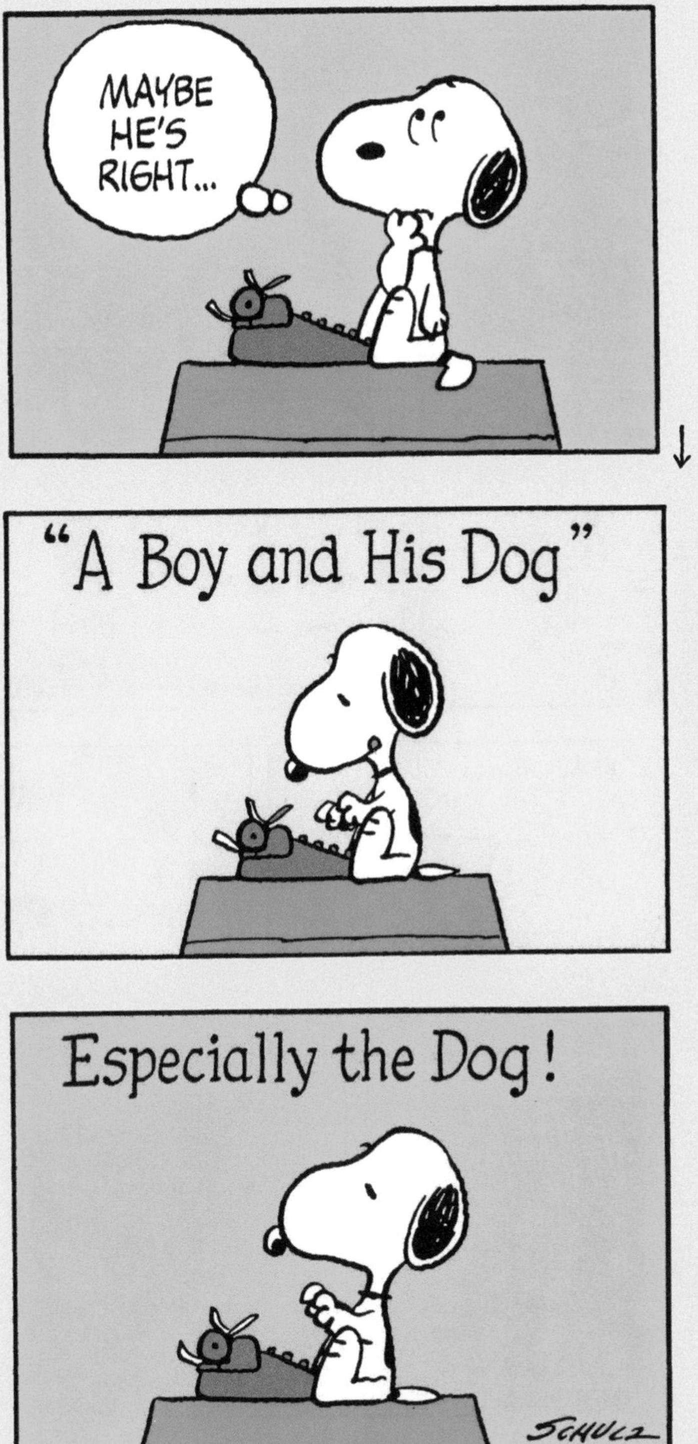
MAYBE HE'S RIGHT...
"A Boy and His Dog"
Especially the Dog!
SCHULZ

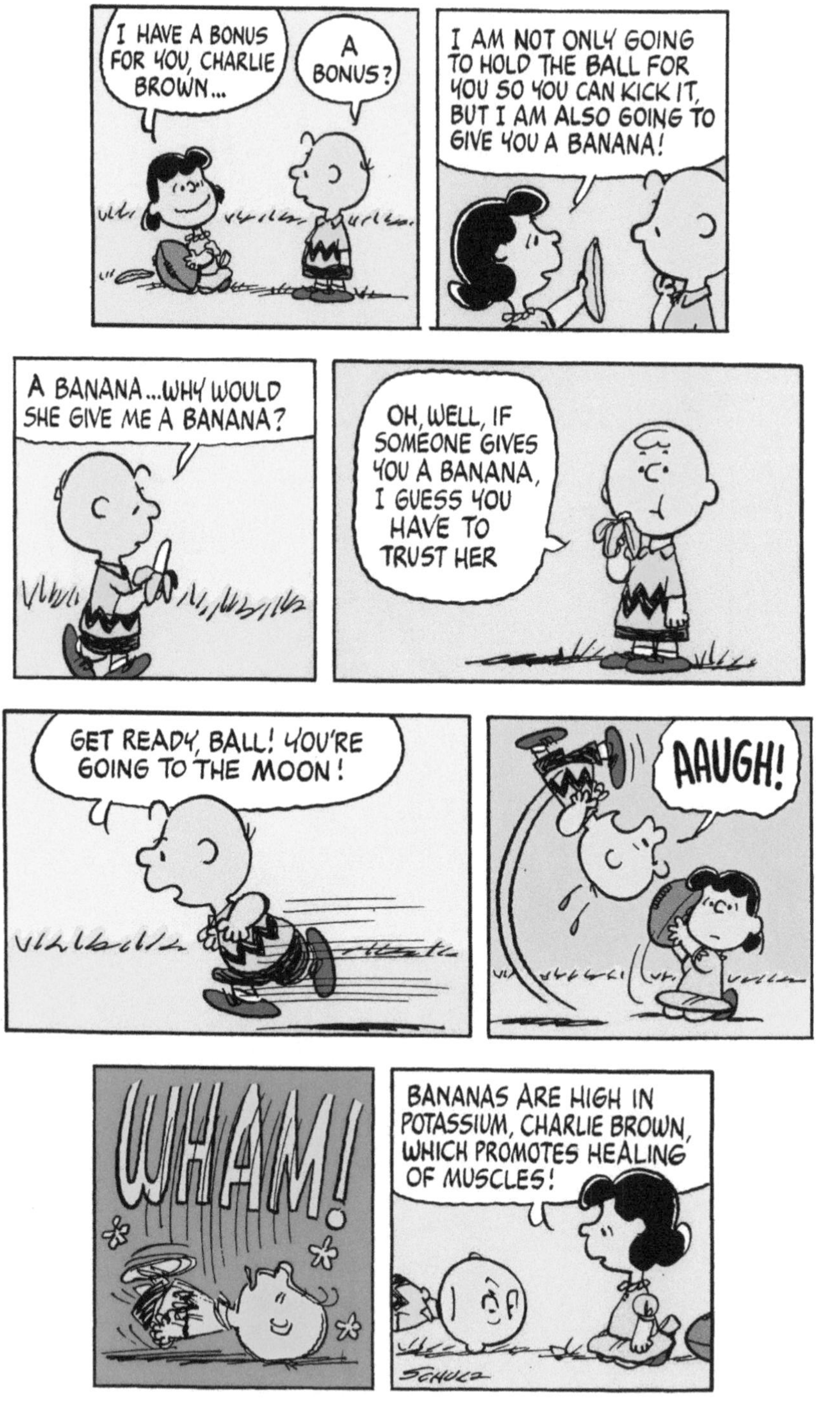
I HAVE A BONUS FOR YOU, CHARLIE BROWN...
A BONUS?
I AM NOT ONLY GOING TO HOLD THE BALL FOR YOU SO YOU CAN KICK IT, BUT I AM ALSO GOING TO GIVE YOU A BANANA!
A BANANA...WHY WOULD SHE GIVE ME A BANANA?
OH, WELL, IF SOMEONE GIVES YOU A BANANA, I GUESS YOU HAVE TO TRUST HER
GET READY, BALL! YOU'RE GOING TO THE MOON!
AAUGH!
WHAM!
BANANAS ARE HIGH IN POTASSIUM, CHARLIE BROWN, WHICH PROMOTES HEALING OF MUSCLES!
SCHULZ

MORE TO EXPLORE! Featuring fun facts!

The *Peanuts* gang loves to dance! During his career, *Peanuts* creator Charles Schulz drew over three hundred strips that featured his characters dancing.

In the following pages, you'll see some famous examples of the *Peanuts* kids boogying down while learning a few of Snoopy's signature dance moves.

Special thanks to our friends at the Charles M. Schulz Museum and Research Center in Santa Rosa, California, for letting us share these with you!

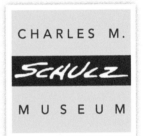

CHARLES M. SCHULZ MUSEUM

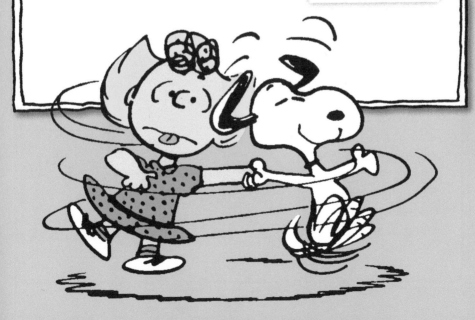

Snoopy's very first dance occurred in October 1952, only two years after *Peanuts*' debut. In the earliest years of the strip, dancing was portrayed fairly realistically, with one or more of the characters dancing for joy if they won a game or dancing while listening to music. Even Snoopy's dances were quite realistic, as he danced around on his back legs for a treat while the gang egged him on.

I'VE GOT TO ADMIT THAT THERE'S NOTHING LIKE THE 'POLKA' WHEN DANCED BY AN EXPERT..
SCHULZ

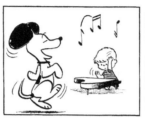

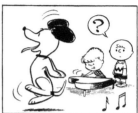

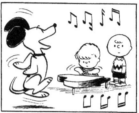

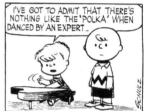

November 12, 1953

By September 1956, Snoopy was dancing purely for the joy of it. By that time, he looked less like a real pooch and more like the Snoopy we know and love today. In his popular "happy dance," Snoopy's love of life is easy to see in his body language: His ears fly up or to the side, and his "arms" open wide as if to embrace the world, while he drums his feet rapidly to the rhythm of the pure delight of being alive.

TO THOSE OF US WITH REAL UNDERSTANDING, DANCING IS THE ONLY PURE ART FORM!
SCHULZ

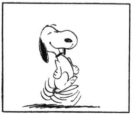

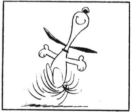

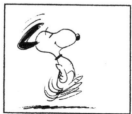

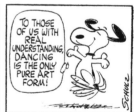

March 16, 1963

Although Lucy has partnered with Snoopy in some slow dances and some wildly exuberant ones, her patience with his dancing depends on her mood.

I DON'T UNDERSTAND YOU!
THE WHOLE WORLD IS COMING APART, AND YOU'RE DANCING!
I CAN'T HELP IT... MY FEET LOVE TO DANCE...
I HAVE AN OBLIGATION TO MY FEET!
SCHULZ

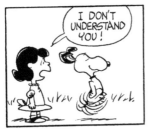

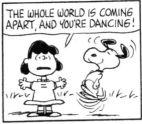

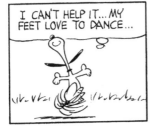

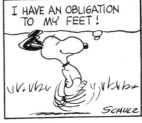

September 22, 1965

One of Snoopy's best-known dances occurs at suppertime. Snoopy's suppertime dance has become something of a standard, almost as iconic as his happy dance.

OKAY, YOU STUPID BEAGLE... IT'S SUPPERTIME!
SUPPERTIME?
OH, IT'S SUPPERTIME! SUPPERTIME, SUPPERTIME, SUPPERTIME!
YES, IT'S SUPPERTIME, THE VERY BEST TIME OF DAY!! OH, IT'S SUPPERTIME! IT'S SUPPERTIME!
I FEEL LIKE I'M FEEDING FRED ASTAIRE!
SCHULZ

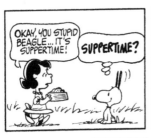

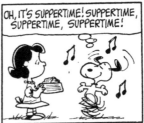

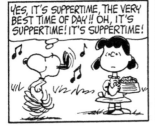

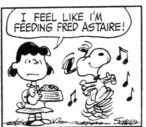

June 19, 1969

By the 1970s, *Peanuts* included story lines about dance fads and the gang's attendance at various social dances. You might have seen some of these in the *Peanuts* animated specials, with the characters showing off their signature moves.

WOW, SNOOPY, LOOK AT ALL THE KIDS!
THIS "TURN-ABOUT" LOOKS LIKE IT MIGHT BE KIND OF FUN...
I'M SORT OF SELF-CONSCIOUS ABOUT DANCING WITH A BOY...
BUT THERE'S SO MANY KIDS HERE, I DOUBT IF ANYONE WILL EVEN NOTICE US...
SCHULZ

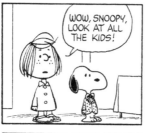

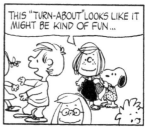

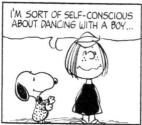

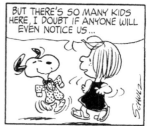

December 3, 1970

In October 1978, Snoopy is seen wearing flashy disco attire and using cheesy pickup lines. To see the Snoopy disco strips, turn to pages 158–159 of this book!

In 1984, Snoopy also starred in the *Peanuts* animated special *It's Flashbeagle, Charlie Brown*, a reference to the 1983 movie *Flashdance*.

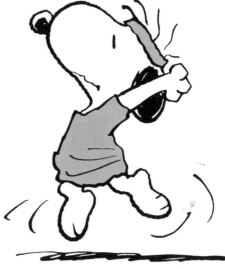

Snoopy may love the spotlight, but he's not the only *Peanuts* character who dances. Check out these strips featuring Woodstock, Peppermint Patty, Pigpen, Spike, and Charlie Brown.

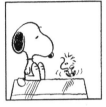

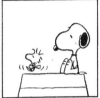

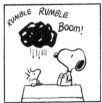

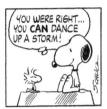

RUMBLE RUMBLE
Boom!
YOU WERE RIGHT... YOU CAN DANCE UP A STORM!
SCHULZ

March 8, 1979

THIS IS SOME WEIRD DATE THAT CHUCK GOT FOR ME...
I MUST ADMIT HE CAN DANCE, THOUGH
WHAT'S YOUR SIGN, PIG-PEN? DO YOU COME HERE OFTEN?
WHERE DID HE GO?
SCHULZ

February 14, 1980

HERE.. A LETTER FROM YOUR BROTHER SPIKE...
"DEAR SNOOPY, WELL, OUR CACTUS CLUB HAD ITS FIRST DANCE LAST NIGHT"
"ACTUALLY, THE DANCING WASN'T AS MUCH FUN AS I THOUGHT IT WOULD BE..."
OUCH! OOO! OW!! OUCH!
SCHULZ

March 29, 1985

HI! MY NAME IS EMILY..WOULD YOU LIKE TO BE MY DANCE PARTNER?
WELL, SURE.. BUT I'M NOT VERY GOOD..
IT'LL BE EASY.. "SLOW, SLOW, QUICK, QUICK"
HOW ABOUT, "SLOW, SLOW, PANIC, PANIC"?
SCHULZ

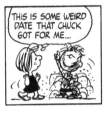

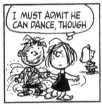

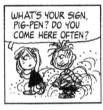

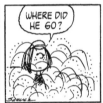

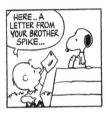

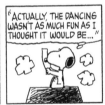

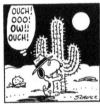

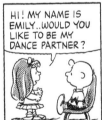

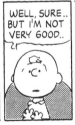

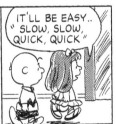

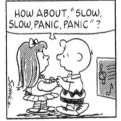

February 11, 1995

To see more classic *Peanuts* strips, learn about the art of cartooning, and take a virtual tour of the Charles M. Schulz Museum and Research Center, visit schulzmuseum.org.

About the Charles M. Schulz Museum and Research Center

The Charles M. Schulz Museum and Research Center was designed as a tribute to the extraordinary talent of Charles M. Schulz. The Museum was created to share his legacy and genius with generations to come.

A tile mural over twenty feet high, Schulz's well-worn drawing desk, and a psychiatric booth are just some of the classics found alongside the largest collection of *Peanuts* artwork in the world. Laugh at original comic strips, explore in-depth exhibitions, watch animated *Peanuts* specials in the theater, and draw your own cartoons in the education room. The Museum features changing exhibitions, a re-creation of Schulz's studio, a life-size biographical timeline, and special programming. Learn more at schulzmuseum.org.

CHARLES M.

SCHULZ

M U S E U M

Andrews McMeel Publishing
a division of Andrews McMeel Universal
1130 Walnut Street, Kansas City, Missouri 64106

www.andrewsmcmeel.com

www.peanuts.com

ISBN: 978-1-4494-9945-7

Library of Congress Control Number: 2018932253

ATTENTION: SCHOOLS AND BUSINESSES

Andrews McMeel books are available at quantity discounts with bulk purchase for educational, business, or sales promotional use. For information, please e-mail the Andrews McMeel Publishing Special Sales Department: specialsales@amuniversal.com.

Check out more *Peanuts* kids' collections from Andrews McMeel Publishing.

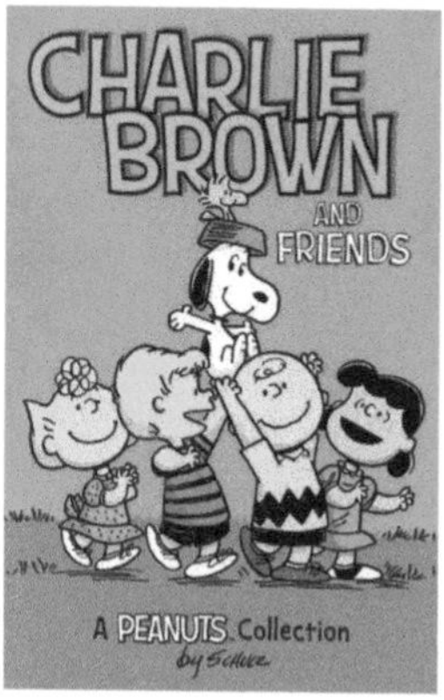
CHARLIE BROWN
AND FRIENDS
A PEANUTS Collection

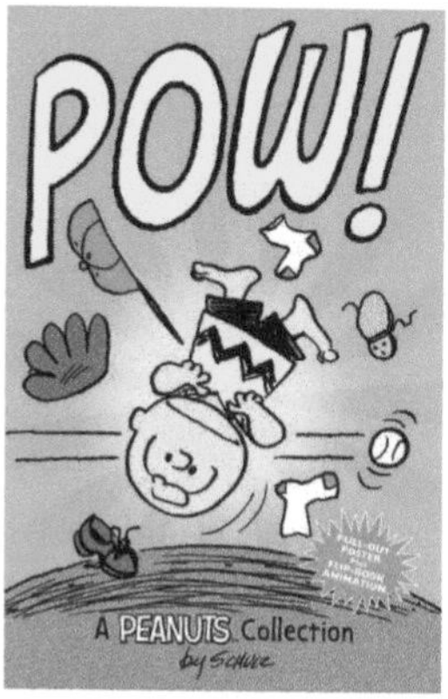
POW!
A PEANUTS Collection

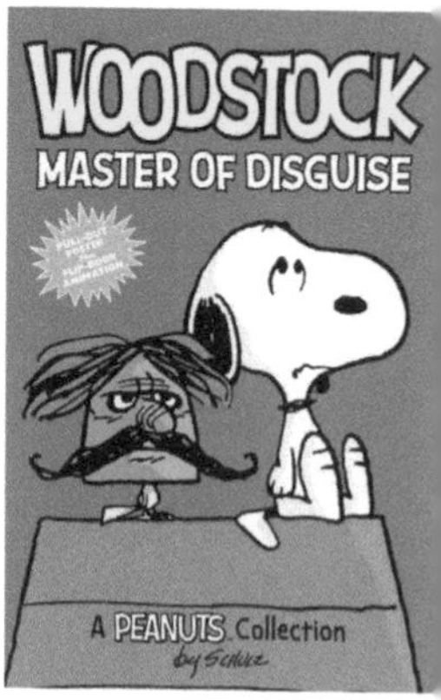
WOODSTOCK
MASTER OF DISGUISE
A PEANUTS Collection

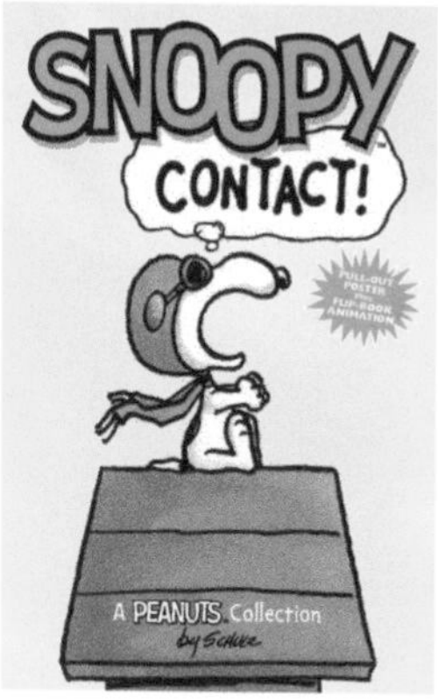
SNOOPY
CONTACT!
A PEANUTS Collection

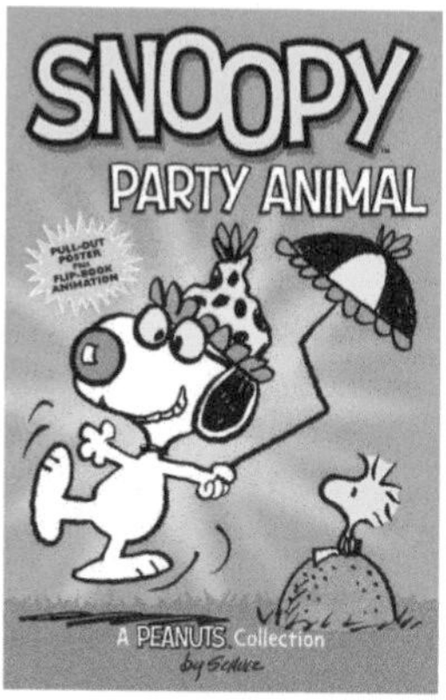
SNOOPY
PARTY ANIMAL
A PEANUTS Collection

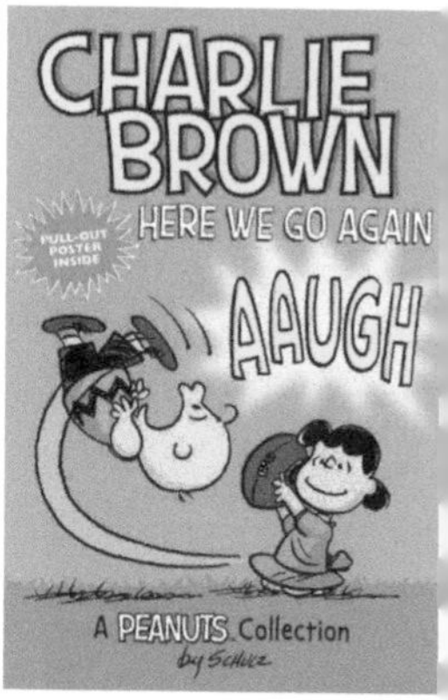
CHARLIE BROWN
HERE WE GO AGAIN
AAUGH
A PEANUTS Collection

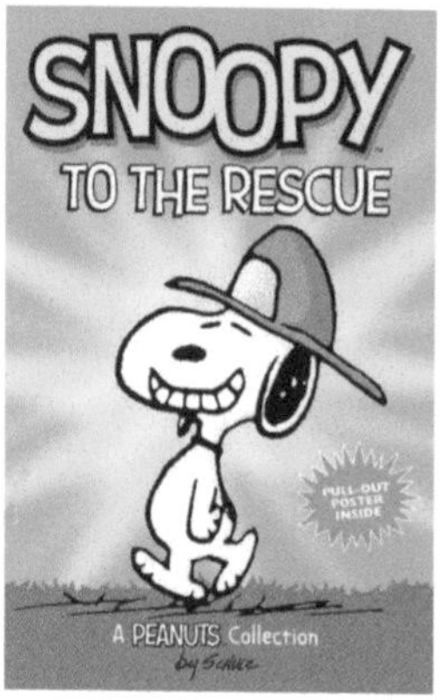
SNOOPY
TO THE RESCUE
A PEANUTS Collection

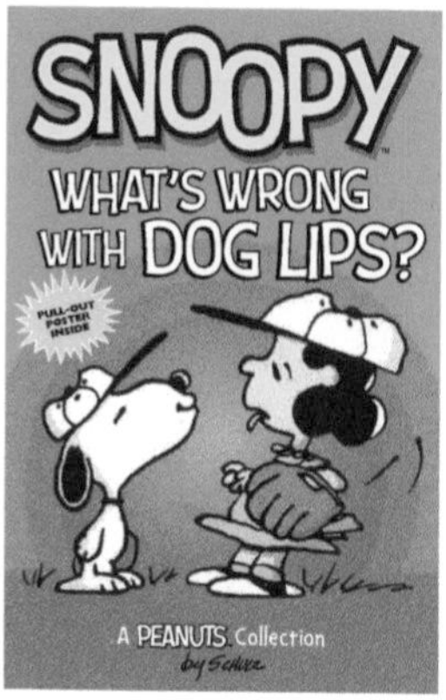
SNOOPY
WHAT'S WRONG WITH DOG LIPS?
A PEANUTS Collection

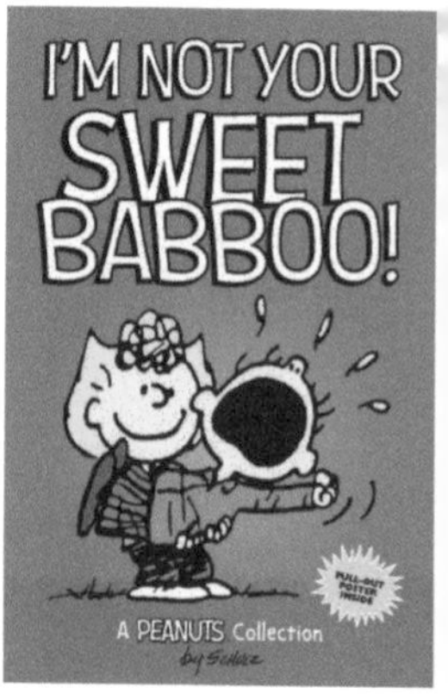
I'M NOT YOUR SWEET BABBOO!
A PEANUTS Collection